The Devil's Stocking

By the same author

SOMEBODY IN BOOTS
NEVER COME MORNING
THE NEON WILDERNESS
THE MAN WITH THE GOLDEN ARM
CHICAGO: CITY ON THE MAKE
A WALK ON THE WILD SIDE
THE BOOK OF LONESOME MONSTERS
WHO LOST AN AMERICAN?
NOTES FROM A SEA DIARY
CONVERSATION WITH NELSON ALGREN
(With H.E.F. Donahue)
THE LAST CAROUSEL
THE DEVIL'S STOCKING

The Devil's Stocking

NELSON ALGREN

*The Arbor House Library
of Contemporary Americana
New York*

 Published in the United States of America by Arbor House Publishing Company and in Canada by Fitzhenry & Whiteside, Ltd.

Library of Congress Catalogue Card Number: 83–45249

ISBN: 0-87795-548-4
Hardcover Edition: 0-87795-547-6

Manufactured in the United States of America

10 9 8 7 6 5 4 3 2 1

This book is printed on acid free paper. The paper in this book meets the guidelines for permanence and durability of the Committee on Production Guidelines for Book Longevity of the Council on Library Resources.

To Stephen Deutch

ALL CHARACTERS IN THIS NOVEL ARE FICTITIOUS.
ALL SITUATIONS DEPICTED IN THIS NOVEL
ARE FICTITIOUS. NO ACTUAL PERSON, OR ACTUAL
SITUATION, IS DESCRIBED HERE.

Contents

Foreword by Herbert Mitgang 1

The Last Interview by W. J. Weatherby 7

I *First Trial* 13

II *The Wall* 117

III *Evidentiary Hearing* 169

IV *Monnigan* 183

V *Athens* 195

VI *Supreme Court Hearing* 217

VII *The Devil's Stocking* 235

VIII *Chinatown* 261

IX *Second Trial* 279

The author wishes to acknowledge the support given this novel by the National Endowment for the Arts.

Foreword

by Herbert Mitgang

The world of Nelson Algren (1909–1981) was not yours or mine and, in a strange way, not his either. As novelist, poet and occasional reporter, he was a deep-sea diver in the netherworld of America. Yet he was not a part of its frenzy and violence; above all, he walked on the wild side as an observant writer. Early in his life, poverty and circumstance had positioned him in the dead-center of political depression and literary realism. There, where his true-life characters dwelled, he chose to do his work of lending them a measure of dignity.

In the last summer of his life, when he was living happily in Sag Harbor, on the eastern end of Long Island, Algren laughed as he told me about his conversation with Otto Preminger, who had produced *The Man with the Golden Arm*. The novel had received the first National Book Award (though, as Algren often noted, no prize money) and brought him fame in the United States and western Europe. He was angry that the film was advertised as if it was not Algren's but Preminger's story.

"Nelson," Preminger asked him, "how do you know *such* people—pimps, prostitutes, vice cops, broken-down fighters?"

"Otto," answered Algren, "how do you know *your* kind of people—actors, directors, bankers and broken-down producers?"

Because of his characters and subjects, Algren's detractors

often have failed to understand his place and significance in American literature. Jean-Paul Sartre and Simone de Beauvoir and other European writers accorded him greater recognition than many critics in his own country. In the United States such neo-conservative defenders of the American Way as Norman Podhoretz complained that Algren "romanticized prostitutes and hustlers," and Leslie Fiedler called him "the bard of the stumblebum," his obituary in the *New York Times* noted. But working novelists knew what he was trying to do. Ernest Hemingway placed Algren in the first rank of American originals, and Kay Boyle, one of America's finest short story writers, regarded Algren as a courageous novelist.

For Algren was in the American grain, rough-hewn, in the tradition of the muckrakers who startled and angered the high and the mighty early in the twentieth century. In fiction and fact, such writers as Hamlin Garland, Lincoln Steffens, Ida M. Tarbell, Upton Sinclair, Frank Norris and Jack London attacked the new industrialists in the pits and stockyards and oil companies, and the old corrupters in political office who protected them. Closer to his own time were the midwestern writers, of whom H. L. Mencken wrote in the 1920s: "There isn't an American novelist deserving the attention of the civilized reader's notice who has not sprung from the Chicago Palatinate." Alongside James T. Farrell, Richard Wright and other angry young men fighting racism and injustice, Nelson Algren was an important voice in the Second Chicago Renaissance, his words walking in the hard and sentimental boots of Theodore Dreiser, Sherwood Anderson, Carl Sandburg, Vachel Lindsay and Edgar Lee Masters.

Of his own adopted town, Algren sounded the alarm in *Chicago: City on the Make,* which bears a strong resemblance to Sandburg's own Depression prose-poem, "The People, Yes." Of the corruption in the city he loved because of its night-colors, its imperfections and opportunities, Algren wrote: "Chicago has progressed, culturally, from being the Second City to being the Second-Hand City. The vital cog in our culture now is not the artist, but the middleman whose commercial status lends art the aura of status when he acquires a collection of originals. The word 'culture' now means nothing more than 'approved'. It isn't what is exhibited so much that matters as where: that being where one meets the people who matter." And so Algren found more reality, less deceit, in his beaten-down characters under the El than in the respectable strivers who bought and owned the town. "All we have today of the past is the poetry of Sandburg," he wrote, "now as remote from the Chicago of today as Wordsworth's."

The slums take their revenge. Algren was a third-generation Chicagoan descended from Jewish, Swedish and German stock. He was born Nelson Algren Abraham in Detroit; when Nelson was three, his father moved to Chicago to follow his trade as a machinist. Nelson grew up in the blue-collar, ethnic streets of the city, worked his way through the University of Illinois and graduated with a major in journalism. "I wasn't sure whether I wanted to be a columnist or a foreign correspondent but I was willing to take what was open," he recalled. "What was open was a place on a bench in Lafayette Square if you got there early. I found my way to the streets on the other side of the Southern Pacific station in New Orleans, where the big jukes were singing something called 'Walking the Wild Side of Life.' I've stayed pretty much on that side of the curb ever since."

Algren became a migratory worker in the south and southwest at the beginning of the Depression, sold coffee as a door-to-door salesman, worked at a gas station in Rio Hondo, Texas, and decided to become a writer. He stole a typewriter and started back to Chicago but was caught and spent four months in jail in Alpine, Texas. He began to write short stores and poetry and turned out his first novel, *Somebody in Boots,* in 1935. For a while, he worked on venereal-disease control for the Chicago Board of Health and, briefly, for a W.P.A. writers' project. His stories began to be accepted, including the often reprinted "A Bottle of Milk for Murder," about a young murderer being grilled until he confesses: "I knew I'd never get to be twenty-one anyhow." His second novel, *Never Come Morning,* was about a South Side prizefighter-hoodlum. The American Academy and Institute of Arts and Letters awarded him a small grant, declaring that the novel had not received the honor it deserved. At seventy-two, in his last year, he was elected a member of the Academy-Institute himself.

Although he was a "name" writer, Algren struggled financially. But his sense of humor and of irony never left him. He and his close friend, Studs Terkel, sometimes would sit in the back room of Riccardo's, the Chicago newspaper hangout, matching cognacs against martinis and testing throwaway lines. Putting on a hick from Manhattan, Algren said:

"Never eat at a place called Mom's. Never play cards with a man named Doc. Never go to bed with a woman whose troubles are greater than your own.

"All the wisdom I acquired in nine months in the Orient can be summed up in one line. Never eat in a place with sliding doors unless you're crazy about raw fish.

"An Oriental woman, even a sixteen-year-old, knows she's a love object. American women don't.

"A woman once told me that I was a devil's stocking—knitted backwards."

Which was the origin of the title of this, his final novel, *The Devil's Stocking*.

The book has a history. In the modest apartment he rented on Concord Street in Sag Harbor, Algren explained how he had come to write it.

"I accepted a magazine assignment to write about Rubin 'Hurricane' Carter, the middleweight boxer, and his trial for murder. I felt it was a miscarriage of justice. What I wrote began to build into a book. I moved to Paterson to be near the court, prison and records. I was in Hackensack later and had the only Puerto Rican landlady in New Jersey with a pacemaker. The trial and appeals were complicated and I tried to put the transcripts into English."

Then Algren perceived the book not as reportage but as a novel. He felt that fiction would give him more turnaround room. For example, he added a mulatto sparring partner in the story who is wholly fictitious, changed the names of all the true-life people to fictional characters, and brought to bear his knowledge of boxing, fallen men and women, gambling, horse racing and the underworld. In an early stage, the novel was called *Chinatown*. The book was first translated and published in Germany in 1980 with the title *Calhoun*, the name of its central character. Early in 1983, Candida Donadio, to whom Algren dedicated one of his books with the phrase, "Not an agent—a possession," renewed efforts to find an American publisher and the novel finally was acquired by Arbor House.

The Devil's Stocking is all Algren, with his imperfections as well as hammerblows in prose. The wisdom of turning fact into fiction becomes apparent immediately, for the novel at its best brings into play the author's imagination, his stacked and sometimes familiar deck of urban jacks and queens and street guerrillas. Had Algren lived, he might have revised some of the "nonfiction" transcripts and added still more of himself; but that is speculation. Certainly the characters he has created speak for themselves, and always in authentic tones. The subterranean world that he knew as well as any living American writer is here. A pimp tells his new woman: "I hope you're not mad at me for making you a whore." And she tells him: "No, don't forget that at the same time I'm making *you* a pimp." And there are touches of language here and there that remind you that Algren could be eloquent: "He began mixing self-pity with Scotch."

For those of us who are not familiar with seedy criminal courts and jails, crummy hotels, the people who live inside the black and brown skins of a white world, Algren still has the ability to shock and outrage. You would not want to spend the night in some of the places where his characters live—where they should not have to live if their lives were not so desperate; but you know that this is not just pure invention. Maybe the author is forcing us to look at what he perceives to be injustice in the dark recesses of the American Way; if so, *The Devil's Stocking* is muckraking in a strong literary tradition.

—Herbert Mitgang

The Last Interview

by

W. J. Weatherby

HE CERTAINLY TOOK Dylan Thomas's advice not to go gentle into that good night. In a last talk only hours before his death, Nelson Algren was as downright, excitable and aggressive as ever. When he told me he'd complained to his doctor that morning of a "heaviness" in his chest, not a good sign at seventy-two, I tried to steer him away from any topic that would excite him. It was a wasted effort.

Whether the talk was of an old lover, racial strife in Paterson, New Jersey, or the prostitution racket as depicted in his new novel, *everything* seemed to send up his blood pressure that last day as the final hours ticked away. Thank God he didn't know what was coming because he was free to rage against the dying of the light the way he had been raging all his life. When I suggested that in old age he resembled Hemingway's old man of the sea, he scoffed: "That guy was one of Ernest's saintly stoics whereas I've always felt more at home with the Devil."

The new novel, destined to be his last, was very much on his mind that last day. Obviously based on the case of Rubin "Hurricane" Carter, the black boxer Algren had written about for *Esquire* magazine, *The Devil's Stocking* had cost him his peaceful retreat (from Chicago) in Paterson, New Jersey. He had gone to live in Paterson, close to Carter, and even tried to rent a room above the scene of the homicide Carter was alleged to have committed.

"The only way I can work is up close," Algren told me, recalling how his experiences as a young man in a Texas jail (he had stolen a typewriter to work on his first novel) had helped him to understand Rubin Carter's feelings in jail. But Algren's "up-close" approach made him a lot of enemies in Paterson when it was learned he was on Carter's side. He began to be threatened and harassed. At first his fighting spirit seemed to enjoy it, but then he realized what he was up against. The memory still enraged him that last day. "The hostility in Paterson was just about as sick as it could be,'' Algren said. ''Eventually it made me leave. The racial conflict of the sixties still persists there between the blacks and the Sicilians, and if you were for Carter, then you had the Sicilians on your neck and that's like fighting the Mafia—you can't win, brother.''

Highly praised by such fellow writers as Hemingway and Carl Sandburg, but attacked by some literary critics for romanticizing prostitutes and hustlers, Algren had researched the New York prostitution scene around Times Square for the new novel. ''It's all changed and it's hardly been touched by writers,'' he said excitedly, as wide-eyed as a boy. ''Prostitution there is very big money now. The women are high class and cost from fifteen dollars to one hundred dollars and up an hour, and that's driven out the poor whore except in the back streets. Maybe it's similar to what's happened in baseball, where players used to work for one thousand dollars a season and now get a million. Some of these women make two hundred and fifty thousand dollars a year without taxes . . .''

He was as fascinated with life as ever, talking as eagerly about New York's massage parlors and peep shows as about the literary world or the boxing business—not bad for a man who was aware that death was close. But the topic that seemed to excite him more than anything was a love affair of twenty-five years ago. His encounter with Simone de Beauvoir, the French author and long-time companion of Jean-Paul Sartre, became a romantic episode in her novel, *The Mandarins*. Algren still hadn't forgiven her.

He told me indignantly, ''She gave me a disguise, another name, in *The Mandarins,* but in a later book, I think it was called *The Prime of Life,* she tried to make our relationship into a great international literary affair, naming me and quoting from some of my letters. She must have been awfully hard up for something to write about or maybe she thought of herself as another Colette. The publisher asked my permission to quote the letters. I thought about it for a few days and then I reluctantly said okay. Hell, love letters should be private. I've been in whorehouses all over the world and the women there always close the door, whether it's in

Korea or India. But this woman flung the door open and called in the public and the press. Other women then began to write to me and even came knocking at my door. God, it was terrible. I don't have any malice against her, but I think it was an appalling thing to do. That's a Continental view of how to do things, I suppose."

Algren had become very excited, and mindful of that "heaviness" in his chest, I tried to get him back to the safer topic of the new novel. So some prostitutes are becoming millionaires, I said. The diversion was a failure. He was too steamed up about de Beauvoir. He confided that in his bare, half-furnished cottage at Sag Harbor, Long Island, New York, was a tin box containing about three hundred love letters from the French writer. As she had published some of his letters, he intended to auction hers. "If one half of a correspondence is made public," he said, "then the other half should be. They're no longer of any sentimental value to me. You can't commercialize half and keep the other half sacrosanct. Let's make it all public!"

He always seemed to have problems in his relations with women. His two marriages ended in divorce and he had been living alone—"to be by the water"—among cheap memorabilia and with newspaper clippings on the walls for decorations. He was obviously living very poorly, but that didn't stop him from planning a party for the next day to celebrate his recent election to the prestigious American Academy–Institute of Arts and Letters, roughly the American equivalent of the French Academy.

A rebel all his literary life, Algren sounded ambivalent about the honor. "I didn't know I was running for office until they informed me I was elected," he commented jocularly. "It puts you in the league of people who are 'distinguished', so I'm told by literary friends. I was a little surprised because I've never been 'distinguished' from other writers very much. In Chicago, where I spent sixty years, I was certainly never accepted. I spent my time feuding with the city. But it's always taken time for people to catch up with the scene I write about. *The Man with the Golden Arm* was a good, solid, journalistic book, but *A Walk on the Wild Side* got off the ground. It was a sort of happening, a very poetic book. If I had only written one book, I'd want it to be that one.'' He paused thoughtfully and then added quickly, "Or maybe this new one, *The Devil's Stocking*."

His excitement seemed dangerously high again as he said intensely, "Writing's a serious business, not just digging up old love letters, which should be private anyway. In this new novel, I've tried to write about a man's struggle against injustice—that's the only story worth telling. I've written it from my guts."

He was a generous man—as generous with his thoughts as with his feelings—but it was getting late and surely time he was resting. But he didn't seem to want to stop. When I insisted on saying good-by, he went into great detail about how to get to the party at his cottage the next day, even quoting the local taxi rates. "I've already bought the liquor," he said cheerfully. They were his last words to me—and his last words to anyone as far as I know. The first guest to arrive next day found him lying dead in the cottage with the unopened bottles of liquor for the party around him. He had had a massive heart attack. I hoped our conversation hadn't brought it on. But at least he had lived life to the hilt and "raged against the dying of the light" right up to the end. The man one met on the last day reflected exactly the writer one had read in all the books ranging from *The Man with the Golden Arm* to *The Devil's Stocking,* and that is an exceedingly rare literary achievement. It means that as long as his books are read, the man will never die—that downright, excitable, aggressive, but, deep down, gentle man known as Nelson Algren.

—W. J. Weatherby

I

First Trial

"I WAS NERVOUS in the dressing room before that fight," Ruby Calhoun's manager later recalled, "it was our first main event and our first time on TV. Ruby kept reading a comic book. 'Sit on the rubbing table,' he tells me, 'and be still. Riccardo's first hook is going to be his last.' What he might do if Riccardo didn't hook, I didn't ask. He wouldn't have told me anyhow. Ruby managed hisself in things like that. I sat on the rubbing table like he told me. Nobody *managed* Ruby.

"If he didn't finish that damned comic book by fight time, would he take it into the ring with him and finish it between rounds? When Ruby got his hands on something, book or man, he didn't let loose until he was finished with it.

"Riccardo was a Puerto Rican Puerto Rican but he had a New York following. When he came down the aisle a gang of his fans held up a sheet on which they had painted, in red:

RICKIE! RICKIE! RICKIE!
GO! GO! GO!

"Ruby didn't wait for Riccardo to go. He hit him with a right square on the chin. Riccardo got up at four and took the mandatory eight. Ruby hooked a solid left to the jaw and followed with another right. Riccardo landed on the apron of the ring, half in half out, on the ropes. His eyes were open but he couldn't move. It had took only sixty-seven seconds. First thing Ruby did, back in his dressing room, before he changed back to his street clothes, was to finish that comic book."

Shortly after that fight Calhoun put his manager aside. The faster he rose in the fight business, the more friends he made and the more trouble he got into. The more trouble he got into, the more friends he needed. Calhoun always made friends when he needed them. Then tossed them aside when they were no longer of immediate use.

He liked people well enough and he enjoyed being liked by

them. Later it began to appear that he enjoyed being hated by them even more. He built up friendships, it began to look, in order to shatter them.

Twelve years after the Riccardo fight, when he was in the state penitentiary at Athens, New Jersey, he told a reporter, who'd reminded him of that fight, "When I fought I fought all out. Like life or death. Me or him. Or not fight at all. If I didn't believe I could knock a man out, I wouldn't sign to fight him. Nothing in between."

There never had been anything in between.

When he'd been a kid of twelve, his parents, fearing his street associations, sent him to an elderly aunt who farmed a few acres in Alabama.

Calhoun recalled that southern holiday with pleasure. He worked a couple mules, and he *worked*. Really worked. And loved it.

He'd never been out of his northern city and the rural South had enchanted him. He would have been content, he still felt, to spend the rest of his life there. His aunt assured his father that the boy was getting along fine. She hoped Floyd would let him stay on.

Sunday, in black Alabama, was church day all day long. After church the farmers gathered to sing and picnic in a grove. The only white in sight was a little old man, selling ice cream on the grove's far edge.

Calhoun wasn't aware of his father's arrival until a heavy blow sent his ice cream flying.

Why had his father struck him for simply buying ice cream from a white? The boy didn't understand. He had never felt fear of whites. But his father contained an inner dread, imbued in him by his Alabama childhood.

"The blow he dealt me didn't make me fear or hate whites," Calhoun recalled, "it made me fear and hate my father. He brought his fears to me."

His father brought him back to Jersey City; he should have left the boy South. He began running the streets with Ed "Red" Haloways, a youth a couple years older.

Red was a wiry, light-skinned rascal who might have passed

for white had it not been for his nappy little mop of red-brown hair and his wide white smile. He named the local street gang "The Elegant Gents" and it was with the "Gents" that Ruby first got into trouble with the police.

A local clothing store kept racks of clothing displayed on the sidewalk. The Gents swept past the racks, grabbed as many clothes as they could and escaped. Their object was not so much theft as it was to elude pursuers. The kids would have returned the clothes had that been possible. Ruby's father came home and found his children all wearing new clothes.

A white woman had given them to him, Ruby explained to his father. "With the price tags still on them? I won't have a thief for a son!" Floyd had begun belt-lashing the boy until his mother stopped it at last. Then the old man had phoned the police.

"I didn't know," Floyd acknowledged, many years later, to his old friend Matt Haloways—Red's father—"that the police would take such hold."

"You know it now, old man," Matt Haloways had assured him.

A thirty-year-old white homosexual assaulted Calhoun when he was fourteen. Calhoun stuck a scout knife into him. "I stuck him everywhere but the soles of his feet. The man survived, I still don't know how. That's right: atrocious assault at age fourteen.

"I don't enjoy hurting people unless they mess with me. Then I enjoy it. If you mess with me I'm going to try to kill you. I don't fight by rules. I go for all. And I don't shake hands when it's done."

"Ruby Calhoun is an antisocial person," an early report warned, "if something is not done soon he will become a dangerous man."

To make certain that that was what he would become, Calhoun was sentenced, for atrocious assault, to the Jamesburg State Home for Boys until he would be twenty-one. When he was sixteen Red Haloways came in, on a mugging conviction, and they locked in the same cottage.

Ruby had been planning escape but he said nothing to Red. Ruby already knew Red's tendency toward screwing everything up for himself and everyone around him. Red looked like a sure winner but was really a loser, Ruby sensed.

Some simpleminded staff member had had the heel of every shoe worn by the inmates cut with a V. The purpose was supposed to be that, in the event a kid ran off, he would show them the way he'd gone by that V. Ruby simply pulled a pair of winter socks over the shoes, got over a six-foot fence in the wintry dark of early morning, and was off. He eluded police patrols back to Jersey City.

His mother's guess was that the boy's best bet would be the army. She shipped him off to relatives in Philadelphia. There, by assuring a recruiting officer that he was a native Philadelphian and of age, he got himself inducted into the 101st Airborne and was shipped to Germany.

The man who had the strongest impact upon him in Germany was a Sudanese, pulling army time in order to earn American citizenship. He was a man most steadfast in his religious convictions, and his religion was Islam. He imbued Calhoun with pride in being black as Christianity had made him ashamed of his color. Islam awakened a moral sense in Calhoun.

"I knew every apostle from Peter to Paul," he explained, "but I could never relate to spirits or ghosts—neither the holy ghost of Protestantism or the Virgin Mary bullshit of Catholicism. I found my discovery of Islam to be good.

"We were in Germany at a new post. There was me and another paratrooper and we were drinking three-point-two beer. Remember three-point-two beer? You'd have to drink a gallon to get a buzz on. We didn't drink a gallon but we did get to feeling good. On the way back to the barracks we took a shortcut through the gym. The boxing team was working out.

"I'd never had a glove on in my life, but that three-point-two kept telling me to volunteer. The coach told me to come back the next day. The next day the three-point-two feeling was gone, but its promise was still in me. I went back and he threw me in with the all-army heavyweight champ. I weighed one-fifty and knocked him cold with a left hook.

"I knew at last what I'd been created for: a fighting man. After that I lived for boxing alone. It became the beginning, the middle and the end of everything in my life.

"When I began fighting I began speaking better. I had had a bad stutter my whole life. Now I went to the Dale Carnegie Institute in Mannheim and they really helped me. I began developing a special feeling for verbal expression. It wasn't like being unable to talk clearly one day and being able to the next. I fought the words as they came at me, one by one, head-on, every day. I forced them into corners in my head until they came out of my lips. Every word was a hard-fought ten-round fight."

The Sudanese encouraged Calhoun's new enthusiasm. Calhoun won fifty-one fights in the army, thirty-five by knockouts, and lost five.

He was honorably discharged, as the army's light-welterweight champion, in June of 1956. He wasn't yet twenty.

He went to work in a plastics plant near Jersey City and was arrested there, while at work, for his escape three years before. He was sentenced to nine months at Annanville.

Full-grown men were forced to wear short pants at this reformatory: like kindergarten kids on their way to a class in coloring.

"The purpose was to make them feel like fools by making them look like fools," Calhoun explained.

He refused to eat and tore the offered pants to shreds. He was sentenced to four months in an empty hollow in a cement wall called "The Graveyard." When he was let out he refused work on the rockpile or in the grain mill; but he accepted a job handling boxing gear.

"When I got out I didn't care for anybody or anything. I'd lost my car, my job and my GI bill. I was mad at the world. I wanted to hit out at everybody in it. Who do I run into at exactly that moment but my old Elegant Gent–Jamesburg buddy Red Haloways.

"Red was fighting here and there, at one hundred seventy-two pounds, under the name of Tiger Keller, picking up fifty bucks here, fifty there. Red couldn't punch the hole out of a doughnut, but he had fast hands and he moved good. His trouble was that he didn't take himself seriously, either as a fighter or as anything else.

"So we'd get a bottle and put our guns in our pockets the way you'd put your wallet into yours. All we needed then was a whim and we'd do it. It was nothing planned. I couldn't begin to tell you how many stickups and muggings we pulled. If I hadn't gone to prison I'd be dead. Somebody would have killed me or I would have killed somebody.

"One night we decided to race one another in stolen cars. We stole the cars, Red in a black Chevy and me in a green Ford. We pull into a gas station and I get the idea of robbing one attendant while the other is filling up Red. I backed the kid toward the washroom when a cop steps out, police special in hand: I dropped my own gun. He could have shot me dead but he didn't.

"Red stepped on the gas and got out. He did the right thing. He offered, through a lawyer, to perjure himself in court in my behalf. I said no because what good would it have done except to get Red named as an accomplice? I pled guilty to felonious assault and was sentenced to four years.

"Most numbers talk out their fantasies in the joint. They're going to do this, they're going to do that. I didn't talk. I *knew* what I was going to do and I *worked* at it."

Billy Boggs, a black man twenty years older than Calhoun, who was Ruby's cellmate for a year, supervised fights in the dusty prison yard.

"Calhoun took to fighting with a passion," Boggs later remembered. "It was never too hot or too cold, too wet or too dry in the yard to keep Ruby from working out. He loved roadwork. He loved to fight. He fought to win.

"We didn't match weights or anything in there. You found a guy willing to box and you boxed, that was all. If the fight got going good the timekeeper might let a round go six or seven minutes.

"Once a year, on the Fourth of July, we'd put up a ring and have a boxing show. I matched Ruby with a strong dude, over two hundred pounds, and Ruby knocked him cold."

"Seven managers bid for my services when I got out," Calhoun recalls, "and I picked the wrong one. I picked Billy Boggs. Well, not exactly. I picked Jennifer Boggs, actually. Boggs's stepdaughter. I used to see her when she came to visit the old man. No, I didn't *meet* her. A tall, light-skinned girl, the quiet kind. She'd bring the old man a package of food and he'd accept it as though she *owed* it to him. That would spin me.

"Jennifer had been only ten years old when Billy made the joint, and her mother had died while Billy was still locked. She was twenty when I first saw her and looked as though she had never had a boyfriend.

"She came to my first fights after I got out. We'd have drinks together after the fight. I'd have a drink, that is to say. With an old man like Jennifer had, all she'd have would be an orange juice. She was teaching grade school, and having her on his hands sometimes got in the way of Billy's drinking. When we told him we planned to marry, he was pleased.

"He took me down to Annapolis to see a boxing show and I'm in the stands eating a hot dog, when Billy comes up running—'Suit up! We got a fight!'—and starts hauling me away.

" 'I don't have a license, Billy,' I had to remind him, 'no more than you got a manager's license.'

" 'I'll take care of *that,*' he tells me. So I suit up and fight some dude head to head for four rounds. They give me the decision."

"Ruby Calhoun, one-fifty, Trenton," the report reads, "gained a split decision over Ritchie Michaels, Baltimore, in four rounds."

Calhoun's purse was held up because he had no license.

"I just fought my stupid heart out for forty stinking dollars," he complained to Matt Haloways, "now they won't pay me. They've got me pitching rocks at the penitentiary again."

"Let somebody else pitch the rocks, Ruby," Matt advised him, and handed him two twenties.

"He was more like a father to me than my own father," Calhoun was later to remember Matt Haloways.

Calhoun began training intensively in a broken-down garage which Billy Boggs called a gymnasium. It had a light bag, a heavy bag and an exercise bike bought by Matt. Old Matt had done a bit of fighting in his youth and still liked to spar with Ruby. Matt had been a heavy in his fighting days and now weighed two-twenty. Yet he had not gone to fat. He was a big-shouldered old boy who, Ruby had learned, was still dangerous. Matt took the game seriously.

It became Billy Boggs's practice to match Calhoun against anyone, any time, any place, license or no license. By fight time Billy would be half-stoned, with a bottle of Old Overholt on his hip. Ruby would go out and kayo an opponent in one round or two, then find that Billy had taken his end of the purse in advance.

"Next time you take my end, *you* fight the guy," Ruby told Billy at last and began managing himself.

Red Haloways was the local fight fans' hero at this moment. He'd won eleven straight, had one draw and no losses. His manager was a local roofing contractor named Yan Ianelli. Yan took Ruby on as a sparring partner for his "Tiger Keller"; but after the first half-dozen sessions Red had complained, "Hey! Rube! Hold it! You're the sparring partner, not me."

By the time Ianelli had signed Ruby to fight one Emilio Sanjurjo, at St. Nick's, Red had become Ruby's sparring partner.

New Jersey fight fans don't buy tickets to witness exhibitions of boxing skill. They pay to see an opponent knocked cold. Red had not scored a single kayo in all his eleven wins. Ruby won his first five fights for Ianelli by early knockouts. Inadvertently, Ruby had thus diminished his old reform-school buddy, both in the ring and out of it.

When Ianelli began giving Ruby most of his attention, Red felt abandoned. Ianelli had matched him for a semi-windup, in Elizabeth, the same night he'd matched Ruby in Union City.

Ianelli went to Union City with Ruby and Red went alone to Elizabeth.

Red had never paid heed to ringside cries for bloodshed, and had been far ahead on points, when somebody near at hand had shouted "Get him, Tiger!" Red had reached over and clipped the opponent on the jaw—just as the opponent reached over and clipped Red. Down went Tiger Keller.

Red made sure he had the full count before he rose.

"Back to the bushes, Tiger!" somebody had taunted him coming out of his dressing room. Red fingered the Band-aid across his nose. He wasn't in a drinking mood but he found his way to the nearest bar all the same. In the bar mirror he saw a brown-skinned girl studying him.

"You got a little careless in there, Tiger," she assured him laughingly. He asked the bartender to serve her another of whatever she was drinking and moved over beside her. She had a broad face, with high cheekbones, which lent her an oriental aspect. She looked to be eighteen at the most.

"My name ain't Tiger," he told her, "It's Ed Haloways."

"Mine is Dovie-Jean. Dovie-Jean Dawkins." She raised her glass and he touched it with his own. "Now give me two bits for the juke," she begged.

She took a small shock at the sight of Red's two rooms: sporting magazines, empty beer tins, sweatshirts, girlie magazines, old fight posters and ashtrays, overflowing, were scattered everywhere. In the room's center a barber's chair rose on its pedestal.

"What the hell do you *do* here—give haircuts?" she wanted to know.

"Oh that. I just thought it would give the place a touch of class," was Red's curious explanation of the chair. He didn't feel it necessary to add that it had been taken, in a raid on a barber shop the year before, by himself and Ruby. Why he'd wanted it he still could not have said.

She curled up in it without taking off her coat and observed this curious, good-looking high-yellow dude mixing her a drink from his beat-up refrigerator. Then he went into the bedroom and came out wearing a crumpled tux, looking like Broadway in the 1920s, with a high white collar and a black string tie. Then he switched on the record player and the voice came sweet and clear:

Night and day
You are the one
In the roaring traffic's boom
In the silence of my lonely room . . .

Then she saw that, though his lips were moving, the voice was that of Sinatra. She laughed, when the record was done, and gave him a hand of applause. He selected another record and the voice came deeper now, slower, less tensely than Sinatra's:

In our little penthouse
Way up in the blue
With hinges on chimneys
For clouds to go through . . .

Apparently displeased with Tony Bennett, he switched the record off and began again:

And every afternoon at five
We'll both be glad to be alive
With cocktails for two.

"I know, I know," Dovie-Jean interrupted in pleased surprise, "Johnny Mathis."

The voice trailed off as the record ran down. Red's face looked ashen. He switched the machine off, tore off his collar and tie and stretched out on the bed, looking at the ceiling with vacant eyes.

"Tiger," she whispered, shocked at the sudden change, "what's happening?"

He rolled his eyes toward her.

"Nothin's happenin'. Nothin' at all. I just don't mime *no* goddamned nigger."

She touched his forehead but he made no response.

"You feelin' all right, Tiger?"

No reply.

She switched off the light and returned to her barber's chair. She heard his breathing deepen then shift to a light snore.

In sleep Red was standing before a full-length mirror wearing his boxing trunks. Behind him a nurse, whose face he could not make out, was holding out a container of some white, unpleasant-looking stuff to him.

"It's the solution we took from you when we were testing," she explained, and he wondered what illness they had been testing him for.

"I'll get an alternate opinion," he told her, and took the container down a long, darkening hall, to another doctor's office. He opened the door and saw a group of mourning blacks in a circle, as if surrounding someone dear to them now dead, and he closed the door and hurried to give the container back to the nurse because he knew now there was something contaminating in it.

He could not find the nurse, he could not find the door from which he'd come, and they were all expecting him. He saw a mini train, the kind that is run for children in amusement parks, and he boarded it.

In a moment he was inside a crowded subway expressing uptown, passing stations in the middle of the track, all the way. He did not know how to get off it, he wanted to go back, the train began picking up speed.

"This is going to cost you nine dollars," somebody in the next room told him, and he looked at the stuff in the container and saw that what it contained was no more than a piece of ham and a large helping of au gratin potatoes.

Light streaming in wakened Dovie-Jean. Red was standing in the bathroom door, freshly showered, a towel around his waist. The Band-aid was off. He was smiling.

"You all right, Tiger?" she asked.

"Of course."

"You didn't look good last night. I thought maybe you'd been hurt. Are you all right?"

"I wasn't even kayoed, honey. Just went down and saw no point in getting up, that was all."

"What got you then, Tiger?" She held his hand.

"Nothing got me. Nothing at all. I get the bad blues sometimes—but who doesn't? Don't you?"

"Of course. But they don't knock me out like *that*."

A shadow fled across his face. "I just lay doggo until the bad blues pass, that's all."

"You're like the devil's stocking, Tiger."

"How do you mean that?"

"You're knitted backwards." She studied him a long moment, wondering to go or stay. Then asked him, "You want me to stick around and clean up a bit?"

"Why not? I'm going down to the gym myself. I want to let my manager know I've retired from the ring. If he'd been with me last night . . ." Red left the sentence unfinished. As it was to remain unfinished the rest of his life.

He carried his boxing equipment in a small green airlines bag, and didn't return until late afternoon. He stopped in his doorway in pleased surprise.

His rooms were bright, clean and shining. There were curtains in the windows. The empty beer cans had been thrown out. Dirty dishes had been washed and were standing neatly on a shelf. His sweatshirts, socks, jockstraps and underwear had been laundered and hung to dry above the stove. He gave her a nod of approval but said nothing.

Later he handed her a twenty and explained, "for groceries."

She bought them, cooked them, served them and cleaned up after. Finally he had to give in, "It looks like we've set up housekeeping, Dovie-Jean."

"If you want it that way, Tiger."

Of her life heretofore spent among a throng of brothers, sisters, cousins, uncles and aunts, she could recall little more than the names of a few. As none had given her a name truly her own.

Red did that. She was Dovie-Jean Dawkins; and she liked it.

"Meet Dovie-Jean," Red would introduce her, and add, "she's my old lady." She could hardly have been more proud.

Until he got dressed by himself, one evening, and left without telling where he was going or when he'd be back. She waited.

"What kind of deal was that last night?" she asked him the next morning.

"The Paradise, honey. I'm getting into the white entertainment world. I mean the *white* entertainment world."

Dovie-Jean said nothing. But when he returned, later that afternoon, from the gym, he knew, as soon as he entered the flat, that she was not there.

She did not show up that night, nor the next. He found her, the following evening, at Rocky's Hideaway, a black dance joint. She gave him no nod of recognition. Finally, following her about the dance floor, she turned on him, smiled quietly and told him,

"I'm getting into the *black* entertainment world, honey."

"Let me talk to you, Dovie-Jean," he asked. "Why not?" was her answer.

"I'm not trying to pass for white like you think, honey," he assured her. "The Paradise is a white joint, that's all. A white dude, Le Forti, he's his own bartender, runs it. I'm his entertainment, that's all there is to it."

"You go right ahead, Tiger. You be anybody's entertainment."

"I have to live, Dovie-Jean. It's a white man's world and I'm in it. I do what I do best, that's all."

She studied him a long minute. What she saw was a schoolboy begging for a passing grade as though she were his teacher. She touched his hand.

"All right, Tiger, don't cry about it. What you want me for, I haven't yet figured out. But I'll keep your house neat, and you go out sucking around your white friends while I look at TV. Maybe someday you'll tell me what you want me around for."

"I don't go for white women, Dovie-Jean," he told her, "I never have."

"Why not?"

"I don't know. I just don't have that feeling for them."

She was uncertain as to whether to believe him or not—and yet it was true. There was dancing in the rear of Le Forti's Paradise but Red never asked a white woman to dance. This was too early in the Civil Rights movement, at any rate, for that sort of thing. Not in Jersey City you didn't.

Le Forti's record player was concealed beneath his bar. He'd hand Red the mike and switch the player on and Red would mime the voice of Eddie Arnold:

You always hurt the one you love
The one you shouldn't hurt at all
You'll always break the kindest heart
With a hasty word you can't recall. . . .

You could never fool everyone at the bar every time. You could always fool some of them.

"Give that redheaded nigger a drink on me!" a white woman had once instructed Le Forti. Red had accepted the drink and had raised his glass to the woman in acknowledgement.

He had ignored Le Forti's wink of encouragement. He might become a pimp, Red realized, but he wasn't about to *be* pimped.

Dovie-Jean said nothing. She doubted that he slept with white women: why should he when he had *her* to sleep with? Yet, night after night they slept side by side and he never reached for her.

"You won't do yourself no good hangin' around a white bar," old man Haloways had cautioned Red; but Red had paid the old man no heed.

"Hardee got more sense," the old man grumbled, referring to his younger son.

Nobody had foreseen the swift color shift, from white to black, which was consummated, within six months, that year in Jersey City.

Hurrying to get in on the big change, old man Haloways and Hardee bought the Paradise from Vince Le Forti and hired Red to tend the back bar.

Red stood behind the same bar behind which Vince Le Forti had only recently been the boss. Now Red could take the mike and sing the songs he chose to sing, when he chose to sing them. He preferred white ballads to black:

It's only a paper moon
Under a cardboard sky . . .

Or:

Come to me my melancholy baby
Cuddle up and don't be blue.

In the early morning hours Red began mixing self-pity with the Scotch and then his voice turned black and guttural and quietly threatening:

Sent for you yesterday
And here you come today

You can't have my love, Baby
And treat me thisaway.

On the morning that Jennifer Boggs became the bride of Ruby Calhoun, in the Newark, New Jersey City Hall, their witnesses were Matt, Ed and Hardee Haloways. The group then retired to a nearby bar to toast the marriage.

"Are you getting decent crowds, Red?" Jennifer asked.

"If what you mean by decent, Jenny, is lots of people, we've got that running," Red assured her, "only not all that 'decent'. The people want to go to church, they go Sunday morning. Saturday night they ball at the Paradise. They come to drink, dance and mess around. That right, Hardee?"

"Mess around, mostly," Hardee agreed sullenly. He was six years younger, two inches taller than Red and was intensely self-controlled. He'd come of age within the Civil Rights movement and shared few interests with Red. Hardee didn't drink, gamble, play games or chase women. He studied law and handled the front bar of the Paradise. He'd never yet been known to say, "This one is on the house."

"Where's Billy?" he asked Jennifer now.

"Sleeping one off in the coach house, more than likely."

"Billy Boggs," Calhoun recalled, "once had me billed for a fight in Trenton on Monday night, and another the following Thursday in Reading, Pennsylvania. 'What are we doing over the weekend, Billy?' I asked him, 'just sit around smoking cigarettes?' Then he tried to match me against Roddy Nims, out of Washington, D.C. Nobody would give Roddy a title fight. He was so fast, cute and strong they were all afraid of him, middleweights same as welters. 'Fight him yourself, Billy,' I told the old man, 'I'm tired.' If I hadn't of left your old man," Calhoun turned to his bride, "he would have got me killed in cold blood."

Two weeks after his marriage, Ruby signed a contract with the roofing contractor who'd been managing Red, Yan Ianelli. His immediate advantage was that he now did roadwork instead of roofwork.

Ianelli, a man of Calhoun's own age, was an enthusiast. He

got Ruby out of bed at 5 A.M. and off the pair would go for an hour's roadwork through the public parks. At 9 A.M. Ianelli went to his office and Ruby went back to bed.

"Calhoun is doing something for me," Ianelli told the press proudly, "he's proved to me that a boy who's been in prison can be helped if he's put on the right track. It's one of the nicest things that has ever happened to me. Ruby is always welcome in my home. He goes to the refrigerator. My wife is a student of astrology and she tells us when the time for him to fight is most favorable."

"In Aries," Mrs. Ianelli would cut into any interview with Calhoun, "the sun is at its most splendid. Ruby is fiery and has a great sense of adventure and an aggressive, pioneering spirit. He is ambitious and, at the same time, possesses the daring and the practicality to realize his ambitions."

Ruby would take off his shades, wipe them thoughtfully, then put them back on.

"He swims in my pool," Ianelli boasted, "he has proved to me that he has a good heart. It is only at his insistence that I have taken money from him. He asked me to take my percentage. So I took it and opened an account, in Ruby's name. I don't want money. I want a champion."

"What you want and what you get are two different things," Elvira would assure him, while the reporter, pencil poised above his pad, would glance across at Calhoun in hope of hearing something worth writing.

"My husband," Elvira went on as though she were the interviewee, "is careless to the point of rashness. He is also willful and impulsive and tends to ignore the counsel of wiser heads." She turned to Yan and reproached him directly. "You often fly into a situation headlong before you have investigated its perils. You act on the spur of the moment and pay no attention to what I'm trying to tell you. You are very likeable. But that doesn't make up for your habit of making a horse's ass of yourself at every opportunity."

Yan Ianelli smiled wanly. Calhoun got up and walked out.

"They say he can't keep hitting that hard for more than three rounds,'' Ianelli defended Calhoun against the growing suspicion, among fans, that Calhoun wasn't able to go the full distance, ''but there are very few fighters who can take that sort of punishment for more than three. You'll have to show me someone who can. My regret is that, when he scores an early kayo, that fans can't see how well he fights in the sixth or eighth.''

Buford Lee, a black man fighting out of Memphis, was the first fighter to give Calhoun's fans a chance to see how their man stood up under pressure. He stayed on top of Calhoun, at Madison Square Garden, with both hands high all the way. He capitalized on Calhoun's wildness, used combinations to body and head, and every time Calhoun took the offensive he fought back.

In the fifth Calhoun sent Lee reeling across the ring, but Lee's jabs bothered Calhoun so much he was unable to follow through.

''I knew I was going to whip you,'' Lee assured Calhoun after taking the decision. ''You weren't fighting your own fight. You were concentrating on the fans instead of on me.''

''We learned a lot from Buford Lee,'' Ianelli rationalized this defeat. ''We silenced people who were saying Calhoun couldn't take a good punch. It was a setback but not a serious one. Boxing isn't a single-elimination game. We'll fight Buford Lee again.''

''When this boy learns to put punches together he'll be better than Dick Lion,'' Sandy Randolph, who had once whipped Lion, observed.

By the time Calhoun fought Buford Lee again, again in Madison Square, he'd learned to put punches together. A terrific right hand started Lee down in the first round. He held on until Calhoun came on with both hands. The southerner dropped, mouthpiece dangling, over the bottom rope. The referee didn't bother counting.

Two minutes and seven seconds of the first round.

''I thought I'd learned a lot about Calhoun the first time we fought,'' Lee acknowledged ruefully. ''It looks now like he learned more about me.''

A host of rooters tried to crash Calhoun's dressing room after he'd whipped Buford Lee. Police were required to control the crowd.

"This is the first time this happened since Marciano beat Louis," Matt Haloways, an old-time fight fan, recalled. "He's the same type fighter as Graziano, but he can do a lot more than Graziano ever could. Graziano went for the head. He couldn't score to the body like Calhoun. I could feel some of those blows to Lee's midsection. They *hurt*."

While training for his fight against Emilio Sanjurjo, one of Calhoun's spar mates told Calhoun he was going out for an ice cream soda; he never came back. He abandoned his equipment and took off, that was all.

"It's bad enough what he does to you, but why does he have to keep *telling* you about it?" the spar mate wanted to know. "The worst part is the blow-by-blow account he gives you while he's doing it. I maybe could take his punch. But not his announcing."

"Why shouldn't I be a fightie-talkie?" Calhoun defended his curious habit of informing an opponent that he was chopping him up while chopping him up. "It's my business, my job. Would you tell a carpenter not to whistle on the job? Would you tell a butcher to keep his mouth shut when he's slicing pork chops? It relaxes me. Sanjurjo is the toughest man I've fought, I know how well he is thought of, that's what I'm telling myself when I work out. If I can whip him it'll be a tremendous boost."

Jennifer, Red and Dovie-Jean, Billy Boggs, Floyd Calhoun and old man Matt Haloways took ringside seats at St. Nick's for this bout. Hardee Haloways was not present. He did not belong to Calhoun's entourage. Hardee had not the faintest interest in sports. He followed the stock market.

Emilio Sanjurjo was an experienced man. He'd fought several times at St. Nick's and had been on Garden cards half a dozen times. He was methodical, working an opponent over before attempting a knockout. He began pecking away at Calhoun with his left. As they swung toward the ring's west ropes Calhoun lashed out with a blurring left that caught Sanjurjo flush on the jaw. Down went Sanjurjo.

He rose before the mandatory eight but was stunned. Groggy, reeling and ducking, he managed to stay clear of Calhoun's left for almost a minute. Then, in mid-ring, a real blockbuster caught him and knocked him almost through the ropes. He slumped against them while the referee counted eight a second time. The fight was over but the referee didn't stop it.

He let Sanjurjo come on until another bone-crushing left caught him. He didn't bother counting Sanjurjo out.

One minute and thirty-eight seconds of the first round.

"Calhoun hits harder than anyone I have ever fought," Sanjurjo acknowledged later.

"A lot of fighters hit hard," the referee added his comment, "but when Calhoun hits you, you don't get up."

Calhoun took his wife, father, Red and Matt Haloways, Dovie-Jean, Yan and Elvira Ianelli and Billy Boggs to a pizza parlor after the fight. Yan and his spaced-out wife were the life of the party.

"They're all going to be quick," Yan assured a couple of sportswriters who had invited themselves to Calhoun's table. "This boy is as powerful as any middleweight in the world. He's going to be champion. Let me tell you how strong and good this boy is. When we fought Hirsch Jacoby and got beat, we agreed to fight three times in one night for charity in Jersey City. The first guy was a heavyweight. Ruby knocked him out in one round. The second was a middleweight. He went out in one too. Then came another heavyweight. This was the main event. It was *rough*. It took Ruby two whole rounds to put him away. What you're looking at tonight, gentlemen, at this table, is the greatest middleweight since Stanley Ketchel!"

Elvira stood up. She was slightly stoned. Elvira was always slightly stoned.

"You are unusually beauty-loving and artistic," she addressed the table but no one in particular, "your sense of proportion, line and color are superb. You vibrate toward balance and harmony. You tend to appreciate music and other cultured entertainments where aesthetic values are involved. You have an excellent constitution and have great powers of endurance. Libra rules the back and kidneys. Afflications to your sun can cause trouble in either of these regions."

She sat down to scattered applause. Nobody knew who she'd been talking about. Or what an "affication" was.

"Anyone who does four and a half years in the joint," one ex-number observed, out of Calhoun's hearing, "can't have no kind of chin. Where Calhoun been, they didn't have no training table. And they don't let you out in the morning because they're not sure you'll come back. The first place *that* shows up is in the chin."

Roddy Nims was a thirty-three-year-old black pro who'd fought the best and had always looked good. Calhoun had declined to meet him when he'd been with Billy Boggs. Because Nims was as workmanlike a fighter as there was in the ring. He had never been knocked down in his career. Calhoun hit him with two left hooks and Nims's legs sagged. It looked like Roddy Nims was going home early.

"Push him off, Rube! Push him off!" Red Haloways shouted to Calhoun from ringside.

Middleweights had been trying to push Nims off for twelve years. Calhoun couldn't. In the fourth round Nims put Calhoun down, for the first time in his life, with a right hand to the head. Calhoun was up at four.

"He had me down," Calhoun said later, "but I said to myself, he got to *keep* me down. I didn't think he could do it. Nims is tough. I'm proud to have whipped him."

"If Calhoun had had the experience I have," Nims acknowledged in his dressing room, "I couldn't have lasted a single round. He is the most determined fighter I have ever been up against."

It had been a good fight, a close fight. It showed Calhoun to be still improving.

A couple of nights after whipping Nims, Ruby walked into the Paradise. Dovie-Jean was at the bar. Red put a fifth of Cutty Sark in front of Ruby, with two glasses, and poured one for Dovie-Jean.

"You going to put something in the juke, Champ?" she asked Calhoun. He handed her a half dollar and she put on a song called

"Back Door Man." Then she asked Ruby to dance.

Calhoun paid her no heed. "You know anything about Rocky Olivera?" he asked Red.

"Rugged," Red assured him. "You going down there?"

"It's an offer."

"He owns the town."

"Which town is that?" Dovie-Jean wanted to know.

"Buenos Aires," Calhoun informed her, then asked "Where you from?"

"Outside Raleigh, North Car'lina."

"I was stationed there one time," Calhoun tried to make conversation, "Fort Bragg. Used to go to Fayetteville on weekends."

"Olivera is a busy boy," Red brought the conversation back to the main track. "He owns two hotels. You stay in one of his joints. Win or lose, he gets dough back like that."

"Dance, Champ?" Dovie-Jean still insisted.

They danced through a song with a catching refrain:

This is a great big city
There's a million things to see . . .

Calhoun caught Red's eye over Dovie-Jean's shoulder. "Take her if you want her," Red's look assured him.

"Where you staying?" Ruby asked her.

She made no reply.

"With Red?"

"Till I get a job."

She didn't sound like somebody in a great rush toward employment. He suggested they go out for a bite to eat, and drove her to a barbecue joint beside a bar. A motel sign gleamed greenly on the other side of the highway:

VACANCY

He steered her into the bar, told her to order what she wanted and one for himself. Then he went across the highway and, when he returned, put the motel key down beside her glass. She smiled.

"It's what I thought you were up to," was all she said.

She sounded contented.

"Red don't care what time I get in," she assured him as soon as they were in the motel room, "so long as I'm with you. You and him been friends a long time, haven't you?"

"Since we been kids," he told her, "we were locked together."

He stretched out on the bed when she switched off the lights. The green VACANCY sign cast a curious glow, behind the curtain, in reverse. She came to him, in her panties, stockings and bra, and sat back on her haunches while he unhooked her bra. Her breasts were full and her nipples pointed. He felt them hardening under his palms while she unbuttoned his shirt, drew it off, then unhooked his belt and drew off his pants. He studied her face while she undressed him.

"I've never done *this* before," she told him, drawing off his shorts, then sat back, smiling, while he undressed her completely.

She studied him, as he lay back, stroking his chest, belly and genitals. Her touch was light, yet her eyes were bright. "I've never seen a man *totally* naked before," she explained.

He put his hands behind his head and encouraged her, "Help yourself, Dovie-Jean."

"You really *mean* that?" she asked. Then, without waiting for further encouragement, put her lips down lightly upon his penis and began a soft sucking which brought the organ up hugely. She sat back, holding it in her hand, immensely proud of her power over it.

He waited as though to say: "Let's see your next move."

Her next move was simple enough: she swung herself over, straddling him, still holding his upright cock, pressing her cunt down upon it.

It wouldn't fit. Either he was too big or she was too small.

Yet, by the way she held her head back, and by the determination of her mouth, he knew she wanted it in. *Deep* in. He put his big hands upon her hips and pressed her firmly down. Her mouth strained back in pain yet pleasure as he entered her.

She began a slow, instinctive woman's dance upon him, working him farther and farther into her belly as she rocked. A pang of pleasure took her, so intense that she straightened up rigidly. Then relaxed only a moment before she came once again. She collapsed upon him, breathless with wonder and surprise. He rolled over above her, and withdrew in order to let her catch her breath.

He waited until she smiled up at him. Then he got his arms about her in a good firm hold and held her so until he'd exhausted himself. She crossed her legs behind his back to help him; he rolled off and lay, mouth parted and asleep, on her breast.

They slept for almost two hours. When he wakened he moved away to look at her. There was something here he did not understand; yet didn't know how to ask.

"Has it been a long time for you, Dovie-Jean?" he asked her at last.

Her eyes gleamed in the dark and she laughed softly. "All my life."

"I don't get it."

"Eighteen years a virgin."

"What about Red?"

"When we sleep together that's what we do: sleep."

"Why? Don't you like him?"

She raised herself onto her elbow. "I like Red *very* much. I like him as much as I've ever liked another person. Red took me in when I didn't have a nickel. Red never looks down on me. I never had nobody, my whole life, to respect me enough to make me feel I was *somebody.* Red done *everything* for me."

"Except screw you," Calhoun mumbled sleepily.

"Is that so important?"

"Don't you feel it's important, now that you've lost your virginity?"

"I would have lost it long ago, if anybody had particularly wanted it. I was never crazy about being a virgin, just for the sake of being one. Now it's gone, I feel better."

"If I'd known you were a virgin I wouldn't have brought you here."

"I know. That's why I didn't mention it until it was over."

Ruby's eyes closed as she was speaking and he began snoring

lightly. She lay back, her own eyes closed yet wide awake, remembering.

Dovie-Jean remembered gumps.

She remembered her father, whom white folks had nicknamed Ironhead Dawkins, and the sack he had taken, every morning, to the poultry market. He had taken her with him many times as a child, to where chickens were being unloaded off boxcars, and the sick and the dying were being sorted from the healthy birds.

A gump was a sick or dying chicken. When they were through sorting Daddy would step up with his two sacks and fill them with gumps, some still fluttering. Then the handler would say, "Take 'em away, Ironhead."

Ironhead Dawkins appeared to be constructed of furnace-forged iron: six-and-a-half feet in height and weighing a solid two-sixty, yet he carried himself with the appropriate air of subservience. "It's not my fault I'm big, white boss," was what his attitude told.

He had to. He had better. His physical superiority over most white men made it more necessary for him than for most blacks to humble himself. Indeed, it was his huge humility that had earned him the privilege of picking up gumps. He sometimes ran into a poultry handler mean enough to charge him a nickel for each gump. No difference. Ironhead sold them in Niggertown for two dollars apiece.

Or he'd go into some black bar holding three gumps upside down which would get them so angry—dying or not—that they would puff out and shake feathers all over the place, looking twice their skimpy size. He'd buy a beer and, sure enough, someone would try to beat him out of his chickens, but Ironhead would refuse. That would encourage somebody to buy him a beer, to loosen him up. After three beers he would appear to be getting drunk. At last he would give in and sell all three gumps for five dollars, and walk out sober. They had only cost him fifteen cents.

Dovie-Jean remembered a rainy summer morning when she'd been playing with an older brother, a boy of eleven, in their barn. She must have been seven or eight.

"Show me your thing," she had demanded.

She'd been studying the powerless little penis when a heavy odor had caught her and she'd looked up to see her father, looking like an avenging Moses, his huge hand drawn back to strike.

She had ducked between his legs and run and hidden, until it had felt safe to return to the house. Her mother had laughed at the incident and had said nothing but, "Shame on you, Dovie-Jean," and it had been forgotten.

Her mother had died that winter of bronchitis. Dovie-Jean had heard her giving a rattle in her throat, and heard it grow louder. Her grandmother, reading a magazine beside her mother's bed, began clubbing the dying woman with the magazine because she was in the middle of some story. Then the rattle had exploded in her mother's throat, the whole bed shook, and the girl knew her mother was gone.

Ironhead had begun drinking after the funeral. The family had broken up. She'd been shipped north, to an aunt in Newark: a woman who already had a houseful of kids. Half-brothers, half-sisters, cousins by the score, in-laws and friends lived in that dark old house. Dovie-Jean was indistinguishable in the crowd. Sometimes some grown-up asked her, "What's *your* name, little girl?"

The little girl didn't feel that she had a name of her own.

Once a teacher, calling her by her first name with an accent of sympathy, had wakened in the child a feeling of great love. For she had great love in her.

Nobody needed it. Nobody wanted it. Love was a drag on the market.

Had anyone encouraged her to continue school, she would have continued. But there was nobody who cared, one way or another, so she dropped out. She went to work as a domestic and, after cleaning some white family's house, sat around black bars, at first, with an I.D. card that belonged to somebody else. She was then not quite sixteen. And was not aware that the life she was leading was not a life but the shadow of living and nothing more.

Until that nice-looking light-skinned dude, with the long, pale, freckled face, a burr-head of reddish hair and a wide white smile, had walked into the bar where she sat, waiting for a live one, hardly an hour after he'd been knocked cold.

She had even liked the Band-aid he'd worn across his nose.

"I just see you settin' here by yourself, and you look *special,*" he told her.

"*Me? Special?* They don't come more ordinary than *me,*" she assured him.

"Not to *me* you don't look ordinary."

He could not have hit on a better approach.

"I think Calhoun will walk right into a right hand," it was José Salazar's expressed opinion before their fight in Union City in August of 1964, "and my right is the best hand I have. I saw Nims drop him with a right. If Benson could have hit harder he would have stopped Calhoun cold."

Salazar opened cuts above Calhoun's eyes, then slashed the cuts with his laces. When Calhoun was told the fight might have to be stopped, he hit Salazar ten successive punches, but Salazar didn't give him room to land damagingly and came back with an offensive of his own. Yan Ianelli began waving his arms and shouting, "Stop the fight! Stop the fight!" The fight was awarded to Salazar although Calhoun had been ahead on points.

"I don't want to fight no more billygoats," was Calhoun's only comment.

"Although he can't box," one critic observed of Salazar, "he can't think too well and he can't punch either."

"If I win as big as I expect to," Emil Griffin assured reporters before his fight with Calhoun, "I expect to campaign as a middleweight. I've fought seven middleweights and whipped every one. Calhoun is going to be the eighth. I'm going after him at the bell and—*BANG!*"

In their bout at Pittsburgh, later in 1964, Griffin started slowly, merely jabbing and ducking. Calhoun, who'd been warming up in his dressing room for twenty minutes, landed a solid left into Griffin's belly. Griffin moved in carelessly, Calhoun pitched another left to the body, pushed Griffin away with considerable force, crossed with a right and drove another smashing left to Griffin's head.

Griffin landed on his back and rose slowly to beat the count, but his legs were rubbery. Calhoun stormed after him and beat him into the ropes. Another smashing left to the body and Griffin slithered to the canvas. He was still trying to rise when the referee stopped the fight.

Two minutes and thirteen seconds of the first round.

The crowd was stunned momentarily by the suddenness of the knockout. Then broke into cheers and applause for Calhoun.

"He's a good little man and I'm a good big man," Calhoun commented. "Though there's only a three-and-a-half-pound pull in the weights, that doesn't tell the story. The comparison is marked in other ways—how I pushed him around proves it. It's silly to match me with welterweights. I've told you that before."

"I was careless and got a lousy break," Griffin complained. "I know I was down twice and I remember everything clearly."

He then proceeded to relate details which had never occurred.

"They should never have stopped that fight," Griffin's mother insisted, "my boy would have stayed up and gone on to win. I wasn't worried about that in the least."

"Griffin was a proud man before he was chosen Fighter of the Year," Calhoun observed, "he was so proud he forced the fight lest he be accused of running away. And I can knock out anybody in the world who comes *at* me like that."

Yan Ianelli announced, at ringside, that he was offering Joey Gardello a hundred thousand dollars to defend his title against Calhoun. "I'm out to do business with Gardello. He's his own manager, I'm going to talk loud and strong," Ianelli promised. "I now hold the key to the middleweight situation."

"You have a towering practical ambition," Mrs. Ianelli assured her husband before the press. "Like your symbol, the goat, you leap over both adversaries and obstacles in your climb to the heights. You have all the attributes necessary to success, since you are hard-working and reliable; you have tremendous initiative and drive, and the only thing that can possibly stop you is that you have almost no brain at all. To tell you the truth, you really *are* a goat."

"I made Ruby Calhoun a contender," Ianelli added without

paying attention to Elvira. "I took him out of prison and straightened him out. Now I'm going to make him a champion."

"I was a contender before I ever heard of Ianelli," Calhoun advised the press. "The man keeps on talking about how he took me out of prison, but he never took me out of anything. I served my time and was released. I'd been out months before I went to work for Ianelli. I was straightened out long before I'd met him. He never knew enough about fighting to whip his own wife. Neither of them have the faintest idea of what they're doing. He told me he lives by 'the Good Book,' but the good book he lives by is one on astrology. When he put Elvira to picking opponents according to their horoscopes, instead of on their records, I told them that was it: forget it. Now he's going to sue me, my father and the Boxing Commission. Let him sue. He claims he's got six contracts with me but he don't have a single legal one."

Floyd Calhoun managed Ruby in his fight with Joey Gardello. Although his father got him little more than his training expenses, Ruby wasn't dismayed by the prospect.

"I'd fight Gardello even if I had to pay him to get into the ring with me," he assured reporters. "Gardello will wind up with the money but I'll wind up with the title. Then I'll show them how to step."

Ruby entrained for Philadelphia with Red Haloways. Red was to serve him as a sparring partner. They took a two-room suite in a downtown hotel that had training quarters.

Red disappeared himself the first morning and Ruby had to work without a sparring partner. After a stiff workout, Ruby was relaxing, in the afternoon, when he heard laughter from the adjoining room. He went to the door wearing only his jockey shorts, and found Red lounging on a divan. A young white girl was mixing a drink for him.

"Rube, I want you to meet Marlene."

Ruby didn't acknowledge the introduction.

"Who's paying for this, Red?"

"I haven't yet got that figured out, Rube," Red answered cheerfully. "Put on some pants."

It was plain enough to the girl that the husky young black man in the doorway had no intention of putting on his pants. Ruby shut the door upon her and Red.

Red was on hand in the gym, early the following morning, by the time Ruby got there. He was suited up and was skipping rope.

"You ready for action?" he asked Red. "Get on your headgear."

Ruby climbed into the ring without headgear. He bulled Red back to the ropes, feinted him to the left, then to the right, moved him around the ring, pulling his punches. He cornered Red, let him go, cornered him again and again let him go.

Red's breath was coming hard not only from the pace. He knew that Ruby was telling him he could knock him cold whenever he chose and hadn't yet decided exactly when.

"Get on your duds, Red," Ruby told him when the round was done, "you're no good to me."

"What do you want me to do, Rube?" Red asked after he'd gotten dressed.

"Go home, Red. Go home. Stay there until fight night. I'll have two ringside for you and Matt."

"No hard feelings?"

"No hard feelings."

"People say he's mean," Red told a reporter. "They ask me how I can get along with him. I'll tell you, you can believe me, that man has no meanness in him at all. If he puts faith in you, and you cross him, he'll hurt you. But if you don't mistreat him, he's the best. Absolutely the best."

"Calhoun's beard is the source of his power," Gardello advised the press, "without it he is helpless. There are big germs in it. I have no fear whatsoever of Calhoun himself, but I cannot fight germs of such size."

The Boxing Commission instructed Calhoun to shave off his beard before getting into the ring with Gardello.

"But the beard makes me feel distinguished," Calhoun protested. "People take me for a musician. I walk down the street and people say, 'Where you playin', man?' and I tell them, 'Down in the Village.' "

"Calhoun gets smarter and smarter," Calhoun's new trainer,

Charlie Goldberg, announced. "Every time he fights he fights smarter than his last fight."

"That's nice," one of Gardello's stablemates observed, "if he lasts fifteen rounds with Gardello he'll be a genius."

"After I take care of Gardello," Calhoun assured him, "I'll take care of you."

Gardello was installed as a nine to five favorite. By fight night smart money, coming in from Scranton, switched the odds to Calhoun, seven to five.

Calhoun looked cool and menacing, wearing a black, hooded robe with a knotted golden belt. He'd shaved off his beard but had kept his Fu Manchu.

Gardello swung through the ropes wearing a ratty terry-cloth robe. Neither man acknowledged his introduction.

Crouched, chin in, Calhoun pressed forward, trying to move Gardello, a counter-puncher, around him clockwise. Gardello was too experienced to let himself be moved into a corner. He kept leading Calhoun back, in a wheeling pattern, leaving himself to move away. Calhoun was the aggressor from the start. He remained ahead the first four rounds because he was landing solidly. But he would not follow up his punches.

"I had to figure I was going fifteen rounds," he explained later. "I'd never gone fifteen before. I knew I had him from the start but I didn't go all out because I felt I had to save myself. Gardello takes a lot of punishment, then comes back. I held myself back. I didn't want to punch myself out."

In the fourth Calhoun staggered Gardello with a head shot and opened a cut above Gardello's left eye. The trickle of blood down his cheek didn't trouble Gardello. He'd been cut before and he succeeded, the remainder of the fight, in protecting that eye.

Calhoun stopped pressing in the middle rounds and didn't keep his hands so high. He was faster than Gardello had thought, slipping punches time and again. Calhoun, however, didn't sustain the pressing attack he'd begun. Gardello kept bouncing away, leaning back and spinning off. In the tenth Gardello took over, scoring with left hooks to the body and head, and sustained that attack in the last two rounds. There were no knockdowns.

"I think it was mine nine to six," Calhoun said after the decision had gone to Gardello. "If I could have made him fall, that was all. That would have made the difference. I staggered him half a dozen times, but he wouldn't go down. I could go another fifteen right now."

"I wasn't in the least surprised at the decision," Gardello told reporters. "I lost three rounds at the most. I hurt him in the thirteenth or fourteenth. I kept getting stronger. Fighting inside won it for me. Calhoun is a tough fighter but he didn't press me as much as I thought he would. This cut over my eye came from a butt. Calhoun told me he was sorry as soon as he did it. Considering he's only had twenty-five fights, he's darn good. Better than Dick Lion."

"If I'd pressed him any harder he would have had to walk along the top rope," Calhoun replied. "I didn't get to sit down once between rounds the whole fight. The ref kept me standing. I couldn't see what was going on in Gardello's corner. He just held me standing there, pretending to fix my cup. Fixed it every round. When it took twenty minutes for the decision to come in, I knew it was going to be a hometown decision."

"Calhoun was doomed before the fight got under way," Doc Lowry, a New Jersey fight manager, claimed. "The fight was in the wrong town."

Ask any ten sportswriters who won a bout, if both men are on their feet at its end, and you'll get six different answers. Boxing is the only sport in which, barring a knockout, any result is so disputable.

The orange-pop carton, and the copy of the Philadelphia *News,* which landed in the ring after Gardello had been declared winner by decision, must have been pitched there by one of the people who'd been predicting a hometown decision.

"If you're a Philly fighter you can win in Philly," one New York sportswriter claimed, adding, "Calhoun *mauled* Gardello."

"Had it been a street fight," another writer observed, "Calhoun would have won going away."

• • •

The Calhouns were now living in a big, tree-shaded old-fashioned farmhouse on the outskirts of Jersey City. They were renting but had taken an option to buy.

There was a half-acre of yard space around the place, half a dozen poplars and a one-story coach house made over from a stable.

Now it was Billy Boggs's home. He paid no rent, but took care of the property in return for his meals and occupancy. Billy didn't take too much care—but then the old stable couldn't have brought in much rent anyhow. Billy mowed the lawn, took out the garbage, trimmed bushes on the street side, and stayed out of the way when he was stoned, which was a blessing.

Because, when stoned, he was the biggest bore on the Eastern Seaboard. He'd found this black kid in the joint, and had seen his possibilities, he'd tell anyone whom he could get to stand still long enough to hear him out, and he'd worked on this kid, and had gotten him out of prison, and then, by careful programming, had set him on the road to a world's title. There was never a word about this kid having married his daughter, thus giving Billy bed and board. He stayed out of Ruby's hearing when explaining his claim to world fame. He watched Ruby's fights on TV rather than at ringside, at the Paradise.

Matt Haloways was tolerant of the old man. He'd dealt with drunks and ex-cons all his life. He was a good listener. The other old man of Calhoun's entourage, Floyd Calhoun, was less tolerant. Floyd came of a long line of backwoods preachers and never took a drink. He enjoyed chatting with old man Haloways, over a soft drink, but he kept an aversion to Billy.

It was their memories of fighters of the thirties and forties that the old men held in common. They could while away a whole afternoon, over a game of five-and-dime rummy in the Paradise, recalling Robinson, Zale, Graziano, Gavilan, Billy Graham and Fritzie Zivic. When Matt was holding a good hand, and a customer came in, Matt would tell him: "Help yourself!" The customer would then go behind the bar, pour himself a shot and a beer and call to Matt, "Put it on my tab." Matt sometimes remembered, sometimes forgot.

"The guy I always liked was Zale," Floyd Calhoun recalled. "You know what he told Jimmy Cannon after he'd been knocked out by Graziano in Chicago? He told Cannon, 'They never should have stopped that fight. Never.' 'Tony,' Cannon told him, 'if they hadn't stopped it you might have been killed on the ropes.' 'I was *entitled* to get killed for my title,' Zale told Cannon."

The Calhouns' house guests were now as often white as black: sportswriters, trainers, fighters black and fighters white, fighters brown and high yellow. Color is secondary among fighting men.

Ruby Calhoun no longer drank desperately. He hadn't been on a real burning-down drunk since his marriage. When Red put the bottle down on the bar for him, at the Paradise, Ruby would take one shot and that would be it.

Although Jennifer regarded Red with suspicion, she never attempted to impose morality on her husband. She knew it could not be done that way. Where another woman might have shrieked reproaches or threats, her silence bore the greater reproach. She had only to give him a certain glance to make his conscience writhe. For a man who'd been such a wild juvenile, Ruby Calhoun was doing well.

He drove Jennifer to the hospital one night, then returned to find his house desolate. He went to the coach house to chat up old times with Billy Boggs, but Billy was stretched out in a paralyzing drunk. He returned to the hospital early the following day, but by evening Jennifer had not given birth. A nurse advised Ruby to go home and get some sleep.

He couldn't find sleep. The moment his head hit the pillow he was wide awake and wondering. Why had his mother permitted his father to call the police that time of the Elegant Gent caper? After he'd gotten back from Germany, who had fingered him, working in the plastics factory, about his escape from Annanville? Why had the police picked him up, during the Harlem riots, and then let him go? Who'd even *known* he was up in Harlem? At last he put on his clothes and went down to the Paradise. It was shortly before the 2 A.M. closing hour.

Dovie-Jean Dawkins was at the bar as if expecting him. The

bar was empty but for her and Red. Red pushed the bottle toward Ruby but Ruby didn't pour.

"Little action, it looks like," Ruby observed.

Red grinned. "When a buddy wants action, he gets *action*." He ducked down and came up, from behind the bar, wearing a huge hawk nose and a wig of orange-blond more fiery than his own reddish mop. He switched on the record player beneath the bar and began miming Frank Sinatra:

And every afternoon at five
We'll be so glad to be alive.
Cocktails for two.

Dovie-Jean sat unsmiling. Her look said: "I've seen this one before." Ruby smiled weakly and nodded to Dovie-Jean. She rose and left with him, leaving Red alone at the bar still miming Sinatra:

In our little penthouse way up in the sky,
With hinges on windows for clouds to go by . . .

They drove, without further word, to the same little highway motel where they'd spent the night of their first meeting.

Ruby talked to women more confidently than to men, and Dovie-Jean was perceptive enough to know that what he wanted tonight wasn't sex so much as having a woman to talk to.

They lay side by side in the darkened room, her head upon his shoulder, his arm encircling her.

"We left Tiger looking like a fool, singing to himself," she remembered.

"Anytime anyone leaves that redhead looking like a fool, it's because Red wants to look the fool."

"I don't understand that, Ruby."

"When people take you for a fool, they're off guard. Red makes his own plans."

"Funny way to talk."

"Why funny?"

"Not friendly. Like you don't trust him. You *are* his best friend, after all, aren't you?"

"We been friends since we were kids. We ran the streets together in short pants. We fought on the streets together. We were locked together. I was his sparring partner till he lost a fight and quit. I started winning. But he never held that against me. He accepted that."

"It's what I mean, Ruby," Dovie-Jean tried to draw reassurance about Red from Ruby's characterization, "he's really generous. He ain't the kind, he does you a favor, he wants a favor right back."

Ruby took his arm from about her waist and repeated the warning he had already given her:

"He will, honey. He will."

They fell to sleep like brother and sister. When she wakened he was gone; but he'd left a ten-dollar bill, for cab fare, on the dresser.

At the hospital Ruby found himself to be the father of a seven-pound girl.

Early on the evening of June 16, 1966, Calhoun kissed Jennifer and drove, in a rented white Buick, to the Paradise.

Matt Haloways was at the front bar. Nobody was at the back. There wouldn't be enough drinkers to require the help of another bartender for several hours.

Dovie-Jean Dawkins was the only barfly at the moment.

"Congratulations, daddy-O," she greeted Calhoun, and sounded as if she meant it.

Calhoun handed her a dollar for the juke. While she was asking the old man to break it into quarters Calhoun told him, "We want you to be the baby's godfather, Matt."

The old man nodded and seemed pleased.

Dovie-Jean put on a song called "Kung-Fu Fighting Man." It made a great deal of noise but very little music.

"Turn that thing down a little, Dovie-Jean," Calhoun asked her, and turned back to Matt.

"I've signed against Rocky Olivera," he told him, "in Buenos

Aires in October. You ever been down that way, Matt?''

The old man shook his head, No. ''I got to New York for some fights once or twice, but that's the farthest I ever got. This Mexican, is he rough?''

''Not too rough,'' Calhoun assured him confidently, ''just a good opponent. Got a big following down there, I'm told.''

''Hope you're getting paid good.''

''Trouble ain't the money. Trouble is sparring partners. Hard to find.''

''Take Red along.'' But the old man laughed uneasily when he made the suggestion.

''Red isn't of any use in the ring anymore, Matt,'' Ruby told the old man what the old man already knew.

''There was a time I thought he was going to get somewheres,'' the old man recalled, ''but it didn't work out. Put your money on Hardee.''

''I'm bringing in a German heavy who moves pretty good,'' Calhoun told the old man, ''but I need at least one more around one-sixty.''

Dovie-Jean was dancing by herself before the juke. She'd put on a roaring record and was enjoying its roar. The old man walked over and turned the record down several decibels. When he looked up he saw a white man, carrying a rifle, coming in the door. Haloways walked up to him.

''How are you, Vince?''

''None of that. I come for my money.''

He was an undersized fellow who could look unkempt even when wearing clothes just out of the store. He needed a haircut.

''I'll have some money for you next week, Vince.''

''Not *some*. *All*. *All* of it. Not next week. *Now*. I want it *all*. *Now*.''

He pulled back the gun and fired. Haloways spun half around, hit in the right shoulder. Dovie-Jean stopped dancing but the juke kept roaring. The little man pulled the gun back and fired again. The shot took off half of Matt Haloways's head.

He fell across the front of the bar with his head on the bar rail. Dovie-Jean came up and stood beside Calhoun, both looking down at the old man. Neither understood.

The little man understood perfectly. He laid the rifle carefully on top of the bar and went behind it. He picked up a bottle of Old Crow then couldn't locate a shot glass.

"To your left on the shelf," Dovie-Jean instructed him.

They watched him pouring himself a shot and, as he poured, the old man dying on the bar rail began a strangled gasping as though he were trying to keep time to the juke:

Blue Moon, you saw me standing alone . . .

the juke cried out, and the old man gurgled something in his throat trying to carry the tune. Then he stopped and Dovie-Jean knew he was dead, and the juke's song sank down to a whisper, then died too.

The little man held the bottle toward Calhoun. Calhoun shook his head, No. Dovie-Jean walked to the door. A dozen people had heard the shots and come running; now they were so near they had become afraid.

"He got a gun, Gallegher," Dovie-Jean warned a white plainclothesman coming in the door.

Gallegher drew his police special.

The man was facing the bar mirror, putting ice into a glass. He grinned, in the mirror, at Gallegher.

Gallegher had arrested Vince Le Forti before.

"I've got you covered, Vince," he gave the man warning.

"I don't have anything against the Jersey City police," he assured Gallegher, turning to face the officer. "You mind if I toss down a shot?"

"Toss it."

"Have one on the house?"

"Hold out your hands, Vince."

Le Forti drank his shot, then held out his hands for the manacles. They waited side by side in the doorway until the ambulance rolled up, with the police photographer just behind in the police van. Gallegher got Le Forti into the van before the photographer had gone to work.

"What was the reason for the trouble?" Gallegher asked Le Forti in the van.

"I sold them niggers the place," Le Forti told Gallegher, "I give them a liquor license. I give them the tavern. I had a contract with them. They refused to pay me. They only paid me seven hundred out of five thousand I was suppose to get. I went down there to collect the rest of it. They begin laughing and making jokes whenever I show up there. They weren't going to pay me.

"That redheaded nigger is the worst. He used to sing for me when the joint was mine. Some singer. I saw him fight once, I decided he'd do better to try singing. Now he's behind my bar and he got the big head. Every time I walk in he hollers, 'Come down to change your luck, honky?' I know what he means all right. As if I'd have anything to do with a nigger woman.

"Always joke time with that damned redheaded sonofabitch. He was real polite when the place belonged to me. Oh yeah. Now he pretends I'm down there looking for a black woman. Oh yeah. That's suppose to be *funny.* Oh yeah.

"I went down there and I took my shotgun. Oh yeah. Just one crack out of that redheaded nigger and he's going to get it. Oh yeah.

"The redhead ain't there. So I shoot the old man instead. One is as good as another, they're all alike, makes no difference which one you shoot. You think I won't talk to a jury the way I talk to you now? The jury will love me. Oh yeah."

Four hours after his father had been shot down, Hardee Haloways walked into the police station in which Vince Le Forti was being held and told the desk sergeant, "If you people don't do something about this, somebody else will. I want to see Le Forti."

"The man is being held incommunicado. When he gets a lawyer you can talk to the lawyer."

"You mean you've already released him? Did you give him his gun back?"

"The man has not been released, sir. He is being held on a charge of homicide. He will be tried in court. If he is guilty he will be sentenced in court. I'd suggest you go home and get some sleep."

It was then around 10 P.M. Two hours later one Eric Heim, unemployed, thirty-seven years of age, was shooting Loser-Buys-the-Beer eight-ball pool, with one Nick Vincio, forty, in the Melody Bar and Grill, some four blocks from the Paradise. The Melody was strictly white.

"I beat him the first three games," Heim was later to recall in court, "then he says, 'Well, you're not going to go home now,' because Nick was a particularly good player. We went to the bar and had a drink and I still wanted to go home. 'Why go home now?' the bartender asks me. 'We'll have breakfast and I'll take you both home.' "

Dude Leonard, fifty-two, had been tending bar for the tavern's owner, Mrs. Elizabeth Vaughn. "He was the greatest guy in the world," Mrs. Vaughn still describes Leonard, "he had a million friends."

All Dude's million friends were white. He'd connected a small buzzer beside the door and he kept the door locked. When the buzzer was sounded, Leonard looked out. If you were white, he opened. If you were black the door remained locked.

"Around midnight," Heim was to testify, "Dude looked out but he didn't open the door. 'Some nigger gal,' he told us, and went back to the bar. Before he got back the buzzer sounded again and this time he opened. It was Helen Shane, a waitress who used to drop in for a drink and chat with Dude on her way home. A nigger gal stepped in right behind her and right behind the nigger gal in comes a nigger man.

"Dude walked right up to the nigger man and told him, 'We don't serve niggers here.'

"The nigger man didn't answer Dude. 'Go to the bar,' he told his nigger gal, 'order what you want. I'll see you get it.'

" 'I'll see you both get it,' Dude told them, and came up with his .38 police special from behind the bar. The nigger gal took one look and walked out. The nigger man studied Dude. He was heavyset. He had a mustache. He was wearing shades. He was wearing some sort of hat. Finally he walked out too.

"An hour and a half later, there were three people at the bar, Dude was behind it, there was no buzz.

"I didn't see the door open, I don't know how the man got

inside. I didn't see or hear the door open. All I seen was Dude pitching a bottle toward the door and then shots—*wham-wham-wham*—like that."

"You saw the bartender throw a bottle? At whom?"

"At whoever was in the door firing into the tavern, *that's* who. I seen him throw *something,* a bottle, whatever you want to call it, I don't know what it was. I heard it crash. I looked at where he'd throwed it. I seen a man with a revolver, a pistol, whatever you want to call it. He fired so fast I never got a clean look—*wham-wham-wham*—and he was gone. A black man."

"The same black man who'd told the black girl to go to the bar and order what she wanted and he'd see that she got it?"

"No, not that black man. This one was tall. The first black man wasn't tall, he was husky. And he was *black*. The one with the gun was slim and light-skinned. All I know is I felt a pain in my head. I looked around. Nick Vincio was still sitting at the bar with a cigarette burning in his hand. Only he was leaning a little forward like he was half-napping.

"Mrs. Shane had changed her position. She wasn't sitting at the bar. She was lying on the floor. I looked around for Dude but I didn't see him. There was a blue-and-white Schlitz sign above the door and it kept flickering blue and white, off and on, on and off. The door must have been still open. It was. It was swinging a little. The neon kept flickering off and on, on and off, blue and white, white and blue."

A bullet had caught Dude Leonard in the lower back, as if he had turned to run. He had died before he'd hit the floor.

Vincio's foot remained upon his stool's footrest. The lighted cigarette remained between his fingers. But he wasn't going to light another.

A broken beer bottle lay shattered on the air conditioner beside the door. Heim, blinded in one eye and his skull fractured, stumbled about the tavern.

"I felt this pain in the side of my head," he recalled in court, "there was a column there or a post, whatever you want to call it. The man didn't know what he was doing and smoke came out and most likely shot the bartender or the other man. I only seen the man briefly. When I seen that pistol, whatever it was, I was in shock. I says, Well my God, what happened here? I heard a door open while I was lying on the bar. I don't know what door it was but a door opened and I heard Helen Shane hollering. Help! Help! Help! Then this door closed. I found myself sitting right back on the stool where I was sitting before."

"What happened then?"

"I had a bowel movement. And I went into the men's room and did what I had to do. And I came back out and I seen Nick Vincio."

"Where was he?"

"Still sitting at the bar."

"Where was Helen Shane?"

"Lying on the floor."

"Where was Dude Leonard?"

"On the floor behind the bar."

"Who else was in the bar?"

"I didn't see nobody else. I just held my head in my hands. I was bleeding and bleeding. I heard someone using the phone but I didn't look up. I knew the cops would come soon. That's all I know. I can't tell you no more than that because that's all I know."

When Ruby Calhoun saw the .38 police special in Dude Leonard's hand, he had second thoughts about forcing the bartender to serve his girl friend. He followed Dovie-Jean out to the car. It was the white Buick.

It had been rented from a New York City agency the week before. He drove off slowly, saying nothing. They drove out to the same motel they'd rented twice before, but there was no sex play this night.

He slept only two or three hours, rose and began dressing. He was putting on his shoes when Dovie-Jean wakened and asked, "Are you leaving?"

He told her, Yes, and she'd replied, "Wait. I'll go with you. I don't like sleeping alone in these little honky joints."

On Sixteenth Avenue they were curbed by a police car. He

made no protest and asked no questions. It was then about 4:15 A.M. The officer, Mooney, checked his registration and let him go. Twenty minutes later, after he'd let Dovie-Jean out in front of Red's flat, the same officer stopped him a second time, instructed him to follow the officers' car to the Melody Bar and Grill. Calhoun still asked no questions. Mooney then drove him to the Jersey City General Hospital, and he was confronted with a man, lying on a stretcher, who'd been shot in the face. He sat up, looked at Calhoun, shook his head, No, and sank down again.

It was not until then, after 8 A.M., that Mooney drove Calhoun to police headquarters in Jersey City.

"They paraded me in front of witnesses brought down from the Melody," Calhoun recalled later, in court, "and I still didn't know exactly what had happened. I decided it was no use asking questions. They wouldn't give me a straight answer anyhow. So I waited. Whatever it was somebody had to be fingered for, there was nobody there to finger me.

"It was almost noon before Lieutenant De Vivani walked in. I knew him and he knew me. 'How you doin', Ruby?' he asked me. 'How are things?' 'I don't know how things are,' I told him, 'I don't even know why I'm here.'

" 'You can answer these questions or not,' he told me, 'that is strictly up to you. But I'm going to record whatever you say and it might be used against you in court—if it should ever come to that.'

"That was when I first started getting worried. If I refused to answer his questions it would look like I was holding back. I thought the best way to do was to answer him right out front. I hadn't done anything, and I thought that way it would become clear that I had not. 'I'd like to phone my wife first,' I told him, 'She'll be worried.'

"I phoned her, told her it was all right, I'd be home shortly, not to worry.

" 'What I have in mind,' De Vivani told me after I'd made my phone call, 'is to send for a polygrapher from the state troopers' barracks. Would you have any objection to a lie test?'

" 'I have no objection,' I told him.

" 'If you have anything to hide, don't take this test,' the state trooper warned me, 'because this machine is going to tell me all about it. If it tells me you had *anything* to do with the killings, I'm going to put your ass *under* the electric chair.' "

The test took almost two hours.

"Do you know a man named Dude Leonard?" Calhoun was asked.

"No."

"Do you know a man named Nick Vincio?"

"No."

"Do you know a woman named Helen Shane?"

"No."

"Do you know a man named Eric Heim?"

"No."

"Have you ever been in a bar called the Melody Bar and Grill?"

"No."

The needle remained as steady, at this question, as it had for the previous ones. But a few seconds after it had been answered, and Calhoun figured he'd beaten it, the needle wavered.

"You can turn him loose, lieutenant," the state trooper assured De Vivani within Calhoun's hearing. "This man had nothing to do with the killings."

De Vivani tossed Calhoun the keys to his car. "Sorry we had to put you through this, Ruby, but it's the only way we have. Three people were shot down last night in the Melody. I'm glad you're not involved."

Ruby was vastly relieved. Jennifer was apprehensive. "I don't think you should have talked into that machine, Ruby," she told him. "You never know how the police are going to use something."

The beauty of that machine lies not in what the suspect says into it, but how he reacts later when he assumes he's beaten it. Calhoun assumed he had beaten it.

He hadn't.

De Vivani had understood, by the state trooper's manner in clearing him, that the machine had involved Calhoun in the murders. He would now be watched without being aware that he was being watched.

De Vivani knew how to take his time.

Fifteen minutes after Calhoun had driven away, Red Haloways walked in on De Vivani, accompanied by Dovie-Jean Dawkins.

"We're here for Mrs. Calhoun," Red told De Vivani. "We understand you're holding her husband. What is the charge?"

"We're not holding Calhoun, Red," De Vivani assured him. "We picked him up as a suspect last night but he has cleared himself. I imagine he's home by now. You want to phone Mrs. Calhoun?" He offered Red his phone but Red didn't take it.

"This young woman witnessed my father's murder yesterday," he told De Vivani. "She's ready to tell you about it."

De Vivani gave the girl a brief glance. "Just leave your name and address, miss. We'll contact you." Then, turning to Red, "We'd appreciate a statement from you on your whereabouts yesterday evening, Mr. Haloways. You don't mind?"

"Certainly not."

"Just step this way then," De Vivani instructed him, at the same time indicating, by touching Dovie-Jean, that she was to remain where she was. "He'll be right back, miss."

"I saw you fight in Union City a couple of years ago, Red," De Vivani became suddenly informal and friendly. "You looked pretty good in there."

The state trooper was already preparing the polygraph, had Red's arms adjusted before Red had given full consent.

"Do you know a man named Dude Leonard?"

"No."

"Do you know a man named Nick Vincio?"

"No."

"Do you know a woman named Helen Shane?"

"No."

"Have you ever been in the Melody Bar and Grill?"

"No."

The needle remained firm.

The trooper later confided to De Vivani: "The redhead did better than Calhoun. He comes up negative. Calhoun possesses guilty knowledge."

De Vivani nodded.

"I believe," De Vivani added thoughtfully, "that if you put Red on the machine again, he'll turn up to have guilty knowledge too."

When De Vivani dispatched an officer, two days later, to invite Red in for another lie test, Red had pleaded delay because of his father's funeral.

Dovie-Jean Dawkins stood at graveside between Red and Hardee. Calhoun and Jennifer stood on the grave's other side. Billy Boggs and Floyd Calhoun, among other relatives and friends, also attended the rites. Floyd Calhoun wept.

Immediately after the funeral Red consulted Gregory Oritano, a white attorney, who advised him against going back on the machine.

"Don't submit to arrest without an arrest warrant," Oritano further advised Red.

"*Don't submit?*" Hardee mocked Oritano to Red. "What does the man mean—not *submit?* You're in New Jersey, man. If De Vivani wants you to submit, you'll *submit*. Don't Oritano know you're *black?* He's giving you advice for a white client, not a black."

Hardee sat behind the front bar of the Paradise and Red sat, like a customer, at the bar. He had a bottle at his hand and occasionally reached over for a piece of ice. He had the feeling of being in deepening water and feeling the bottom giving way. He poured himself a heavy shot.

"What in God's name, Red, you went for that lie test for is something I'm still trying to figure. What were you thinking of?"

Red stirred his Scotch thoughtfully. "Two reasons, Hardee. First, I didn't want to arouse De Vivani's suspicions. Second, I thought I could beat it." He didn't add that he'd found himself undergoing the polygraph test before he'd had time to figure out anything.

"De Vivani's suspicions, for one thing," Hardee assured him, "are already aroused. With or without a lie test you're a prime suspect because of Le Forti."

"So are you, Hardee."

"I have no criminal record, Red. You have. A long one. You've been busted for crimes of violence: assault, armed robbery, mugging. You've been busted for carrying a concealed weapon. I don't know one end of a gun from another. I'm not a violent man. You are. That's the record."

"I beat the lie test, Hardee."

Hardee put his head into his hands and shook it slowly and sadly. *"Dummy, dummy, dummy,"* Red heard him saying into his hands. When Hardee looked up again he was pale with anger: "You *dumdum, dumdum sonofabitch*. Don't you ever learn *anything*? They let you go so you beat them, is that it? I suppose because they give Ruby his car back he's running around thinking *he* beat it too? I'll tell you something. You didn't beat that test. Neither did Ruby. There's an awful lot of things in this world you think you can beat, Red. The trouble seems to be that they keep beating you. Now you got yourself involved in a triple homicide with your ex-con buddy, Calhoun. There's only one nigger in this town crazier than you and that's him. How is this going to reflect on *me*—a man preparing to practice law?"

Red's face cleared. "I didn't do that shooting, Hardee."

"You're saying Calhoun did."

"I didn't say that."

"What are you saying?"

"I don't know *what* to say, Hardee."

"You don't know what to say and still you stagger into De Vivani's office, sit down for a two-hour lie test in which you shoot off about everything. Man, if you don't know what to say to me it has to be because you've already said it all to De Vivani. You don't *deserve* to have a lawyer in the family."

Red sat with his face down above his glass, shaking his head unhappily.

"I don't know what to do, Hardee."

"Then I'll tell you what to do. Here."

Red glanced up to see Hardee handing him a roll of bills. "Make this last, Edward. There won't be any more. Don't phone and don't write. Don't go near Harlem."

Hardee wrote a name on a slip of paper, folded it and handed it to Red. "Here's your connection. I'll get in touch with you through her. Don't contact me. Repeat. I'll contact you."

Red put the roll of bills in his pocket.

"Hardee," he asked his half-brother reflectively, "Hardee, who shot those people?"

"There's only two niggers in this town crazy enough for that," Hardee assured him. "One is Calhoun. The other is you."

Dovie-Jean walked in.

Hardee didn't give her so much as a nod, far less a hello.

Red rose and said "Let's get out of here, honey." She followed him out and up the backstairs to his small flat.

"That man don't like me," she assured Red.

Red was throwing shirts into a battered suitcase.

"It's just his way. Hardee don't like many people. I think you better start getting your things together, sweetheart."

Sweetheart?

"What's up, Tiger?"

He urged her into the big barber's chair, swung her playfully about as if playing a game, then grew serious.

"We have to move, baby. We have to get out of town."

"I figure that much," she told him, "but what about Ruby?"

"Ruby's in the clear. He beat the lie test. They even give him back his car. He's out of the case."

Dovie-Jean shook her head as though struck dumb by incredulity. Then simply studied him a long minute. Her eyes never left his face.

"Tiger," she told him, "there are times I don't dig you at all. What do you mean 'Ruby's out of the case?' I told you the argument him and me had with the bartender. Hour and a half later the bartender is dead and two others. What do you mean, 'Ruby's *out* of the case?' Ruby is going to need help. So am I."

"It's why we're moving, Dovie-Jean. To help you. Also me. Also Hardee."

"If running is what you need to do, Red, *run*. I'll stick."

"*Sweetheart*"—he'd never before called her "sweetheart"—"Sweetheart, what good would sticking in Jersey do? Ruby don't need your help, sweetheart, believe me. He's been all around the pisspot and he knows where the handle is. He's better off with you out of the way. You'll never get loose once De Vivani gets you under his thumb. Start packing, Sweetheart."

Dovie-Jean shook her head, No. "Red," she told him, "you can't expect to beat a homicide rap by crossing a bridge into another town. We'll look better sticking it out right here. Face up to it, Tiger, if you run you'll draw attention."

He took both of her hands into his own and, holding her with his eyes, went slowly down to the floor before her onto his knees.

She recoiled inwardly. She'd never had a man humble himself before her. It didn't seem right. She didn't know how to react. Was he miming again? He put his lips to the palms of her hands, one by one. And when he looked up at her his eyes were wet.

"I *need* you, Dovie-Jean. I *need* you, sweetheart. You're all I have to make me feel *real*. Without you I don't know who I am. I'm not even sure what *color* I am. Unless I'm with you I have no *hold*. No hold on *anything*. Don't make me go alone, sweetheart."

He gave Dovie-Jean her first insight into his two-sided personality. He gave her her first chance to be kind to another person in a way that no other person could be kind.

"Tiger. Please get up. Yes, yes, of course if that's what you want. Just get up off your knees, for God's sake." He got up and she went for her clothes.

Along the New Jersey turnpike she looked out the window, in order to avoid looking at Red. If she looked at him, she felt, he would be embarrassed by their recent scene. She didn't know Red.

At the Port Authority they cabbed to the Hotel Chester, on West Twenty-third. In their room, eight stories up, she looked down at the moving traffic, moving in a kind of pantomime, and felt a curious mockery of her down there.

"We're on our own until this blows over," he told her apologetically. "I can't contact Hardee until he contacts me."

"Blows *over?*" She turned to face him at last. "Blows *over?* Do you actually think this thing can blow *over?*"

"I meant until the heat is off."

"Who is going to turn off the heat when three whites have been shot down, for God's sake? Tiger, I just can't *figure* you. You think something like this can be *forgotten?* Somebody is going to take the rap, Tiger, and take it hard."

"You think you can do Ruby any good by doing time yourself? Hardee got his career to think of. I got myself to think of. You got yourself to think of. All me and Hardee are trying to do is to get you to protect yourself, Dovie-Jean. That way we protect ourselves."

Dovie-Jean lowered her head. You're born somehow. You live somehow. You play out the hand that's dealt you somehow. Then you die somehow. Whatever little she had, Red had given her. Whatever she had of friendship, Red had given her. Whatever she had had of trust, had been Red's trust. She had had nothing and he had taken her in. She looked up.

"I got no way of going *against* you, Tiger. I think you're playing your natural part of a fool. But I got no way of going against you."

He put on a huge cap of black and white checks. It looked like something a burlesque comedian would put on in mockery of a golfer.

"What the hell is *that?*" she asked. "On your *head.*"

He took it off and inspected it gravely. "I picked it up on Eighth Avenue opposite the Port Authority. Snappy, eh? I call it my businessman's cap." He yanked it down over his ears and looked out at her with shadowed eyes. They were not smiling.

"I can't tell when you're serious or when you're jiving."

"I got to see a guy," he told her, "dude name of Moonigan. He can get me on night bartending over on Eighth, he claims."

"Is he a bartender?"

"No."

"What does he do?"

"Bouncer."

And he was gone as though reluctant to say more.

There was someone, in the room next door, who made sucking sounds. Sometimes it sounded like a baby gurgling; other times it just *whooked*. Then, again, like a woman sucking in breath for dear life.

Oath of God, Dovie-Jean thought, left now alone in the room, What is *that?*

"Let it alone," Red had cautioned her, "it ain't no business of ours."

She had let it alone. But aloud she'd told him, "It turns my stomach just to think what kind of man that could be."

Now it began again, so she switched on the TV loud to drown him out.

She caught a program called the Uriah Yipkind show. Uriah was a small white-haired fellow wearing a face which appeared to be a kind of mask representing every phase of ingratiation, from simple, straightforward servility to open solicitation. He had a black comedian on.

"I understand you have recently married again, Redd," Uriah was saying.

"That's right," the comedian assured his host, "to a Korean lady."

"*Korean?* What does it feel like to marry outside of your race?"

The comedian turned in genuine surprise.

"Outside of my race? What do you think I married? A duck?"

Dovie-Jean fell asleep in her chair and was sleeping soundly long after the station went off the air. When Red came in the set was on, the picture was off and Dovie-Jean was snoring. He carried her to the bed without waking her and fell asleep beside her.

Dovie-Jean was dreaming she was driving a white Buick through crowded traffic. She had never driven a car in her life, yet she felt in perfect control of this one. She saw, on her right, a dark car pull alongside and force her to the curb. An old woman, wearing a mauve veil, was at the wheel. She leaned toward Dovie-Jean, apparently smiling, and asked, "Do you think I'm going the right direction, sweetheart?"

Behind the mauve veil she saw Red's long, pale face, immensely aged.

"I have no idea where you're going," Dovie-Jean told the old woman.

"Then you better get in with me, sweetheart," the old woman advised her. "We're both going the same route."

"Stop miming!" Dovie-Jean heard herself cry out as she struggled to waken. "Stop miming! Stop miming!"

And knew, at last, that when he had gone to his knees before her he'd been miming.

Miming whom? Himself? Or the man he sometimes pretended to be?

She looked down at him, in the earliest light of morning. And knew that, behind his closed eyes, he was not asleep. He had heard her cry.

He had read her suspicion.

"You're going to see the big city today," he told her calmly, opening one eye. "I'm going to show it to you. Get on your duds."

They cabbed to the foot of West Forty-second and boarded a Circle Line boat for the three-hour trip around Manhattan.

Dovie-Jean had never before seen a big river. It was a morning in which sun and cloud alternated on the water, blinding her momentarily with flashes of light on the waves. She sat, dazzled, trying to follow the flights of the big gulls along the docks, then trying to grasp the height of the great towers they were passing.

Red brought her an ice cream cone and she licked at it as the boat pulled along.

"On your left," the spieler filled them in, "is the site of the duel between Alexander Hamilton and Aaron Burr in which Hamilton was killed."

"Who was Alexander Hamilton, Tiger?"

"Early president. One of them between Washington and Lincoln."

"Who was Aaron Burr?"

"A very big man in the government. He'd run against Hamilton and Hamilton had beaten him."

"Is that why he shot him?"

"He couldn't stand defeat."

"Did he do time?"

"Not a day."

"How come?"

"You've seen yourself how it works. When you're high up enough the government can't touch you. It's like you're the government. All they can do is impeach you."

"Impeach?"

"It means getting tried by a jury of your peers, in this case the Senate and the House of Representatives."

"And what if he's found guilty?"

"He has to resign."

"Did Burr get impeached?"

"No. He quit so he wouldn't lose his pension."

"He got away with murder then, didn't he?"

"He surely did."

Dovie-Jean finished her ice cream while studying the skyline of Manhattan.

"Which is the Empire State, Tiger?"

Red pointed to the spire of the Empire State building.

"I'd like to go up there, Tiger."

"On your right," the spieler continued, "is the pier that was featured in the film *On the Waterfront,* starring Marlon Brando. It is the old Hoboken pier. Hoboken is Frank Sinatra's hometown."

Red brought her an orangeade, then sat holding her hand. He had never been so attentive.

"Two weeks ago," the spieler filled them in when passing under the Verrazano Bridge, "two trucks collided in the middle of the bridge. One was carrying chicken, the other was loaded with barbecue sauce. Fortunately, neither driver was hurt. But the gas tank of one truck exploded, roasting a thousand chickens under rivers of barbecue sauce. Thank you, we are now approaching the Statue of Liberty.

"Give me your tired, your poor,"

The spieler recited.

Your huddled masses yearning to breathe free
The wretched refuse of your teeming shore.
Send these, the homeless, tempest-tossed, to me
I lift my lamp before the golden door."

She was sitting alone as they passed the great monument. Red came to her, carrying a paper cup of coffee; he was puzzled to see tears in her eyes. He did not ask her for a reason.

The reason was simple, albeit mistaken. The girl thought she had been included among the homeless and tempest-tossed yearning to be free.

She hadn't even been invited.

"I want to ride the subway, Tiger."

They took the Seventh Avenue line and the ride was as exciting, to Dovie-Jean, as a ride in an amusement park. Stations flashed past like stations on some gigantic Ferris wheel. She felt dizzied by its speed and roar and was at last glad, when they reached Canal Street, to get out into the sun of Little Italy.

They took a couple of chairs outside a capuccino café on the northeast corner of Mulberry and Hester.

Ropes of golden tinsel, arching high above Mulberry Street, shook in the September wind and flashed back the sun of September. A great Italian clamor rose on every side, challenging them to games of chance, to kebab and sausage stands while smoke drifted above bright pennons: the festival of San Gennaro.

Grandiosa Festa Annuale—Omaggio al Nostro Miraculo—they walked past the stuffed shell and baked ziti stands, where the smells of calamari, calzone, zeppole manicotti and braccioli merged in the smoke and the gaiety. Cries for ice cream, for games, challenges to try this then that, rose on either hand. Red stopped before the Duck-Water-Balloon game, and paid fifty cents for a chance to win a prize. He was given a water pistol, with half a dozen competitors, and when the woman running the game said, "Go!" he took steady aim at the target on the duck and a blue balloon began rising, and inflating as it rose, behind the duck. The balloon which burst first won the prize and Red won it. It was a fist-sized puppy made of cotton, which Dovie-Jean fastened proudly to her coat. Red looked proud too.

Dovie-Jean had never eaten in a Chinese restaurant. He took her to a second-floor place, overlooking Mott Street, and ordered martinis for them both. She had never had a martini before. She sipped at it, wrinkled her nose in distaste, then returned to it, surprised to find she liked it after all.

He ordered chicken almond ding for her and a shrimp dish for himself. By the time the meal was half over Dovie-Jean was almost on the nod; it had been a long, exciting day.

Back in their hotel room, when she was half-undressed, Red took her into his arms for the first time. She was too tired to respond; yet was pleased that, after all, he should want her.

Late in the night she wakened to find him making serious love to her. She lay back, first accepting, at last responding. When the first light came across their bed she was lying with her legs crossed passionately behind his back, her arms about him, giving herself completely.

It was the first time Red had made love to her.

A whore who works in a house is less likely to go down the drain than is the woman who cruises the streets. She is protected from muggers as well as from police, from men who may whip her and take back their money, and she has a biweekly physical examination. She always has help, close at hand, in event of a trick getting rough or crazy. She gets every other week off and earns as much as a thousand dollars a day—untaxable. Would you believe that that sad bespectacled cretin lounging in the corner and looking like a titless chipmunk, makes a hundred dollars a day without even *trying*?

She does. Whom she spends it on, don't even try to imagine.

Entrance fee to the thousand-a-day house is fifty dollars and the girls call you by your first name—or by whatever first name you choose to give at the desk. Drinks are on the house, there is muted music in the walls, a valet will take your clothes and show you to a shower. Rooms are tastefully appointed, your credit card is good and there's a jacuzzi.

Red Haloways's connection wasn't good enough to get Dovie-Jean into a thousand-a-day house. His connection was one Amanda

Dillon, who ran an escort service and conducted interviews for half a dozen houses in midtown Manhattan.

Miss Dillon, an ample, middle-aged party, had never seen the South. But there was very little that had gone on, along the Eastern Seaboard, since she'd been born, of which she was not aware. The sympathy in her voice sounded like a put-on to Dovie-Jean, who wasn't yet accustomed to that dreadful Barbara Walters nasal sniffle now current. But she possessed a judicious eye for a girl's possibilities.

Dovie-Jean, outfitted in a gypsyish dirndl and oversized earrings out of a Village shop, didn't appear overly promising to Miss Dillon. It wasn't the oversized earrings or the dirndl so much as a feeling the girl gave her of vulnerability.

The freckle-faced high-yellow dude who'd brought her in was confident that he had nothing else to do but to turn his charm upon Miss Dillon and she would be immediately swept away.

She'd met him a thousand times before: these bartenders who kept a deck in one pocket and a pair of engineered dice in another, these pimpified pool hustlers, bag men, three-card monte operators, all experienced street-wise cats: agile, fast-talking, sharp dressers who, often as not, drove Caddies—not one of them, she knew, but was a total fool. Not one who realized that, while he was victimizing everyone within reach, his biggest victim was himself.

She'd asked him to excuse himself while she talked to the girl—not because he constituted any threat to her conversation but in order to establish her dominance. Miss Dillon was very good at establishing dominance. Black women have inherited the pants of the family because, for so long, their men's pants had been taken off them. The black man, having been weakened by the white, has passed his strength onto his wife. Thus she and the white man remain rivals of equal strength.

"Report to this address," she decided at last. "Your joint togs will be a hundred dollars. Cash. Payable now," she added with a smile.

Dovie-Jean stepped out into the hall. "I need a hundred, Tiger," she informed Red.

When they returned from Miss Dillon's agency, they had hardly gotten back into their room before Red began undressing her. Again he made love to her, and again she responded to him.

She was half asleep when she heard him telling her, "You hate me now, don't you, Dovie-Jean?"

She opened one incredulous eye.

"*Hate* you? What for? I'm glad you made love to me. I wanted you to make love to ever since our first night."

"It's not what I meant. I meant you must hate me for making a whore out of you."

Dovie-Jean sat up and switched on the bed lamp.

"Look, Tiger," she told him, "you're not making a whore out of me. I'm making a pimp out of you. Now get to sleep."

Between Seventh Avenue and the Avenue of the Americas, on Forty-eighth, an upward-pointing arrow is painted in red against a whitewashed wall:

PLAYMATES OF PARIS
ONE FLIGHT UP

One flight up the door is locked, but through its window you can see a girl seated at a littered desk under a fluorescent light. She presses a buzzer, you step inside and are confronted by an aging, oversized Jew in a pair of frayed corduroys and a faded plaid shirt, wearing a tiny pink-peaked baseball cap. You raise your arms, he pats you down and then steps to one side.

"You a member, sir?" the girl asks.

You show her a small red card stamped P.P. that brings the entrance down from fifteen to thirteen dollars.

Your next impression is of a dozen lightly gowned women in a spacious parlor, but there are only half a dozen and the parlor isn't all that spacious. Mirrored walls do the trick.

Somewhere someone in the parlor has a transistor playing music too faintly to be identified. The muted breathing is that of an air conditioner.

"Hi, children!" you may greet them; but you won't get a "Hi, Daddy!" in return. The women have been disciplined not to compete by smile, voice or laughter. The most you'll get is a conjectural glance. Smiles cost money and so does laughter here. Credit is not extended. If you want a friendly look or a welcoming glance, pay off, daddy, pay off.

Three of the women are white; one is dusky; one is black; one is yellow. All are good-looking. None is over thirty.

It was a wintry autumn afternoon. There'd been only one trick the entire morning and little prospect, in midweek, of many more before midnight.

"The character trade," Spanish Nan observed, "is something else. Poor things, they can't help theirselves. I was working escort service and a dude sent for me by phone.

"I go to his apartment house uptown and get by the doorman, who gives me a look like from the morals squad. The elevator leaves me off inside the apartment.

"Dark. Curtains drawn. Music, sad and low from somewhere. Two tall candles flickering. What century is *this* trick living in?

"Then I see the coffin.

"I was more puzzled than anything. I go up to that box and there's a dead dude in it. What do you know. His face is rouged and powdered. He has on gray gloves and they're folded across his chest. I felt a little sick, a little like laughing; and very much like I better get out.

"Then he sits up smiling and I screamed.

"He climbs out of the box, a short, fat, middle-aged trick in his stocking feet, and holds out his hand with money in it. I took the money without touching the glove.

" 'Thank you, miss,' I heard him say as I was getting into his elevator.

"I was mad as the devil at him, having such a joke at my expense, until I realized this was his only way of making it with a woman. His *only* way. Two hundred dollars he handed me in conscience money. Poor man. Poor clown.

"For all my hustling, in and out of jail like a fiddler's elbow, I'll still take my life against his any day. The man is walking dead, dead, dead."

"Weirdos don't scare me," Fortune put in. "You have to realize he has no other way to go. Yet he *has* to go. If the only way he can make it is by hanging from a chandelier by candlelight while petting a white chicken—so what? Who's he hurting outside of the chicken?

"What the man is doing is letting the sickness inside him come out. Once he does that he's all right for a couple of weeks. You don't have to worry about him. The one you have to worry about is the one who *can't* let it out. He's like a man who can't dream. If he doesn't dream, it'll come out in real life. Then somebody gets hurt. You read about it in the papers."

Spanish Nan was a slender woman in her early thirties, her dark hair bleached blond but still black at the roots, who'd been brought to the States through Mexico, by a professional "fiane." By the time she realized his promises were fraudulent she was knocking doors on Doyers Street and saying "me-me" to Chinese men without women.

"Me-Me" were the only words she knew outside of her own language. She had survived by learning English and wrenching herself free of her "fiancé." Now, after eleven years in the trade, she had a twenty-three-year-old husband whom she was supporting through courses in media communications at Columbia, and owned a tiny *botanica* in a Ninth Avenue cranny.

"He never miss a day," she assured Dovie-Jean about her young husband, "he *like* going to classes. Every day I give him ten dollar. *I* handle the money."

Big Benjamin, the oversized flunky, came in bearing hamburgers, cokes and coffee. His jacket and cap were wet with rain. He shook them while the women divided the food. When everyone had what she had ordered, one super burger remained unclaimed and yet neatly wrapped.

"That one is yours, King," Spanish Nan assured him, and he took it into his shadowed corner like a well-disciplined mastiff and ate it there in two huge gulps, by himself.

"How do you know it's kosher, King?" Tracy asked him.

"Kosher, shmosher," he murmured.

Big Benjamin was not an Orthodox Jew.

"I know that coffin deal," the girl from Buffalo, who called herself Ginger, recalled, "except my operation was different. I was working escort service and my madam came with me because, like she said, 'Special handling, honey. You've never done anything like this before.' 'Ain't anything I ain't done before,' I told her, but all she said was, 'Wait, you'll see.'

"The apartment was so full of flowers it smelled like a funeral—and there, in the middle of the flowers was a casket. 'Take off your clothes, honey,' madam tells me before I could ask who had died, 'then climb into the box. Somebody will be coming through that door and he wants to see you daid. Don't be afraid. I'm standing by. Just lay still with your eyes closed.'

"I kept one eye barely peeled. Sure enough, here comes an old boy, stark naked, past sixty, skinny, gray below and bald above, he's coming to the coffin, he walks up on tiptoe all around it. He kneels, rises, puts his arms around me, kisses me, very light, on my forehead.

"He never touched me further than that. Just walked around the box once more, then left.

" 'How much does he pay for *that,* for God's sake?' I asked madam.

" 'Come back to the office and you'll see for yourself,' she tells me. He comes into her office—this time he has his clothes on—and hands her a five-hundred-dollar bill. Then he hands me a C-note without so much as a smile. And I get a hundred-fifty from my madam just for playing dead."

"I never heard anything like it," Dovie-Jean admitted.

"One time," Tracy added, "one of these no-laugh clowns comes in carrying a briefcase and tells me, 'I must ask you not to laugh.' 'What's to laugh?' I ask. 'Get undressed,' is all he tells me. And he tells it to me in such a cold tone, like I felt right then he wasn't going to touch me.

"He opens the briefcase and pulls out a long, colored feather, like off a peacock's tail. 'I won't let you whip me,' I tell him, still not knowing what he has in mind.

"He sticks the feather between his buttocks and begins taking short, hopping steps like a chicken with its legs tied saying, 'Caw! Caw! Caw!' Then he reverses, hopping the opposite way, saying, 'Beepie! Beepie! Beepie!' Is he going to fly or lay an egg, I wonder.

"I started to laugh and couldn't stop. I was helpless. He stopped his crazy hop-hop-hopping then and stood looking at me, his feather now in his hand, just so *sad*. Then he put the crazy feather away and got dressed. I finally stopped laughing.

"When he was almost dressed he looked at me and I saw he was trying not to cry. Like a little kid. I turned away, it was the only thing I could do. I *had* to feel sorry for him. But I still have to laugh when I think how foolish that trick looked.

"No, I didn't get paid. I didn't expect to. I'd ruined his day."

A youth of no more than twenty came in, carrying a book under his arm. He glanced about self-consciously, as though he had come in only to browse, and sat down in one of the large armchairs provided for tricks. None of the women looked directly at him: they were accustomed to this type of youth. He hung around the main reading room of the Public Library, on Forty-second, trying for a pickup, but always failed. The Chinese woman, Fortune, remembered him because he'd chosen her once before; and then, as now, he'd been carrying a paperback copy of *Catch-22*. She remembered him as a tight trick, a poor spender, and tried to avoid his eyes. But when he handed her the ticket she led him to the room.

"I was living in a twenty-dollar-a-month basement flat on Chicago's Near Northside," Ginger recalled, "when I get a knock. A man maybe sixty, dark suit, looked like he'd cabbed down from Lake Forest. Not a word, not a smile just hands me a blank letter.

"It was on business stationery. I kept him standing while I read it: 'Dear Madam: Bearer has made application for Membership in our fraternal order. In accordance with our constitution he is to receive twenty lashes upon his naked buttocks. We would appreciate your administering them at the current rate of two dollars per lash. Cordially yours,' I'd never handled this type of trick but I knew I wasn't supposed to hurt him for real. You're suppose to fake the hurting, as a rule. I let him step inside.

" 'You got a big whipping coming to you, you four-legged

alley fink,' I began on him as soon as he was inside, 'and I'm going to give it to you. Get your clothes off.'

"I could see by his expression I'd made the right beginning. 'Now get on the bed, face down and take your punishment like a man,' I told him. 'You've been very *very* bad.'

"He's been a bad boy and he knows it. I took off my own clothes down to my garter belt and slapped him lightly with his belt but not with the buckle. Just kind of slapped him with it but not hard enough to draw blood. But I gave him perfect hell with my tongue: 'you piece of pigshit, you motherless degenerate.' By the time I'd given him twenty lashes I'd called him everything in the book and he was crying like a baby. Finally he dries his eyes, gets dressed and hands me a fifty. 'Keep the change,' he tells me.

"How did he find me? God knows. A week later he showed up again with another business-type letter. This one says something like, 'Regret to inform you applicant has failed his recent initiation. We propose your cooperation in giving him fifty lashes, somewhat severer than previously. May we have your assistance in this matter? Payable at current rate.'

"For God's sake—I'm a psychiatrist! I whipped him till my arm tired, but still not with the rough end of the belt. He paid me a hundred but he never showed up again. Maybe I should have used the buckle end. He might have come back and brought some of his business-lunch friends."

"You didn't whip him hard enough, Ginger," Tracy decided, "he was *serious* about being whipped. All businessmen are serious. If he could laugh he wouldn't be paying you outrageous prices to whip him. Why is it that *all* these characters are businessmen? What is it about *business?* Masochism, sadism—that's all bullshit. *Nobody* likes to be hurt. But if the only thing a man can feel is pain, he has to settle for that, else he's dead. He pays you so he can feel alive, in any way at all. It has nothing to do with sex directly. I don't know why business kills. But I know it does."

The kid from the Public Library came out of Fortune's room still carrying his paperback. When he'd left, Fortune shook her head and sighed, "What a *yossarian!*"

"What's that?"

"I just meant he does a lot of evasive flying," Fortune explained, "a character out of a book."

"Don't mess with young dudes if you can help it, that's *my* experience," Ginger expressed a private opinion. "The younger they are, the meaner. One thing I learned in San Diego—they used to come up there in gangs. Nineteen-year-olds trying to prove their manhood to each other. They'd gotten the word on every perversion known to man and wanted to try them all out without ever knowing what they were. Like kids in an amusement park who want to try all the high rides, and knock off all the rabbits in the shooting gallery and eat all the cotton candy at once. Here's one with egg stain still on his chin asking me, 'How about up your old keister, sis?'

" 'I'm not accustomed to being addressed in that fashion, young man,' I told him. 'I'm a real lady, so fuck the hell out of here,' and I shoved him out the door. Thank you all the same, sonny. I appreciate the honors, but no, no, no. I'll take an old man who takes out his dentures every time."

"There's no single way of handling men," Fortune added reflectively, "but he'll be easier to handle if he's a little scared inside—and most of them are. Once he has clothes off, he's *always* a little scared.

"Myself, I'm scared of a thousand things—dogs, the wind, bridges over water—I have had dreams I'm back at that big black sewing machine in Chinatown and the door is locked.

"But the one thing I *ought* to be afraid of—me—I have no fear at all."

"Here comes the Blinky, girls!" the girl at the front desk whispered into the mike before she pressed the buzzer to let the Blinky in.

The Blinky was a tall, stout boy, wearing blue-tinted glasses and well dressed; he was led by a young German shepherd.

The dog, a male, leaped wildly, tail wagging furiously at the scent of the women. He went from lap to lap wriggling with pleasure. When Big Benjamin took his leash, however, he went to a corner and lay quietly.

The Blinky always picked Fortune, yet now he stood perplexed.

"There's a new woman here," he announced in the high-pitched voice peculiar to the blind.

Nobody enlightened him.

"Speak up, new girl," he demanded.

"I'm the latest," Dovie-Jean acknowledged at last.

At the sound of her voice a thin, knowing smile flicked his lips.

"I see," he decided, "Okay. Let's change my luck."

In the room he stood, naked, holding the basin of water while she washed him. "I've never gone down on a black woman," he admitted. "What is it like?"

"Like eating a sardine through a Brillo pad, I've been told," Dovie-Jean assured him.

"I was a whore before I knew it," the square-faced little blonde, Tracy, picked up the reminiscent mood of the strange twilit afternoon. She took off her rimless specs as if the better to remember.

"I took on guys now and again and if they felt like buying me a little something afters—a hat or a blouse or a pair of shoes—I took what was offered. I didn't have any clear idea of what I was doing." She laughed a light, airy laugh and tossed back her blond bangs. "The guy who cleared it all up for me was the only one who cared about me. He was even more innocent than me, for God's sake.

"Blakey was a skinny little clown, a little on the silly side but not too silly. What he was good at was spotting leaks for the gas company. He used to hang head down in attics and crawl hands and knees through tunnels, looking for leaks. The company valued Blakey. They said he had a good nose. Sometimes he could spot a leak when the gas-smelling machine didn't give a flicker.

"Blakey had a good heart, a real good heart. He was the kind who wasn't bright enough to stay out of trouble, and Blakey's trouble was his wife. She'd been bedridden two years when I met him.

"He didn't spill his guts to me about her. It just came out in conversation. Later, in bed, he told me I'd been his first lay in two years. His old lady's trouble was her heart, he said. He was the kind of man you got to believe because he ain't smart enough to lie.

"Once a week we'd have dinner in some cheap chop suey joint, the kind without a bar. He thought I was a lady, for God's sake. Even though he knew I still took on half a dozen tricks a week. I know he knew because he told me once, 'We can get along without *that*.'

"Only we couldn't. Whatever extra he had went for doctor's bills.

"It's nice to have someone like that, who really needs you. It's how Blakey made me feel. For the first time in my life, I was a human person. Blakey did that for me without even knowing he was making me a human person.

"We used to walk around the Village Sunday morning unless his old lady had took a turn for the worse. She took a bad turn whenever she got suspicious and she was suspicious most of the time.

"We got a knock Sunday morning, we're in bed, there stand two cops, one in citizen dress and one in uniform. 'Come along,' the citizen dress says, and we go along without even asking for a arrest warrant! *Green?* Greener than green. They told Blakey at the station, 'Testify against her that you gave her money and you make the street, no sweat. We won't even have to talk to your boss.'

"His boss was the least of it to Blakey. Blakey wasn't afraid on his boss's account. It was on his wife's account he was scared. The cops had already talked to her doctor. If Blakey didn't testify how they wanted him to, they'd talk to his wife. In Blakey's simple mind that would be the same as knifing her.

"Which struck me as a pretty good idea, myself.

"He told everything straight up to the point of whether he'd paid me money. Then he lied. He saw the citizen-dress guy standing there and he got the shakes. I got thirty days.

"That was when I found out I'm a whore.

"I never been held since longer than overnight. Those thirty days on Riker's Island taught me something: there ain't a man on this earth who won't send you up in the clutch.

"When I think of little Blakey now all I feel for him is sorry. If I ever saw him again I'd turn him off fast. Once is enough. Never give a square an even break.

"I just don't believe in them squares. I'm scared of the way they live. I don't even know what they're laughin' at. They make the laws that make it so hard on cats, and that makes it all the harder on themselves. They make it so we know we got to be punished hard. So why shouldn't we get to them if we can?"

She put her grandmotherly looking specs back on and brushed back her bangs, then smiled wistfully, without bitterness. "That's how it goes in the Big A, girls: the less you know them, more time you do."

"That joint had a steel door and two armed guards," Fortune recalled, a syndicate joint she'd worked outside of Buffalo, New York, and a killer police dog they kept half-starved. "But that wasn't what got me down. What brought me down was the crazy nigger who ran it. A real space cadet, that one was. He wore a white football sweater with eighty-eight on the back, and a whistle around his neck like a football referee. Why the syndicate would send anybody with as little brains as that nigger had, I still can't figure.

"He was *big*. *Very* big. All that meat and no potatoes. He'd been a pro football player—I was told—with the Rams. He'd been concussed. I believed it.

"He'd put six or eight of us whores into a huddle, early in the evening. A real huddle: we'd stand around him in our joint togs, our arms round each other's shoulders, like we were playing for the N.F.L. championship, and he'd give us a locker-room pep talk.

" 'The more you make for the joint, the more you make for yourselves, girls,' he'd let us know. 'And you, Miss Foo,' he'd tell me, 'you're the mainspring of this squad. Your spirit is what is carrying us on.'

"Honest to God, you'd think we were suppose to score against the tricks instead of screwing them.

"We'd hit the hay, dead beat, about four A.M., and here he'd come busting in to our rooms, without a knock, four hours later, and blasting that stupid whistle. 'Morning practice, girls! Rise and shine! Everybody out!' And he really meant it. We'd be out of bed, in pajamas, he'd toss us all heavy sweatshirts, and start us jogging around the joint!

"Some of these women, especially the ones who'd been in the trade awhile, were all out of shape. I'd usually get out in front, being the youngest, just a long-legged kid is all I was then, but I remember one old-timer—she'd been in the trade twenty years if she'd been in it a day—just *gasping* to me, 'What for God's sake *is* this?'

"I was lapping the field at that point, but I couldn't tell her. I didn't know. I suppose what that fool thought was he was getting us into shape. He had us practicing everything up to drop-kicking. We'd run until he'd blast the whistle and holler, 'That's all, girls! To the showers!'

"We'd tumble back into the sheets and get us some rest then, till early afternoon and the daily pep talk."

"I never heard anything like it," Dovie-Jean repeated.

"I've heard worse," Spanish Nan commented.

Spanish Nan had a slot-machine habit. All her quarters went into it but very few came back. Sometimes as many as three, four or five came back, which she immediately replayed. When she ran out of quarters she began changing bills. All she usually got for a two-bit piece was a dull, metallic, *"pshdang!"*

Into those twilit hours which fell between the timeless gray afternoon, and the flaring sexual panics of the late-night tricks, when the only sounds were the air conditioner's breath beating beneath the whirr of the big electric fan, and the occasional *pshdang! pshdang!* of the slot machine, there sauntered in a sixty-year-old horse player with a *Form* stuffed into his bright sports jacket, his collar open, his tie askew, his hearing aid in one ear and his attitude that of a kid of twenty-one, announcing the latest flash from Aqueduct.

"Summer Girl win driving!" He tossed his program, marked and torn, into Dovie-Jean's lap, then circled the parlor waving a green tip sheet. "Fromarco wire to wire! Win going away!"

"This is a whorehouse, Flash," Spanish Nan reminded him, "not a bookie. Sit down." Then added, turning to Dovie-Jean, "He'll be all right once he's settled down. He acts like a goof but he got good sense. You have to know how to take him."

Flash sat down beside Dovie-Jean on the divan and adjusted his hearing aid. "You want to see me turn up the level on it?" he asked her, and turned it up. "Now you want to see me turn it down?" And turned it down.

"Haven't I seen you somewheres before?" she asked him.

"I know, I *know.* Only it ain't me. Every time Art Carney shows up on TV I get it the next day. I *ain't* Art Carney. I ain't nobody. I never been on TV, I never met Art Carney. I never met Jackie Gleason. I never met *nobody*—and thank God for *that*. Now, what do you think I do when I'm down two hundred sixty at the end of the seventh? What would *you* do?"

"If I were down two hundred sixty at the end of the seventh," Dovie-Jean answered thoughtfully, "I'd go back of the grandstand and shoot myself."

"Don't do it, honey," Flash assured her gravely. "*Don't* do it—keep in mind when you're losing—*your life don't go with it. Your life don't go with it*—say it after me—"

"Your life don't go with it," Dovie-Jean accommodated the simple fellow. *"Your life don't go with it."*

"That's *right*. Now I'll tell you: Popular Victory may be closing—that was the tip I took and here comes Popular Victory, off at thirteen to one. I get two hundred eighty back for my twenty! I'm twenty ahead for the day! What do I *do?* What would *you* do?"

"Get the hell out of there with my money," Dovie-Jean assured the old sport.

"Okay, then I'll *show* you. I don't even look at the odds this time. Just run my eye down the entries till I hit a number—nine. All Our Hopes. Don't ask me why, I just go to the window and put that extra twenty on Hopes's nose. I don't look at the odds till I'm back to the rail. Nineteen to one! And the horses are entering the gate! Too late to switch my bet. All a sudden, as the flag goes up, odds on Hopes drop to fourteen to one. Last minute money! Somebody else believing in Hopes too! He breaks fourth, at the far turn he's third and moving up." Flash started to rise.

"Stay in your saddle, Flash," Spanish Nan commanded him, and he sat down once more and resumed. "He moves up to third, he's running second at the turn for home and here he comes head and head down the stretch—he's a nose, he's half a length—he wins by a length and a half!" He grinned triumphantly all around the parlor.

"I pick up three hundred twenty-eight dollars and eighty cents!" He took off his straw hat and, twirling it gently on one finger, began to sing in a rasping, not unpleasant old timer's voice:

Oh, I get by with a little help from my friends,
Mm, I get high with a little help from my friends
Mm, I'm gonna try with a little help from my friends.

He wouldn't leave the parlor now until he'd spent the greater part of his winnings. The women knew this and Big Benjamin knew it too. The old sport would send out for whatever they wanted—except booze. Big Ben never interfered because he'd make a twenty for bringing in the order.

Flash no longer remembered how long he'd been following horses, but guessed it must be about as long as he'd been following women. Strangely, when he saw horses entering the gate, he felt almost the same excitement he'd first felt, so long ago. As, when seeing a woman undressing for him, he felt the same rise of passion as he'd felt it the first time he'd seen a naked girl.

"Did I tell you about the time I hit a million-dollar daily double?" he asked Spanish Nan. Nan, disregarding the question, went to the slot machine, slipped in a quarter, and got nothing in return except a metallic *"Pshdang!"*

"Did I say a *million?*" Flash persisted, turned to Dovie-Jean, "*Five* million! I hooked up a horse named Moon Red in the first with a filly named Jealous Widow in the second. Both short-price entries. Here comes Moon Red into the turn for home a head out front—and falls. He'd hit a hole in the track and broke his right foreleg. They had to shoot him right on the track. Here comes Jealous Widow a head out front into the turn for home—and falls. Same hole. Same leg. They have to shoot *her* right on the track. I ask you, how's that for a daily double? Any bettor wishing to pick two horses in the double which won't survive either race, will be paid ten million to one!"

"I don't know how many million-to-one that is, Mister," Dovie-Jean assured him thoughtfully, "but I'm sure it's better than even money."

Spanish Nan put in another quarter. All she got in return was, *"Pshdang!"*

The whores' indifference to his story didn't trouble Flash. He went right on yakking of this and that, breaking off only to start singing, in a hoarse, off-key, somehow pleasant bass:

Would you believe in a love at first sight?
Yes, I'm certain that it happens all the time.
What do you see when you turn out the light?
I can't tell you, but I know it's mine.

"You got change for a dollar, Flash?" Spanish Nan asked him, and he gave her four quarters for a dollar.

"Pshdang!"
"Pshdang!"
"Pshdang!"
"Pshdang!"

When she came back, offering another bill for changing, he took her hand. "Let's save you some money," he told her, and she led him into her room.

Dovie-Jean sat idly on, a paperback book half-read on her lap and Flash's program, from Aqueduct, marked and circled. Glancing into her handbag, she found a quarter. For lack of anything else to do, just to kill time, she rose and put it into the machine.

She heard a far-off whirring as of gears within gears, then a rising note as a plane taxiing in down a runway. She stepped back as though to escape an explosion.

It was. It did. *"Pshdang! Pshdang! Pshdang! Pshdang! Pshdang!"* A month of quarters poured forth so furiously, rolling across the whorehouse floor and under the whorehouse divans, whirling into whorehouse corners as though some inner brake had slipped or broken and here comes Spanish Nan stark naked screaming, "*My* jackpot! *My* jackpot!" And sees Big Benjamin on his knees grabbing quarters right and left. *ZAP!* She kicks him from behind and he swings about without rising and grasps her knees. Down goes Spanish Nan head over heels and all the women screaming.

Benjamin goes back to scrambling for quarters still on his knees, Nan mounts him, gets both hands into his hair and haul-haul-hauls his big gray head back while he waves his clenched fists wildly. When he got to his feet she put him up flat against the wall and emptied his pockets as he stood, making no protest, with his cap in his hand. Then Nan took Dovie-Jean's handbag and poured her loot into it. Dovie-Jean stepped forward and opened her palm, revealing two quarters.

"I guess these must be yours too."

Spanish Nan, having recovered her breath along with her jackpot, studied the two coins for a moment.

"No, honey," she told Dovie-Jean, "they're yours. After all, it was *your* quarter."

Everyone turned their heads to Spanish Nan's door: there stood Flash, naked as a baby, holding his penis in his hand.

"What kind of a whorehouse *is* this, for God's sake?" he complained.

"I'm sorry, honey," Spanish Nan apologized, and moved him back into the room.

"Be careful what you pray for, girls," Big Benjamin gave them all warning from his shadowed corner, "you may get it."

Flash came out of Nan's room, now fully dressed and looking cockier than ever. He did a loose-limbed jaunt around the parlor, passing out dollar bills to each of the girls as he passed, then put his head back and sang:

Oh you trifling women
You say you love your men
When one leaves by the front door
The back door lets a new one in.

When Calhoun arrived in Buenos Aires to fight Rocky Olivera, the only sparring partner he could find was Dietrich Kroskauer, a German heavyweight who'd looked good against the best heavies in Europe. Calhoun knocked him cold, with a left hook, in their first round of sparring, although Kroskauer had been wearing a head protector. He packed his bags and took a flight back to Mannheim. Calhoun was left without a sparring partner.

He cut off training a couple days before the fight and lost to Olivera by a split decision. When he paid his bill at Olivera's hotel he found he'd lost again.

Dick Lion had taken the middleweight title from Gardello. Calhoun signed to meet Lion at Madison Square Garden in December.

"I know Dick Lion like a book," Calhoun assured the press at his signing, "he'll be easier for me than Gardello."

The following morning he drove to Doc Lowry's gym, one flight up above the Italian-American Club. It was a dimly lighted room, lined by posters of old fight shows, with a roped ring in its center. A Puerto Rican was skipping rope in one corner. A black light-heavy was working combinations before a full-length mirror. Lowry was standing beside him when Calhoun came in.

"I got a good-looking boy here, Ruby," he told Calhoun. The light-heavy began punching more energetically.

Lowry picked up fighters from all over the country and fought them up and down the Eastern Seaboard. He'd once tried to get Ruby from Yan Ianelli but Ruby had not been ready to make the move. Lowry had never yet had anyone to come close to a championship of anything.

Calhoun liked Lowry. Most people did. He'd been a puncher in his day and tried to make punchers out of his fighters. Most of them weren't. You could teach a kid balance, how to move and how to throw combinations; but you couldn't teach him to have power. He might be strong as seven, but that wasn't the name of the game. It was in sensing how to use it, and few had that sense. Watching Lowry's latest 'good-looking kid', a light-heavy out of North Africa who'd already won half a dozen fights here with great ease, Calhoun's guess was that he'd be back in Casablanca in six months.

He suited up and saw a middleweight, moving about the ring, whom he recognized.

"How you doin', old billy goat?" he greeted him.

It was Salazar, to whom he'd lost, after being outbutted, in Union City. Salazar came to the ropes and looked down. His right eye appeared to be slightly crossed and he gave Calhoun no sign of recognition. He merely gestured, with his glove, inviting Calhoun into the ring.

Lowry handed Calhoun headgear. "José don't remember too good," he warned Calhoun.

"I remember *him,*" Calhoun assured Lowry.

Salazar came at him as though he were still fighting the bout in Union City, forcing Calhoun to his right. He had to keep wheeling to the right to avoid Salazar's left. Calhoun jolted him twice with left hooks. The man still, after all these years, had no defense. When Lowry called time, Calhoun climbed down out of the ring.

"This dude is still fighting-mad," he told Lowry laughingly, handing him the headgear. "I don't need no billy goat like *that.*"

Calhoun drove two blocks from Lowry's and stopped, against a red light, still thinking of that poor punch-drunk Salazar, and wondering whether the Boxing Commission still permitted him to fight, when a police car drove up beside him.

" 'Keep your hands off the wheel!' " Calhoun recalls, was his first police warning, "and I can tell you I kept my hands off. Two squad cars, both loaded. They handcuffed me behind my back. When they shoved me into the police car I thought we were going to the station, it was only a couple of blocks away.

"No way. They drove me up to Garrett Mountain, above Paterson, by then there were six squad cars behind us in unmarked cars. What they had in mind, at that moment, I didn't know then and I don't know now. Two detectives in front of me and one on either side—one of them a black dude. I'd seen him somewheres before but I hadn't known, wherever that was, that he was on the force.

"When we got up on that stupid mountain we just parked and waited. Their microphone kept chattering, it was real excited. But I couldn't make out what about. We stayed up there the whole afternoon until somebody said 'Bring him in.'

"They locked me and I couldn't get in touch with nobody two whole days. The second day a trusty slipped me a note from somebody held in protective custody on the third floor. Name of Baxter. So I knew who the witness was the papers had been talking about.

"Baxter wrote me that a conspiracy to charge me with murder had begun while I was in South America. He himself, he told me, was in no way implicated! He was only being held as a material witness. This dude *has* to be a space cadet, was what I thought.

" 'Nobody living in Jersey City,' he wrote to me, 'could have committed those murders and remained in the city because there are too many paid informers for the police not to have heard something. Rewards,' he wrote, 'of twelve thousand five hundred dollars had been posted for information leading to the conviction of the killer or killers.'

"I realized that he was trying to collect the reward money and at the same time to protect himself against getting killed for it."

"Do you feel vengeful toward Baxter?" a reporter asked Calhoun.

"Toward that pitiful boy?" Calhoun appeared surprised by the question. "No way. Baxter is merely a product of the penal merry-go-round. He is like one of those creatures who are born without a digestive tract; he had to live off the tracts of others. When I feel vindictive it has to be toward a man worthy of my vindictiveness."

Calhoun named no names.

The judge's forebears had been German Jews of that highly assimilable tribe who had made such excellent Germans of themselves; and, the moment they'd passed the Statue of Liberty, had become the most American of Americans. Grandfather Turkowitz had changed the family name, at Ellis Island, to Turner. His grandson, now presiding over the criminal court in Jersey City, had been named after Grover Cleveland.

The Turners had never seen Delancey Street, nor Hester. Their friends had never been Jews. Their friends, from the beginning, had been Anglo-Saxon suburban types who belonged to country clubs with constitutions limiting membership to white Christians.

Judge Grover Cleveland Turner had himself married into a Christian family; his two daughters were blue-eyed blondes. Yet he had always been privately aware that he owed his rise, from practicing attorney to district attorney to a judgeship, to some shadowy figure chanting, head bowed, in a long-abandoned synagogue of Galicia. He had retained a talmudic mind.

New Jersey vs. Ruby Calhoun was the first occasion in which Judge Turner had presided over a criminal case. He was not made uneasy by that: he liked the challenge. He was a small, slight man who carried himself with the cockiness of the actor Claude Rains; and, indeed, in his youth, that actor had been Judge Turner's model for the face and figure he now turned to the world.

"Capital punishment may exist as something distasteful to you," Judge Turner advised one prospective juror, "but what you are being asked here is whether you will be able to support a first-degree murder conviction without recommendation of mercy—should the evidence so warrant—despite your personal reluctance."

A first-degree murder conviction, without recommendation of mercy, automatically demanded the death penalty under New Jersey law. Recommendation of mercy reduced it to life imprisonment.

"What the court is trying to do here," Calhoun's attorney, Ben Raymond, protested, "is to seat a special class of jurors, all of whom believe firmly in capital punishment." Raymond was a black man.

"Helen Shane was on the floor between the bar and the air conditioner," Eric Heim recalled on the stand, at Raymond's opening query. "I didn't touch nobody, I just set on the stool. I was bleeding and bleeding. I just waited for the police."

"How tall was the man with the revolver?"

"I only seen him like, I just turn here and see this woman, I wouldn't even know if she had glasses on. I seen that miserable gun all right. I seen *that*. I think he had a little mustache, like I said, and that's all I can say about it."

"I show you a report," Raymond persisted, "indicating you had told the police you had seen a light-skinned black man wearing a pencil-line mustache, about six feet tall or slightly taller. Is that correct?"

"No!" Heim shouted. "I told Gallegher the man had a dark mustache, well, it was a mustache, whatever you want to call it. I didn't look at him that long, I told Gallegher I couldn't identify him. Do I have to say this or do I have to?" Heim turned to the judge to ask, "because at that time I was in shock."

Calhoun is five foot eight, dark-skinned, and was wearing a Fu Manchu.

Miss Violet Vance had been watching television, one floor above the tavern, while Heim and Vincio had been shooting pool.

"I was lying on my couch," she remembered, "I'd fallen asleep. I was wakened by a loud noise. It sounded like a big bang. I heard two more noises, I thought Dude was closing up. I saw the neon sign still lit. I heard a voice saying, 'Oh no.' An excited voice. It sounded like a woman's. It was coming from the tavern, it sounded. I went to my bedroom and saw a white car double-parked in the middle of the street. I saw a colored man come running out of the bar to the car. It was white and he had taillights like two triangles starting at the outside of the car and narrowing at the center. He jumped into the driver's seat and wheeled off. I didn't see any weapon."

"Did you see anyone else in the car?"

"No. But the way he took off I figured something was wrong. I tried to get the license plate numbers but I couldn't make out the lettering or the numbers, but I saw they were dark plates with yellow or gold lettering, not a Jersey plate. I saw the car pull away and threw on a raincoat and went downstairs into the tavern. I saw Eric Heim holding on to a pole. I started to walk toward him and just past the pool table I saw Helen Shane. Her head was by the juke, laying on her back. Then I saw the man."

"What man?"

"The man standing in the door. He was holding it open. I just looked at him. He just looked at me. Finally he said, 'Stay where you are. Don't move.' It was like in a dream.

"Then I saw Eric had blood on his head. I saw by the way he was holding the pole he needed help, and I went to him."

"Was the man who told you to stop where you were white or black?"

"White."

"Had you ever seen him before?"

"In the tavern."

"What was his name?"

"All I ever heard him called was Nick."

"Do you see him in this courtroom?"

"Yes." (Rising, she approached a short, heavyset youth of twenty or twenty-one, sitting on the witnesses' bench, and pointed to him.)

"When you heard the command: 'Stay where you are! Don't come in!' it was from this man, and he was inside the bar?"

"That's right. And he kept coming toward me, walking along the bar, then he went behind the bar."

"He went past Mrs. Shane?"

"Yes."

"He went past Vincio still sitting at the bar?"

"Yes."

"What did you do?"

"I went to Helen Shane. I knelt down alongside of her. She asked me to phone her boyfriend. She was shortwinded, very faint. She had on a black uniform and the whole top of it was like a rust color. I called her boyfriend. I saw a police car pull up and a civilian car behind it. Officer told me to go look at the tailgate of the civilian car. I walked around behind it and looked at the taillights and they were the same as the ones I'd seen from my bedroom window."

"Did you look behind the bar?"

"Yes. I saw Dude Leonard lying on the floor with money all around him."

"When I brought Mr. Calhoun into the operating room," Detective Mooney recalled, "Eric Heim was incoherent, hollering and mumbling. The doctors were trying to subdue him and treat him all at the same time."

"Did he have a full chance to look at Calhoun there?"

"He did, but he was not able to identify Calhoun as the gunman. He was unsure of what he'd seen. He said, 'All niggers look alike to me.'

"In the latter part of July," the same detective went on, "I spoke with Mr. Iello in a tavern then called Pete's Playpen. He brought a beer to where I was sitting and asked me did I remember him and I said I did. 'I never told the police,' he then told me voluntarily, 'but someone else was with me that night.' And gave me the name Dexter Baxter. We'd been on the hawks for Rabbit Baxter for a stickup and an escape. He wasn't hard to catch but he was hard as hell to hold. We apprehended him along with Esteban Escortez, and tied him into four armed robberies. Then we questioned him about the triple homicide at the Melody. Every question we asked Baxter, he made a wild dash for the door—in his mind. Fortunately, we had him shackled.

"He admitted he was with Mr. Iello and that he'd seen a car with two occupants, one of whom had been a woman. He'd heard shots, but had seen no shooting, he told us. Two weeks later I saw Mr. Iello going into a tavern and followed him in.

" 'You look scared, Iello,' I told him, sitting down beside him.

" 'I'm all messed up since that shooting,' he told me. 'A black gal hit on me, 'Forget the whole thing or you'll regret it,' she told me. 'You talk to the police you'll take the consequences.' There was a redheaded nigger a few feet away. I'd seen him around, he used to be some sort of fighter. I seen him once in the Jersey City Armory. He said nothing but I thought they were together.'

" 'Who do *you* think did the shooting?' I then asked him. 'You had the man and you let him go,' he tells me. 'What man was that, Iello?' He just shakes his head, No, he ain't talking. 'Was it

Tiger Keller, Iello?' He shakes his head, No. No again. Then he says, 'His initials are R.C.'

" 'Why has it taken you so long to tell us this?' I asked him.

" 'R.C. has friends,' he tells me. "I'm a parolee. I have a brother in Trenton. I have to think about him. If you try to use this conversation I'll deny everything.'

"He had to have protection, that much was certain. So we brought him in handcuffed but not under arrest. Handcuffing was his own idea. He wanted to give the impression that he was being taken by force. He didn't want to look, in the papers, like a man volunteering information, which is what he was. The poor clown was really caught. He'd caught hisself."

"The handcuffing," Sergeant Mooney added, "was just to make him feel a little secure. He feared for his life. That was why we quartered him in Atlantic City. He felt he was in peril of suffering great bodily harm. De Vivani promised him protection and made good on that promise."

"We got a call there was trouble at the Melody," Sergeant Conroy supported Mooney's testimony. "At the intersection of Jefferson and Twelfth a white car shot across our lights, it had a foreign [out-of-state] license. We shot down McLean to Route 4 and came over the underpass into East Jersey City where you can look down Route 4 for quite a distance. We didn't see it so we did a U-turn and just as we reached the bus station we seen a white car cut across Jefferson at Twenty-ninth. We stopped it at Thirtieth. A black man was driving, and there was a girl lying down in the rear seat. It was a rented car."

"Who was the driver?"

"Ruby Calhoun. We checked them out and let them go. Half an hour after, at the intersection of Eighteenth and Broad, we came up against the same white car. We pulled it over to the curb. Now there was only one person in the car—Calhoun. We told him to turn around and follow us back to the station."

"Do you have testimony sir," Raymond asked Mooney, "that this *was* the same car you'd seen speeding past you toward New York City?"

"What testimony?" Judge Turner interposed. "Testimony from whom?"

"The officer's own testimony, your honor," Raymond assured the judge, and turned back to the witness. "How many police cars were at the scene when you returned there with Calhoun?"

"Six or seven."

"How large a crowd?"

"Enormous."

"What was your reason for bringing him there instead of directly to headquarters?"

"After all, sir, he was only a suspect. I had no reason to actually take him to headquarters."

"What was your purpose in pursuing such a roundabout route to catch the car that got away?"

"I felt that, it being an out-of-state car, when they reached Thirtieth Street they'd find themselves in a dead end. They would have had to make either a right or a left turn there in order to get out of town."

"And what happened?"

"We lost it."

"You have no specific knowledge of what happened to that car?"

"It could have proceeded, turned around, done anything. And when we returned to the scene of the homicides a man told us he'd been chased down an alley by a black man with a revolver."

State prosecutor Scott then took over the examination of Nick Iello.

"Mr. Iello, do you see the man whom you saw coming out of the Melody Bar and Grill immediately after three persons had been shot dead inside it?"

"I do."

"Please point him out."

Iello rose, moved half a dozen steps toward Calhoun, then pointed directly at him and returned to the witness chair.

"What did you do then?"

"I went inside the tavern through the side door. I walked over to this side here [pointing at photograph of tavern's interior] and down this way here. There was a man right here wearing a white shirt. He was sitting up. There was blood down the side of his face. There was a broken bottle on the floor and there was blood all over the floor. There was a woman lying right about here. She was holding her stomach bleeding profusely. Very bad. I knelt down there and she says . . ."

"Don't tell us what she said," Judge Turner cautioned Iello.

" 'Please help,' " Iello went on all the same, "then she grabbed my arm and I just backed up because there was blood over everything. I stood up. As I stood up two things happened. This man sitting at the thing. He stood up and said something about going to the men's room. But just about the same time in the door came a girl. She stopped for a minute. She walked over and screamed. She left. I walked down here. Around the bar. To the cash register. I took a dime and went back around the bar and phoned the police."

Ben Raymond took over the witness:

"Did you tell Sergeant Mooney that whoever you'd seen had chased you up the street?"

"Yes."

"That's not true, is it?"

"Not actually."

"You served in the armed forces?"

"Yes."

"How were you discharged?"

"Fraudulent enlistment."

"Undesirable discharge?"

"Yes."

"You served some time in the stockade after a general court-martial, did you not?"

"Yes sir, I have a fradulent enlistment discharge. Undesirable conditions because I was on parole from Jamesburg when I entered the service. I was seventeen."

"And because you beat up another soldier and served time in the stockade for that?"

"The charge was not for beating up anybody. The charge was because I hadn't mentioned I was on parole."

"Now sir, with respect to the indictment number nine-eight-eight-dash-six-one, did you, with another individual, plead guilty to nine-eight-eight-dash-six-one, which indictment states that you unlawfully and feloniously made an assault upon one Imogene McElway against her will and by violence and putting her into fear, from the person and against the will of the said Imogene McElway then and there did feloniously, forcibly and violently to steal, take away and carry the same. Did you plead guilty to *that?*"

"Would you mind repeating all that?"

"You were not listening?"

"No sir."

"Do you remember pleading guilty to the indictment charging you with assault and robbery of Imogene McElway?"

"Everything ran concurrent. I'm not definitely sure which was first or second."

"This is not to be taken lightly, sir. You are charged with robbery of Imogene McElway. Do you remember it?"

"Naturally, I remember it. I confessed it. I was charged and found guilty of it. I went to an institution and was punished thoroughly for it. I accepted the punishment. I served the time imposed by the court. It should be obvious to anybody that I'd remember it. Or are you trying me for that all over again? What became of the murders in the Melody bar? I thought that *that* was why I was brought here today."

Raymond stepped to one side, glanced at the judge as if for help and received none. He took a deep breath and began all over:

"You have never been charged with the offense of robbery in connection with the events of June seventeenth, nineteen hundred and sixty-six?"

"You might say larceny."

"You have not been taken back to Bordentown for violation of your parole, even though you are an admitted thief?"

"No sir."

"You are still walking the streets?"

"No sir."

"You're incarcerated?"

"I'm limited, as you might say."

"I can see you're not unlimited. You still go to work every day?"

"In a manner of speaking."

"Is it, or is it not a manner of speaking, that you stood outside the Melody Bar and Grill shouting, 'Everybody in here has been shot!' "

"What I said was to the police officer, 'Sir, I think you'd better call for an ambulance. There are people inside who've been shot.' "

"You went to the cash register to get change to make a call?"

"I went in there to try to help. I did go to the cash register to get that dime. When I seen the money, knowing myself, that I'm a thief, I took more. Basically I *am* a thief. But I am no assassin. Remember *that,* mister. I am *not* an assassin."

"Nobody has accused you of assassination," Judge Turner assured Iello. "Please answer the questions only. I am striking it."

"I would prefer it to remain," Ben Raymond requested the court.

"I'm certain you would," Judge Turner replied. "I am striking it."

"You are not, then, an assassin?" Ben Raymond turned back to the witness.

"Don't answer that question," Judge Turner cautioned Iello, and turned back to Raymond. "I told you I struck it, Mr. Raymond. That means it is an improper question and it is stricken. I hope I make myself clear."

"You told the police that you didn't see the face of the man coming out of the bar," Raymond resumed questioning Iello. "Is that correct or not?"

"It is possible."

"It is a *fact*. Is it *not?*"

"I had a reason why I didn't."

"I didn't ask you, mister, anything about your reasons. I asked you one simple question and that one alone. Is it not a *fact* that you informed police, the morning of June seventeenth, nineteen hundred and sixty-six, 'I didn't see his face.' Is that correct or is it not correct?"

"Whatever the officer wrote on his report I would have to say I said it."

"That is not the question, Mr. Iello," Judge Turner interrupted. "Do you remember saying . . ."

"No, I don't. I don't remember that, your honor. I remember only the highlights. I told them it was the same car I seen on the corner. At the station I told the officers, 'This looks like the same man, but forget it, I don't want to get involved.' I didn't identify anybody at the station. In the morning De Vivani accused me of stealing some money and I told him, 'Go screw yourself, De Vivani. You may be the chief dago around here but you're just another wop to me.' "

"What money was he talking about?"

"Who knows what he was talking about? I sure didn't. I don't remember hardly any of the conversation except telling him it was a New York plate."

"Did De Vivani at any time suggest you were a possible suspect in these murders?"

"I don't remember anything like that."

"Where were you when you saw the car's taillights?"

"Out on the street looking at the back of the car. As it hit the brakes it lit up. I was in a good position because I was back in the crowd. I didn't want anyone to see me was why I faded back."

"And isn't it a fact that the statement I've just shown you was given after you saw a car occupied by Ruby Calhoun returned to the vicinity of the tavern under police escort? Is that not correct?"

"Correct. But I didn't identify him."

"When you got to the register by climbing across Dude Leonard, did you realize he was dead?"

"You could tell he wasn't alive."

"And when you went back you had to go across him again—and you didn't stop, in all that time, to make a phone call?"

"No sir."

"Did you go back to see if Mrs. Shane could be helped?"

"Sure I came back."

"And what did you do for her?"

"What *could* I do for her?"

"Did you call for an ambulance?"

"I called the operator."

"After or before you took the money?"

"After. Obviously."

"How long did the police keep you in protective custody in October, nineteen hundred and sixty-six?"

"I don't recall."

"How long have you been in their protective custody?"

"I don't recall."

"You have used drugs, have you not?"

"Under a doctor's care."

"And within three weeks of this date you have been under the influence of narcotics, have you not?"

"What date?" Judge Turner wanted to know. "What relevancy does it have whether he uses narcotics or not three weeks ago?"

"It would have relevancy in that it has been necessary to reduce him to custody for this reason. The police want to keep him in a position where . . ."

"You are going off the subject, sir. Dangerously off the subject."

"You talked to someone on the prosecutor's staff last night," Raymond assured the witness, "did you not?"

"Yes sir."

"Did you discuss what reward you were to receive?"

"I have never been promised anything from the prosecutor's office."

"Have you been promised anything from anyone?"

"No sir."

"You are, of course, aware of the reward offered by the Tavern Owners' Association?"

"I'm not sure about anything."

"Are you or are you not aware that the mayor of this city declared that reward, the very day of the offense, in every newspaper in the city?"

"That could be hearsay. I don't recall. No one from the prosecutor's office ever offered me anything except protection."

"You went behind that bar because you saw the cash register was open. Right?"

"I went behind the bar to get a dime to make a phone call."

"Even though you had two quarters in your pocket?"

"I thought more of a dime than a quarter, somehow. I could have gotten it off the bartender."

"There was no bartender in view, sir."

"Not after he'd been slain, I guess not."

"When did you do that?"

"Do what?" Judge Turner asked quickly.

"Slay the bartender," Raymond replied.

"*What*?" Judge Turner demanded.

"*When did he slay the bartender*—that is addressed to the witness."

"It is not to my knowledge," Iello replied.

"The jury will disregard the question," Judge Turner ruled. " 'When did you slay the bartender?' is a question which has nothing whatsoever to support it in the proceedings of this court."

"The witness Baxter has been sitting here," Raymond advised Judge Turner before presenting the next witness, "trying to write notes to us. If he were unshackled he could do this more comfortably. It is extremely difficult for a man to write while handcuffed, your honor."

"The witness has a record of escapes," Judge Turner replied, "every time they take off the handcuffs he escapes."

"He couldn't very well escape in this courtroom, your honor."

"Remove the handcuffs."

"Mr. Baxter," Raymond asked the uncuffed witness, "is it not true, sir, that, at the time of the murders in the Melody Grill, there were pending against you the following charges: armed robbery of the Burnbrook Motor Lodge in Morristown, New Jersey?"

"I have that charge pending."

"Armed robbery, Raven Motor Lodge, Fort Lee, New Jersey?"

"I have that pending."

"Theft of a motor vehicle in Saddlebrook, New Jersey?"

"The charge is larceny, not theft."

"How about breaking and entering, Bergen County, New Jersey?"

"I broke but didn't enter."

"How about escape from the Hackensack, New Jersey, police?"

"When they woke up they caught me."

"Armed robbery, Royalton Hotel, Linden, New Jersey?"

"Pending."

"Possession of stolen property, city of Paterson, New Jersey?"

"Paterson or Elizabeth, I forget which. Maybe Union City."

"After you testified before the grand jury, Mr. Baxter, did you talk to Lieutenant De Vivani or state's attorney Scott?"

"Correct."

"Correct what?"

"Correct sir."

"What did they ask you?"

"They wanted a statement to the effect that I went back to the Apex Supply Company and broke in. I didn't want to give it. Later I gave it anyhow."

"What were you doing behind the Apex Supply Company early on the morning of June seventeenth, nineteen hundred sixty-six?"

"I had all black clothes on and I hid my face so no car going by could see me. I started looking for a tire iron and I couldn't find it. A car came past going on Adams toward Eighteenth Street. It was a white car. The make I wasn't sure about. Maybe a sixty-three Ford. I saw a Negro in the front seat, driving."

"Who was he?"

"Ruby Calhoun."

"Did you know him before?"

"Not personally. But I knew his face."

"You had seen him on television, I assume?"

"I'd saw him once in Paterson. I was in a car with a friend and he pointed Calhoun out to me."

"How long prior to this night, the seventeenth of June," Raymond asked, "had you seen Ruby Calhoun?"

"About in February. I seen him in a magazine."

" 'Prior' means 'before.' How long before June seventeenth had you seen Ruby Calhoun?"

"I'd saw his picture often during that time."

"Did anything happen while you were working on that door?"

"I wasn't actually working on that door. I stopped when I heard like backfiring or a gunshot. I came through the alleyway here and came out on Jefferson Street. I seen someone in front of me on the sidewalk walking toward this corner here."

"Could you describe anything of the physical characteristics of the man directly in front of you or anything of the clothing he was wearing?"

"He was short and stocky. He was walking down the sidewalk on the inside of the shadows. He had on a dark shirt and dungarees."

"Did he have high heels, a little higher than ordinary, like a Cuban heel?"

"I don't remember."

"Do you recall that Mr. Iello had rather long hair?"

"His hair wasn't ever that long."

"Did you ascertain that the person you were following was Mr. Iello?"

"I wasn't sure and I didn't want to call out and arouse suspicion. I thought maybe I could catch up with him and make sure before he got to the bar, if it really was him."

"Although you had been with him from early evening, you weren't sure that the man you were following down the street was Mr. Iello—is that correct?"

"Correct."

"You'd known him for how long?"

"A few hours."

"You'd only known Nick Iello a few hours?"

"No, I've known him a long time."

"Although you didn't recognize the man in front of you, a man driving a car very fast, whom you'd seen once, you recognized in a flash? Is that right?"

"That's only a statement," Judge Turner decided. "Don't answer it."

"Where are you at the present time?" Raymond asked Baxter.

"Morris County jail."

"Have you ever told the jury that you own a thirty-three caliber revolver?"

The prosecution objected and the objection was sustained.

"What happened next?" Raymond asked the witness.

"I saw a Negro carrying a revolver. I walked away from the scene. I went back to Kenneth Kelley's and he drove me back to Apex Supply. I finally forced the padlock. But all I found inside was a safe behind a partition. I knew I couldn't make that type safe with the sort of equipment I had, so I left."

"Do you see the man who was carrying the revolver in this room?" state's attorney Scott asked Baxter.

"Yes sir, he's right there." (Pointing at Calhoun.)

"Do you know a man named Esteban Escortez," Raymond resumed his examination of the witness, "who was with you in the Passaic County jail on August third, nineteen hundred sixty-six?"

"Yes."

"Do you recall telling Mr. Escortez that you were going to play off the Calhoun case against charges you were then facing?"

"No. I have no such recollection."

"You never made such a statement, either to Mr. Escortez or to someone else?"

"Never. No way."

Esteban Escortez was a man of twenty-seven, of short stature but robust physique, of Mexican-American ancestry. Although his face had a defiant tilt, his manner on the stand was shy; and his voice, slightly accented, was low.

"Why were you in the Passaic County jail, Mr. Escortez, with Dexter Baxter, on or about August second of last year?"

"We was arrested for armed robbery."

"What did Baxter tell you about this case?"

"He told me he had only one chance. That was to testify for the state against Calhoun. If he didn't he was going to go away for long."

"Did Baxter ever tell you that he was going to play off the Calhoun case against charges, so he and you would benefit?"

"Yes sir. He did."

"And did he tell you in fact that Iello had never seen Ruby Calhoun at that scene in the Melody Bar and Grill?"

"Yes sir, he did."

"Did you have anything to gain by coming here today, Mr. Escortez?"

"I spend eight dollar, my own money. I get nothing."

Calhoun appeared relaxed on the stand. He wore a dark, conservative suit of good material, collar and dark tie. He still wore a heavy mustache but had not let his beard grow back; that he'd been forced to shave off before the Gardello fight.

"Mr. Calhoun," state's attorney Scott began his examination, "were you a witness to the murder of Matt Haloways?"

"I was."

"Had you known the victim previous to his murder?"

"All my life. He was my daughter's godfather."

"Naturally, you were angered at his killing."

"No. Saddened. He was a good man."

"His sons, Ed and Hardee, were your lifelong friends, were they not?"

"No. I knew Ed for many years. I only know Hardee to say hello to. We have nothing in common."

"But you do have a great deal in common with Ed Haloways?"

"We're the same age."

"Did you know him when you were serving time in Jamesburg?"

"We locked together."

"Naturally you shared Ed's desire to avenge his father."

"I'm not aware that Ed Haloways had such a desire. If so, he never expressed it to me."

"He expressed it to the police. He came down to the police station, shortly after his father had been shot down, and warned the police that something would be done about the murder if the police did not do something."

"That wasn't Red. It was his brother."

"Nevertheless, the police *did* do something. They arrested a man named Le Forti, who was found guilty by reason of insanity and is now confined in a state institution."

"I'm pleased to hear that."

"What is your trade, Mr. Calhoun?"
"I fight professionally."
"Are you successful at it?"
"Reasonably so."
"It is, then, your purpose, when you get into a ring to knock your opponent unconscious, is it not?"
"It is not. If the opponent should expose himself to a knockout punch, I'll throw it. But the purpose is simply to win, that's all."
"I see. What was the charge for which you were convicted and sentenced to the state prison?"
"Objection," Ben Raymond rose to interpose, and was immediately sustained.
When Ben Raymond examined Calhoun, he replied in a low voice devoid of tension. When asked to account for himself on the evening of the murders he answered without urgency in his voice, "I was in the Paradise before midnight. They had a jukebox and space to dance in the rear. I stayed for half a dozen records. I don't remember who I was dancing with. Then a young lady asked me to drive her home. I don't know her name. She lived about four blocks down from the Paradise. We'd only driven two blocks down when we got the police-car flash. It was Officer Mooney. I showed him my registration.
" 'What's the trouble, officer?' I asked him.
" 'Nothing, Ruby,' he told me, 'we're just looking for a white car.'
"I dropped the girl off, drove to my own house, took my shoes off because my wife and daughter were sleeping. I got some money, came down and drove down Highway 40 to Rocky's Hideaway. That was what I was doing the second time the police car stopped me. It was Officer Mooney again; but this time he wasn't friendly."
"How long had it been since you'd left the Paradise?"
"Hour, hour and a half."
"Did you go to the Melody Bar and Grill?"
"No sir."
"Mr. Heim informs us there was an altercation in the Melody between the bartender and a black couple. Can you tell us something about this?"

"I have never been in the Melody Bar and Grill in my life. I can tell you nothing."

"What happened after Officer Mooney stopped you for the second time?"

"He said 'Follow my car,' then I seen three, four other police cars behind me. I followed Mooney and when we got in front of the Melody, Mooney told me, 'Get out and open the trunk.' I got out and opened the trunk. He kicked my boxing equipment around for a while. Then he told me, 'Close it and get over by the wall.' So I closed it and got over by the wall. There was quite a crowd in front of the Melody. A police van drove up and Mooney said, 'Get in,' so I got in. We left my car parked by the Melody and drove to General Hospital and I saw a man lying on a stretcher.

" 'Is this the man with the gun?' Mooney asked him.

"He raised hisself up and looked at me: 'No,' he said, 'that ain't the one,' and sank down again."

Heim had not recognized Calhoun as the man who'd had the altercation with Dude Leonard.

Calhoun's first fear was that, if he acknowledged his presence at the Melody he'd be volunteering for the electric chair. The only way he'd have out would have been to finger Red Haloways.

When Ben Raymond had put that question to him, privately and directly in the attorney's office, Ruby had replied without hesitation: "I have never been inside the Melody Bar and Grill in my life."

Ben Raymond had believed him.

"How were you dressed, Mr. Calhoun," he asked Ruby in court, "when you went to the hospital where you saw the man on the stretcher?"

"The same as I am dressed now."

"Did you object to going to the hospital?"

"No sir."

"Did the police search you?"

"They never searched me. Only my car. I just stood there. There was a procession of officers in and out of that room the whole night. Some asked me questions. De Vivani didn't come in until morning. No, he gave me no Miranda warning. How could he? Not even federal judges had it figured at that time. 'We want to question you about the Melody Bar and Grill shootings,' was the only clue he gave me about why I was there.

" 'You've never used a gun?' he asked me then. 'That's in the past,' I told him. 'When I say, "I don't use guns" now, I mean my profession is my hands. It's how I make my living.' "

"He didn't tell you, specifically, what had happened at the Melody?" Raymond asked.

"All he told me was 'shootings.' When I was released I was told my car was in the police garage, and it was: all tore up. The panels had been tooken apart. The radio was hanging out. Every conceivable place somebody might hide something had been tore out."

"Did you remain in Jersey City, available to police?"

"I went to Buenos Aires. I was arrested the day after I returned."

"Were you on the corner of Jefferson and Sixteenth on the evening of June sixteenth, nineteen hundred sixty-six?"

"Never except when I was brought there by the police."

"Mr. Iello testifies that he saw you on that corner, coming out a tavern, carrying a gun."

"Never."

"Did you know a man named Dude Leonard?"

"Never."

"Nick Vincio?"

"I did not."

"Helen Shane?"

"I did not."

"Eric Heim?"

"I did not."

"What was the name of the bandleader that night at Rocky's Hideaway?"

"Valentine Easter."

Prosecuting attorney Scott now took up the witness.

"Mr. Heim informs us that there was an altercation in the Melody Bar and Grill involving the bartender, Donald Leonard, and a black couple, a young man and a young woman. Were you the young black man involved, Mr. Calhoun?"

"I have never been inside the Melody Bar and Grill in my life."

"Were you the young black man involved, Mr. Calhoun?"

"No. How could I have been?"

"When Officer Mooney drove you to the hospital, you were confronted there by a man who'd been shot in the face. Was he still so drunk that he was unable to identify you as the man who'd shot him?"

Raymond took immediate objection. "Nowhere in the record is there anything to indicate that Mr. Heim was drunk at any time during the course of the evening of June sixteenth, nineteen sixty-six. Was he drunk when he went to his lawyer's office later in the year, and described the killer to his lawyer as 'a man six feet in height, light-skinned, with a pencil-line mustache'?"

"Objection sustained," Judge Turner ruled.

"From the day that you were picked up until today," Raymond then asked Calhoun, "you have protested your innocence. Is that not true?"

"True."

"Now you are charged with discharging a weapon causing the deaths of three people. Would you turn to the jury, Mr. Calhoun, and tell them how much truth there is in this charge? Take off your glasses."

Calhoun removed his glasses with deliberation. He put his hand to his eyes as though to rest them; then turned his face slowly to the jury.

It was a face sculptured in dark bronze. The strength of the jaw was supported by the absolute firmness of the eyes. Calhoun looked at each juror, individually, one by one.

"I had nothing to do with the killings," he repeated. "I use my fists, not guns."

Humphrey Scott was a Civil Rights attorney, an activist who had opposed the war in Vietnam. "Good law enforcement is cheap and bad law enforcement is expensive." He put himself on record as politician as well as lawyer. "I am philosophically opposed to the death penalty—unless I can be satisfied that there will be no significant effect upon the crime rate; I could then overcome my reservations. Too often we employ social conditions as an excuse in enforcing the law, saying we cannot reduce crime until we improve those conditions. I say we ought to stop making excuses and do the best with what we have.

"The original report on Mr. Calhoun," Scott continued, "was knowing, intelligent acknowledgment of the man's rights. Lieutenant De Vivani did not have to inform Mr. Calhoun that he could have a court-appointed attorney if he wanted one."

"Is Mr. Iello telling the truth?" state's attorney Scott asked the jury, "or do you think he is merely hopeful of the reward? Is his statement tailor-made? Just look at the discrepancies. If Iello and Baxter were so interested in that reward, why didn't they get their stories straight? Baxter said he had seen Calhoun only once. He could have said he'd been Calhoun many times."

Scott then emptied three bags of bloody clothing onto a table directly in front of the jury; each bag into a separate heap. Beside each heap he placed a photograph of the murdered person.

"There was once a man," he continued gravely, "a human being by name of Donald Leonard, a bartender at the Melody Bar and Grill in Jersey City, and he wore this shirt I now hold before you. And he looked like this (holding Leonard's photograph up before the jury) when he was sent into eternity by a gunman with a thirty-eight caliber pistol in his hand.

"There was once a man, a fellow human being by name of Nicholas Vincio, and he had the misfortune of going to the Melody Bar and Grill on June sixteenth, nineteen sixty-six, and this [holding Vincio's photo up to the jury] is how his life ended, murdered in cold blood by a thirty-eight caliber revolver.

"And there was once a human being, a woman by name of Helen Shane, and she wore these clothes, these bullet-ridden clothes, when she was shot not once, but twice. Two of the bullets passed through her body and she clung to life for nearly a month, and finally passed away, and this is what became of this human being from a thirty-eight caliber revolver shot.

"Ladies and gentlemen, on the question of punishment, the

facts of this case clearly indicate that, in the early morning of June seventeenth, nineteen sixty-six, Ruby Calhoun forfeited his right to live. The state asks that you extend to him the same measure of mercy he extended to Donald Leonard, Nicholas Vincio and Helen Shane. And that you return a verdict of murder in the first degree to all charges without recommendation."

"The most incredible thing you have heard in this case," Raymond assured the jury, "was from a man who admits to having a lengthy criminal record. 'Yes, I *am* a thief,' he tells us. While his pal was breaking into the Apex Supply Company, he decides to go down to the Melody to buy a pack of cigarettes. In front of a smoked-fish place he hears two shots coming from the bar. Yet he continues to walk directly toward the sound of gunfire.

"That is fantastic. That is incredible. A parolee, acting as lookout for his pal trying to break into a supply house, hears gunfire and heads right toward it as though it were a promise of terminating his parole. The witness may be none too bright, but he is not insane.

"As he approaches the bar, his story becomes yet more incredible. He sees a Negro approaching him, carrying a revolver, but he doesn't say, 'I turned and ran.' He says, 'I kept walking toward him and it was only when I got to nine or ten feet away that I turned and ran.'

"If Mr. Iello saw a man who just shot down four people coming around a corner, you can be certain that Mr. Iello would not be here to tell us about it today.

"What Mr. Iello did next was yet more amazing. He went back into the tavern, he says, where, seeing the carnage, he demonstrates his compassion by pushing Mrs. Shane's hand away when she tried to hold him and said to him, 'Help me!' Instead of helping her, Mr. Iello ran around the bar, stepped over the dead body of Mr. Leonard, grabbed money, stepped back over the body, ran out into the street, didn't stop to phone for an ambulance or for anything like that. He ran back up the street and delivered the money to his pal. Then ran back to the tavern because he had glimpsed Violet Vance in the window and knew he'd better get back there and explain what he was doing around the place and called the police—the operator testified she had heard only a low male voice and a brief message—'Everybody is dead here and I'm the only one alive.'

"The interesting thing about Mr. Baxter is that he saw this white car going in a directly opposite direction from what his pal Iello saw it. That one factor is enough to raise doubt in our minds and to demonstrate that they are both lying.

"When Baxter heard the shots he too ran into the alley and over to Jefferson to see what was going on, and observed what appeared to be his pal in front of him. Iello was rather distinctively dressed, with that kind of outfit on, that kind of hair; but yet Baxter wasn't sure this *was* his pal, but he kept closing in on him because he was pretty sure it *was* his pal. And then he makes identification of a man who was *behind* his friend whom he cannot recognize, identification of a man he'd seen once in his life, riding in a passing car. He then turns about and runs back up the street into the alley where he waited for Iello to bring him the money from the register. This may make sense to you. It makes no sense at all to me.

"Iello and Baxter don't tell their story to the police until some time in October, four months after the murders. They tell it at precisely the time when they are in desperate need of a story to get them off the hook. Iello faced twenty years worth of charges at that time and Baxter was facing eighty.

"Baxter then withholds information that he returned, after the shootings, and finally broke into the place. This is the type of witness you are supposed to heed when a man is being tried for his life.

"There is an air of desperate tragedy in this procedure. I represent a man sitting here with his life in the balance, and the state keeps presenting evidence which is altogether mysterious. I don't have the gall to suggest that Iello, or Baxter or Kelley committed this terrible crime. I wouldn't have the gall to suggest that because these jackals, now bearing witness, are not killers. They are sneak thieves.

" 'Why,' Mr. Scott will protest, 'he sounds as though he is putting Iello and Baxter on trial.' Not really. I'm fighting for a man's life here,'' Raymond explained, looking directly at the black juror. ''If Iello and Baxter live forever, that's all right with me. But I do wish to point out to you people of the jury that their brand of testimony entitles you, if you disbelieve any part of it, to disbelieve it all.

''And if you disbelieve their tissue of lies, you must find the defendant not guilty. I submit you can make no other finding.

''Is there any accounting for either of these young men? They are suave, well dressed, self-assured. Iello, when asked why he did not identify Ruby Calhoun immediately, replies, 'Because I recognized the fact that I was on a conspiracy to break and enter, and as I walked up the street I got involved in murder. I realized that if I had recognized Calhoun, he had recognized me. I realized that if I ever took a fall and went back to the reformatory, then there was another objection, a seriouser one, so I thought I should just tell my crime and the court said, 'Proceed' and the witness said, 'I don't have anything further to say.'

''Perhaps you ladies and gentlemen can make some sense of all this. I cannot. If he is afraid of Mr. Calhoun why did he not identify him immediately and thus get him off the streets? Why permit him to walk around free for months if he were guilty? Mr. Calhoun walked out of the police station, having been cleared by the polygraph and was given back his car. 'Drive away!' he was commanded.

''I asked Mr. Iello, 'Did you tell Officer Greenleaf that the man coming around the corner carrying a gun was thin built, six feet in height, light-skinned?' His reply was, 'Yes.'

''Can you condemn a man upon the strength of such memory? The bench has stopped me from implying that Iello and Baxter had something to do with the murders. Yet I will imply, with all my might, that there is more to the story of Iello, Baxter and Kelley than has yet appeared.

''I know that Mr. Scott, when he sums up, will present the evidence of the white car. But the manager of the Citgo station, from whom it had been rented, stated clearly that this was not the only car of its color and its kind in the area.

''But from beginning to end,'' Raymond added, looking once

again at the black juror, "the question which has gone to the heart of everything here is Baxter saying, 'That Negro over there.' What is *'that'?* An animal? Why didn't he say, candidly, 'That animal over there'? Because that is what was in his voice, and that is what has been in the prosecution's voice from the very beginning of this case.

"The prosecution has depended upon a single accusation, *'Negro, Negro,'* I have heard it in Baxter's voice and in Iello's voice and I have heard it from every living soul in this courtroom. When Mr. Scott told, specifically, how this *Negro*—the *Negro* sitting over there—the *Negro* with the shaven head—walked into a tavern with a revolver, how he shot this one then that one, all of *that,* I was shattered. Its lack of evidence was so bizarre that it sounded like a soap opera. I still cannot believe that anyone would have so little sense of responsibility as to make such statements in a court without a shred of evidence to support them.

"Because neither of these two ghouls—Baxter and Iello—saw Ruby Calhoun coming around the corner of a tavern. Nobody found a weapon. Did the police stop the right man? Have they proven to you, beyond a reasonable doubt, that *this* man is the *right* man?

"The issue here is not merely life or death, ladies and gentlemen. The issue is: Who counts? A man because he is white and wears a badge? Or because he is black and forthright? I challenge you to find a single instance wherein Mr. Calhoun did not come forward. He has faced you wearing the same jacket as he did that night, and with the same attitude he has carried all his life.

"Could anything be more contradictory than that any man who'd done such a dastardly deed would ride slowly about the streets and be stopped a few blocks from the scene of his crime? Calhoun showed no fear. He took no flight. He offered no resistance. He abused nobody. 'Here is my license,' he told police, 'the registration is on the wheel. What is wrong, sir?' 'Nothing. Routine check. Have a good night.'

"But what of the white car that went streaking out of town? What about that car first seen by the sergeant? What about the people he chased and made all those loops out to Route 20 and then came rushing back? What about *that* car? It could not have been the same as the one in which Calhoun was stopped, could it? Would you not think that that was important if *you* were a Jersey City police officer?

"And then where was one little witness whom nobody wants to talk about. The police just wish he would go away. A little man, who came in early this week, named Esteban Escortez. He came from Bordentown and he went back to Bordentown. He is in custody in Bordentown. 'Did Baxter tell you,' I asked him, 'that on that night he had not even seen the defendant?'

" 'Yes, sir,' Mr. Escortez told me, 'Baxter said to me, "How would you like to make it easy on yourself?" I said, "I don't want to get involved worse than I am now. I'd only get hurt. Calhoun has friends who will do anything for him. If I should get sent away I could get hurt bad." '

" 'What," I asked him then, 'did Baxter tell you about the case?' 'He told me he was pulling a breaking and entrance.' 'Where were you when he asked you to cooperate with him in informing?' 'In the cell next to his.' 'What cell was that?' 'The first cell.' 'Where was Baxter?' 'In the next cell.'

"Mr. Escortez departed," Ben Raymond continued, "without extensive cross-examination. No rebuttal. Would you say then that a young man like Escortez, who told a story not favorable to the state, would be more likely to say, 'I will tell the truth regardless of consequences,' than a Baxter with five armed robberies, breaking and entering and an escape to account for to the state? The price is high, ladies and gentlemen, but the state is prepared to pay.

"Calhoun is a young man in fear of his life. Iello and Baxter have only to gain here. Can you believe that this man, who did not run, who did not hide, did these things?

"But that is not, of course, the question. Did the state prove its charges beyond a reasonable doubt is the question. Of course you have to answer No. Violet Vance could not identify Calhoun within feet. Eric Heim said, No, the gunman was six feet in height and light-skinned. Do you write that off? Or do you feel that the crime is so terrible *somebody* must be sacrificed?

"You must decide whether Iello and Baxter testified for the sake of truth, or for the hope of obtaining leniency in sentencing on the charges both are facing.

"I ask you to consider a maxim: *Falsus in uno, falsus in omnibus:* False in one thing, false in all. Both Iello and Baxter have testified that under prior judicial proceedings they testified falsely. This entitles you to disregard *all* their testimony."

Judge Turner judged the testimony of Esteban Escortez and ruled it out of court. He then turned to the woman who'd been seated beside the bench throughout the trial.

"You may proceed," he instructed her.

She rose and began to turn the lottery box containing names of fourteen jurors.

Calhoun didn't understand. He looked questioningly at Ben Raymond.

"Two of the fourteen have to go," he explained.

The first to go was the black juror.

"The killings for which you were indicted and tried were of innocent persons wholly unknown to you," Judge Turner advised Calhoun on June twenty-ninth. "There is no single factor in these murders which might serve as mitigation of the offense. There is no understandable reason for the commitment of these murders. And the killing of each person represents a separate crime.

"Upon the charge of the murder of Donald Leonard, this court sentences you to be imprisoned in the New Jersey State Prison for the remainder of your natural life.

"Upon the charge of the murder of Nicholas Vincio, it is the sentence of this court that you be imprisoned in the New Jersey State Prison for the remainder of your natural life. This sentence shall be consecutive to the sentence of the first count.

"Upon the charge of the murder of Mrs. Helen Shane, it is the sentence of this court that you be imprisoned in the New Jersey State Prison for the remainder of your natural life, and this sentence shall be concurrent with the sentence imposed upon the second count."

Calhoun turned and, without a flicker of change of expression, lifted Jennifer's hands to his lips.

• • •

"You have performed a public service which should be encouraged," Judge Vito Carrera congratulated Dexter Baxter for Baxter's demonstration of good citizenship. "You gave the state great support in the trial of New Jersey vs. Calhoun. I am therefore going to modify your sentence in order to express the state's appreciation. Is there anything you care to say, Mr. Baxter?"

"Just on the point of the reward."

"I have nothing to do with the reward, Mr. Baxter."

"I wrote to the mayor of Jersey City. I told him I planned to use the money to fight juvenile delinquency. But I haven't yet received it."

Judge Carrera appeared momentarily confused.

"I'm not certain that you are motivated by being a good citizen or by hope of money. But thank you for coming here all the same," he finally decided, "and I wish you good luck in your courageous battle against juvenile delinquency."

II

The Wall

MULTITUDES HAVE MOUNTED this midnight stair. Students risen from 2 A.M. beds have taxied down here. Husbands, young and old, have spent whole nights here. Here comes the young man off a date with a girl who permitted his hand to fondle her breast until its nipple had begun stiffening and had then wriggled free.

Weirdos' time is the early afternoon: they don't want to sit waiting, in the night hours, among other men. They don't like being observed lest they be identified. They are weirdos because the attraction of sex does not derive, in them, from love, but from a deep sickness of the soul. They buy secondhand copies of Playboy and read them secretly.

One was an unemployed fry cook, a man in his mid-twenties, slight of frame and passably handsome. He was dressed neatly albeit not quite up to Fifth Avenue standards; nor standards of Harlem or the Bronx. Nor could he be placed as identifiably New Jersey. The fact was that he was nothing at all, and this was why women did not respond to him. It wasn't looks or dress or some ugliness that stopped them. It was that he could awake no interest in others. Others' eyes did not perceive him. As if he were a zero.

He was a zero. He had no personality of his own. How he lived, in his hours away from frying onions, wandering the city day after day, looking for someone he had never seen, without knowing it was his own lost self he pursued, nobody knew. Nobody cared.

"I'm Ezio Pinza's favorite child," he would present himself to some waitress after someone whose name he'd recently seen in print. "Who is Ezio Pinza?" the waitress had asked. He had also tried being an illegitimate grandson of Charlie Chaplin: "My mother was Lila Lee."

"Lila who?"

Then he had tried being the illegitimate son of Warren G. Harding.

"Why brag about something like *that*?" a bartender had put it to him.

Teachers of biology, mailmen or neurologists, waiters out of Chinese restaurants, subway motormen, janitors, unemployed water-ski instructors, jockey's valets and some lonesome all-night hackie with his meter still running when he ought to be dead—heading home.

All come in search of love.

Young lake-boat sailors off Lake Huron and old-time seamen from seven oceans wander in, from the Seaman's Home, in search of some ship long foundered and beached. Railroad porters from the Deep South at the end of their runs come here, and saxophone players from the East Bronx; and officers of the U.S. Marine Corps.

There is also the black from the Village who mixes an ancestral awe of the white woman with an equally ancestral contempt of her: it sometimes makes him hard to handle. Like a child, he tries to see how far he can go; he goes so far then gets slapped down. Now he knows.

And always the senior citizen who's just cashed his Social Security check to prove to himself he is still among the living, though a lifetime of lusts have all now settled dustily behind his ears: he'll hang in there till he dies.

All come in search of love with money in their jeans.

Masters of industry, politicians, clergymen Christian or Jewish, TV celebrities, members of the Bar, professors of ancient Greek, violinists with perfect pitch and editors of newspapers with a million circulation: all come in search of love with fifty-dollar bills in their wallets.

The women saw such a variation of naked males, some so undersized they were almost dwarfs, to great gangling dudes so tall they'd been rejected for army service: no regulation army uniform would fit them.

There were men of such mottled hue they were neither white nor black nor red nor brown nor yellow. There were those with skins so white they gleamed and some so black—perhaps a seaman from Senegal—that his skin held a bluish sheen.

On occasion there appeared some youthful athlete, boxer, dancer or first baseman who moved with such natural grace that a secret homesickness crept into the hearts of these women who had so long forgotten that a male body could be beautiful. To be followed immediately by some trick whose belly was so swollen that he had to walk with two canes to support its terrible weight.

Some came in smiling faintly in self-mockery. Others with a serious air as if to say: "I won't put up with nonsense. I'm a busy fellow. My time is limited. Here's your money. I want exact change."

"When I found out my mother wasn't dead," Ginger recalled, "like my father had always told me she was, I was sixteen then, that was how it began with me. She was living in the next town with the guy she'd took off with. I begun going down on every dude in town, I can't tell you to this day exactly why. It felt like I was taking revenge on her. If I hadn't of got out of town, the wives and girlfriends would have *run* me out.

"I got off the bus at the Port Authority and before I got to Eighth Avenue I had one runner walking beside me and two more following. I let the one beside me buy me a meal, then I took off through the ladies' room. I never been pimped and never will be."

"Pimps," Fortune interrupted, "pimps—God bless them. He gives the girl what her daddy never gave her at home. He never gave her affection. He never gave her the feeling like he cared what became of her. He made her feel she wasn't of use. She never had an older brother, she never had a kindly uncle, she never had a lover. She never had anyone to tell her right from wrong. The pimp is her daddy. He's her big brother. He's her kindly uncle. He's her lover. He tells her right from wrong. If what he says is right, and the world says is wrong, she'll take *his* word. The world gave her nothing. He gives her everything. And he tells her out front she'll go to jail sooner or later. By that time she's *anxious* to get locked. Just to prove herself to him. And when she is, he's the one, not her daddy, who comes down and gets her out. She may have been brought up in a four-bedroom home with two cars in the garage and servants, too. She may have gone to a private school and had a summer place on the shore, as well. But she's never had a home. "We do everything we can for her," her parents boast; yet they do nothing at all.

"The pimp parks her in his attic above the alley, two flights down to the bar, and he's brought her home. Best of all, she learns how to hold her own on the street. It's exactly the sort of life her parents spent a lifetime guarding her against and it's exactly the life she needs the most. Ten days of it and it would take two cops and a matron to get her back to her four-bedroom home. And, the first chance she got, she'd run away back to the Village looking for her pimp. He doesn't have to chase *her*. She'll come to him. Thank God for pimps, they do more for kids coming out of the suburbs than the kids' parents ever did."

"Like I was saying," Ginger went on as though Fortune hadn't said a word, "I was eighteen and looked fifteen. I sat in the lobby of the Manhattan Hilton with my shoulder bag slung over my shoulder and begun fixing my hair. That hikes the skirt up like accidentally. A middle-aged dude at the bar caught the flash and I knew I had him pinned.

" 'Waiting for somebody, honey?' he wants to know, sitting down beside me. . . ."

"I used to get up in the dark and get down to the bus stop rain or snow," Fortune picked up her own story as if feeling it was, basically, of greater interest than Ginger's. "I'd ride crosstown to sit all day at a sewing machine, and go back home dead beat and then do it all over again. Now I sleep till noon and make as much, even on a poor day, as I used to make in two weeks of sewing.

"Of course you have to keep on top of the situation. The police have to be provided for. Taking a cut is what cops are for.

"Men are men, of any color, but the tightest ones are the white dudes. They don't like paying off. Once—I was still so young I didn't collect off him first—refused to pay and called me a dirty chink. If I want money off him, he tells me, I can wash his shirt.

"I brought out a springblade knife and sprang it.

" 'You're not going to leave this room alive, mister,' I told him.

" 'I was only fooling,' he told me, laying out the ten-dollar bill he owed me. 'Put a twenty on top of that,' I told him. 'I'm fining you ten for trying to beat me and another ten for what you called me.'

"He paid off. White guys are tight but they're easy frightened. Black guys aren't so tight, and they don't scare so easy, but they're mean. Really *mean*. They get pushed around so by their own women, when they come to a woman who isn't black, they try to push *her*. . . ."

" 'For my Uncle Mike,' Ginger resumed her own story, "lowering my eyes and trying to keep that skirt down. He didn't try to touch but there were only two tiny pearl buttons between his hand and my tits, and he's a tit man, I can tell. I'm wearing a type of bra that pushes the nipples right up into a trick's face.

" 'Can we have a chocolate soda, sweetheart, while we're waiting?' he invites me, 'or do you prefer strorberry?'

" 'A double martini, is what I would prefer, sir,' is what I thought but I didn't say it. All I said was, 'What will I do if Uncle Mike shows up, sir?' Putting on a baby lisp.

"The lisp did it. 'We'll have him paged.' he tells me, and takes my hand. 'Pertend *I'm* Uncle Mike.'

" 'Uncle Mike *always* been like a daddy to me,' I tell him, "account my real daddy died," and I go with him toward the restaurant where he decides, 'Room service will be better, sweetheart,' and we go eight floors to his room. He pulls the shades and gives me a chance to go on the nod on the bed. After all, I'm only a child and I've had a hard day. When he thinks I'm asleep it's off with his pants and I don't wake up until he's on top and *in*.

" 'You like this, honey?' he starts, 'ain't this better'n *both* chocolate 'n strorberry?' I could barely feel him but he still keeps trying to get me hot. I wanted an awful lot by way of room service.

" '*Oooooo—Da-ady!*' I finally let out a whoop at the very top of my voice, '*Ooooooo—Da-aad-dee!*' You could have heard me hollering down in the lobby, '*Give it to me Daddy! Give it to me!*'

" 'No, honey, No! No!' he tries to tell me, and I could feel him getting limper as he begun getting scared. I kept it up until he'd gotten out of bed and was pulling on his pants, scared to death of the knock on the door.

" 'Before you leave, Uncle Mike,' I told him in my grown-up voice, leave a hundred on the dresser. I'll be sixteen come Sunday.'

"He was so relieved to get out at that price he was shaking. I could have made it tougher but I didn't want to get into a big hassle with the house dick and then have to split it down the middle. I gave him time enough to pack and get out. Then I went down to the bar and broke his hundred.

"The house dick was at the bar, not drinking just watching. He knew his trade. When the bartender asked for my I.D. card, he gave the bartender a nod. He knew a baby pro when he saw one.

"He'd caught on to the play in the lobby and hadn't interfered. We worked together half a dozen times after that, but he never took money off me. All he wanted was a piece of the same once a week. Maybe he wasn't getting along with his old lady, I don't know."

"White guys are the most boring," Fortune decided, "because they want to put their story on you—their big business deals, their wife troubles, all of that. Sometimes I think they come to put out a story as much as to screw. Their wives won't listen to them anymore and I can't blame them.

"I only had one white trick worth listening to. He'd been at sea most of his life and he knew about the far-off ports, how it was in Cebu—that's in the Philippine Islands—and the Port of Marseilles—that's in the Mediterranean Sea. It's all blue and sunny in that sea, there are dozens of ships and big restaurants and women who sell fresh fish on the harbor front. And there's a ship that takes tourists out to an island that used to be a prison. It's empty now, but it used to be like Alcatraz. But a guide will take you through and show you the cells where the prisoners were kept. And one prisoner, nobody knew who he was, and the government didn't want anyone to recognize him, so he wore an iron mask all day, and he wore it for twenty years, and he was buried with the mask on, so nobody knows even today who he was—isn't that a *killer?*

"My favorite way of spending a day is going to movies. Especially ones about far-off places in the world I know I'll never see.

"Have you been to the zoo, Dovie-Jean? The one in the Bronx? I never been, but I'd like to go, only I got no one to go with. You want to go out there one day with me?"

Dovie-Jean nodded. "I'd like that."

"I'd like to too," Big Benjamin told them, looming above them like a huge child. "I'd like to go to the big zoo too."

Late in the night hours and the lights too bright, the women's faces becoming careworn and the big electric fan no longer able to blow off the odors of tobacco mixed with cheap perfume and Benjamin's transistor sounding weary, all heard Spanish Nan scream.

King Benjamin came out of his shadowed corner, crashed through Nan's door and clamped a full nelson onto a stark naked stud wielding a knife. The stud dropped the knife as Benjamin lifted him, lashing and kicking off the floor, aimed his skull at a corner and crashed him head-on. The stud went limp: out cold.

Hauling the stud like a leg of mutton down one rear flight, Nan following with the stud's clothes and one of his shoes, across the areaway and into a tiny walled patch of garden, Benjamin dumped him. Nan tossed the clothes and the single shoe, then followed him back up the rear flight.

If the police picked up the stud, that was okay with the King. If he came to before and tried to figure out, while putting on his clothes and casting about for his missing left shoe, how he'd gotten to wherever it was he was: that was all right with the King too. And if he lay in a pelting rain until the homicide detectives arrived, that was just as well with King Ben too.

The women of the parlor gave him welcoming smiles when he returned. A wide shy smile came to the King's big weatherbeaten face, to see how proud they all were of him.

Spanish Nan tossed him the stud's left shoe. It was a brown oxford. Benjamin fingered it shyly.

"I used to rassle, too," he explained, as if to apologize for his enormous strength.

"Where did you wrestle, Benjamin?"

"At the rasslin' place," he assured them all.

One night a middle-aged dude, who'd gone to fat around his middle, but whose arms and legs still looked thin, walked in. He entered so expensively dressed that he looked cheap.

"I wonder what he's so scared about," went through Dovie-Jean's mind.

He bought two tickets and handed both to Fortune, who nodded to Dovie-Jean. The three of them crowded into Fortune's small room, decorated with plastic dogs and cats off Woolworth's novelty shelf. An ad for a condom guaranteed to prevent "premature ejaculation" was thumbtacked to one wall.

"Tell us what you want, honey," Fortune asked him.

"Whatever you girls do, do it," he instructed them, and handed a hundred-dollar bill to each. Then added, "I've never been in a whorehouse before."

It appeared, the way he lay stretched naked and smiling innocuously, that he may never have been with any woman at all before.

Dovie-Jean had had a dream the night before: she'd been on some kind of a houseboat, among many people whom she did not like. She had gone into a cabin and had had a baby without pain. Sitting on the bed's edge, washing it, she saw its mouth was filled with feathers and it began to gasp for breath. She began taking them out, but there was always more and they kept coming until she wakened.

When Fortune used her mouth on this trick, he smiled down with faint amusement yet did not react. Finally she reached for the bottle of Signal and told Dovie-Jean, "You try, honey."

Oral sex was something Dovie-Jean could handle, when paid for it, but for which she had no strong desire. For the sake of the hundred dollars the trick had paid, she tried it now.

It was like munching a moldy turnip.

"You want to go down on one of us, honey?" Fortune asked, trying to find some way to give the fellow his hundred dollars' worth.

For a full half-hour they tried by turns to rouse him. He watched with a smiling detachment, as though they were nurses searching for the cause of some obscure illness. Nothing availed.

"We've done everything we know how, honey," Fortune finally advised him.

He sat up then. "What I'd really like," he confessed at last, "is for one of you to blow me, hold it in your mouth and put it into mine."

Dovie-Jean felt herself cringe inwardly. Fortune didn't cringe for a moment.

"Put on your clothes, mister," she told him, "you don't want a whorehouse. You want a hospital."

"I wish they were all that easy," Fortune observed after he had gone.

"I don't understand," was all Dovie-Jean could say.

"The man is dying, that's all," Fortune assured her. "They die inside years before their time. They know they're dying and they try to make themselves feel alive inside again, and there ain't no way. No way at all. They're dying because of the way they lived and it's too late to fix *that*."

The next day Dovie-Jean saw the trick's photograph on the inner pages of the *Daily News*. He had shot himself in the head, in the hotel directly across the way, shortly after leaving them. The story mentioned missing racetrack funds.

"It looks like we finally got a winner off the Big A," Fortune said cynically.

"Why be so hard about it?" Dovie-Jean reproached her.

"It's why they call me Fortune, honey," the Chinese woman explained, "because I'm a hard little cookie." She laughed and asked Dovie-Jean, "What do you do on your days off?"

"Just set around thinking how things are going back home."

"Where is 'back home'?"

"Jersey City." Then she added, "I got no real hometown. I've just kicked around here and there."

"Why don't you take a bus ride and find out how things are in Jersey City?"

"I've got a small legal problem it's best to stay away from."

"Is that why you came to New York?"

"My old man told me that if we went to New York we'd have all kinds of fun. I think if we'd stayed in Jersey City it would have been even funnier. Using the plural of course."

Dovie-Jean was cautious about telling Fortune that she was working the Carousel on her week off. She had no specific reason for holding this back; it was only that she'd learned that the less information a person gave out about himself, the better off he'd be.

"What do I do with *this?*" King Benjamin asked Spanish Nan, holding out the stud's shoe.

Spanish Nan shrugged. "What does anybody do with one shoe?"

"Give it to me," Fortune asked, "I'll have it bronzed," and she took it from the big bouncer.

"You can come with us to the big zoo, King," she added.

At the Bronx Zoo's bird theater a girl was displaying two great green-and-gold parrots.

"Folks," she addressed the half-filled little open theater, "I want you to meet Lucifer and Robert, two very nice boys. Now we're going to give Robert a head start."

She placed Robert at the top of a pole from which a tin cup was hung by a cord. She put a peanut in the cup and Robert began hauling it up.

Lucifer sat calmly atop his pole and paid no heed to the peanut in his cup until the girl urged him, "Lucifer! Robert is way ahead of you!" Upon which Lucifer flew down, snatched his peanut and flew back atop his pole.

"Lucifer!" the girl cried, feigning indignation, "Lucifer! You bad bird! You *cheated!* Come here immediately!"

Lucifer trundled over to her, rolled over on his back and raised his claws pleadingly.

"Lucifer says he is sorry," the girl assured her audience, "he wants to be forgiven. Shall we forgive him?"

The crowd applauded and a couple of children cried, "Forgive him!"

Lucifer struggled to his feet and acknowledged his appreciation by bowing to the audience.

"Now," the girl announced, "we're going to have another

contest. We're going to see who can pick up these hoops and put them over the stakes the fastest. Robert, you begin."

Robert trundled to a hoop, picked it up and placed it over a stake and trundled back for another; placed it over the second stake. Lucifer swept down, picked up all three hoops at once and placed them over stakes before Robert had completed his chore.

"Lucifer!" the girl denounced the smarter bird, "you *bad bad* bird! You cheated *again!*"

The children were immensely pleased with the disobedient Lucifer.

The girl then went into a plea for funds, for conservation of endangered species in the South American jungles, and Benjamin became restless. He left them and returned, grinning with pleasure, at a small silver-and-blue pinwheel he held in his hand as it whirred. The women smiled at each other.

He led them to a line of carriages below a sign saying:

WILD ASIA

Benjamin bought the tickets and they climbed into one of the open carriages, where a black family was already waiting to start the trip high across the African plain. This was a family of one small girl, a mother and an elderly man, apparently the little girl's grandfather, who was gray-haired and two sheets to the wind.

As the train began to move, the driver began describing a herd of deer grazing below. "Oh!" the old man cried out, "if I had a gun! Bang! Bang! If I had a gun!"

"Sit down, grampa," the little black girl ordered him. "We can't hear the driver with you hollering!"

The old man sat down. The little girl's mother nodded her approval.

"Looka them rhinoceros-eros!" The old man was on his feet again upon the sight of two great beasts almost submerged below.

"They aren't rhinoceroses, grampa," the little girl corrected him, "they're *hippotami*—and we *all* want you to shut *up!*"

The old man sat down looking abashed and the carriage rolled on. Benjamin's pinwheel whirled green, silver and blue and he looked so foolishly happy that Fortune nudged Dovie-Jean to look at him: his big face was beaming like a child's taken to the country for the first time.

The carriage stopped directly above a great striped alley cat that looked like any cat looking for a home. "Siberian tiger," the driver announced. "When you see him face-to-face there are only three things to do: Remain calm. Second: Run like hell. Third: Keep running like hell."

The old idiot was on his feet again. "Oh, if I had him at home nobody bother *me* then! Oh, I'm gonna take you home with me! Oh . . ."

Big Benjamin stood up and his pinwheel was whirring madly.

"Shut you *opp!*" he commanded the old clown. "Shut it *opp* right *now!* Sit down and shut it *opp!*"

The old man looked up at this huge dude towering above him as if he didn't quite understand.

"You don't sit down," Big Benjamin warned him, taking a step toward him, "I t'row you over down to *tiger!*"

There was the rail. There was the tiger. There was the big man with huge hands. It looked perfectly possible.

The old man sat down and said not a word the rest of the trip. The little black girl smiled up at Benjamin as she left. "You scared my grandpa!" she told him and seemed pleased that he had.

Dovie-Jean and Fortune led the way, pausing to look at a dreaming polar bear, monkeys one could hold in the palm of one's hand, elephants with children riding them, and Big Benjamin following them with his pinwheel.

He stayed so long staring at the elephants bearing children that Fortune nudged Dovie-Jean, "He wants to ride but he's scared to ask." Dovie-Jean looked at the big dimwit's open-mouthed face, the pinwheel whirring as he watched, and saw it was true. They led him to the camels that also gave rides to children, but he wanted to go back to the elephants.

"Let's eat," Fortune suggested, and all three sat at a picnic table under a great green tree, and ate chicken and french-fried potatoes.

After lunch they wandered into a great open square, where a red-and-gold Chinese dragon, made up of two boys, on all fours, carrying the silken costume above their backs, fought with a sword-bearing warrior, consisting of one boy, while a masked fellow leaped about the pair. It had a battle to the death, one judged by the great booming of drums, and the masked man was, apparently, the referee.

Big Benjamin didn't seem able to make sense of the dance. He looked troubled by it, shaking his head in bewilderment.

It didn't make sense to Dovie-Jean either. The beating of the drums was so monotonous she became bored.

"What's it all about?" she asked Fortune at last.

"How in God's name would *I* know? I've never hung around clowns like these in my life," and she walked away, Dovie-Jean following and Big Benjamin still holding his happy pinwheel above his head.

Fortune was a slight woman with an alert, bird-like habit of cocking her head to one side.

She had been orphaned early and had gone to work, in her teens, on Mulberry Street.

"I was the only girl in that shop who could speak English," she remembered, recalling her early life to Dovie-Jean. "It was piecework on big, black, beat-up Singer machines. Their lights had been broken, so we worked by desk lamps placed on tables behind us. *Noise?* You have no idea how much noise thirty sewing machines, behind locked doors, can make. It sounds like a battle. Mr. Lee locked us in. Mr. Lee was *boss*. The place was airless and women had to bring in their kids and keep them there all day. How could they complain? To who?

"Seventy-two hours a week, forty-fifty cents an hour. The women would do nothing to help themselves, they were that afraid of losing their jobs. Without English, there was no other work for them. If they took off for being sick, they got fired. Lee worked those women like he was an old-timey villain.

"He wasn't the real villain. He was running scared from the apparel firms uptown. The minute he let his shop get organized, he was ruined.

"Every time we'd finish a dozen pieces we'd get a receipt and a time card with instructions on how to fill it out. If a woman had worked eighty hours and had earned fifty dollars, the card said she had worked thirty hours and that made her appear to be earning the state minimum of a dollar sixty-five. She was getting a bare half of what she had earned. Lee was stealing fifty hours, every two weeks, from every woman in the joint.

"The women knew, of course. But where else could they go for work? They were all off the boat from Hong Kong except me. If I got up a petition, which I did, who would sign it? In their homes they'd talk your leg off about what a terrible screwing they were gettng, but they dummied up in the zone, on shop premises. There they wouldn't even say good morning to me; they were that scared of being fired.

"I got sick and applied for unemployment insurance. They told me I'd have to have a letter from Mr. Lee and he refused to give it to me. 'The sickness is all in your head,' he tells me. This much we had in common: we were both born in New York City.

" 'If you don't give me the letter,' I told him, 'I'll sue.' 'So sue,' he tells me.

"I went to the ILGWU. I had proofs of my time and the ILGWU got me eleven hundred dollars in back pay and Lee had to pay a fine also.

"That was the last job I took seriously. I was sixteen by then and I had learned how much easier it was to hustle a dollar than to sweat it out at a sewing machine.

"The first job I got was sitting with a phone booth for a furnace outfit, calling homeowners. I'd tell them this time of year, summer, was the best time to think about their furnace because it would cost them a lot more come winter. 'What would a checkup cost me now?' the furnace owner would want to know.

" 'Not a dime, mister,' I'd tell him, 'we're giving free checkups now in order to create goodwill; so you'll call us in case anything should go wrong in the future.'

" 'Fair enough,' he'd tell me, 'how long will a checkup take?'

" 'Only a couple hours, sir. All our team does, in weather like this, is to remove vital parts so that, when the cold sets in, you'll have to call us to reinstall them. That'll be a neat fifteen hundred dollars for parts you can buy in any hardware store for twenty-five dollars in cash. What time would you like our team to drop by, sir?'

"He'd hang up very slow. The boss has put in ten years building up that business and I drove it into the ground inside of two weeks. That was when I went to the Walrus."

"The *who?*"

"Walrus. He was in art films. 'New-Wave Classics' he called them."

"New what?"

" 'New Wave.' I called this dude I worked for the Walrus because he was big and heavy and had a walrus mustache and wore ground-gripper shoes. That was to help him keep his balance when he was drunk, which was every day. He never used shoe trees, so his toes bent upward like a clown's.

"What was so awful about those ground-grippers was that they were *yellow!* I'm telling you, Dovie-Jean, they were *yellow!* When I tell you he carried a briefcase with nothing in it but a fifth of Cutty Sark, you can believe me.

"The Walrus was wonderful at inheriting money, but that was all he was good at. Every six months he'd inherit a new bunch and every six months he'd go broke. What he was trying to do, he told me, was to see if he could go broke in five. 'That'd save a full month,' he told me, 'with your help, sweetie, I think we can do it.' The art-film business was just his way of seeing if he could go broke in five.

"I rented an old retail-outlet store that had a big window onto the street, but no front door. The door was in the alley. People could look in all day, but they couldn't get inside.

"Film festivals were real fun. I strung paper pennants, every color, like gas stations put out on opening day, and hung life-size photographs of Laurel and Hardy, W.C. Fields and Hubert Humphrey. I got old posters: *Return Of The Vampire* with Bela Lugosi. *Mary Burns, Fugitive* with Sylvia Sydney—she loved a psychopathic killer—that was Alan Baxter. I got a poster showing Chester Morris saying to Jean Harlow, 'Your hair is like a field of silver daisies. I'd like to run barefoot through your hair.' I was glad he was going to take off his shoes.

"We got fair-sized crowds at the big window. People trying it out, wondering if they might not be missing something. One woman brought a signboard that asked, 'What about Frances

Farmer?' Frances who? Never heard of her. I just looked up and smiled sweetly.

" 'You're sure booking some ungodly stinkers, sweetie,' the Walrus congratulated me. 'Don't think I don't appreciate it.' 'I have to give credit where credit is due,' I told him. 'You were the one who booked *Hurry Sundown.*' 'Yeah,' he agreed, 'but you were the one who got Kim Novak and Kirk Douglas into the same picture! And who else could have thought of renting a place without a door?'

"When New-Wave Classics went broke I went to work for Far-Ways, a travel agency. I'd sell a couple of airline tickets to a pair of newlyweds and book one to Bermuda and the other to Trinidad. I figured that, down there, they were both going to latch onto someone else anyhow so what was the difference, in the long run? Probably both would wind up better off.

"Once I put a twelve-year-old girl onto a plane for Jamaica and her uncle onto one for St. John's. I'm sure somebody has found work for that kid by now.

"But I still have bad dreams," Fortune confessed in a changing mood, "the worst one is when I'm back in Chinatown and I'm at one of those big, black beat-up sewing machines, with a desk lamp behind me, and the doors are locked."

As the early afternoon hours moved toward dusk, the voices of the women in the little parlor above Forth-eighth street, became quieter. Spanish Nan played the slot machine once or twice but got no return. Tracy went on the nod with her head on Ginger's shoulder. Big Benjamin's small radio kept murmuring behind his shadowed screen.

Flash came in but not in his usual exultation. He merely sat and smoked a cigarette and listened to the dull murmuring of Big Benjamin's radio.

"Had a bad day, Flash?" Spanish Nan asked him.

He nodded to assure her that it had been a bad day at the fight. "Turn up the sound, Ben," he instructed Big Benjamin.

The voice of the mayor came on, high-pitched and plaintive: "We're going to call it the John Hour," the mayor announced over WNYC, "because 'John' has become the slang phrase for a prostitute's customer. We will announce the names of all men against whom convictions have been obtained for patronage of prostitutes. The threat of public scorn will be a severe deterrent to patronage of prostitutes. Not only will men now fear to patronize them, but the present imbalance, in the law, of punishing the prostitute but not her customer will be corrected."

Flash cocked his head toward the radio. "No wonder that guy looks so much like a chicken," he commented, "he *is* a chicken."

"Some people," the mayor assured the parlor full of whores, "just don't seem to know what the real world is like. I have been in office twenty months and what I am advocating has the overwhelming support of the ordinary folk who live in this city."

"What this dude thinks the real world is like," Flash commented sadly, "is nothing like it is. He thinks that a man who goes to a whorehouse puts on tinted shades and wears a false beard, for God's sake. He takes it for granted that, when the man comes out, he is so filled with guilt that he's ready to kill himself if his name is broadcast on the radio, for God's sake. Who does he think comes up here but the ordinary folk who live in this city?"

"Don't *you* feel guilty, Flash?" Dovie-Jean asked just to try him out.

"Guilty? About what? I come here the same way I go to the track. I lay my money down at the mutuel window and hope I picked a winner. If I felt guilty about laying a woman I'd be dead for forty years, for God's sake."

"Although the state legislature has seen the unfairness of the present approach," the mayor's voice went on, "some judges have not been carrying out the law in this area. Many of them set their own standards about what the law should be. Judges have no right to nullify statutes."

"Mayors have no right to tell me who I can screw, either," Flash muttered.

"The *New York Times* editorializes, this morning, that 'The police and the courts have more important things to worry about than either prostitutes or busted johns.' Yet this is the same newspaper which has repeatedly condemned vice and lewdness in the Times Square area, and has demanded that the area be cleaned up. Now the paper takes a new direction: let Forty-third Street between Broadway and Eighth be a combat zone where prostitutes, pimps and johns can frolic freely without let or hindrance by the police.''

''How can prostitutes, pimps and johns frolic freely when the street is already so overcrowded with businessmen from the suburbs,'' Flash wanted to know, ''and with middle-class kids from Yorkville and Queens? Does he think that hookers make their living off *single* men, for God's sake?''

Uriah Yipkind attempted, that same evening, to resolve the conflict of opinions about the mayor's views on prostitution.

Yipkind had already run a program featuring three male patrons of prostitutes and many prostitutes had taken exception to comments made upon that show. They had demanded equal time and Uriah had given it to them.

The three hookers were shadowed. Yipkind named them Jane, Joan and Jenny. They were all three—by their voices—in their early twenties, and all three were hundred-dollar-an-hour women.

''One thing I resented on your program, Mr. Yipkind,'' Jane led off, ''was your use of the phrase 'pimped off.' You used it three times. I've never seen a pimp in my life. If I've ever talked to one I didn't know what his business was. No woman is forced, physically, into prostitution, from what I've observed. We are in it because it pays ten times as much as other trades, it is much more interesting than most positions open to women, and you are your own boss. I enjoy the life I lead and the money I make is not taxable.''

''Where do you work?''

''On Park Avenue near a first-class hotel.''

''Do you have a steady boy friend—not a pimp, just a friend?''

''No boy friend.''

''And you, Joan?''

''I'm married.''

''How does your husband feel, about your making it with other men?''

"He approves."

"Approves?"

"He could hardly object. He's a male prostitute."

That was the first of several shocks Uriah was to sustain in the course of the program.

"We have two bedrooms," the girl explained further. "He works one, I work the other, then we compare notes."

"But don't you feel this is *degrading?*"

"What's *degrading?*" Jenny came in, "to me it's more degrading to be an average housewife, cleaning house, shopping, taking care of her husband's needs, and getting nothing for herself. Except respectability—another name for a dog's life."

"I'm a college graduate," Jane came in, "and I wanted to work with people. I went into social welfare but I never *reached* anybody. All paper work and the male social workers assuming you'll be flattered to sleep with any one of them, for the honor of the thing.

"Now when I sleep with men I make them feel *they* are being honored. I reach them because they come to me with problems. I'm of help to them. They need a woman to talk to and, as often as not, to let them indulge in fantasies. I wish that, just once, somebody would have the nerve to write 'therapist' instead of 'whore.' Because that's closer to what I do. This town is full of men who lead secret fantasy lives and who have the money to support it. I have a hundred-dollar-an-hour psychiatrist—and that's exactly what *I* charge *him*. He needs me more than I need him."

"In what way does he need you?"

"I help him get born. He gets into a warm bath which he fantasizes as a womb. When he comes out I put him on the bed and diaper him, exactly as though he were a newborn infant. Then he puts on his clothes and keeps appointments with patients in one of the classiest offices on Park Avenue."

"It depends upon the value you put on yourself," Jenny added. "You can go to a massage parlor in the Village for twelve dollars, of which the girl gets five. If that's all the value she puts on herself, that's all she's worth. I put a higher value on myself, that's all."

"Five bucks?" Yipkind asked incredulously. "It sounds like

Pakistan. But do you feel yourself to be superior to the Village hooker? Basically, you do the same joyless thing—you take money for the use of your body. The trick hands you cash so you take off your clothes and lie down. What can be more degrading than *that?*"

"I don't get it," Jenny protested. "What does your nice little housewife do except take off her clothes and lie down in exchange for room and board? What can be more degrading than *that?*"

"It doesn't work the way you think, Mr. Yipkind. For one thing, he doesn't *hand* you money. He comes in, you make him feel at ease, he puts the money under an ashtray. You don't even talk about it. You deal with every man differently, but most of mine like a story. I tell him, 'I was born in Bimini last week—just went for a week of sun you know—and I still can't believe what happened to me. I'm lying on the beach, suntanning myself, when this gorgeous man comes along, sits near me and smiles. At first I pay no attention but I do notice his *gorgeous* body.' It's all cock-and-bull, of course, the sort of story schoolgirls read, but all the while I'm telling it I'm loosening my clothes as if I don't know what I'm doing. By the time I get to the hotel-bedroom scene, I have everything off but my panties and the trick is so hot it takes him very little while in bed. Sometimes I get myself so hot I come with him."

"You come with your tricks?" Uriah asked all three. Joan answered, "No, not usually, but now and then, when a trick has become a friend, I do."

"Who *are* your tricks, your johns?" Uriah asked. "Where do they come from?"

"Businessmen," Jenny answered, "politicians, clergymen, cops, lawyers, judges . . ."

". . . and TV celebrities," Joan added laughingly.

"Your best customer is your past-middle-aged successful businessman," Jane puts in.

"Especially if he's Jewish," Jenny added.

"Jewish?" Uriah asked as though he had never heard of such a thing as a Jew who patronized prostitutes.

"Half my clients are Jews," Joan put in.

"At least," Jane supported her.

Jane put her head down to stifle her laughter, then explained, "I'm from the Deep South. Small town. I never saw a Jew my whole life until I got into hustling. One day a john shows up dressed like no john I'd ever seen. He's wearing a tiny skullcap, he's got long curly sideburns and he's wearing a long black topcoat. He must be some sort of priest, I figure. I'd never seen anything like it.

"I'm a Chasidic Jew," he explains while taking off his clothes. He takes off everything except the skullcap and a black-and-white scarf he's wearing under his underwear."

"Talith," Uriah, being a Jew himself, was able to help.

"Talis-shmalis," the girl agreed, "so all right, we got along, I didn't try to hustle him, he was ready with the money. Next week here comes another dressed just like him, a beard just like the first one had. Next week I get two-three! Where the hell are all the rabbis coming from, I wonder."

"Where *were* they coming from?" Uriah asked.

"From their homes, Mr. Yipkind, from their *homes*. These are men in their fifties and sixties, they have grandchildren, the old lady is fat and has lost her looks . . ."

"It isn't entirely a matter of losing her looks," Jenny explained, "because when she was a young beauty she was still a dead mackerel in bed. All she knew was that for a woman to share sexual pleasure was a sin. And she's never learned anything since."

"They do sleep separately in orthodox homes," Uriah was helpful again. "Sex is only for purposes of procreation."

"That's the craziest thing I ever heard," Jane put in.

"There you have it," Jenny picked him right up, "sex is *evil* to her. She was brought up to think so. *Oral* sex? She never heard of it. If you told her she wouldn't believe you. If she believed you it would disgust her."

"I think it's lovely," Jane put in.

"But where does that leave her old man?" Jenny continued. I'll tell you where it leaves him: he becomes a successful businessman and he has no love life at all. All he has is a fantasy of a young blond *shiksa,* naked, with a marvelous figure, going down on him! He keeps this fantasy going for years until he discovers that, for money, he can realize it. What a discovery! It's like he's born again! He runs and tells his friends in the synagogue—what a bargain!"

Uriah appeared to be talking to himself. The idea of a Jewish businessman pimping his colleagues was something he didn't seem able to grasp immediately. "What were you laughing at a moment ago?" he suddenly turned on Jean accusingly.

"I was thinking of one of my Jewish johns," Joan answered. "He takes off his clothes but keeps his yarmulke on. He gets into a pair of black satin panties. I bought them for him because my own wouldn't fit because he's short and fat. Then he puts on black hose and stands looking at himself in the mirror. That's my cue to put *the* record on: 'Sleepy Time Down South.' "

Joan paused to see that she had Uriah's interest.

"Yes? Yes?"

She had his interest for certain.

"Why, he begins to dance to it. He can't get enough of that record. He *chants* it. He chants it all around the room, dancing to it and you can't tell whether he's in a whorehouse or a synagogue, the way it sounds. His eyes are closed, he's smiling to himself, I'm on the bed, ready. Four times around the bed and he's ready too."

"A hundred an hour to dance to 'Sleepy Time Down South,' " Uriah said aloud, yet as if talking to himself, "in women's panties."

"The hundred an hour is only a part of it," Jenny explained, "the Jewish trick is usually in jewelry or women's clothing, something like that. I have one who has brought me at least five thousand dollars' worth of jewelry. All he asks is that I wear it when he visits. If I don't he is offended."

"The Jewish johns are what makes the trade so expensive," Joan told Uriah. "They have money and expect to spend it. I'd much rather deal with an old Jewish businessman than with a young trick—say Irish or Italian. The old Jewish guy is a *business*man. He knows you don't get anything for nothing. He knows you get what you pay for. He's *appreciative*. He's polite, he's respectful, he tells his friends about you. The young guy is likely to give you a kick in the head and take his money back."

"The Jewish trick is also good for tips on the stock market and in real estate too," Jane added. "One of them invested money for a friend of mine, so now she has an income whether she works or not."

"And where is the *harm,*" Jenny asked, "what is all this stuff you put about being *degrading?* You give a love-starved man a taste of good old-fashioned belly-to-belly raunchy sex and he feels better than when he came in. You squares act as if having an orgasm does big social damage. Maybe if men had more orgasms they wouldn't run around firing bullets at everybody who don't act like they think he should act."

"Do *you* have orgasms?" Uriah wanted to know, asking all three women.

"Not every time," Joan replied, "but if you like a guy, and he keeps coming back and always enjoys himself, you begin coming with him. I've got half a dozen tricks I come with."

"You haven't hit on half the story, Mr. Yipkind," Jane advised him, "such as, what else can a woman do if she's not a specialist in some line? She can work as a secretary, as a receptionist, as a cloakroom attendant for a hundred dollars a week and tips. That doesn't mean she isn't sleeping with men. She sleeps with any male higher than herself, whether it's in advertising or in television. She does that just to keep her job. She is dependent upon every male above her in the pecking order.

"I'm dependent upon nobody. I run my own business and what I make is untaxable. And I take satisfaction in taking care of men. When I see a big man in politics on the TV screen, and know that, in a couple of hours, he'll be in bed with me, I have a sense of power."

"How big?" Uriah wanted to know. "Municipal? State? Federal?"

"State."

Uriah shook his head. There was something else he wanted to ask: "Is this big man in state politics Jewish?" He wanted to ask, "Is the Park Avenue psychiatrist whom you diaper Jewish?"

Uriah stopped himself from asking. He wanted to know, yet he didn't want to know.

• • •

The wall is thirty feet high, fourteen feet into the earth and is two feet thick; it encloses forty-eight acres, houses two thousand men, and has twelve gun emplacements.

Three years after his sentencing to three lifetimes for triple murder, Calhoun appeared, to Barney Kerrigan, to resemble a brown barn owl.

Kerrigan, of Calhoun's own age, was a state investigator.

Calhoun was sitting with a book spread on a table and with a magazine article below his hand. The book was *The Idiot* by Feodor Dostoevsky.

"How can a man," Calhoun asked Kerrigan, "whose life has been spent inside a campus fortress, have the faintest flash notion of what it's really like to live in a cell, a few feet from the electric chair, and the death sentence upon him?" Then answered himself. "No way. No way." He swung the magazine around.

"In Favor of the Death Penalty," by one Professor Barzoom, was the title and author of the piece he'd been reading.

"He tells us here," Calhoun informed Kerrigan, "about a man who spent a year in prison due to a miscarriage of justice. When the man got out his wife was dead and his children were in the workhouse. This man, the professor tells us, was not so lucky as Tim Evans, who was hanged in another miscarriage of justice. 'Rather be Tim Evans dead,' " Calhoun read the professor's decision, " 'than to emerge, after twelve months in prison, to find all reason for living gone.' "

" 'Ask Tim Evans,' " Calhoun answered the professor's question.

"A sailor," Calhoun explained, "might travel around the world nineteen times and remain the same man he'd been when he'd first gone on the ship. He's seen everything and seen nothing. He can't judge because he is not capable of *experiencing*. I'm sure the professor has attended funerals; yet nothing about death has ever touched him. He is wrapped in cellophane. Listen to this, Kerrigan:

" 'The propagandists for abolition speak in hushed tones of the sanctity of human life—but most of the abolitionists belong to nations that spend half their annual incomes on weapons of war and research for more efficient means of killing. These good people vote without a qualm for political parties that arm their country to the teeth.'

"What he's saying," Calhoun interpreted, "is that, if you live in a Western nation which uses military means to assault a country, say of Southeast Asia, you yourself are doing the killing. Even though you may be sitting in jail for protesting the assault, the responsibility for it is still yours, he says. You are therefore a hypocrite for demanding abolition of the death penalty if your state reserves the right to impose capital punishment. You voted for the governor, didn't you?

"All the professor is doing is putting the old tribal belief of an eye for an eye, into academic language. Thank God, Kerrigan, for people who don't believe in an eye for an eye and a tooth for a tooth. Were it not for them the world would have gone toothless and blind long ago. Here," Calhoun picked up the novel, "is a man who *knew:*

" 'But the chief and worst pain,' Calhoun read from Dostoevsky, " 'may not be in the bodily suffering but in one's knowing for certain that in an hour and then in ten minutes and then in half a minute, and then now, at the very moment, the soul will leave the body and that one will cease to be a man and that that is bound to happen; the worst part of it is that it's certain . . . to kill for murder is a punishment incomparably more terrible than murder by brigands. Anyone murdered by a brigand, whose throat is cut at night in a wood, must surely hope to escape till the very last minute . . . but in an execution, that last hope that makes dying ten times as easy, is taken away for certain. There is the sentence, and the whole awful torture lies in the fact that there is certainly no escape, and there is no torture in the world more horrible.' "

"It isn't all that certain any longer," Kerrigan reminded Calhoun. "Very few death sentences are now carried out."

"All the worse—now the man must live between living and dying, neither being able to feel himself alive nor knowing when he will be dead. Death isn't merely a matter of the body ceasing to breathe. Death comes to many before the actual death sets in. I doubt, for example, that the professor has ever been really alive. Men who are truly alive possess sensitivity to death.

"What I would enjoy seeing," Calhoun reflected, cocking his head at Kerrigan like an owl sitting in judgment, "would be to see the professor in a cell and the death sentence upon him. I can picture him on his knees and he wouldn't be Walter Mittying it anymore with Joan of Arc.

"Joan of Arc chose death, the professor writes, in preference to imprisonment. No way. Joan of Arc chose imprisonment in preference to death. It wasn't until she learned that the imprisonment would be solitary confinement that she chose death.

"Joan of Arc wavered in the face of death, but the professor never wavers for a moment. He stands atop his desk and challenges death to take him.

"What a complacent little humbug. He doesn't know that, even in a campus sanctuary, death can still look in. He's not as safe as he believes he is. And when death does, the professor will fall to his knees with tears in his eyes and plead for another day, another hour. 'No! No! I'm not ready to go! Take the head of the department, not me!'

"And to think," Calhoun marveled sadly, "a man like that gets paid good money."

He and Kerrigan were seated in a corner of the penitentiary library with a guard stationed within hearing distance. Calhoun rose and, confronting the guard, asked him, in a courteous tone, to station himself out of hearing distance.

The guard shook his head. No. He'd been instructed to stand where he was, and where he was standing was where he was going to continue standing.

Calhoun tried again. Kerrigan couldn't hear the words yet caught the tone of threat.

Again the guard shook his head, No.

For a long moment then the two men stood eyeball to eyeball. The guard then turned and walked to the back end of the library, out of hearing distance.

Calhoun returned to his seat without showing any indication of having been, momentarily, disturbed.

"I can't let myself be treated like a criminal," he told Kerrigan when Kerrigan commented on Calhoun's dress: he was wearing a black dashiki and a headband, both against prison regulations.

"If I let myself be treated like that, I'd begin to *think* like a criminal. Most of the men in here feel that what has happened to them *ought* to have happened. I don't. Dressing in prisoner clothes would be to acknowledge openly that I belong here. I don't."

"How are you getting on with the Muslims in here?" Kerrigan wanted to know.

"I try to have as little to do with them as possible. They want me to play the part of a black nationalist hero, and I'm not a nationalist. Nobody's nationalist.

"This means, of course, I lead a lonely life, somewhere between the antiestablishment establishment and the prison establishment. It leaves me with nobody to *reason* with.

"It's like being the only sane man in a madhouse where the doctors are as mad as the patients if not more so. In here it's a perpetual three-way war between an army of mourners, an army of cripples and an army of thieves. The mourners are our mothers, brothers, daughters and wives. The cripples are ourselves, because we have no power, no choice, not even names. The thieves are the administration. They give us everything we want but nothing of what we need. When a politician opens his mouth, saying he wants to improve our conditions, it's like an alligator—you can't tell whether he's smiling in friendliness or preparing to swallow you alive. Chances are it's to eat you.

"Prisons have only one function: to break the prisoner's ego. His own true function must be to hold onto it. Even though he is doing thirty-to-life, he *has* to hold on."

"I have to agree with you," Kerrigan assured Calhoun, "that the prison is set up to guarantee the prisoner's failure. Parole is good business for the prison and they aren't about to give it up. When you guys get out you're on a yo-yo; they can yank you back any time. And they will yank you back, because they need you. You get out just long enough to prove you can't make it out there."

"The prison is set up to conceal the basic hostility between administration and inmate," Calhoun assured Kerrigan, not being certain of how deeply Kerrigan's perception may have gone. "This is the place where the man who has never had a chance to finish grammar school is made to feel he's a Madison Avenue executive.

He has an office, a staff of six, a title like 'Personnel Counselor' or 'Editor' or 'Liaison Executive'—and a coffee percolator available only to himself and his staff.

"This makes for the greatest possible security within the prison system: the warden owns these people body and soul. They used to be sulking in their cells or scheming in the yard.

"Now all they want is to keep doing what they're doing. They never had it so good. All their lives people been telling them what to do. Now they're telling others. All their lives they've been unimportant—the most unimportant men on earth. Now they're important. Now they matter. What they say goes. Wait till they get outside and find out they're not important at all. Wait till the first day it rains. When the prisoner gets back on the street he's been destroyed morally—which is what the prison system is aiming at. It's easier for a man to become a shadow in prison, and to believe that shadow to be real, than it is to become a responsible human being.

"That's where the tension comes from," Calhoun continued. "It isn't, chiefly, between black and white. It's between young and old. The old boys are the ones who buy the Madison Avenue image. They remember the time of the lockstep and this seems now to be too good to be true. To the young one, it's no big deal that he doesn't have to work fourteen hours a day in a quarry. Having a basketball hoop in the square doesn't make him warm with gratitude. He's not a criminal, in his own mind. He's a victim. And when you tell him he doesn't have a name, he's only a number, he shuts up tight. Look out then: he's dangerous.

"The farther you remove a man from the real world, the more dangerous he becomes. Rehabilitation, in the sense the super means it, and rehabilitation, the way we mean it, are two absolutely opposed beliefs. To the super it means making the prisoner presentable: one who has adjusted himself to things as they are and as they always will be. This is the same prisoner who used to get his soul saved by Baptist do-gooders. Now he gets it saved by a visiting analyst whom he has conned into recommending him for parole. There isn't a psychiatrist living who can outthink *these* dudes.

"What *we* mean by rehabilitation is giving up booze, junk,

punks and all the foolishness the prisoner plays at to make time pass. Because when he wakes up in the morning he's always in the same old cell, facing the same routine, with all that time still to serve. To the super, the prisoner who is now willing to fink has been rehabilitated. To us, rehabilitation means a determination to become a man instead of a number.

"We can make this a place where alley finks and old-time scumbags learn how to become men. We can put men to work who have never had an honest trade. We can guard ourselves better than the guards can guard us.

"You can feel the tension in here. It comes from the administration's realization that the prisoners can run this place better than they can—and that they might, one day, just try it. The administration has the old men on their side but they can't reach the young men. The officers are scared of the young guys and I don't blame them."

Kerrigan took Calhoun's report directly to the super.

Kerrigan began with small matters first. He worked up gradually to the question of the tension within the walls.

"Prisoners complain about censorship of their mail," he assured the super. "Can you tell me what your method of censorship is? What are your guidelines?"

"If I come on something objectionable I send the book or paper to Dead-Mail," the super explained. "I never approve of books on psychology, physics or chemistry. We are here to teach the prisoner to rehabilitate himself; not how to become an amateur psychoanalyst or a bomb-maker. The book is marked, in Dead-Mail, for the prisoner upon his release."

"Rehabilitation," the super went on, "cannot be achieved at the expense of security. Security comes first here, Mr. Kerrigan. The more you do in security the less you do in rehab.

"Security is what the people of this state, who pay me, want. I cannot go against the voice of the people."

"I don't know what you mean by security," Kerrigan told the super.

"When I say security," the super confided to Kerrigan, "I mean, first, no grab-assing with inmates. Because the first thing an inmate is going to do is ask you for a light. You give him a light and the next thing he asks for is a cigarette. Next he wants marijuana. Then cocaine. By that time he's so far into you that, when he asks for a gun, you better get him a gun or he'll report you to the front office. Prisoners are smarter than guards, you know—inside.

"Outside, they have no brains at all. If you put a hundred of them out of the front gate and told them they were free, eighty of them would not have the faintest idea of where to turn. They would stand about waiting for someone to tell them what their next move ought to be. There would be a few who, when told they were free, would make a short dash for freedom. All the others would do would be to steal the officers' cars and make it to the nearest bar.

"There is a right length of time for each prisoner—but you must never let him know how long he has to serve. What is most essential to security in uncertainty. When he goes into isolation you don't let him know how long he's going to be in there."

Kerrigan wanted to hear the super tell him in the super's own words, what isolation was.

"Isolation," the super told Kerrigan, "is a stripped-down cell, coveralls for the prisoner but no shoes or socks, a blanket but no mattress. Two plates of vegetables a day and a regular meal every seventy-two hours. Along with the possibility that, any day he is in there, he may be forced to begin his sentence all over again. He'll come out straightened out."

"Isn't there any other way, sir," Kerrigan inquired courteously, "of straightening a prisoner out?"

"The best way to straighten a prisoner out is to straighten the country out," the super advised Kerrigan, "and that would be to post the same rules in every courthouse in the country and make them apply to every criminal, rich or poor, white or black, weak or powerful. Rape should be twenty years. Robbery should be fifty. Robbery using a weapon, the death sentence. No probation, no pardon. If this is applied, with force, without discrimination, and immediately after the crime, our crime rates would drop eighty percent overnight."

"Eighty percent, sir?" Kerrigan asking, keeping his face straight;

outwardly marveling that a man so asinine was yet shrewd enough to draw a fat salary.

The super looked pleased at having made a strong impression on this young fellow.

"I am proud to tell you, young man," he was proud to tell Kerrigan, "that the men are living better here than they did at home. They are better dressed and better fed. When a man is released here he is usually in better shape, physically, than he was when he came in. I have achieved this by banning contact visits between inmates and their wives or girl friends. Because that is how weapons and drugs are smuggled in here. I don't believe visits by children are healthy either. Because it leads to emotional problems in the child. Investigators I have to bar because time after time they have lied to me. I believe that the public should be less concerned with the prisoners and more concerned with their victims."

All recreation at Athens takes place in a square a hundred yards long and a hundred yards wide, with a basketball court in one corner and a baseball diamond at the other. Thus an outfielder sometimes finds himself in the middle of a basketball contest.

The hundred-odd men who report every morning for sick call don't get physical examinations. Chronic physical or emotional disabilities are not assessed. If a prisoner appears seriously ill, he is sent back to his cell. If not quite sick to death, he is given a pill. He retains the privilege of complaining loudly and bitterly. So long as he does not sustain his complaint too long, too loudly or too bitterly, he is tolerated. He can be dispatched, at a doctor's word, to Vroom City: the Bug Ward.

Once in the Bug Ward, the Bug Ward is your home. For keeps. If you're not a real bug when you enter, you soon will be.

Two doctors try to minister to over a hundred men in the time it takes to minister to one. "If I get sick in here," Calhoun told Kerrigan, "that's it. Good-by. That's all she wrote."

A white guard told Kerrigan: "You won't find any racism in here."

"What about the self-segregation in the mess hall?"

"Well, for God's sake, you don't want to sit down and eat between two coloreds, do you?"

Two establishments were confronting each other at Athens: the establishment as represented by the Police Benevolent Association; and the antiestablishment establishment, represented by the Nation of Islam.

Of the pitiful wage paid the hundred and twenty five metal-shop workers, half was held back against the day of their release. Calhoun was one of five prisoners appointed to request a higher wage, and full payment to the men on regular paydays. The shop supervisor passed the request on to the super and all five were keeplocked.

Two hours later the super received a decision of the U.S. District Court apprising him that his prison was failing to afford due process to prisoners. It added a restriction upon the administration's right to censor mail addressed to prisoners' lawyers or to public officials.

The grapevine carried the good news from cell to cell that night. The next morning more than three hundred men crowded into the metal shop and sat down.

"We didn't threaten anybody," Calhoun told Kerrigan. "Our watchword was: *No violence*. We sat there the whole day and not once did anybody holler, 'Pigs!' And not one lick of work was turned out. We went back to our cells peaceably."

The district court decision seemed eminently fair in the councils of the court. Fair-minded, yet mistaken. Because it left the brunt of its enforcement to a tiny group of half-educated white country boys whose sole skill was to hold men in custody. They were men who were suspicious of the big city.

They had not the faintest hazy notion of what the Black Muslims were all about. When they saw a New York City bus bringing wives, daughters and sisters to the penitentiary, one of them was certain to say, "The African Queen just pulled in. Watch the Zulus coming off."

"I intend no derogation of these officers," the Prison Commission's chief psychiatrist advised the commission about the prison guards, "but they are not skilled for this particular job—*if* this particular job *is* rehabilitation. If the prison's purpose is simply to keep men off the streets, and to keep them from killing one another inside the walls, these men can do the job. But for anything more than simple custody, they are not fitted."

Supervisory positions, for prisoners, paid as high as eighty cents a day. But prisoners were not allowed to handle their own money. The chief psychiatrist suggested that, if the men were paid a realistic wage and allowed to handle their own money, the effect would be rehabilitative.

Nobody heard him.

The metal shop was a cavernous two-story barn. Its ostensible purpose was to teach prisoners a trade. Yet only a fourth of the men assigned to it actually worked at the fashioning of shelving and cabinetmaking. Three had to stand about while the fortunate fourth ran a machine. A dozen men were assigned to the print shop's two presses, each of which required a single operator. The other ten stood and watched.

The metal shop earned a quarter million dollars annually. Whether they worked or watched, the men were paid thirty to forty cents a day.

When the same crowd jammed into the shop the following day, the super called J. Pat Wilson, the commissioner of prisons, to speak to representatives of the Prisoners' Council. Wilson granted the men an increase to a dollar a day across the board.

For the first time in American penal history, prisoners had improved their living conditions without violence and without outside help.

No greater error could possibly have been committed from the establishment's point of view.

Calhoun—it was to become increasingly clear—in his concern for prisoners' interests, had not abandoned his own.

He had obtained the interest of two energetic, effective people. One was the man with whom he'd once boxed in the Police League, Barney Kerrigan. The other was Adeline Kelsey, a mulatto woman of forty, who'd been bullied into prostitution in her teens. Before she'd reached twenty she'd gained domination not only over her first pimp—by the simple expedient of slicing him from forehead to lip with an ivory-handled springblade (which she still carried)—but also over every other pimp within reaching distance, black or white. She'd gained a name for being a dangerous whore.

She'd gone legit by investing in a fleet of taxicabs. Before that year was out she was running a dry-cleaning establishment. By the time she was thirty she owned four dry-cleaning plants and still ran a fleet of cabs. Now, nearing forty, she was into bail bonding as well.

A woman so strikingly successful was bound to be ugly as sin, Calhoun assumed. Instead he found himself confronted by a beige-hued Elizabeth Taylor. One who carried herself just as dramatically.

No public relations firm could have devised a finer camouflage for her irresistible aggressiveness than Adeline Kelsey had devised for herself. Slight, low voiced, she concealed a relentless drive beneath a manner almost shy.

Her hidden fury, when it burst out, usually burst out against white men. Kerrigan was standing in a queue before the visitors' desk at Athens, when a woman's voice behind him said, "Excuse me," and stepped in front of him, "if you don't mind."

Kerrigan was not a man to be pushed lightly to one side by anybody. "I *do* mind, madam," he assured her and stepped in front of her.

He felt a sharp kick on his ankle and backed out of the line. He stood back, rubbing the ankle contemplatively. Almost all the people in the line were women, most of them black. All were smiling quietly at Adeline Kelsey's triumph. They had, most of them, seen her in action before.

Kerrigan lifted her off the floor, put her down toward the end of the line and told her, "I can get rougher than this, if you want."

The other women appeared pleased to see her put into her proper place; some of them smiled softly but said nothing.

"Oh, I see the kind *you* are," Adeline informed him; but she did not try to get in front of him again.

While waiting for Calhoun in the prison library, neither acknowledged the presence of the other. Neither knew that both had come to visit the same prisoner. When Calhoun came in, smiling, and introduced them, Kerrigan gave her a small nod but she gave him no nod at all.

It wasn't until Kerrigan began speaking to Calhoun about Don Kessler that Adeline began getting interested in him.

Kessler, a white man not yet thirty, had put twelve years into New Jersey prisons, six of them locked with Calhoun.

He had also locked with Baxter at Bordentown.

Kerrigan had gotten wind of Kessler through Esteban Escortez. When Kerrigan found Kessler, Kessler had served his time and was living with a girl from Fort Lee in Hackensack. He was on parole and was planning to marry the girl.

Kerrigan had found him in an expansive mood. He assured Kerrigan that Baxter had told him the same story to which Esteban Escortez had already brought witness. Baxter had told him, too, that he had never laid eye on Ruby Calhoun; and that he had borne witness against him for the sake of reducing the sentences he had been facing.

"Take me to meet him," Miss Kelsey demanded of Kerrigan.

Kerrigan shrugged, "Why not?"

He drove her over to Kessler's place the following week. Less than a week after that she had Kessler on an afternoon TV show for a full hour. Kerrigan watched it from his office; Calhoun watched it in the auditorium at Green Meadow.

Adeline had tried to get a black interviewer, but had not been able to swing that. It was the only aspect of the program that did not swing her way.

"Baxter was in Bordentown," Kessler explained to his interviewer, Mark Sellinger, "because the prosecutor had made arrangements to keep him out of Athens. His life would be in peril there.

"Baxter's job was sweeping the block down," Kessler recalled, "what we called a runner. He brought in candy and cigarettes, on the sneak, and other prisoners accepted them without accepting him. They'd take the stuff but they wouldn't talk to him.

"I asked Baxter why he had testified against Calhoun, and he told me he had not only been facing eighty years, but that the prosecutor had threatened to charge him with the murders if he failed to support Iello's identification of Calhoun.

"Over and above that," Kessler went on, "Baxter felt he had a good chance to collect the reward. I asked him whether he didn't feel badly about sending another man to prison for life and he told me, No, because as soon as Calhoun appealed, he (Baxter) was going to cut him loose."

"How did Baxter get money for candy and cigarettes?" Sellinger asked Kessler.

"The only people Baxter had outside was a mother and a sister and they didn't have a dime between them. Somebody was putting walking-around money on him, but he didn't say who."

"Where was he coming from?"

"He'd been at Brookhaven but he was going to Yardville, he told me. The prosecutor had arranged that, he told me, because after testifying against Calhoun, it was dangerous for him to be anywhere else. He was very nervous about who he came into contact with. If a new inmate came in, Baxter would go to his own cell and have himself locked. He talked to me like I was some kind of leaning block, like he needed to get his troubles off his chest.

"He and Iello had stumbled into this bar, he told me, and these people had already been shot up. They began robbing the dead, he told me, Iello going through Mrs. Shane's handbag. That was how they got involved, he told me. Then he said he had seen Iello pitch a gun into the river—but whether this was right after the murders, or long after, he didn't tell me."

"Did Baxter tell you he had seen Calhoun after he had left that bar?"

"He'd seen nobody, he told me. All he wanted was to get the hell out of there."

"Is your recollection of this clear?"

"Perfectly clear. 'Do it our way,' he said De Vivani told him, 'and you make the reward money and the street, both. Do it the other way and we really stick it to you.' "

"Did Baxter tell you he concocted the whole story as he told it on the stand?"

"He told me that that story was made up between De Vivani and Iello. He was just there, that was all, Baxter said."

"Would you like to be of help to Calhoun?"

"I'd like to see the man get a fair shake, that's all. The way Baxter explained things, there's no way Calhoun *could* be guilty. No way. I was locked next cell to his when he got the news that the New Jersey Supreme Court upheld the verdict in the first trial, and the way he took it convinced me he is not the man who committed the murders."

"How did he take it?"

"He went clear out of his gourd. Simply raved for four full days. A couple of Black Muslims came up and stood guard at his cell to keep the P.B.A. people from moving him to Vroom City. We wondered would he *ever* come out of it. I listened all the while his mind was at large, raging and raving. Not once did he so much as mention the Melody Bar and Grill, the names of the people murdered there, or the previous shooting at the Paradise.

"That was what convinced me he hadn't been there. How could he have been there, and yet not recall it in a delirium? Calhoun took, to me, the truest type of lie-detector test right there: there is no way of lying when you've lost control of your mind, is there?"

"What kind of guy is Baxter outside the joint?"

"I never knew him well outside the joint. I know that, inside, he could stand up under some pressure. Iello was, to me, the weak one. Definitely the weak one. How they arranged things between themselves I have no idea. Baxter seemed to know what it must be like for Calhoun. He seemed to have some touch of feeling about Calhoun doing all that time."

"Was Baxter lying to you or telling you the truth?"

"He had no reason to lie to me."

"How many conversations about Calhoun did you have with him?"

"Quite a few. I listened because I didn't want to blow the cigarettes and candy and stuff he kept bringing into the unit."

"How much time have you spent in prison yourself?"

"Almost thirteen years."

"How old are you?"

"Twenty-nine."
"Are you telling the truth?"
"I am."

Hardee Haloways stopped by Jennifer Calhoun's house, accompanied by a white man whom he did not introduce beyond mentioning his name: Kerrigan.

"I've been hanging around the Melody," Kerrigan explained himself to Jennifer, "looking for Esteban Escortez. I haven't been able to find him."

"Are you an attorney?" Jennifer asked.

"No. State investigator. I knew your husband before the shooting."

"Bordentown," Jennifer decided to let him know.

Kerrigan shook his head, No. Escortez had been released from Bordentown. "I know a bar in Fort Lee where he hangs out. But where he hangs out when he isn't hanging out there, they won't say."

"Are you assigned to Ruby's case?"

"It isn't a case yet, Mrs. Calhoun. I just have a gut reaction, nothing more. I've got to have more than that for the state to get into it."

Roddy Nims came in with Doc Lowry and his new light-heavy, Eddie Sykes of Dublin; then Max Epstein and Floyd Calhoun; then Don Kessler and his new bride.

Kerrigan was a man of quiet energy. Even while sitting still, his confident spirit lifted spirits around him. A feeling rose among these people that the world was starting to come right-side up once more. Somehow, people *believed,* when Kerrigan announced that he was in pursuit of recantations from both Baxter and Iello, that he was going to get them.

Both informers possessed a unique capacity for disappearing themselves. Whenever one of them was jailed, Kerrigan would show up immediately after his release; and no one would give him a clue.

The occasional anonymous phone call was the only encouraging aspect of his search. These came usually fast and hushed and Kerrigan was seldom home when they came. His mother would take them, but could never keep the caller on the line for long. These leads led Kerrigan nowhere. Then one came of just two words: "Bergen County."

Kerrigan wheeled over to the Bergen County jail, found Iello there and arranged to talk to him.

Iello didn't offer to shake hands. The county pants and jacket hung on him loosely. He'd lost weight.

"I got nothing to say to you, mister," he assured Kerrigan. Had he had any choice, it was plain, he would have remained in his cell.

"At times he seemed to be listening a little," Kerrigan told Jennifer, "other times he would just shut me out. It was like talking out of the window then. Only when I told him that the statute of limitations on perjury suits had run out on him, he perked up a little. I saw that this information, that he was now protected against suit by the state, had impressed him. 'Think it over, Nick,' I told him, 'I'll be back.'

"It was a week before I got back to him. This time he asked questions. He got scared when I told him Baxter was going to recant. He knew this would leave him holding the bag. Then I told him about Kessler's interview. He hadn't viewed it directly, but he knew about it. He had more to fear now, I told him, from street people than he had from the law. And I think he had.

" 'That goddamned De Vivani,' I heard him say," Kerrigan reported to Jennifer, "and I knew what he meant. I knew exactly what he meant. He meant that, although De Vivani had gotten him off various charges before, and had given him protection, too, he hadn't done a thing for Nick Iello lately.

"Iello had assumed he had gained immunity from imprisonment, that he could now steal at will, and De Vivani would always be there to keep him out of jail. Now that goddamned De Vivani was no longer lifting a finger for him. There wasn't anything more, it looked like, that De Vivani was going to do for Iello.

" 'He thinks,' Iello told me, 'he's the chief dago. But if I once start talkin' he'll find he's just one more wop.' "

Kerrigan talked to Iello again in the following week. Two days later, and just out of jail, Iello phoned Kerrigan that he was ready to sign a statement that he had perjured himself in identifying Ruby Calhoun.

"I recognize now that I made a grave mistake about Ruby Calhoun," the statement read. "I realize now that, at the time of the trial, I identified the wrong person. I spoke in a moment of fear and instantly regretted it. I was under constant pressure and was confused at the time. The pressure came from the prosecutor's office and from the police. The police suggested to me constantly that it was Ruby Calhoun I had seen. If I didn't testify that it was Calhoun, they'd put me in jail for not testifying, they said.

"Then they were talking about the ten thousand-dollar reward; I told them I wasn't sure that I wanted to do this and they told me I'm going to do it whether I want to or not."

Kerrigan dropped in on De Vivani without an appointment. De Vivani didn't mind people dropping in. If he was occupied he ignored them; if he was unoccupied he was pleased to have company. De Vivani was not a hard man to get along with.

He was over six feet and put together solidly: tough cop. Yet he was not as tough as he appeared. When he saw a chance to give some prisoner a break, he gave it. De Vivani was not a mean man.

"A friend of Ruby Calhoun's is a friend of mine," he greeted Kerrigan, "coffee?"

"Ruby was the best middleweight in the world for a while," Kerrigan made conversation, blowing on the coffee in the paper cup, "but who I want to talk to you about is Vince Le Forti."

"*That* poor sonofabitch." De Vivani laughed wryly. "He was committed and released, then the black kids began beating him up on the street. He couldn't go down to the corner without getting slugged. So he had himself recommitted, voluntarily. He's at Marlboro now."

Kerrigan was only half-listening. He was casing De Vivani's office with an investigator's eye and Kerrigan had an extremely shrewd eye. He took in every drawer of both big desks. He studied the files without touching them.

"How'd he get out in the first place?" Kerrigan asked about Le Forti, just to feign interest. He was eliminating the files, in his mind, where the tape could not be.

"Vince had a smart lawyer," De Vivani answered.

A black officer came in holding an envelope up to De Vivani's view.

De Vivani nodded. From the corner of his eye, Kerrigan observed the officer pull out the middle drawer of the big desk and deposit the envelope. "Did they beat him up bad?" he asked De Vivani.

There was no beating victim upon earth which interested him less than Vincent Le Forti.

"The first time they hospitalized him for a week. They seemed to let up on him, just a little, after that. All they do is punch him out until he's unconscious. Vince was always crocky, of course. Now he's really punchy. We can't let him carry a gun like we used to. He'd mow down anything he saw that was black, even if it were a cow."

"I knew he had a sheet before he shot old man Haloways," Kerrigan told the detective, "What was that about?"

De Vivani shook his head, No. "A public investigator ought to know better than to ask a police officer a question like that," he reproached Kerrigan. Officer Motley appeared in the doorway and gestured to De Vivani. He rose and talked to Motley, low-key, just beyond the door. Kerrigan sat tight. Then heard their footsteps fading down the narrow hall.

He went directly to the middle drawer, ran his fingers down the file to "Iello," yanked it, put it in the briefcase, locked it and returned to his chair opposite De Vivani's.

When De Vivani returned, ten minutes later, Kerrigan was at ease. He had what he'd come for.

De Vivani was grinning.

"Had to pull a couple of Puerto Ricans apart," he explained, "over a woman, of course. It's always over a woman. Good thing we took their knives off them or they'd both be dead or in the hospital. They don't fight like *us,* you know."

"How do they fight?"

"They pull hair, go for the eyes with the fingernails. Like women. More coffee?"

"No thanks," Kerrigan extended his hand. "Thanks for the

information on Le Forti, Vince."

"Always pleased to help an old enemy," De Vivani assured Kerrigan.

Kerrigan took care not to walk hurriedly to the door.

He didn't hear the tape until he got to the recorder in his office. He was alone when he put it on. At its first sound Kerrigan knew he'd had a lucky day.

"After you've read your statement over," Kerrigan warned Iello, "and have made any changes you feel are necessary, I'll get it notarized and have you swear that everything in it is true, so help you God."

"So help me God," Iello agreed.

Iello had agreed.

STATE OF NEW JERSEY	AFFIDAVIT
COUNTY OF HUDSON	June 15, 1974

I, Nicholas Iello, of full age and of sound mind, upon my oath do swear that the following is a complete and true statement which I give to State Investigator Barney Kerrigan for the purpose of making sure that the truth is told.

On the morning of June 17, 1966, Kenneth Kelley drove me and Dexter Baxter to the Apex Supply Company. Baxter went to work on the company's back door and I walked into the Melody Bar and Grill while he was trying to force the door.

I was sitting inside having a beer when a colored broad walked into the bar then walked out. Right after that everything went down.

Right after the colored broad left a black man came in the front entrance and fired five shots into the bar. I was sitting next to this broad who wound up with three bullets in her. I heard her say, "Oh No, My God, Oh No." I believe I might have used that broad to get out of the bar. She was more or less a shield for me.

Baxter never seen anything. He wasn't around there when things were going down. I believe the colored broad who came in earlier was involved.

I never told the cops I was in the bar at the time of the shooting because I didn't want to get involved.

I am willing to take a lie-detector test on everything I have said in this statement because it is the truth, so help me God.

(signed) *Nicholas P. Iello*

"Baxter dear," Mother Baxter insisted on filling Baxter in after supper, "your parole officer dropped by this afternoon. He was most polite. He asked whether you had found work. I told him you were looking and looking, every day."

Baxter had come out of prison with nothing more to show he had aged than a gray streak in his brown mop. He was a tall, pale youth who would have been passably good-looking had it not been for the look of apprehension in his eyes: like that of a cat with one paw raised ready to scamper. Everything Baxter had ever gotten in his life had been on the scamper. Snatch and run was how he made it. Local police had nicknamed him Rabbit Baxter.

Rabbit didn't answer his mother. Didn't even look at her. He looked, instead, at Melissa, his sixteen-year-old sister sitting across the table from him.

"How's school?" he asked her. Although he knew she had dropped out months ago.

"Fine, Dex, fine," Melissa assured him, "school is fine. I walked past it a couple of weeks ago and it's still standing there looking fine."

"I'm disappointed in you, sis,"

"*You're* disappointed in *me?*" She was smiling.

"You had a chance to go to school and make something of yourself, Melissa, I never had that chance."

"Now Dexter dear," Mother Baxter corrected him, "you know how I *begged* you to finish high school. Purely *begged* you."

Again he did not, apparently, hear her. The fact was that Dexter was as deeply disappointed in his mother as he was in his sister. Dexter Baxter kept high moral standards for both mother and sister. Both continually let him down.

Nor were his mother and sister the only people who had ever

disappointed Dexter. He had also been disappointed in the court that had sentenced him to three-to-five instead of handing him the reward money and letting him make the street.

Not only had the court forced him to serve two years and eight months, but he still had not seen a penny of the reward. People never tired of taking advantage of Dexter Baxter. Here they were still at it.

"It would be good if you could find *something,* dear," his mother persisted.

"They need a weekend bartender at the Easy Street," Melissa informed him, "ten until closing time. No experience necessary. All they ask is that he put *some* of the money into the register." She smiled.

"The landlord phoned too, son," Mother Baxter put in. "He was polite too. He reminded me we're two months behind."

"Mother dear," Dexter finally turned toward her, "you've worked for me all your life. Now why don't you go out and find a job of your own?" Reaching his open palm against her face, he shoved her over backward, chair and all.

"Are you hurt, mother?" Melissa asked as the old woman rose, blushing in humiliation. She turned, breathing hard because she was a heavy woman, and walked to her bedroom dabbing at her eyes. Only her feelings had been injured.

Melissa cocked her head to one side and, pertly as a bird, studied her brother. He'd never try anything like that on her, she knew. He'd tried it once but he wouldn't try it again. He never tried force on anyone who might strike back; she knew that much about Dexter Baxter.

"What are you hanging around Easy Street for?" Baxter asked, though he could not have cared less. Where Melissa spent her nights, whose bed she slept in, was the least of his concerns. If the wench didn't come home at all, so much the better. All he wanted was to talk about something else than going to work. Talking about work was as boring as work itself. Even for a weekend in a bar where he could steal as much as he earned.

"I got a steady boyfriend there," she lied, "he thinks the world of me."

"I'm glad you've settled down to a single man," he congratulated her. "The last time I got locked, you were going steady with the whole town."

"He's not single," she chose to misunderstand, "he's married."

"How come we're two months behind then in the rent?" he jumped right in there.

"Dexter *dear.*" Mother Baxter was back, standing now in a tweedy pink bathrobe, in her bedroom door, "Dexter dear, you ought to be *ashamed* to talk like that to your sister."

" 'Going steady,' " Melissa ignored her mother as completely as had her brother, "doesn't mean what *you* think it means. Our relationship is purely flatonic."

"It's *what?*"

"Flatonic. That means . . ."

"I know what it means, sis," Dexter grinned, "it means you don't neck. You just converse about books. What was the name of that last book you read, sis?"

"You know, Dexter," she smiled at him, "every time you come out of the can you look fruitier than when you went in?"

" 'Fruitier?' " Mother Baxter needed to know, "what is 'fruitier'?"

Nobody explained to Mother Baxter. Nobody ever explained anything to Mother Baxter. How this young girl with the morals of a mink, and this skinny thief, who was in and out of jail like a fiddler's elbow, came to be flesh of her flesh, was more than the old woman could grasp.

"Different strokes for different folks, sis," Dexter answered his sister, and turned away from both her and his mother as if, between the pair of them, he felt he were being asphyxiated.

Melissa's latest affair of the heart actually was platonic. It was platonic because her friend was not even aware of Melissa. Barney Kerrigan had been sitting around Main Street bars, in Hackensack, chatting with this barfly then that, in hope of running down Dexter Baxter.

He'd bought this good-looking young redhead a few drinks, had wondered whose I.D. card she was drinking on, but hadn't paid much heed to her chatter until she'd volunteered her name.

Kerrigan had invited her into a booth.

He was sitting with his back to the door when Baxter came in and, spotting his sister, strode up to her with the intention of giving her a talk on morality loud enough for the barflies to overhear. But Melissa spoke first.

"Mr. Kerrigan, this is my brother."

Dexter Baxter took one look, swung about and was out the door.

Kerrigan stared after him. "What got into *him?*" he asked.

"He don't take to cops, that's all," Melissa explained.

"I'm not a cop."

She touched him lightly on his hand, as much as to say, Stop kidding.

"Of *course* you're a cop. *Some* kind of cop."

"What makes you think so?"

"A cop is a cop, that's all." Melissa gave him her whitest, sweetest smile, "you just *know,* that's all."

"That's funny," Kerrigan told her, "because I'm really not. I'm an investigator with the public defender's office."

"It's what I said. Some kind of cop." Her smile had become teasing. "Look, don't feel bad. It don't mean you're a bad guy. It just means people got to be a little careful talkin' to you, that's all. Why else do you think Dex took off like that?"

"Well," he told her, "all I can tell you is what I told you already. I'm *not* a cop. Quite the opposite in fact. And it's Dexter I've been hoping to talk to."

"We were talking about you earlier this evening, Mr. Kerrigan."

"I don't understand."

"I told Dex I had a new boy friend. That we were going steady."

Kerrigan still didn't get it.

"Well," she laid her hand onto his, "we *have* had a couple drinks together, haven't we?"

Then, having gotten it at last, he didn't know how to handle it. He'd found a person who could bring him to Baxter—but there seemed to be a price tag attached. She handled it for him by picking up her coat. "Let's get out of here," she decided.

They sat in a pizza parlor for an hour before Melissa said at last, "Dex will be home by now, if you want to see him."

Kerrigan nodded. It would suit him fine.

"It's a long walk," she told him, hoping he might hail a cab.

"Let's walk anyhow," he told her. It was too easy to get involved in the back of a taxi.

When they came into her small front parlor, Mother Baxter greeted them, smiling her short-sighted smile.

"Are you the man who called from the parole office?" she asked Kerrigan.

"No," he told her. Then, looking up, he saw a shadowy figure leaning, as though listening, in the shadowy hall. Kerrigan felt alarmed until Melissa called out cheerfully, "Come out, Dex, we have company."

Dexter came out unsmiling but did not sit down.

"Can we have coffee, mother?" Melissa asked. The girl was enjoying the situation she had created.

"Sit down, Dex, so we can talk," Kerrigan suggested.

Baxter stayed standing.

"Sit down, dear," Mother Baxter urged her son, "the man isn't going to hurt you."

"Sit down, Dex," Melissa commanded him, and he sat down.

"You think I'm going to talk to you about Calhoun, mister, you're wrong," Baxter assured Kerrigan. "That's done. Over. Through."

"It isn't done, through or over for Calhoun," Kerrigan reminded him. "It's every day for him."

Baxter shrugged his indifference. Kerrigan felt himself getting angry, but cooled it.

"You put the man in there, Dex. You know what it's like in there. I don't blame you, in a way, considering the time you were facing."

Baxter looked Kerrigan up and down. He didn't care much, it appeared, for what he saw.

"I'm not talking about Calhoun, mister."

"Mister," Kerrigan assured him, "you *have* to talk about Calhoun."

"Meaning what?"

"Meaning it isn't the state you have to be afraid of anymore. It's the people behind Calhoun you're standing in danger of now."

This was straight bluff. Baxter was not in imminent peril of physical assault. Calhoun regarded him as a man whom the judicial system had used and had now tossed aside. The man was, in a sense, a victim too. He didn't feel vindictive toward Baxter, but toward the forces behind Baxter.

This kind of thinking, Kerrigan perceived, was totally alien to Baxter's own vindictive mind. There blacks and whites were forever at swords' points; that blacks were out to kill him there could be no doubt. Kerrigan read Baxter well.

"Sleep on it," he suggested to Baxter. "I'll drop by tomorrow night."

When Melissa opened the door to Kerrigan, the following evening, she saw, beside Kerrigan, a big blond fellow. Don Kessler was well over six feet and had put on weight since his marriage. He weighed close to three hundred pounds.

When they stepped inside, Mother Baxter came out and told them to make themselves at home while she made coffee. Dexter was sleeping but she'd wake him up. She didn't ask Kessler who he was.

If Melissa knew, she didn't say. She retired to a corner to listen and watch.

Dexter came out, in pajamas and a bathrobe. He gave Kessler a cursory nod of recognition.

"I've been talking to Iello," Kerrigan began.

Baxter, sitting on the edge of his chair, looked ready to take flight. Except he had nowhere to fly.

"I don't have anything to do with Nick Iello. I haven't seen him for years. We don't have anything in common anymore."

"You've got plenty in common with Iello, Baxter. If he goes into court and testifies that he lied about Calhoun, that makes you out a liar too."

"I've been called a liar before. So what?"

"A man is doing triple life because of it, that's so what."

"Don't make *me* responsible for *that,* mister. That whole deal was made up between Iello and De Vivani. They didn't even tell me what to say. I had to figure it out for myself. What do you expect me to do? Go up for eighty years for God's sake?''

"Let's forget about then and talk about now, Baxter," Kerrigan suggested. "You're out of the reach of the courts now, as you know, for perjury. But you're not out of reach of others." He turned toward big Don Kessler. "You tell him, Don."

"Get yourself off the hook, Dex," Kessler advised him. "You'll be going up again, you know that as well as I do, and you won't have the protection you had till now. How long do you think you'd last at Leesburg?"

"I don't have any plans to make Leesburg," Baxter assured Kessler, "none whatsoever. I'm out and I'm going to stay out."

"Be that as it may, and I wish you good luck, too," Kessler filled him in, "but if you're not inside then you're out. You've used up your protective custody, Dex. If you don't get off the hook by yourself, there are people who are going to put you on it."

Mother Baxter appeared in the doorway bearing a tray on which she'd arranged a dish of chocolate cookies. A moment later she was back with three cups and a coffee percolator still perking.

"Help yourself, boys," she invited them, and sat down to watch them eat and drink. Mother Baxter always felt contented when she had the privilege of serving people.

"And what line of work are *you* in, Mr. Kessler?" she asked big Don.

"Oh," big Don rambled a moment for a reply, "I'm in television," he told Mother Baxter.

"On the morning of June 16, 1966," Dexter Baxter's statement read, "I was in the alley behind the Apex Supply Company's plant in Jersey City. My purpose was to break in and rob the place. My partner, Nick Iello, was lookout. He told me he was going down to a bar on the corner for cigarettes before they closed, so it must have been around 2 A.M. I heard a couple of shots shortly after, but thought it must be a car backfiring. A few minutes later Iello came running, hands me a handful of bills and tells me to get out of the area, there's been a shooting, there's going to be cops all over the place and he has to get back because he's been seen. Somebody had seen him running out of the bar.

The money was from the register. I never saw anybody come out of the bar. Iello mentioned a man named Ruby Calhoun, a prizefighter of whom I'd heard. When I got picked up, because of Iello, the police tied me up to nine charges of armed robbery, in four different counties. They could charge me with the murders, they told me. I could do eighty years for armed robbery, they told me. Then they began handing me mug shots. What else could I do? I identified the one they wanted me to identify."

Kerrigan got the recantations of Baxter and Iello notarized and handed them to a *New York Times* reporter. The reporter promptly attached his own byline to them and made the front pages, accompanied by a photograph of Calhoun. He had never met Calhoun.

The reporter accepted full credit, nevertheless, for an admirable job of reporting and his long association with the man who'd been perjured into the penitentiary. There was talk of film rights.

The reporter was so busy accepting honors that he neglected to mention it was another man who had built up Calhoun's case by two years of determined pursuit of the witnesses.

New Jersey vs. Calhoun became a national issue.

"Both men are sticking their necks out," Max Epstein told the press. "They're making themselves liable to prosecution for perjury."

Neither Iello nor Baxter were making themselves liable to anything. Neither was a man who left himself open to anything, for a moment. Both knew that the statute on prosecution for perjury had run out for them.

"If they recant their original testimony in court," state's attorney Scott warned both witnesses, "we will establish that they are now lying, and we will prosecute."

More hot air. Prosecutor Scott, too, knew that the statute had run out.

III

Evidentiary Hearing

DID THE RECANTATIONS of Iello and Baxter make the first trial of Ruby Calhoun null and void? Calhoun's defense thought so. The state did not.

Calhoun's attorney was now Max Epstein. The evidentiary hearing, convened to decide the legality of the original trial, was presided over by the same judge who had conducted that first trial.

"We are not here to retry the criminal case," Judge Turner forewarned Epstein at the evidentiary hearing of October 1974. "We are here on a limited procedure. Kindly attune your evidence to such procedure."

Epstein immediately asked Iello whether the testimony he had given, identifying Calhoun as the man emerging from the Melody Bar and Grill immediately after the killings, had been true.

"No," Iello replied.

"You lied under oath?"

"I did."

"Now you have come forward and have spoken to Barney Kerrigan of the office of the public defender. Barney, will you stand up? Have you not?"

"Yes."

"Were there any threats to you by Mr. Kerrigan, or by anyone, which would cause you to volunteer this information? Promises? Inducements?"

"Nothing at all."

"Why did you not come forward before?"

"I was afraid of retaliation from the prosecutor's office."

"Have you been visited, recently, by any member of that office?"

"I seen Lieutenant De Vivani three times the past year, more or less. He'd promised me I wouldn't have to worry about going to jail because I had testified for the state. So I told him, 'I'm having quite a lot of trouble here, lieutenant. Can you do something for me because I'm under a doctor's care?' He told me,

'You got yourself into this, now get yourself out.' Then he tells me, 'Don't try to rearrange your story or I'll get you a hundred years.'

" '*A hundred years?*' I ask him. 'For what? If Calhoun gets an appeal I'll take the Fifth. I won't testify no more for the state. The state is a stinker.' That is why I'm getting pressured now from the prosecutor's office. The prosecutor's office is also a stinker."

"In what form is this pressure applied to you, Mr. Iello?"

"I never realized until after the trial how I had been fashioned by Hudson County. They molded me into that and made a stool pigeon out of me and then they made me a scapegoat. You know who the real victim in this whole business is? *Me*. I'm the *real* victim."

"How did Hudson County fashion you, Mr. Iello?"

"By continuously and constantly questioning me. I was told of a reward I was supposed to have. I was told that a certain man ought to be in jail, if not for this crime then for some other, and that it was up to me to send him there. Why *so?* Am I the prosecuting attorney for God's sake? 'They really gave me the business' is what I said to myself when I seen the papers. And when I ask them, 'What do I do now?' after I had perjured myself for them, you know what they told me? 'Move to another town,' they told me, 'it won't look nice for you to be hanging around Jersey City.' How do you like *that?* I'm born and raised in Jersey City, now they tell me, 'Get out!' Then the police broke my ribs and I was back in jail."

"Mr. Iello," Judge Turner put in, "may we have questions and answers instead of a story?"

"Mr. Iello," Epstein continued, "were ethnic matters mentioned before members of the Hudson County prosecutor's office?"

"I heard the term 'niggers' mentioned several times. 'They're all criminals,' I heard them saying. And that was in my parents' home, right in front of my mother and father."

"Who are 'They'?"

"De Vivani and another officer. They said, 'Oh, your son has to do this for the families of the people who were murdered.' That crack upset my stomach. I became extremely nervous. I couldn't figure out why it had to be *me* to do something for people I never even knew and don't want to meet. If I had an attorney I wouldn't have been there, I would have been out of town. Far out."

"When you were asked what reward you hoped to get, did you not answer, 'I was never promised anything from the prosecutor's office?' "

"I gave that answer. It was a lie. De Vivani had told me I was going to get a reward of either ten thousand or twelve thousand five hundred. I forget which."

"Then you were aware of this reward before the trial?"

"Of course."

"When was the last time your attorney requested this reward?"

"The last time he mentioned it I told him, 'Forget it. You aren't needed. Leave me alone. Don't bother me.' "

"You gave the police a description of Mr. Calhoun sitting in a white car. Was that true or false?"

"I remember saying I had seen a white car. I forget who I told that to."

"Do you recall seeing Mr. Calhoun in it?"

"How should *I* know where Calhoun was that morning? He may have been in his car. He may have been fighting in Madison Square. He may have been home in bed with his wife. I don't try to keep track of things which are none of my business."

The first thing state's attorney Scott asked Iello was whether he remembered telling detectives Conroy and Motley, in a diner in Paterson, that he had seen Calhoun coming out of the Melody Bar and Grill with a revolver in his hand.

"I remember telling them I wasn't sure who it was," Iello replied.

"Do you recognize these initials?" Scott asked him, showing Iello his own initials—K.P.I.—on the margin of a statement he had made for the prosecuter's office, identifying the killer as Ruby Calhoun.

"Is this not your signature?" Scott demanded.

"Yes," Iello conceded, "but at the time B was under pressure. I just went ba-ba-ding ba-ba-ding, just ripped it right off."

"I regret we don't have music for that lyric," Judge Turner observed.

"You were going ba-ba-ding, ba-ba-ding for two complete pages," the prosecutor reminded Iello. Do you recall *that?*"

"I just wanted to get out of there and get it over with."

"Do you remember that, in the police van, you made certain statements about how you were going to get De Vivani?"

"What was the statement I was supposed to have made? I just came out of a hospital for being a chronic alcoholic. I don't even remember what happened two months ago. How can I answer a question when I don't even know what you're going to tell me?"

"He's asking you," Judge Turner interposed, "whether or not, on your return trip to Bergen County jail, you said anything about Lieutenant De Vivani. That's a simple question."

"I don't remember offhand."

"Did you say this to Detective Zileski?" Scott asked. "I'll let you look at it."

"That doesn't mean a thing to us," Judge Turner decided. "If you want to ask him you have to ask him so it's on the record, sir."

"I'll ask him so it's on the record. Do you remember saying this: 'They fucked me again, I'll get all those cocksuckers back. I should have signed that fucking statement the other day when I had the chance. I'll get all the motherfuckers back starting with the prosecutor's office. I don't give a shit if they give me five hundred years. They fucked me long enough. Tell De Vivani I'll fix his ass. You'll read about it in the *Times* Sunday. I'm going to sign that statement.' Did you say that?"

"Not in words like that. I seldom use foul language."

"What words did you use?"

"I don't remember."

"You swore in an affidavit that a couple cops jumped you in the street and broke a couple of your ribs. Did you say that to Mr. Kerrigan?"

"That ought to be rephrased."

"Rephrase it."

"The cops were standing right there while I was getting worked over by one of their heavies. That is just how it went. It's on the record where I got my ribs fixed. Those could be gotten."

"Has your memory improved since you talked to the officers?"

"What officers? Look, the night all this happened I'm not even sure I was talking to Baxter. Look, you don't go into and out of a bar and have a murder without being a little excited. I may have talked to somebody. I don't remember exactly because there was such a crowd there. I believe, for a time after that shooting and way up into the trial and through it, I must have been in some type of shock or something. I was under strain. I didn't even realize what was happening until years later."

"Were you under the same type of strain," the prosecutor asked, "when you talked to Mr. Kerrigan?"

"I was under pressure for three months in that lousy Hudson County jail. It's where I got my back sprained and I had a tooth pulled with the roots left in the mouth and now I'm in P.C."

"Please give me the names of the people who kept harassing you in the county jail."

"If I did there'd be only two people left in there."

"When was the first time, and to whom, did you say, 'When I said the man I saw was Ruby Calhoun, I was lying'?"

"When I gave that statement to Mr. Kerrigan."

"Was this the first time you had seen Kerrigan?"

"I'd seen him once or twice before, last year. He wanted me to talk but I didn't want to come forward at that time. Later I thought, why not get it off my chest once and for all?"

"What is the present charge against you in the Bergen County jail?"

"There is no charge against me in the Bergen County jail. I'm there because I sprained my back in the Hudson County jail. I was sent to the hospital because Hudson County said I was insane. The nurse there said to me, 'You ought to be on the cuckoo farm. You're nutty as a fruitcake. There are only forty-four cards in your deck.' 'That's eleven more than there are in yours, Butch,'

I told her. 'Your oil don't even hit the dipstick. You been around the bend so long you can't see ahead of your ass.' So they said, 'We don't know what to do with him, let's ship him to Bergen County.' So they shot me down here. For two years I was tellin' De Vivani I wouldn't have anything further to do with *New Jersey vs. Calhoun*. I washed my hands of that case. 'Count me out,' I told De Vivani, 'I'm doing all right on my own without all that.' "

"Can you explain to us, once again, what you meant when you told us you had been fashioned by Hudson County?"

"I was in a room with fifteen cops and one of them said to me: 'This is the way it's to be. No other way.' That was how Hudson County fashioned me. Hudson County promised to take care of me in event I should get jammed up. I believed I was doing the right thing. Then things got worse after De Vivani visited me. They stopped my mail. The whole reason was so I wouldn't testify against them. I'm testifying all the same, just to let people know exactly the way they are and just what happened."

"Testify to what?" Judge Turner asked Iello.

"To exactly what I did know at that time, just about what I can recall, *that's* what."

"Mr. Baxter," defense attorney Epstein asked the second witness, "you know that I am Ruby Calhoun's attorney, do you not?"

"Yes."

"Mr. Baxter, on the morning of June seventeen, nineteen hundred sixty-six, at about two-thirty A.M. . . ."

"Hold it, Jack. Hold it. I don't want to hear nothing."

"I'm sorry," Judge Turner asked with some surprise, "I didn't hear you. You want to say something?"

"Yes."

"What do you want to say?"

"Nothing."

"Did you talk to your lawyer before you came on the stand?"

"I don't want to say anything, your honor."

"You don't want to say anything. May I ask you why not?"

"Just don't."

"Just don't?"

"No."

"Under our law, when you are subpoenaed as a witness you must testify under oath unless there is some good reason which you assert why you should not. So far I haven't heard anything. You can't just come into court and say 'I don't want to say anything.' "

"Just don't."

"Let me warn you, sir, that unless you testify the court will issue an order compelling you to testify. If you violate such an order you face confinement for contempt. Is that clear?"

"Let me talk to my lawyer."

The court waited while the witness conferred with Max Epstein. He was back on the stand in minutes.

"Mr. Baxter, you met with Mr. Kerrigan and myself last night, did you not?"

"Yes."

"You told us both that you wanted to do the right thing, to come here and testify. Is that right?"

"I said I'd testify. So all right. I'm here."

"Mr. Baxter, on the morning of June seventeen, nineteen hundred sixty-six, at about two-thirty A.M., were you at the rear of a supply plant called Apex Supply?"

Mr. Epstein, do you *have* to go through all this detail?"

Epstein turned to the judge. "Your honor, I think the witness is nervous."

"I'm not nervous," Baxter corrected him, "I just didn't see what I said I saw, that's all."

"That doesn't mean anything to us," Judge Turner informed the witness. "What did you say you saw that you didn't see?"

"I didn't see anything. I wasn't even on that corner. That's it."

"Do you remember going *toward* the Melody Bar and Grill?" he asked the witness.

"No. I was never going toward there. I was never going toward there my whole stupid life."

"Did you identify Ruby Calhoun as being at that scene?"

"I did."

"Was that true?"

"No. That was false. I lied."

"Why did you lie?"

"I was facing charges. Numerous counts. Four different counties."

"Did anyone ever tell you that, in return for your testimony, you would be helped in respect to those charges?"

"More or less, yes. By the county prosecutor's office."

"An office, a room, tells us nothing," Judge Turner pointed out. "Do you have information as to *who* told you that?"

"It isn't a question of that, your honor."

"What is it a question of?" Judge Turner persisted. "Can you answer my question or can't you answer it?"

"No one ever really threatened or pressured me. I knew myself what I was facing. Nobody told me."

"So it wasn't anybody in the police department or in the prosecutor's office who said to you, 'Look, we want you to say there was a white car and that one of the people in it was Ruby Calhoun?' Did anybody tell you to say that?"

"No."

"Then you lied of your own accord and not through the suggestion of somebody else?"

"I was told that the prosecutors in each county would be advised of my testimony and would probably help my sentencing."

"Who told you that?"

"Lieutenant De Vivani."

"Did you feel," Epstein resumed, "that you were going to be helped by testifying?"

"I wasn't helped as much as I ought to have been. They were questioning me, showing me photographs and telling me this and that but all I had in mind was just one thing—to get out of there. I didn't care about anything except that I was fearful of just one thing: all the time I was facing."

"The first day you were in custody," Judge Turner reminded the witness, "you took off and they caught you on the police range. Is that right?"

"Correct."

"Ten days later you escaped once again and you were gone

two days before an officer rearrested you and returned you to headquarters?''

''I wasn't confronted by just one officer.''

''You mean that a couple of them grabbed you as you were coming out the back door with Esteban Escortez?''

''Correct again.''

''When you were in Bordentown, how many officers came to see you?''

''Two.''

''Did you discuss the Melody Bar and Grill murders with them?''

''That's what they came there for. To feel me out.''

''And when, in reply to your question, 'Who was the person in front of you?' and your answer was, 'I wasn't sure,' you are now telling us that that was made up?''

''Right. Iello came running back up to me and handed me money. And all he kept saying was, 'Get out of here, get out of here. Take this stuff and get out of here.' He wasn't acting right.''

''Were the officers around you discussing the murders?'' Epstein asked the witness.

''Mr. Epstein,'' Baxter complained, ''you are asking me questions I have no way of answering. All I remember is how they went over my statement. I saw a way out of the mess I was in. I bought my way out. Then I came home one night and Kerrigan was waiting for me with Don Kessler.''

''Who is Don Kessler?''

''Someone I knew from jail.''

''Is he a friend of Calhoun's?''

''He was locked with Calhoun.''

''Was he locked with you?''

''Correct. And what I told Kessler was that I had no doubt but that Calhoun had been framed by the Jersey City police.''

''Thus the trial judge must himself consider where the truth probably lies,'' the State Supreme Court of New Jersey decided in *State vs. Baldwin,* ''and if the trial court is satisfied that the present testimony of the recanting witness is unbelievable, the application must be denied.''

Judge Turner's opinion, on the motion for a new trial, was

based upon the above precedent. In assessing the credibility of both recanting witnesses he felt that a cloak of suspicion was upon them because it took them seven years after the trial to confess their alleged perjury.

"Baxter claimed he had created the details of his own testimony," Judge Turner decided. "He did not attribute his alleged perjury to pressure from anyone. He repudiated his previous testimony about hearing shots and observing a white car. That had been a figment of his imagination, he told the court. He had said that he had withheld information out of fear of involving himself in the break-in at the Apex Supply plant and also out of fear of retribution from friends of Calhoun.

"There is also evidence of a revenge motive, on Iello's part, toward Lieutenant De Vivani. In both witnesses there exists an overwhelming fear of bodily harm from followers of Calhoun.

"Finally it is appropriate to discern motives in witnesses; but this pair are so devious, and so immoral, this court cannot analyze their mental gyrations or their actions.

"The jury, not the court, determines the witness's credibility. The jury decided that the defendant committed a triple homicide. In absence of such recanting evidence as would indicate a miscarriage of justice, such a verdict must stand.

"There remains no support for the contention that the state knowingly permitted a witness to perjure himself. This court therefore accepts Baxter's answer, that no promises or guarantees have been made to him.

"I believe in the jury system. The jury said Calhoun was guilty. It is not my privilege to alter that finding.

"I am therefore compelled to refuse a second trial to Ruby Calhoun."

"Any man can make a mistake," Nick Iello commented upon Judge Turner's denial of a new trial to Ruby Calhoun, "but only a man who totally wants to become part of society will take the stand and admit he has made a mistake and will correct it openly. I put myself into jeopardy with the authorities by testifying against the prosecution. But this is a small thing when one considers how much Ruby Calhoun has taken in his years of confinement. Judge Turner doesn't understand that in nineteen hundred sixty-six and nineteen hundred sixty-seven I was a sick, confused alcoholic. He assumes I was lying now, but it was then that I was lying. This time I did tell the truth."

"You tell the truth, they don't believe you," Dexter Baxter complained, "when you lie they suck up every word. I should have known something like this would happen. The judge is *so* wrong. Why should I go up there to admit I lied? No one gave me fifty thousand dollars to do a thing like that. I had nothing to gain. The judge disregarded how convenient it had been, how I'd been allowed to overhear what the detectives had in mind, so I could get the story they wanted to hear together without they're having to tell me directly."

"Two statements from known criminals," Iello added, "become two very small voices. They believed me in nineteen hundred sixty-seven because what I said then fitted into what the prosecutor wanted said. I'm willing to testify again, right now, for Calhoun."

Iello, at this time, was serving a nineteen-month sentence in the Bergen County jail for burglary.

IV

Moonigan

DOVIE-JEAN HAD STARED unbelievingly at the price list of the Carousel when Red first showed it to her:

BEER . . .	$3.75
SMALL SPLIT BOTTLE . . .	$30.00
COCKTAIL . . .	$10.00

"Strictly legit," Red assured her, pointing to the official sanction of these outrageous prices:

> These prices are registered and approved by the State of New York Department of Consumer Affairs.

"That's some department," Dovie-Jean observed. "Who they suppose to be protecting, anyhow? I'd like to see one of *them* get trapped thirty bucks for half a glass of Virginia Dare. Wouldn't he purely *howl?*"

"He'd be making a big mistake if he did," Red nodded toward a massive youth, wearing steel-studded leather wrist bands, sitting down the bar: Moonigan. Emil Moonigan. Moon Moonigan. Moon-the-Bear Moonigan. "The Bear'd *eat* him," Red assured Dovie-Jean.

All Dovie-Jean had to do was to strip and jiggle about at the far end of the bar. She jiggled for twenty minutes, to juke-box recordings, then put on a leotard and invited the bar-mooks, one by one, to buy her a drink. With a 25 percent cut on drinks, she earned more at the Carousel than at Playmates of Paris.

She was working the Carousel on the week she was off at the Playmates of Paris. Red had gotten her the job, but she did not give him a nod of recognition when she came in. Tourist traps are cautious about hiring a couple: sooner or later they'll conspire to defraud the joint. Moonigan was unaware of any relationship between his redheaded bartender and the new black go-go girl. In fact, he was not even aware that Red wasn't a white man.

Now, in the forenoon hush before the other girls had arrived for the day, Moonigan motioned Red toward him and began speaking low and confidentially. Dovie-Jean, sitting with her back turned to him, could still distinguish his words.

"They should throw every rotten slut-whore in this town into jail and throw away every key," Moonigan assured Red. She wondered, Is he kidding?

Red, washing glassware, went on washing it; neither agreeing nor denying Moonigan's Draconian measures.

"I say," Moonigan insisted as though he felt he wasn't being understood, "I say lock up all these filthy pigs and give the city back to the *clean* people. How are you going to protect virtuous women, like my wife, like my little girl, with a hundred and six of these sluts in every block? Throw them in the clink—throw them *all* in the clink. Don't let them out until they're willing to work for a living."

"Live and let live, Moon," Red ventured to suggest.

" 'Live and let live'—Is *that* what you're saying?" Moonigan was fired by Red's casual remark. "Live and let live? Let me ask you, would you let a person with a contagious disease walk around in contact with normal people? Of course not. Yet you let these alley animals hang on every corner and God knows how many diseases *they* got. What do *they* care? 'I'm going to infect every man I can' is what your alley animal is thinking."

"What kind of disease is it *you've* caught, mister?" Dovie-Jean asked herself.

Every midtown tourist trap employs one Bear. He's so big that barflies, trapped between paying an extortionate price and fighting him, almost invariably choose to pay.

Yet the Bear is not a fighting man. If he were he'd be working out in a gym instead of a bar. Because, when you're six feet tall and weigh two hundred pounds before you're thirteen, you don't get into fights. Your size suffices. Lacking, thereafter, an ability to earn a living by other means, Bear's size becomes his livelihood: his proportions become his trade. He can't fight, he can't wrestle, he can't make the police force. He's too big for the army yet not big enough to travel with a circus. He becomes the bar-room conquerer who has never fought a battle.

Moonigan had been engaged in only one battle and that had been because the Carousel had only one john.

The joint hired a big gooney broad who looked like she'd screw on the head of a pin to waggle her gooney-looking ass about atop the bar. That she was stone deaf appeared to be only a slight handicap. When one of the bar mooks propositioned her—"How much, honey?"—she'd answer, "Milford Junction, Ohio." Later, when he asked where she came from she'd tell him, "Ten dollars for the room and twenty for me." She had the right answers but put them in the wrong places.

This was not due entirely to deafness. She was usually so high, on this or on that, that she wouldn't have understood even with good hearing. "I'm an Alanol Cat," she explained when asked why she walked tilting forward. "I have to take care not to break all them eggs." She'd forget she'd already taken one Alanol and would take two or three more still thinking it was the first of her Alanol Day.

Milltown. Thorazin. Serpasil. Atanax. It was all one to the Alanol Cat.

Two well-set-up customers walked in one evening and ordered a beer apiece. One was a young dude, the other one in middle age. She gave them no greeting and they gave her none. They merely sat at the bar and sipped beer.

It wasn't until the Alanol Cat went to the john that it happened.

There was only one john and it had no lock.

The girls had to hold it from the inside. One of the mooks, a small, bespectacled man, having failed to notice the Alanol Cat go into the john, went to it. He pulled at the knob but the door didn't open.

"*Yank it!*" Moonigan, out of some perverse sense of humor, instructed him. He yanked it and out flew the Alanol Cat with her pants down.

Everybody laughed except the Alanol Cat and the two sullen men at the bar. They merely continued drinking their beers.

A few minutes later the younger one approached Moonigan.

"Air you the fella who said, 'Yank it'?"

"I am," Moonigan acknowledged.

The other customer came up and stood behind Moonigan.

"In that case," the younger man assured Moonigan, "no hard feelings," and clipped Moonigan right on the button with a solid right hand. Moonigan reeled and, as he turned away, caught another solid punch, this one a left, from the older fellow. Down went Moonigan.

"Get on your clothes, Mary Lou," the younger one then told the Alanol Cat. This time she understood immediately.

She left, walking between the pair of them, without stopping to ask for pay for her night's work. Moonigan sat and watched them leave.

He looked pleased to see them go.

"Bisexuals!"

The Uriah Yipkind show was coming on at the far end of the bar. Uriah himself explained that he was about to present a TV show which, for simple daring, had never been surpassed.

The bar mooks looked dully at the screen.

"Children should not be permitted to view this program!" Uriah warned all parents.

Actually the children, say fourteen-year-old David and his sister—call her Judy—had their own TV on upstairs but weren't sharply interested.

"I've seen it before," David explained. "Do you want to see it?"

"What is it about?"

"About people who fuck both ways."

"So what's new? Let's look at 'The Gong Show.' "

Their parents, down in the front room, were caught by Uriah's assurances.

"Tonight," Uriah assured them, "we are going to present two young women who have had sex with both sexes, and a man who has also had sex with both sexes!"

Well what do you know.

The camera shifted to a serious-looking young woman in her twenties, who might be a student of anthropology or of dietetics.

"Who did you first get interested in, Jo-Anne," Uriah asked her, "men or women?"

"I fell in love with my teacher in the sixth grade," Jo-Anne recalled. "She was my music teacher. Then I fell in love with a cleaning girl. Then I fell in love with my roommate at college. When I was eighteen I had my first date with a man and I fell in love with him. Then I fell in love with his boyfriend. Then I fell in love with the boyfriend's older brother and we got married and I have a lovely little girl now, only we aren't married anymore, because he fell in love with the first man I was in love with, so it all worked out beautifully."

"Time for a commercial," Uriah announced, looking bewildered.

"Now," he said cheerfully when he returned to the air, "we have Jack Woodburn of Santa Barbara, California. Tell us how you got started as a bisexual, Jack."

"I started chasing men when I was twelve. I scared the bejesus out of them. I was sixteen before I met one who let me make a connection. After that it was men, men, men. Then I met a bisexual woman and we hit it off so well we got married. Yes, we're still married and have two sons. Yes, my wife has women lovers, and now and then I have a little affair on the side with a man. I believe my life has been greatly enriched by my ability to love someone of any sex. Don't *you?*"

Moonigan switched the program off onto "The Gong Show."

Nobody in the bar protested.

"I once had a broad," Moonigan began reminiscing after the incident of the Alanol Cat, "who was so perfect I was hard put to find a reason to belt her. She kept herself so clean, and the apartment so spick-and-span, she cooked so good and kept bringing me a thousand a week between washing the dishes and feeding the cat. What did I have to belt her about?

"You can't let things go on like *that*. Before you know it you will have lost your leadership and she'll take off with some dude who needs no reason for belting her. *Wham!* He just knocks her on her can. If she asks him what was *that* for—*wham!* he cracks her for asking. Then, while she's holding a knife blade to her swelling eye she realizes that what she got is a real solid stamped-on-every-link pimp, a jewel among pimps, and a swollen eye is a small thing to pay for a possession like *that*."

"You'll have to use more hot water if you want to get the feathers off that bird," Red answered enigmatically.

Moonigan stared at him, trying to figure out Red's remark. Its meaning evaded him, yet revolved slowly in his head.

"Of course," Moonigan answered at last, "I *go* with whores. Of course. Love is one thing and sex is another. Right? Does that mean I don't love my wife? I just bought her a Corvette. If *that* isn't love, you tell me what love is. She knows I love her because I refuse to act toward her like an animal. She's as pure as my mother was. My mother was so pure she never permitted talk of sex in the house and our house is run just the same."

"How'd you ever get born, for God's sake?" Dovie-Jean asked Moonigan in her mind.

"Why should I act like an animal toward my wife when I don't want her to act like an animal toward me?" Moonigan wanted to know. "Husband and wife aren't suppose to be animals. It's why I go with a whore once a week. Then I can return to my wife and treat her with respect and no unclean thoughts."

Red had never seen Moonigan's wife but he'd once answered the phone, when Moonigan was momentarily out of the bar, and talked a minute or two with Mrs. M. She'd put on a tone of such sultriness, the moment she realized she was talking to a man other than her husband, that Red had been as shocked as if a strange woman had thrust her tongue into his mouth.

"I was sixteen when I had my first girl," Moonigan assured Red. "She was like an animal and that's *all* she was—a damned animal, a damned goat, a sow in heat, a damned alley cat for God's sake, a monkey in a tree. That filthy little slut let me do *anything!* Oh, she was a dirty little thing, the things she encouraged me to do! No shame, no shame at all. The moment we're alone she zips open my fly and down come her pants! They should have pitched her into jail and let her rot."

"How old was she?" Red inquired.

"Fourteen goin' on fifteen! Old enough to know better!"

"Just young and foolish," Red suggested.

"Just *foolish* you say? I suppose it's just foolish, too, when they say, 'I give a damn if I give this clown syphilis if I can get twenty bucks off him.' Oh yeah, sure, just *foolish*. You think a whore considers the risk I'm taking? Does she stop for as long as one moment to think she may give me an infection I may take home to my wife? Don't give me that 'just young and foolish' bit. She knows exactly what she's doing and she don't give a damn."

"Everybody's struggling to get by, Moon."

"Look," Moonigan ignored Red's observation, "I'm not a doctor. I have no way of knowing, when I go with one of them, whether she's sick or well. You call that *fair?* What am I supposed to do? Drag her to a clinic for God's sake? Have her inspected? I say a whore who makes me a carrier of some dirty disease, and I infect my wife, ought to be kept off the streets. It's a fact, and a fact *is* a fact. I'm only talking sense, Red."

Dovie-Jean caught his face in the bar mirror: he wore his hair blond and long and carried a jade earring in his left ear. He had a big brown walrus mustache and a heavy jaw. When he caught her eye he gave her such a wide white smile she thought he must be showing off his dentures. He's been kidding all along, she thought. He's been putting us all on.

"Every whore in this town should be made to wear a red tag saying: *Prostitute: Dangerous to your health.*"

He'd withdrawn the wide white smile. Now he looked at her sternly and spoke enough for her to hear him clearly, "Black or white, they ought to be treated like animals, every one."

Moonigan had no suspicion that the bartender and the black go-go girl were living together. Tourist traps, such as the Carousel, don't hire couples knowingly, whether married or common law. Such couples inevitably conspire to defraud the house.

He had been taught two things: to *loom* and how to make ominous-sounding noises like: "You ordered the lady a drink, didn't you? Okay, now *pay.*"

Dovie-Jean always felt uneasy when Moonigan was at hand.

She always felt relieved when her week at the Carousel was done. The presence of Big Benjamin, at Playmates of Paris, gave her the feeling she was being protected. But this big blond's conversation made her feel threatened.

"One thing you have to say for a cat," she once heard Red telling him, "that you can't say for a dog. You can't poison a cat."

"Try dissolving five cigarette papers in a saucer of milk," Moonigan answered immediately.

"How about a dog?"

"Two yellow jackets in a hamburger."

Big Benjamin was as illiterate in Yiddish as he was in English. This Delancey Street alley fighter, this ghetto lumberjack in the faded plaid shirt, this matzohfied Marciano with a broken nose, this pimpified kingfish who knew nothing of the Talmud and less than that about women, was nothing more, in fact, than a muscular schlemiel who went up and down stairs a dozen times a day fetching Cokes, coffee and hamburgers to the house's whores.

He could gulp a superburger in a single gulp, then look up like a masterless mastiff for more. Yet he never bit a hand that fed him or even barked when kicked about by one of the women.

Janitor, runner, bouncer, between his chores he stayed out of sight in a shadowed and curtained corner, occasionally peering around the curtain's corner to see that everything was all right.

He was also the local handyman. When one of the ceiling bulbs burned out, Dovie-Jean kept a trick waiting so she could watch Big Benjamin fix it. Up the ladder the women saw him mount step by heavy step. Everything the King did was step by heavy step. As though he had to think out every step beforehand. "I want to see this," she explained to her trick.

There was nothing, really, to see except the man's deliberativeness. He unscrewed the old bulb slowly, dismounted the ladder with it, placed it carefully on a table and remounted with a new bulb in his hand. When he'd gotten the new one screwed in, and the light came on, he beamed down upon the parlor with a look of such pride in his achievement that the women gave him a brief burst of applause.

"Can we go now, honey?" Dovie-Jean's white trick pleaded.

"Just one minute, dear, he isn't quite through."

She wanted to see the King come down. Step by heavy step. Then saw him pause, at the ladder's foot, take off his cap and make a low bow of acknowledgement.

"Do it again!" Spanish Nan asked, but the girl in the front office spoke into the audio system. "That's enough fooling around, King. Back to work, girls."

The voice was no more than that of one of the whores, but she was the receptionist for the day and felt herself to be a lady executive.

"What team is that cap from, King?" Tracy asked him.

The cap had been faded, by many Manhattan rains, to a pinkish white. Its peak bore the letter C in red.

"Cincinnati Reds," he decided, "I used to play for them." Why embarrass the clown by asking what position he had played? If he knew first base from left field, that would come as a surprise.

Benjamin's forebears had reached the Lower East Side in the 1880s and their descendants were still on Delancey Street. Of that whole sad clan, in a hundred years, Benjamin was the only one who'd made it as far uptown as Forty-eighth. He'd never made it to Fifty-ninth.

He slept on an army cot in the rear of the joint beside a broom closet where he kept the bucket and mop he used to clean the parlor, before the women began arriving at ten A.M. The girl at the front desk handed him seventy-five dollars every Saturday morning and he never asked who was paying him.

The girl at the desk could not have told him. The house was owned by two uptown lawyers who never came near the place and who discussed it, between themselves, as "our Forty-eighth Street property."

Benjamin was not curious. Being provided with food and shelter satisfied him. He was being paid well, he felt, for his single skill.

For make no mistake: Benjamin really was skilled. No other bouncer in all Manhattan could rush a complaining trick onto the street faster than King Benjamin.

He seldom had need for violence. Most of the tricks came up the stairs half-intimidated by the time they pressed the buzzer. Some of them, once in a room with a naked girl, lost their nerve and left. Most were polite and respectful. All Benjamin had to do was to watch for the springblade and the .22.

"Does that big Jew really dig what goes on here?" Dovie-Jean wondered aloud.

Yes, oh yes, Fortune filled her in. "I caught him staring at my tits once. I stared right back until he looked the other way. If it weren't for having to pay, I think he'd like to come on."

The women were skilled as nurses as well as whores. When a whore gave a trick a short-arm inspection (while he held the basin in awkward docility) she was less casual than a doctor or nurse might be, because her own health was at stake.

Sometimes it wasn't an easy matter to find out what a trick wanted because he was either too ashamed to ask or else did not know how to express some curious urge. The women would have to help him then.

Most of the women rejected men who wanted to sodomize them. Spanish Nan claimed to prefer it.

"I think your milk been poisoned, honey," Dovie-Jean told her.

"What I *don't* like," Spanish Nan complained, "is the trick who wants to suck my toes. I put up with it all the same." Then added thoughtfully, "Afternoon is the time for weirdos."

"What do you want me to do with *this?*" Big Benjamin asked, holding the oxford the stud had left.

"I'll take it," Fortune offered. "I'll have it bronzed. It'll bring good luck."

V

Athens

60
45
49
13.5
9
32

179.7

"THE LID IS about to blow," a fellow-officer phoned warning to Captain Carlos Connery at Connery's home that morning. Connery left his watch and wallet behind when he went to work.

"Back off from any attempt to provoke you," he instructed his officers at roll-call. "If a man calls you a pig, you take it. We don't have the force to handle a confrontation."

Connery assigned Officer Gavin DeJohn to handle D Company. DeJohn, a young relief officer without experience in handling a company, opened the lockbox of the cell-locking system but left lever twenty-two up. He'd been ordered to keep that cell's occupant deadlocked.

"Why is Calhoun being keeplocked?" one black prisoner demanded to know of DeJohn.

"I only follow orders," DeJohn replied.

"Hell then," the man decided, "lock me up too," and walked off down the corridor to his own cell. Several Muslims followed him back to theirs.

As the rest of DeJohn's company passed the lockbox, one prisoner reached in and pulled down twenty-two without being observed by DeJohn. A few moments later Calhoun came up and joined the group quietly and sat down to breakfast with them.

"There's a man supposed to be in keeplock having breakfast down here," Officer Urquhardt phoned Connery in the administration building. "What do we do?"

"Finish breakfast," Connery instructed him, "then get them into their cells. Don't let them into the Square. I'll be right over. I know what it's about."

Connery had no idea of what it was about. A rumor had spread, cell to cell, that one of the keeplocked men had been taken out during the night and beaten so badly that he was now in the hospital in critical condition. Coming out of the mess hall, the men spotted an officer holding a gas gun. This confirmed the rumor to them. That the rumor happened to be false made no difference whatsoever.

Connery considered the incident to be only one more schoolroom prank of Calhoun's. He possessed perfect confidence in his own ability to get the men back into their cells without upsetting the whole cellblock. As he was walking a voice behind him said, "You no-good mother," and he felt himself struck on the side of his head.

Urquhardt turned just in time to see Connery fall. He rushed up and caught a hard smash to his jaw, knocking him cold on the cold stone floor.

When Urquhardt came to, he was lying on the ground in a corner of the Square. He sat up and saw DeJohn sitting up on one side of him and Connery, bleeding from his head, on the other.

"I'm glad I left my wallet home," Connery told Urquhardt.

The administration had always depended upon the Big Gate to guarantee its security. This was the gate, leading to the administration building, which was locked by a three-point bolt system. It was only necessary, in order to contain rioting men, to lock it. It was so stoutly made that it was not conceivable that it would give way.

It gave way all the same. "When those fifty men hit that gate," one guard reported, "it didn't slow them down for a minute. The gate bounded in against its hinges." One of its big bolts had been welded and the weld painted over so often that it was no longer detectable. When Calhoun's company began hitting it, the gate swung back upon itself.

Eight correction officers were surrounded in the Square the minute the Big Gate gave way. Nobody, least of all the rebels, grasped what now began happening. A riot had begun upon momentum accumulating for months, and swept everyone before it.

Every security measure the P.B.A. had taken now turned against them. Their impregnable gate left the officers outside while lending protection to the rebels within. The officers' keys, hidden in the arsenal in the administration building, left officers trapped in offices, toilets, broom closets and storage rooms.

The super began getting calls from all over the prison as the rebellion spread. The super phoned the state police and the commissioner. The steam whistle in the power house began sounding a general alarm. But since this whistle was also used to announce individual escapes, the townspeople did not assume that this time it meant not escape but riot.

A shout greeted the officers being marched across the Square: "Kill the pigs!"

A protective ring of Black Muslims surrounded the officers almost magically. The shout died down and was not repeated.

Gary Stein, a convict clerk, twenty-two years old, was sweeping the corridor with used coffee grounds, to keep down dust, past a cell in which officers Dowdy, Harridan, Halstead and Durso had barricaded themselves. They had nightsticks but no guns.

"Maybe they'll just forget you're here," Stein told them hopefully. "Just stay quiet."

Stein had served two years for check forging, had been released and was now back for some violation of parole. He had six weeks yet to serve.

"Get ready," he warned the officers, "here they come," and stood to one side, holding his can of coffee grounds and his broom.

"If you come out you won't be hurt," one of the prisoners advised the officers.

"If I were you I'd take their word," Gary Stein put in. He was a well-meaning boy who had never learned to keep his mouth shut.

Halstead handed Stein his wallet. The four men were then blindfolded and led off to the Square. Halstead got his wallet back three days later but not from Gary Stein.

"Do you want to leave with us or do you want us to hide you?" the men working under Officer John Sheeley, in the tailor shop, asked him. Sheeley chose to be hidden. They locked him into a storeroom on the shop's second floor before the rebels reached the first floor.

"There's an officer locked upstairs," one of the workers informed the rioters.

"He'll have to figure how to get out by himself," was the answer. Then they set fire to the building.

The Muslims had now set up a large tent in the center of the Square to house and protect their hostages. Hostages had been given prison clothes and their uniforms hung neatly in one corner.

"It made us feel hopeful," one survivor later recalled, "to see our own clothes ready to be put on again. It made us feel they were ready to deal fairly with us, and they were."

There were now eleven hostages. The Square was getting crowded.

Block Nine is off the Joint's nerve center and houses prisoners also off-center. Some cannot cope physically; some cannot cope mentally. Others have been on Cloud Nine for years. They are old broken plates long overdue for the ashcan.

A dozen of them were in their dayroom getting a touch of September sun. Some were playing cards with beat-up decks. Others sat dreaming of times long gone that seemed, always, to have been golden times.

What the rioters thought a psych ward might yield them they never asked. They broke down the door into a long white corridor, housing nothing but these old time-servers: some on crutches and some in wheelchairs. When Bixby, the officer in charge, was stripped to his underwear, some of them began whooping in mindless joy. Others began groaning in despair. Bixby was forced to lead this straggling mob of wildly happy, deeply despairing, whooping, groaning old men, on crutches and in chairs, into the Square.

"The dingdongs!" They were greeted by cries of welcome as if they were a winning baseball club returning to its hometown after a winning road trip. "Welcome, dingdongs!"

The rebels began pushing ice cream lily cups into the old cripples' hands, then lit cigarettes for them and stuffed their pockets with chewing gum and candy. The old broken cons sat lapping pink, vanilla and chocolate ice cream. Somebody stuffed a pill into one of the ice cream cups, and, in no time at all, the dingdongs were all lapping up pills of every color. Some of them went on the nod and others tried to get out of their wheelchairs. One of them kept shouting, "Bananas! Bananas!" but nobody knew why. A holiday spirit began pervading the Square.

Every color, shape and size of pill could now be had for the asking—or the grabbing—under the basketball backboard, most of them unidentifiable. Stimulated by a pill he could never name, one dingdong shook his crutch challengingly at a gun-tower guard, clenched his emaciated fist and shouted, "Come on down here and get us, pigs!"

A young prisoner, tall, dark and bespectacled, mounted a bench in the center of the Square with a bullhorn to admonish everyone in the Square:

"Men! This is not a holiday! Not a picnic! No time for pills! We are challenging the administration! There are no blacks, no whites or Puerto Ricans anymore! This is not a race riot! Do you want to be treated like men? Then *act* like men!"

This was Elvie Barker, serving eight years for a hundred-dollar stickup. After years of battling each other on the streets and in prisons, Barker was now asking Black Muslims, Black Panthers, Young Lords and whites to put aside their differences.

The whites may have been willing but they were wary. Seven of them hung together in a tent on the handball court. They kept to themselves and were left alone for the first hours of the riot.

Then one of them heisted a white flag on the tent. Five black security guards walked over and ordered all seven prisoners over to the big new tent, housing the hostages, that the Black Muslims had just constructed. Elvie Barker charged all seven with treason, and they were shoved into a corner of the tent, opposite the corner where the hostages were held, to await trial on Barker's charge.

Half a dozen groups, five or six men in each, no one group all black or all white, began bringing in more officers and stripping them to their underwear. They also brought in half a dozen more prisoners, three blacks and three whites, and put them in the corner with the seven whites already taken. One of the new "traitors" was Gary Stein.

Teeney Sweeney, a big white man in for life for first-degree manslaughter, who had managed the prison infirmary for two decades, set up an infirmary in the Square: a medical aid station equipped with drugs and bandages. Through the four days of the riot, assisted by four prisoners, he treated both hostages and prisoners. Although Sweeney had never performed a suture in his life before, he made them successfully now.

Rumors, rising out of the old contempt of the officers for the prisoners, claimed that hostages were being abused sexually.

Townspeople accepted these rumors. All were false.

Two hundred state troopers had arrived under Major Marcus Hanrahan. Two hundred were not enough, Hanrahan decided, to retake the prison. He would wait, he announced, for three hundred more before attempting an assault.

Long-haired demonstrators heightened tension by materializing across the street from the prison, bearing signs sympathetic to the rebels:

FREEDOM TO OPPRESSED PEOPLES!
WE SHALL OVERCOME!

When a bus from Spanish Harlem wheeled up, local people felt they were being invaded from abroad.

One of those who came off the bus was a tall black man wearing flowing white African robes. He hitchhiked to the prison and identified himself there as Kenyatta Islam. In the tumult of events Pat Wilson had no chance to check his credentials; he accepted the man at face value.

The youthful civil rights lawyer, who had already gained a national reputation defending radicals, Max Epstein, and a black mayor, a black judge and a white journalist, as well as Kenyatta Islam, were the first members of Pat Wilson's negotiating group.

"You're undermining yourself, Mr. Wilson," the super assured the commissioner. "The only way a prison can sustain itself is through exercising absolute authority. Once you start negotiating over hostages, whether you get them back unharmed or not, you've lost. Lost heavily. Because you have given the green light to every prison in the country to take hostages."

Wilson had been trying for prison reform for years. He disregarded the super's counsel. He now perceived an opportunity not only to implement old hopes, but to avoid bloodshed as well.

"There's a first time for everything," he advised the super.

This was the first time TV cameras and press photographers had been permitted inside a prison to witness negotiations. An audio system enabled every man in the Square to hear what was transpiring in the hostage tent.

"Had it not been for the cameras around us," Calhoun observed later, "negotiations would have taken a different turn. Our people weren't used to all that publicity; they began role playing. We lost sight of what was real and what was not real. Amnesty and flight to a third world was a soft-headed dream that looked beautiful on color TV. It had nothing to do with reality. Getting more than a slave wage in the metal shop would have been more real. Getting in touch with lawyers without censorship would have been real. Getting machinery into the metal shop, or typewriters into the typing school, would have been more real. Conjugal visits were real. Seeing visitors without a screen or glass between was real. Demanding to be treated like men, instead of dogs, that was the realest of all. Amnesty was no real way at all."

"We have come to the conclusion that if we cannot live as people," one rebel assured them from the table set up in the center of the Square, "we will then die like men."

From being faceless numbers, whose voices were unheard and whose agony was unheeded, these men had leaped overnight into the nation's spotlight. Helpless all their lives, they now held their society helpless. They felt a confidence they had never felt before: one out of all proportion to their true capability.

The cameras created an illusion, in their view, that the outside world was passionately sympathetic to them. They felt a rising tide of international love for them, of pity for their pitiable lives, and encouragement of all their hopes.

Which simply did not exist.

"We've got Connery here," the rebels' bullhorn let the super know, "Do you want him?"

"We want them all."

"Remains to be seen. Do you want Connery or don't you want Connery?"

"Why Connery?"

"He keeps passing out. We can't do anything for him."

"We want them all."

"Do you want Connery or don't you want Connery?"

Two black security guards assisted the officer to the administration gate. He collapsed there into the arms of correction officers.

When Carlos Connery collapsed, the bitterness of his fellow officers, particularly over the Supreme Court decision limiting their control over men in their charge, deepened. It was *their* friends who were now being held, *their* colleagues. Therefore it was their right to free them.

They were only country boys feeling they'd been wronged, and were entitled to right that wrong themselves. Some had brought old hunting rifles to do the job.

Which was the very reason, of course, that the governor was holding them back. What he wanted was not reprisals, but order out of chaos.

The rebels now controlled the Square, the metal shop, the auditorium, school and commissaries. The establishment held the hospital, the powerhouse and the kitchens.

Small groups of uncaptured officers began attempting to regain parts of the prison without orders. They drove a forklift truck up to the tailor shop, pried open the bars of a second-floor window, and got John Sheeley out ahead of the flames.

Down a corridor they encountered a stout young Puerto Rican chewing a candy bar and toting a bucket full of candy bars still to be chewed. He'd finished one bucket, he admitted, and was on his way back to his cell to finish this second bucket. He gave up the uneaten candy reluctantly and was led to the administration building.

Len Reedy, a civilian supervisor of some thirty men in the coal gang, was standing beside the powerhouse, talking to an officer on the wall, when another officer opened a gate to let a garbage truck through. Three prisoners leaped off the truck and assaulted Reedy. Reedy, a big man, did not go down. The officer in the gun tower gave warning: "Stop or I shoot!" The prisoners fled. The powerhouse remained in the administration's hands.

"We're not dealing here from strength," Calhoun advised other leaders under the hostage tent, with Wilson's group facing them. "What strength we have can last only until the administration decides to use force . . ."

"Brothers!" Calhoun was interrupted by Kenyatta Islam, standing a full head over most of the men present and a head and a half over Calhoun. "No amnesty! No transportation! We are going to stay and die here! The world revolution is at hand! It is beginning here!"

Calhoun looked at Wilson. Wilson looked at Epstein. Epstein looked at Calhoun.

"The masses are on their way!" Kenyatta went on. "They shall overcome! Overcome state police! Overcome the national guards!"

"What about the air force?" somebody inquired quietly.

"I am an authorized representative of the Intergalactic Mission," Kenyatta finally disclosed his credentials. "I have a message for the Planet Earth. We are beginning to enter the period of Aquarius. Many corrections have to be made by Earth people. All your weapons of evil must be destroyed. You have only a short time to learn to live together in peace. You must live in peace"—here he paused to gain everybody's attention—"you must live in peace or leave the galaxy!"

It appeared high time for the representative to leave the galaxy himself. A couple of security guards muscled him out, still raving, to the administration building. Correction officers there found him to be unarmed.

"What we have to demand," Calhoun picked up his interrupted counsel, "is protection against reprisals. We have to demand an injunction restraining the correction officers when these negotiations have ended."

A federal injunction might be obtained, it was then suggested, from the same judge who had handed down the decision limiting the administration's powers of censorship.

"She doesn't have jurisdiction over the prison," Wilson advised the prisoners, "but a federal injunction isn't necessary anyhow. A state injunction will serve the same purpose."

"A state injunction will *not* serve the same purpose," Elvie Barker assured Wilson. "It has to be federal."

"Then I'll get you a goddamned federal injunction," Wilson promised.

He left that afternoon, by plane, caught a federal judge vacationing in New England, and was back at Athens the following morning with the signed injunction in hand. He handed it to the Prisoners' Council with a sense of triumph.

Several prisoners read it yet said nothing. When it got to Barker he tossed it back at Wilson.

"This is worthless," Barker told him.

"Why?"

"It doesn't have a seal."

"It doesn't *have* to have a seal."

"Mister, you're not dealing with the Mohawks here," Barker told Wilson.

"All right," Wilson gave in once again, "I'll get you a goddamned seal."

He dispatched the injunction, by police car and by plane, back to the federal judge. He got it back the following morning, with a seal. Once again he handed it to the Prisoners' Council.

"We're not talking about reprisals today," Barker informed Wilson. "Today we're talking about amnesty. Complete amnesty. And flight to a third world nation of our own choosing."

"Aren't you going to read the signed and sealed federal injunction you've been demanding for days?" Wilson asked.

Barker picked it up. Then, conscious of the TV cameras upon him, tore it in two and flung away the pieces, seal and all.

"I've given everything, I've gotten nothing," Wilson grieved. "I can give you no more assurances."

The man was confronted by a dozen prisoners adamant on amnesty; behind him were three hundred correction officers of whom many did not even understand the word.

Some of the officers had fashioned slingshots and were slinging at prisoners from crannies in the administration building.

"All we could do," Wilson tried later to explain, "was to try to keep buying time in hope of getting personal support from the governor. Even the hostages' wives asked the governor to come down. Just to talk to us. He didn't have to go into the Square. They would have known he was here and that alone would have made them listen closer. One of the wives suggested that the prisoners be asked if they would release one hostage every morning at nine A.M. in return for one hour of negotiation. I thought it was a good idea myself.

"When we told the governor that his presence would gain us time, he asked, 'Whom do you want to buy time from? Are you worried that the prisoners are going to move and kill the hostages? Or are you worried that the state is going to move?' I told him I was more afraid of the move the state might make than I was about what the prisoners might do."

Max Epstein, acting now for the prisoners, quoted examples of criminal amnesty already granted: the Canadian government had flown twenty-six people to Cuba in return for a British economic advisor from Montreal in 1970. The British had released a suspected Arab terrorist in return for the safety of passengers aboard a BOAC plane down in the desert. Brazil had released a hundred political prisoners for the life of a Swiss ambassador.

"That's dishonest," Wilson rejected Epstein's argument. "Either it's amnesty or it isn't amnesty."

The hostages wanted amnesty granted. "If they would have granted them transportation," one hostage reflected, "and transportation to a nonimperialist country, each one of us hostages would have paid for one airline ticket for anybody who wanted to leave. Amnesty was a small price to pay for our lives."

"We must give them clemency," another hostage sent a note to Wilson, "clemency from criminal prosecution. Anything else than that is as good as dropping dead. It's cut and dry. That's all there is to it."

Then it was too late. Connery was dead. And everyone, inside the Square or not, realized that everyone inside the Square could now be charged with murder. A fresh desperation began pervading the plea for amnesty.

The seven white men held in one corner of the hostage tent to await charges of treason, were given a choice between digging a large trench in the Square or of being executed. They chose to dig a trench.

Calhoun was escorting Wilson across the Square where the seven whites were digging, when someone called, "Hold him! Hold him for hostage!"

Calhoun stopped in the middle of the Square, picked up a bullhorn and answered the shouts:

"Brothers!" he advised the crowd, "we have given our word that Mr. Wilson will be returned safely to the administration building. That is where he is being taken now and that is where he is going to go."

Black Muslims, including Calhoun, got Wilson to the gate and into the hands of correction officers.

He wouldn't be coming back; everyone knew that. The only question now remaining was whether the men assembling outside could, once inside, be controlled. They made up a small army: 587 state troopers; 250 sheriff's deputies; a contingent of park policemen and—unofficially—over 300 correction officers determined, despite the governor's specific order, to take part in the assault.

This little army also had two helicopters and its troops were equipped with rifles with telescopic sights, sidearms and twelve-gauge shotguns loaded with 00 pellets, ordinarily employed for hunting big game at distances exceeding thirty yards. Their commander had forbidden them to engage in hand-to-hand combat. When they apprehended danger they were to fire.

The men inside had baseball bats, iron pipes and homemade knives. They thought that, as traditional in warfare, the side possessing overwhelming force would offer terms of surrender. That is only what they thought.

They didn't expect troops to come in firing. They were already on the verge of surrender. They'd been sleeping for four nights on the ground in a season of rain and mists. Their food supply was dwindling. They were tired, tense, disappointed and afraid. They'd begun talking, among themselves, of resisting their own leaders.

A small group of men, between a dozen and twenty, were running the whole show. Their security guards were their officers and the mob in the Square were peasants: they had no voice in anything. In the name of democracy they had set up a despotism more tyrannical, by far, than the administration's tyranny.

Many of the men in the Square were doing time only for violation of parole. They wouldn't have wanted to fly out of the country even if given such a chance. They had had no say in the negotiations.

At 9:44 A.M. Major Hanrahan gave the order to switch off the prison's electricity. Then a yellow helicopter rose above the Square.

Some prisoners conjectured that it must be the governor, arriving at last to settle everything. Others said, No, the plane had come to offer transportation, to those who desired it, to a third world country of their choice. It didn't occur to anyone, apparently, that the helicopter's message was simpler, much simpler, than that. Its message was that the hostages had now become expendable.

When troopers appeared on the walls, eight hostages were blindfolded and made to kneel on the catwalk below the wall, plainly visible. A Muslim security guard stood behind each hostage with a knife at the hostage's throat.

"Why me?" one hostage asked.

"Because you're white," he was told.

A black liberation flag was unfurled above the heads of the hostages.

"Hold your fire," Hanrahan instructed his troopers, "until you see an overt act by the executioners." Then, to the rebels, he added, "Release the hostages. The Citizens' Committee will meet with you."

"Negative," the reply came back without hesitation. "Negative."

"Do not harm the hostages," Pat Wilson made a final desperate plea. "Surrender peacefully. You will not be harmed."

Then a yellow gas began descending from the helicopter and the correction officers opened fire. Troopers, not knowing where the firing was coming from, fired back blindly. The park policemen then joined in, just as blindly, into the gas-filled square.

"Put your hands on top of your heads," Hanrahan hollered into the drifting mist in which men were milling about, falling, crawling and stumbling. "Sit or lie down."

"The gunfire was necessary," one state inspector said later, recalling an occasion when he'd been involved in civil disturbances among blacks in Newark. "There were no fatalities in Newark and this was because we were dealing with people, not criminals. Here we were up against something else, a situation entirely unparalleled in the history of the United States. These were less than people and could not therefore be treated with the slightest leniency."

The inspector knew history as little as he knew people. In 1929, and again in 1964, state police had been called upon to quell prison riots.

To the accusation of the prisoners, that they were treated like dogs, the inspector gave full justification: twenty-nine prisoners and ten hostages shot dead.

No one inside the walls had committed a crime so heinous.

A crime perpetrated needlessly, mindlessly: the prison could have been retaken without loss of a single life.

"Most of the people in there deserved to be in there," one correction officer explained. "Some of them were three-time losers. They were hard criminals. That is what aroused our emotions so much. We felt we had a job to do and we did it. The confrontation was forced upon us by inmates already confined for heinous crimes against society."

For the most heinous crime, that of demanding that men be broken to dogs, committed by society against the criminal, no mention was made.

Yet, there had been a job to do. And, yes, they had done it.

For what reason thirty-eight men, criminals and civilians alike, had to be murdered to achieve this, no explanation was brought forth. The same job could have been accomplished without a single killing.

The confrontation was the state's. Because men are everywhere going to resist at being treated as less than men.

The uprising had not been a race riot until the correction officers made it into one.

"If a prisoner took his hands off his head," one survivor reported, "the officers circling him would swing from the floor. When he fell he'd get hit for minutes. One guard would step up and slug him, then step back and give another a clean shot. One officer hit another by mistake—a glancing blow. The officer who got hit yelled, 'This is for his hitting me, you black sonofabitch!' and gave the man a resounding blow."

"You want your amnesty?" one correction officer kept asking. "Here's your damned amnesty!"

"We've taken your guff," another officer warned the prisoners, "now you're going to take ours!"

Six minutes of gunfire left the men in the Square stumbling among their collapsed tents in a yellow mist. After they had been ordered to lie down on the grass, one officer told a prisoner to take off his watch. "He pushed my head down with his foot," the prisoner said. "I handed the watch up to him. He tossed it onto the ground and stomped on it. 'You aren't going to need to tell time anymore,' he told me."

When a thousand men were lying face down in the mud, the officers went about strip-searching them and identifying them, here and there, as "executioner," "security guard," or "negotiator." Men so suspected were chalk-marked with an X across their backs. The correction officers acted as if they felt they could not feel themselves to be men again until they had made every man on the ground feel he was less than a man.

A big black man was forced to lie, stripped, across a recreation table, with a football beneath his chin. "If the football falls," he was assured, "you're dead." An officer then explained to a national guardsman, "He castrated a hostage. Some of our men were disembowelled and abused sexually."

The guardsman phoned the administration building for help. "Watch your people," he told the super, "they're talking and acting bonkers."

None of the hostages had been abused sexually, disembowelled or castrated. They had been fed and guarded. And one officer repaid his treatment in kind. "This guy took care of me," he indicated a black prisoner, "take care of him. He's all right."

When several young doctors arrived to volunteer their services they found a dozen young blacks and Puerto Ricans stretched out in the hospital corridor. "Nothing but first aid for them," the doctors were instructed by a correction officer, "they're ring leaders." Other correction officers stood around but refused to lend doctors or nurses a hand.

Elvie Barker survived the shooting. He was found dead in his cell the following day with a gunshot wound in his head. Gary Stein's body was found two days later. He'd been beaten to death. Two of the men stretched out in the corridor died while awaiting treatment.

Prisoners could not be moved to a local hospital because the prison had no contract with that particular hospital. Next, use of ambulances was out of the question because insurance had not been taken out. Then it developed that no wounded man could be moved without the specific authorization of the super. And the super was nowhere to be found.

When he finally materialized, he decided that every prisoner transferred to a hospital would first have to be photographed and fingerprinted, although all of them had been fingerprinted and photographed when they'd arrived at the prison.

Every prisoner so released, the super added, would have to be accompanied by two correction officers. He was finally persuaded that one officer would suffice. Two more men died while the red tape unwound.

"The deaths of the hostages," one paper reported, "reflect a barbarism wholly alien to our civilized society. Prisoners slashed the throats of utterly helpless guards whom they held captive through round-the-clock negotiations, while making increasingly revolutionary demands. Others they stabbed and beat with iron pipes. 'I saw seven throats cut,' one trooper assures us. 'Those cons didn't wait a second, they just slit throats. We were hit by gasoline bombs, makeshift spears, rocks and iron bars. It's a marvel more of us weren't seriously injured."

Other papers followed this lead. It was only following the autopsies, and then only after the original false story had been implanted, that reluctant admission was made at last: all ten of the hostages had lost their lives by gunfire. None had had his throat slit. None had been castrated or abused sexually.

Nothing was reported about the beatings, administered by groups of correction officers, five or six in a group, upon blacks and Puerto Ricans held naked in their cells.

No reference was made to Governor Nelson's demonstration of physical and moral cowardice.

"One little lie," Calhoun assured Kerrigan, "covers the whole world by the time the truth can get its boots on."

"They came down on me at twelve midnight," Calhoun told Barney Kerrigan at Green Meadow, a couple months after the collapse of the riot at Athens. "Must have been fifty men in helmets, with shotguns and movie cameras. In the event I balked for a moment they could show how they had been forced to gun me down in order to keep me from raping their wives. 'We had to fire in self-defense,' would have been the story—'he's a murderer.'

"People will believe anything that supports their prejudices—particularly where there are promotions to be had.

"There are no people more brutal, nor more cowardly, than those who control our prisons. Army people are disciplined: they have learned to control their fear. Not these P.B.A. creeps. The P.B.A. people panic at every rumor. We learned that from the correction officers at Athens.

"We lost at Athens," he added, "but we learned something. We learned about bringing in the outside world. There's no way of bucking an administration from inside. So long as they have barbed wire and censorship they'll do whatever they want with you. Which is simply to crush you as a human being.

"I remain a threat because I remain uncrushed. I never acknowledge guilt. I dress in my own clothes here according to my own taste. I do no work. That would be an act of repentance and I have nothing to repent.

"We've had visits here from doctors, lawyers, editors and clergymen; sometimes singly, sometimes in groups. Twenty-two of us lifers—we call ourselves 'The Lifers' Club'—met for lunch here with a citizens' group. Of course we couldn't talk too much because of the guards. It worked all the same. We weren't out to complain or to proselytize them. All we wanted them to realize was that we are men like other men. Not, after all, monsters. We wanted them to catch some faint notion of what it's like to be locked in a cage for life. They caught it.

"Myself, I'm a man walking a fence at high noon. I cast shadows on both sides. The administration thinks I'm a black nationalist because I'm on the Prisoners' Council. Not so. I'm not a nationalist. No way. I'm a human being among other human beings, nothing more or less. The administration sent a psychoanalyst to see me. He needed help, poor fellow, but I couldn't do anything for him. I just walked away.

"It isn't fear of another riot that makes the administration here handle me with kid gloves. We accomplished more, at Athens, by appealing legally to the state than we did by threatening them with violence. They can always handle violence. What they can't handle is the appeal to reason. They fear it because the don't live by reason themselves. When it pops up they reach for a gun.

"What would you do if you were a correction officer, and you came to work and found the prisoners guarding themselves? Wouldn't that scare the living bejesus out of you? What would you do if you were a civilian supervisor and found that nobody needed supervision? What would you do if you were a warden and found a warden was no longer needed? Nothing is more dangerous than making the state feel useless. What if it became apparent that prisons themselves are unnecessary? What would happen to the contractors and politicians whose whole lives are invested in protecting society from criminals? What if it looked as if there were no real difference, no basic difference, between people inside the walls and people outside? God almighty, what a fright that would be, top to bottom. The P.B.A. would be running in circles. If you told them, cool it, you'll stay on the payroll two full years, that'll give you plenty of time to look around for another type of work, they wouldn't even hear you. Just trying to *reason* with this kind of man infuriates him.

"When you get an enlightened warden he is horrified at the waste and degradation of human beings held within walls. But he is never free to relieve conditions. He is always caught between the League of Frightened Men—the P.B.A.—and the antiestablishment people who want to bring the house down just to see it fall.

"Guys come in here with two-to-three-year sentences for breaking and entering, and when they walk out I *know* they're going to kill somebody.

"I have as many problems here with prisoners as with guards," Calhoun went on. "This place is dangerous from both sides of the fence. If I weaken I can get it from either side. I've reversed my hours, like sleeping during the day and staying up at night. Chiefly, I stay in shape."

"You still look to be in good shape," Kerrigan assured him.

Calhoun appeared not to have gained a pound since he'd fought Gardello.

"I can still whip any middleweight in the world," Calhoun assured Kerrigan.

Billy Boggs went off on a weekend toot, somehow found his way back to his army cot, pitched himself onto it and rolled over dead.

Jennifer found him lying face down, clutching a half-pint bottle of vodka. Funeral arrangements were made that night. Billy was buried two days later, with his daughter, Hardee Haloways and a couple of ex-cons at graveside. Jennifer shed a tear or two, not so much for the old man as they were for the way he'd wasted not only his own life, but the lives of those around him.

When they returned to the house they found a well-groomed black woman waiting for them in Jennifer's parlor.

Adeline Kelsey had come to offer her condolences. She only stayed half an hour. As she was leaving, she held out a check to Jennifer. "Take it, honey. I know you need it."

It was for twenty-five hundred dollars and more than covered funeral expenses.

Jennifer told Ruby, while visiting him, of the gift. Ruby grinned.

"That's my big honcho broad from Harlem. Watch out. She has plans for when I get out. Let her have them. They won't be *my* plans."

By September of 1975 the big honcho broad from Harlem had made *New Jersey vs. Calhoun* so controversial that the governor appointed a state assemblyman to investigate the case, and was shrewd enough to make him a black assemblyman. He also intimated that he was considering granting executive clemency to Calhoun.

Thousands of black votes went to the governor when he was elected to a new term in October. But the wide publicity for Calhoun, attending his re-election, aroused a white backlash. An ironic comment on the governor's contemplation of clemency for Calhoun appeared in the *New Jersey Legal Journal:*

Dear Editor:

Right-thinking lawyers and judges should be grateful to the governor for his recent action in requesting attorneys for Ruby Calhoun to file a petition for pardon with his office for review.

The burden of making decisions from the shoulders of the Appellate Division is herewith lifted. Defendants will now no longer have to waste time appealing convictions. The governor's innovation will also save countless hours in the criminal justice process. May we suggest the following procedure to applicants for pardon:

1. Attorney for defendant should file a nonspecific request for pardon. Proper grounds need be no more than the claim that defendant was denied fair trial.
2. Governor assigns any legislators who haven't anything else to do to report their findings. Transcripts, and judicial opinions not necessary; attitude of the public should, however, be sampled with specific interest in the opinions of sports personalities, such as prizefighters, wrestlers, football players, tennis and softball players.
3. If the public reaction is favorable, governor shall pardon; if unfavorable, he will deny. If public reaction is mixed, use may be made of the qualified pardon.
4. Governor's decision should be made publicly, in an amphitheatrical setting, using 'thumbs up' or 'thumbs down' signals.
5. This simple guide is the one that has recently been employed in State vs. Calhoun. The governor, following the new process in granting pardons, has avoided reading judicial opinions in State vs. Calhoun as such reading might prove counter-productive.
6. There is no danger that the public's respect for the judicial process will be modified. Because, should a pardon be granted, it will be interpreted by the public as a grave warning to all judges that they had better play ball or else. And, in event of a denial, it will be plainly seen that the judges are attempting to avenge themselves upon the governor. It is well known that no judge has ever yet admitted to having been mistaken.

VI

Supreme Court Hearing

THE PUBLIC CLAMOR for an executive pardon for Calhoun, supported by pleas from film stars, sports heroes and TV celebrities, was silenced by a decision of the Supreme Court of New Jersey to conduct a hearing on Calhoun's appeal for a new trial. The court met in the state capital in the first week of January, 1976.

"Eight years after his conviction," Defense Attorney Max Epstein advised the court, it "develops that Iello's statement was perjured. Notes proving that he perjured himself have shown up in the prosecutor's files.

"Neither Judge Turner nor Ben Raymond had any awareness that such notes existed. This left Raymond at sea without even knowing he was at sea. And it enabled the prosecution to argue that there was no substance to the defense's claim of pressure and promises to Iello and Baxter.

"Yet there *was* substance: the testimony of Esteban Escortez that Baxter had assured him, in jail, that he was going to play off the murders to gain leniency on charges of his own. His testimony was ruled hearsay by Judge Turner.

"Your honor," Epstein pleaded, "I am forced to suggest that there is a deliberate pattern here. I don't ask you to conclude that it was invidious. It could have been no more than sharp practice. But even though only one member of the prosecution's staff knew, the staff remains an entity."

"But," Judge McCormick asked, "did not the defense deliberately try to prevent exploration of the premises? Raymond objected so strenuously that he finally succeeded in blocking that line of interrogation."

"Mr. Raymond knew nothing of the heavy promises like, 'I'm going to every prosecutor, to every county detective to do the same thing I'm going to do for you here.' "

"Is it your contention, sir, that the lower court's decision—that the recantations lacked credibility—was not the correct standard to be employed?"

"The correct standard was *not* employed, your honor. The

judge first regarded the witnesses as people not of criminal minds, then, in their recantations, chose to regard them as men of criminal intellects. Although these are, admittedly, bad people in one sense, still you cannot regard them in such a truncated fashion. When the story which *should* have been told at the trial, but was withheld, due process went down the drain."

"Do you feel it is correct to say that failure of the prosecution to disclose evidence could be the basis for the granting of a new trial?"

"Correct. In asking this court to sustain it, in keeping evidence from the jury, the prosecution is substituting itself for the jury."

"The rule of the law in New Jersey," Judge McCormick recalled, "is that, when recanting testimony appears to be truthful, a new trial should be granted."

"I don't think," Epstein replied, "that probable truth is necessarily the correct standard. Promises had been made prior to the original testimony. We think the judge isolated issues from issues; that he dealt with the recantations as if it were one piece that could be separated from the suppressed material."

"One matter that has always troubled me," Judge McCormick inquired of Epstein, "is that the same judge who presided at the trial is now asked to surmise whether his trial was fair and just. I don't know that I have ever encountered a judge who might say, 'I was unfair at the first trial. If you give me a second chance I'll try to do better.' Do you have any observations upon the propriety of such a procedure?"

"The idea behind this rule, your honor," Epstein filled the judge in, "is judicial economy. How could we tie up another judge to learn the whole thing and then hear witnesses for the first time? There is confidence, in the judiciary, that the judge will be sufficiently impartial to say he had been wrong in the first place, if he had been wrong."

"Nothing in Judge Turner's opinion indicates the slightest impropriety," prosecutor Scott asserted for the state. "I find no misconduct, gross or small, on the part of the prosecutor's office. I have reviewed this case, your honor, and I must say I cannot help but wonder that allegations of conspiracy must be intended for some media other than this court."

"Would you have gotten to the jury without the identifications of Iello and Baxter, Mr. Scott?"

"Yes, your honor," the prosecutor replied promptly, "because of the identification of the car by Violet Vance. The testimony of Iello and Baxter was never more than material."

"But if their testimony is discarded, Mr. Scott, what is left to indicate that Calhoun committed the crime?"

"Your honor, Violet Vance described that car as it wheeled away, and a short time later that same car, with Calhoun in it, was found by officers."

"You would permit a conviction for first-degree murder to stand upon the facts you have just set forth, Mr. Scott?"

"Correct, your honor."

"There remains the question of whether a revelation of promises made to the witnesses would not have so impaired the credibility of both witnesses that it could easily have disbelieved both."

"I conceded that the testimony of Iello and Baxter were material."

"Do not the interests of justice therefore now require the setting aside of the original verdict?"

"If this were a close case, your honor, then possibly a retrial could be granted; but this is not a close case, your honor. How about the evidence they did not hear? They did not hear that Iello, the morning of the murders, said to Ken Kelley, 'It was Ruby Calhoun who shot up the bar.' And when Kelley asked him, 'How do you know?' Iello replied, 'I know because I saw him. He had a gun.' They didn't hear that, your honor."

"Then why should we?"

"And still out five hours . . ."

"Then why should we?"

"Given the question . . ."

"Given the question we are called upon to consider today, why in the name of God do you put *that* to us? Evidence that did not come out before the jury, was no part of their considerations and—I suggest to you—should now be no part of ours?"

"If there is any feeling in this court that there is some innocence here . . ."

"Then is not the place to meet it at a new trial?"

"When one survivor has already died? Is that fair to the state, your honor? You must be as fair to the state as to the defendant, your honor."

"As between the possibility of an innocent man standing convicted, and continuing to bear a lifelong stigma, and the possibility that guilty people may get away with something, which choice would you make, Mr. Scott?"

"The former, of course. And that is why I am arguing that this case does not indicate innocence and that this evidence does not tip the balance."

"You are evading the issue, sir. Is not the basic and overriding issue before us that of whether the jury could not have regarded the credibility of these two witnesses as subject to fair doubt had they heard it?"

"If there is a possibility of innocence, I think there is justification for opening up a nine-year-old case."

"How do you tell whether the suppressed evidence would not in fact have been vital to the issue of credibility?"

"No defendant, your honor, has a right to a perfect trial. Judge Turner concluded that there had been no perjured testimony and that the material which had allegedly been suppressed would not have altered the jury's decision."

"If the undisclosed testimony *had* been part of the original trial, Mr. Scott, would you not be willing to concede a possibility that this would have tipped the scale?"

"Your honor, if those items had become part of the record, the jury would have been in in less than five hours. Mr. Raymond failed to ask Baxter a single question about promises and not one question about leniency."

"But don't you think, counselor, that had Mr. Raymond known of De Vivani's promises, he would have confronted the lieutenant directly with them?"

"I don't think that knowledge would have had any effect upon the trial," Scott replied promptly.

"On the contrary, counselor, I think he would have landed on the lieutenant like a ton of bricks. Mr. Raymond could have inflated that two-bit promise into a sixty-four thousand dollar question. Do you mean to tell me that the jury is going to sit there and assume that that doesn't mean anything? If they admit making *those* promises, you can imagine how much more they probably *did* promise. I have no doubt whatsoever that that testimony would have strengthened Raymond's hand considerably."

"Judge Turner found Iello's statement, that he expected to do time, not perjurious," Scott replied, "because at that time he did expect to serve time and had no presently existing promise of nonprosecution."

"Promises, counselor," Judge McCormick assured Scott, "in order to constitute basis for a new trial, need not be exact, concrete, definite and unequivocal. In De Vivani's tape Iello was uncertain of his identification of Calhoun. What then is your comment upon the argument that, if defense had had that taped information, it could have been most effective in cross-examination of Iello?"

"They would have had to be very careful how they employed that taped conversation, because if you read the entire transcript it is so inflammatory and so nonexculpatory that any defense counsel worth his salt would stay away from it with a ten-foot pole."

"Should that not then be the choice of the defense to make?"

"In a perfect world, yes, your honor. But the U.S. Supreme Court rules do not hold that treading in a risky area entitles a defense to a new trial."

"Why in the world should not defense counsel been afforded opportunity to accept or reject the risk incumbent upon treading in this area?"

"We must not put unbearable burdens upon prosecutors."

"What is unbearable about giving the defense a tape? How does that become an unbearable burden?"

"It makes it unbearable in that it means when a prosecutor has missed, then there is going to be a reversal of the conviction. I concede that a prosecutor's primary duty is not to convict but to see justice done. But, after all, this is an adversary system and your adversary's points are not exactly in the forefront of your mind when in the middle of a murder trial. A reversal of this case will mean that, if a police officer gives a witness some assurance, and the prosecutor doesn't know about it, the case is going to be reversed. That is an unbearable burden upon a prosecutor."

"Are you implying that everything that was done here should not be binding upon the prosecutor's office? That a promise made is not binding upon the prosecutor?"

"The question is whether we're going to say that a prosecutor is responsible for everything a police officer might say in the course of an investigation."

Epstein had only been waiting for the strategic moment to bring forth the tape, which De Vivani had made of Iello's conversation before the first trial, and which Kerrigan had stolen from De Vivani's files. It was played to a courtroom which held itself breathlessly still for fear of missing a word:

DE VIVANI: Here he comes now. See if you can get this thing working. Hi, how you doing?

IELLO: Good morning.

DE VIVANI: Let me take the handcuffs off, Nick, and we'll get going.

DETECTIVE CONROY: Vince, just so you know, I've told Nick you want to hear it straight from the horse's mouth.

DE VIVANI: Who is your parole officer, Nick?

IELLO: Eugene Barker.

DE VIVANI: A white man?

IELLO: Colored.

DE VIVANI: Reason I ask this, Nick, is for your own welfare. I am interested only in the truth, Nick. Not the truth that makes me happy, but what really is the truth. You give me that and I guarantee I will do everything to protect you within my power, and have your parole transferred to another state.

IELLO: Isn't there some way I could get my parole dropped?

DE VIVANI: That I cannot promise. I'm taking this one step at a time. I asked you whether your parole officer was a colored man because I know you have fear of the colored people and their supposed movement where they are strictly for colored. Hear me now, I assure you I will go to the top people. I am not bullshitting. I'm trying to help Iello and I hope Iello is sincere with me. For example, if you were in that area because you were attempting a burglary, there would be nothing done on that. Even if I have to go before the grand jury for you. Because, look, this isn't a case of attempting burglary, it's a matter of triple murder: three people sitting in a bar minding their own business. Now I want the complete truth. You said Calhoun was the boy. You were evasive about the money in the register. That pulled us apart. I'm just trying to do my job to the best of my ability, Nick.

IELLO: Yeah.

DE VIVANI: Because I live by the good book. Now you've probably been living out this crime in your mind. Suppose you tell me, in your own words clearly and slowly, what your actions were on that Thursday night or early Friday morning. Who were you with when you first came into that area?

IELLO: Baxter and myself, we were gonna do a B and E on this plant. Dex says I'll go in and you stay on the corner and watch for police. After a while I walked across the street, there's a soda machine there. I was drinking soda and I seen a white car come this way. I thought it was a Pontiac or a Chevy, I didn't take a close look. So Baxter says to me, Who was that, so I says, just some fool nigger cruising around. I said that because the guy driving looked at me as he passed, just glanced. I seen a kind of brown hat, I think there might have been somebody in the back seat. I seen a dark figure there. Then I walked all the way down Garfield Boulevard.

Down there they got trucks and stuff. I was lookin' at a couple of pickup trucks they got there. They had a telephone number on them where you call if you want to get hold of the owner. I walked all the way back and talked to Dexter. What's the matter, I ask him. I can't get in, he tells me.

So I told him I only got four cigarettes left, I'm gonna walk down for a fresh pack. You want anything? He says, No, he don't want nothing, do what you want. I says I only got four left. He says, get yourself some more, stop bothering me for God's sake. So I walk down to the bar as much for the hell of it as anything. Then I heard like two shots. I stopped and lit a cigarette. I thought they were shots because I didn't think the Melody had any entertainment. Then I noticed a white car parked about three feet from the curb facing Jefferson.

DE VIVANI: You thought it was the same white car you had seen earlier?

IELLO: The same.

DE VIVANI: Were you later shown photographs of the driver?

IELLO: Let me finish. I thought it was Ruby Calhoun.

DE VIVANI: I now show you a photograph of Ruby Calhoun. The face appears light because of the photo.

IELLO: It's possible. I'm not completely sure.

DE VIVANI: Do you know the man when you see him? Had you seen him before?

IELLO: I know Ruby Calhoun. I knew it was him unless he got a twin brother. You see, when the police came back with him he was dressed the same way and everything. I knew it had to be him, the same man I'd seen coming around that corner. When I seen him first he was wearing a light jacket, sports type, salt-and-pepper pattern.

DE VIVANI: What corner?

IELLO: The tavern corner. He was coming out as I went in.

DE VIVANI: What did you do then?

IELLO: I went inside.

DE VIVANI: Now let me say this, Nick. You don't have to mention anything that happened inside that bar that might incriminate you. You can tell me everything else. Now you know I have a suspicion. I firmly believe that this man with the gun went there purely for the motive of revenge because there'd been a shooting, a few hours earlier, of a black man by a white, only a few blocks away. I firmly believe that this man with the gun did not go anywhere near the cash register. All he was thinking of was getting even. Don't tell me anything that might incriminate you.

IELLO: I don't intend to incriminate myself into anything. Are we going to go through that whole bar scene again?

DE VIVANI: We don't have to go into detail. I want to know exactly what happened when you went into the Melody Bar and Grill.

IELLO: Exactly?

DE VIVANI: Of course. No, not exactly. You can eliminate certain phases. Was it true you went to the woman on the floor?

IELLO: Yeah. She, uh, there was a man sitting at the bar, but I could see he was like, uh, he didn't know was he coming or going. Before I had a chance to say anything, he stood up and staggered off. Where the hell he staggered to I have no idea.

DE VIVANI: Did anyone else appear in the tavern?

IELLO: The girl. I said, "You better stay outside." She didn't stay outside. She walked into the bar an', uh, fuckin' screams. She went out.

DE VIVANI: Did you telephone the police?

IELLO: Yeah. I looked in my pockets for change. I didn't have one fuckin' dime. I had some quarters. I didn't have no dimes. I went behind the bar and I seen the money been thrown around and, uh, a guy was twisted up back there. I knew he was dead. So, uh, I went to the cash register. There was money layin' on the floor. So I, uh, took out a dime. That was all I took. Just a dime. Then I stand there lookin' at the rest of it, and I took a two-bit piece. Just a two-bit piece. Then I look again and this time I took a couple singles, and then a couple more singles, and then a ten-spot, and that was all I took.

DE VIVANI: If that's the truth, stay with it.

IELLO: That's the truth.

DE VIVANI: Isn't it possible that, in your hurry, you dropped money onto the floor?

IELLO: No, the money was already on the floor. I'll tell it like it was. When I came around the bar the register was open. Money was laying all over the floor. I knew that there was no robbery but I said to myself, Should I clean the fuckin' place out? On second thought I said, Fuck it, I'll take a little spendin' money is all, a little pin money. I put a few bills in my pocket then like I told you. I took it outside and said to Baxter, Here.

DE VIVANI: Where was Baxter?

IELLO: Still working on that goddamned door. He couldn't get it open. I told him, "Dex, there's been a shooting down at the bar. You better split because there's gonna be cops all over this place. I gotta stay because when I came down here a broad was in a window and seen me. If I take off they'll say I was involved." "Well," Dex tells me, "don't do *that*." "Look, man," I tell him, "get the fuck out of there. Just *go,* man, *go*. For your own sake—*go!*" "Well," he tells me, "I might as well wait around for you." "Don't wait for me, Dex. I'm *in* it. You are *not*. Save your hide, man—*go!* There's been a *shooting!*" All he says is, "Did you see the car?" I tell him again—"Are you going to go or not?" "Iello," he asks me, "who do you think was *in* that car?" "I think it was Ruby Calhoun was in that car?" I tell him. "Listen, man, why don't you just *go?*" "That's who I think it was, too," he tells me. I could not get him to *move*. Not one solitary inch. All he says is, "What is this?" And I tell him *again,* "Take the fuckin' money and *go!go!go!* Man, *go!*"

DE VIVANI: You never took an exact account of this money?

IELLO: I'm levellin' with you, it could not have been much. Then I figure if I call the police maybe they'll get there and save somebody's life. I called the operator and said, "Everybody is dead in here. I'm the only one alive. Give me the police." I don't think she believed me 'cause she asked me what street I was on. I'd been in that tavern before but I couldn't think what street, I was a little fucked up myself. I went out the front door and looked to see what street. There's a street sign on the corner but I didn't notice it. I went back inside and told the operator, How do I know what street, it's the Melody Bar and Grill and there's dead people all over the place—look it up. So she says all right, I'll look it up.

DE VIVANI: How was it that when the police brought Calhoun back, you did not identify him immediately?

IELLO: I was scared to do that. See, uh, I'm no fuckin' good and I been in a lot of jails, and everybody is out idolizin' Calhoun. If anything should happen, how I figured, I'd be provoked and harassed every time I walk down the fuckin' street.

DE VIVANI: Have you been harassed by anyone since that time or warned to keep your mouth shut?

IELLO: I told Officer Mooney about the day I got cut loose I went into the R and R Grill and there was a colored girl and a redheaded colored man setting there. I know a good many people momentarily, so I said "Hi!" and the girl said, "You were mixed up in that Melody Bar and Grill thing." So me like a fuckin' jerk I say, "Yeah." So the guy says, "You know who this is?" and he pointed to the girl. I says "No." "This is Ruby Calhoun's girl friend," he tells me. I figured right then it was time to split. I turned around and walked the fuck out.

DE VIVANI: Were you given warning not to talk to the police by either of these people?

IELLO: Not in so many words. But what I took it to mean, when I was told this was Calhoun's girl friend, was I'd better not mention Calhoun to the cops. Look, in my own mind I know you can't do a thing about that money from the register. No matter what happens, you're going to bring me to court whether I fuckin' lie or tell the truth. So why shouldn't this Calhoun pay for a fuckin' crime? This was me, I'd be hung long ago.

DE VIVANI: There are laws of men and laws of God, Nick. If Calhoun did this he not only violated the laws of man, he also violated the law of God which says, Thou Shalt Not Kill.

IELLO: I know that's right.

DE VIVANI: There's people innocently drinking beer and minding their own business . . .

(Tape cuts off here.)

"Was there any time," Epstein continued to question De Vivani, "when Baxter and Iello were together long enough to compare statements?"

"There was no contact beyond the men greeting each other. After Iello had made his statement I spoke to Baxter. 'I understand you want to give us a statement?' 'Lieutenant,' he answered me, 'do you know how long I'd last out in population if it ever got out I gave you a statement?'

" 'I'll tell you this much,' I told him then, 'first of all, we've already gone before a court in order to have you remanded here. Secondly, I guarantee you protection around the clock.' Then I went back in and we had coffee while he was reading the statement. Iello took longer than Baxter. He'd make changes and initial the statement to one side after he had read it. Then we brought Baxter back in."

"How did you first meet Baxter, lieutenant?"

"I was in the detective bureau, on another matter, when an officer told me, 'Baxter wants to talk too.' The following morning he escaped. He walked out of the visiting room, away from his sister, went down to the river and swam across it. We didn't pursue him. Just waited on the other side and brought him back soaking wet. Then he got mad at all of us and tells us we can all go to hell including his sister. What he's bringing in his sister for I have no idea. His big fear was of being locked with friends of Calhoun. I advised all county detectives to do whatever they could to protect him.

"All Iello had to do was to walk down to the corner mailbox and there would be charges. Then the receptionist would ring me and say, 'Your adopted son is here, lieutenant.' 'You would do well to lay off booze, Iello,' I tried telling him. 'Every time you drink you come on like a Comanche.' When I'd ask him what he wanted from me he'd give me an ultimatum: 'Either you get me out of this fix or I'm going to tell them New York newspaper bums what they're after me to tell them.'

"I tried to warn him not to tell me about taking money from the register but he blurts it out anyhow—'I took the money'—all the same."

"Did you threaten to get him a hundred years?"

"Certainly not. But when he was in the Hudson County jail I got a hurry-up call from him. When I asked him why he'd sent for me he said, 'Them bums threw ammonia on me.' 'Why don't you go to work, Iello?' was all I had to say to that. When I got back my phone was ringing: Iello's father. 'You've let my boy down,' he tells me. 'Now you have got to be putting me on,' I told the old man, 'I've done more for him than you have done as his father. Every time he would break up your furniture and you'd send for me to quiet him down. Mister, you have got to have one crazy hell of a nerve, tell me now how *I'm* letting him down. You must be as nutty as he is. Who did that little alley fink of yours ever know that *he* didn't let down? I can only tell you one thing, Mr. Iello. Kindly go fuck yourself.' Then I hung up."

• • •

"It is our hope," one of De Vivani's notes read, "that the Morris County sentence will be concurrent with the Union County sentence and that the same thing happens in your county."

Epstein then asked De Vivani, "Do you consider this some sort of promise?"

"I do."

"Did you ever tell prosecutor Scott you had made such a statement?"

"Never."

"Was Mr. Raymond furnished with a copy of Iello's testimony?"

"I do not believe so."

"You wanted to follow through on your promises to Iello and Baxter, did you not?"

"To the best of my ability."

"Baxter was extremely hesitant," Sergeant Mooney recalled of his interview with Baxter. "I then asked the guard to leave the room so that Baxter might speak more freely. He then told us that the man he had in mind was Ruby Calhoun. We assured him we would try to get him yanked out of the place as soon as we got back."

"Had the jury been apprised of the true facts," Epstein advised the court, "it might well have concluded that Baxter had fabricated testimony in order to curry favor from the state.

"Lieutenant De Vivani is a professional detective who knows," Epstein summed up the lieutenant's testimony, "that it is the tiny particulars that make a case and not the direct interrogations, and not the flat statements, and not the open no-yes answers. This is attributable to training and skill. De Vivani is . . ."

"All right," Judge Turner interrupted, "he's not trying for promotion here. He is an able man doing his job, that's all."

"*Able?*" Epstein countered bitterly. "I *know* he is able. I know *how* able. *Very* able. He is the clever guy who tricks the little guys who don't know the tricks. Calhoun didn't even know what the lieutenant was talking about, but the lieutenant knew. Calhoun was not told he could remain silent. He wasn't told that what he said might be used against him. He was not charged with anything but he was charged all the same. He was not given a single warning, not a single cautionary word, as he surely would have been had he been white."

"I don't blame Calhoun for wanting to be free," De Vivani interrupted Epstein, "but if I were responsible for any man spending a single night in a cell for a crime he had not committed, I could not live with myself."

"Lieutenant De Vivani," Scott immediately supported the lieutenant, "told Mr. Calhoun that he was questioning him in connection with the shooting at the Melody. Further, Lieutenant De Vivani advised Mr. Calhoun that he could answer his questions or not as he wished, and that whatever he said might be used against him in court. He was cut short by Calhoun when Calhoun told him, 'I don't need a lawyer, I use my fists, not guns.' "

"When the prosecution," Epstein explained, "rather than a jury, screens evidence, we know something has gone wrong; the sanctity of the jury verdict has been violated. The prosecutor is required to disclose any evidence which might prove helpful to the defense. Should this plea for disclosure be upheld, rights of defendants to inspect police records will be greatly enhanced."

Epstein then presented affidavits to the court, from a dozen businessmen, offering Calhoun employment.

Vincent De Vivani, a corrupted racist, arrogant, contemptuous and cunning, was the living epitome of what had gone wrong with justice in New Jersey.

That, at any rate, was the implication made daily by the New York City TV establishment. New Jersey justice no longer existed, was the story; and De Vivani was its most representative voice.

Celebrities of the films and the stage, each with a film or a play to plug, fighters and soccer players and everyone in the public eye who was dependent upon TV and radio, jostled one another for the chance to denounce De Vivani as a bigot.

De Vivani made no reply. Either he didn't read the papers, or look at TV. Was it possible he didn't *care?*

Not even when TV people, irritated by his refusal to sit stage center on a talk show (while being derided on both sides by famous people) employed a blow-up of him looking ominous, did he deny any charge.

Justice, it now became plain, could never miscarry in New York as it had in *New Jersey vs. Calhoun*. Not only were New York policemen more efficient than New Jersey cops, but they were more compassionate to the common man as well. New York judges and New York lawyers, it further developed, were—compared to those in New Jersey—compassionate and just. The glow of utter righteousness, which filters so lovingly through stained glass upon a pulpit, began to shine just as lovingly about the heads of New York TV talkers.

The TV talkers continued to exploit the public fear of a bad guy wearing an officer's badge. De Vivani began appearing ominous and threatening. The talkers left the impression that De Vivani and his goons might come through the Lincoln Tunnel any night.

New Yorkers have always looked down, from their million-windowed metropolis, upon those two-story houses across the river. They smile when they say "New Jersey" as though being told, "I'm off the farm." They speak of New Jerseyans as clam diggers. A New Jerseyan had always appeared clownish to the New Yorker, now he also looked like a hoodlum. The TV talkers put down the New Jersey police, the New Jersey courts and the New Jersey politicians day after day.

Neither the NAACP nor the Southern Christian Leadership Conference would touch *New Jersey vs. Calhoun* in the years when his support came from white law-and-order New Jerseyans, many of them in enforcement, some merely old-time fight fans. Now both organizations, sensing the political value of supporting Calhoun, came in swinging both fists.

The New York talkers never mentioned, even once, the name of the clam digger who had stuck by Calhoun from the beginning and had built up his case independent of any organization: Barney Kerrigan.

Bob Dylan, whose poverty of spirit could be sensed in the emptiness of his voice, slapped a few words together, called it a lyric and sang it to a packed house in Madison Square:

Jedge said you crazy nigger
Woo-woo
You done pulled the trigger
Woo-woo . . .

and when he entitled this wheezing whinny "Calhoun" a million liberals bought it before he could get to the bank. The Southern Christian Leadership Conference announced it would construct a tent city in Trenton which it would sustain until Ruby Calhoun was a free man.

The Supreme Court of New Jersey, by a vote of 7-0, threw Calhoun's first trial out of court.

This decision was based upon the rules of discovery: that the prosecution had had in its possession tape recordings which it had concealed.

This was the tape made, involuntarily, by Nick Iello, while being interrogated by Lieutenant De Vivani, and which had been brought to the light only by the vigilance of Barney Kerrigan. The tape revealed that an offer of immunity from prosecution had been offered the witness in return for his identification of Ruby Calhoun as the man with the gun.

Thousands of black youths milled about the streets outside the courtroom in Jersey City when Calhoun was released. Ruby Calhoun had become the symbol of the black man victimized by white society.

Black Muslims protected Calhoun from the crowd when he came out of the courtroom. He was escorted to a fleet of five Cadillacs chauffeured by Black Muslims. The heavyweight champion of the world served as one of Calhoun's guards.

VII

The Devil's Stocking

THE FIRST TASTE of freedom had a strong, sweet taste to Ruby Calhoun.

Judge Gregory Oritano had been Red Haloways's counsel in 1966, and it had been Oritano who had advised Red against taking a second polygraph test. But because of this association Oritano was now disqualified as judge of Calhoun's second trial. Then Epstein was advised that, unless Oritano were so appointed, there would be a delay of several months.

Epstein feared delay. The prosecution was already putting pressure on his witnesses, and Calhoun was not to be kept in hand. Epstein agreed to have Oritano preside so long as they could go to trial immediately.

"Take care, Ruby," Epstein tried warning Calhoun, but the warning went unheard. Every Friday afternoon Calhoun took off for New York City "to consult his lawyers," he assured Jennifer, and returned, the following Monday, looking as if he'd been playing poker with them and had lost midtown Manhattan, the Bronx and Queens.

Everyone in the world, it seemed to Calhoun, had been having a ball for ten years. Now that he wanted a ball for himself, for just a weekend or two, people began talking to him as though he were still locked. He'd fought too long for his freedom, Calhoun assured himself, not to use it now.

On Christmas Eve Ruby Calhoun walked down Fifth Avenue like a man who had never before seen Christmas.

Shish kebab stands were steaming on either side of the avenue. Their smoke kept rising between the faces of the December twilight. There were nearly as many horse-drawn carriages on the street as there were automobiles.

"Ho! Ho! Ho!" a Santa Clause shouted at him and he felt that the Santa meant that particular Ho! Ho! Ho! just for himself.

Later a cold Christmas rain began around the peep shows down Eighth Avenue, pelting the male burlesques and the bars.

It wasn't until he saw Adeline, sitting at the bar of the hotel cocktail lounge waiting for him, that he felt he was free at last. When he'd kissed her, and ordered a drink, she asked him, "Why so *stern?*"

She knew, all the same, that his deadpan expression concealed a feeling of deepest happiness. He had always gone at life deadpan, in the ring as well as out: the less you showed an opponent the less were his chances of getting to you. The more joyous you felt, the more careful you had to be to cover it, lest it be snatched away.

"Bad news," she filled him in, "our best witness has taken it on the lam. Rabbit Baxter has disappeared himself."

"Who needs him?" Calhoun asked. "It isn't up to me to prove my innocence. It's up to the state to prove my guilt. How are they going to do that now? They don't have a single witness. In fact I think they'll drop it now. It's going to cost the county two million bucks to retry me. The ball is in our court, honey."

"It's not that simple, Ruby. For one thing, the press will say an innocent man was framed. That opens the possibility of a lawsuit of a million dollars a year for every year the innocent man served."

"I don't want a nickel. Just my freedom, that's all."

"But if the prosecutor's office drops it, it's going to leave the Jersey City police hot as possible against the prosecutor's office."

"Tell 'em to get their best hold. We won't even miss that rabbity witness. We got Dovie-Jean Dawkins. Remember Dovie-Jean?"

"How do you figure she'll do on the stand, Ruby?"

Ruby reflected a long moment.

"She won't be ill at ease, I can tell you that much," he decided. "She's never ill at ease. Still, she's simple. No put-on. When she talks, the jury will *know* she isn't lying."

He talks, Adeline thought to herself, as if this little country whore had class.

"The jury," he added, "will *have* to believe her."

"I've never met her," Adeline reminded him; he looked to be lost in thought.

"Why don't we go upstairs and finish our conversation there?" he asked.

The legal light faded in Adeline's eyes and a slow-burning gleam, at once dark and golden, began shining forth.

Upstairs, he switched on the radio and she came to him, swaying to the rhythm of some band playing on the Jersey Shore. She parted her lips at his kiss and he stretched his tongue deep into her mouth. She closed her lips upon his tongue and drew upon it.

His big hands slid down until they clasped her buttocks; beneath the silk of her gown he felt her pressing them tightly together. He led her to a chair and handed her a glass of champagne; her hand trembled when she took it and a few drops spilled.

She had had many men in her teens. And had felt not the faintest passion for any of them. When she had gained control over her own life, she had diverted her sexual energies into a drive for power. She'd stopped drinking and had become celibate. She had had enough sex for a lifetime, she had felt.

For twenty years now, she had lived a harsh, austere and driving existence. Her needs, so long submerged, began to overwhelm her now like a wave which hits before it is seen.

"Just the dress," he instructed her, standing before her with a clothes hanger in his hand.

She raised her gown over her head and handed it to him. He hung it neatly but unsmiling onto a hanger and put it into the clothes closet. He was pleased that she wasn't wearing pantyhose. Brief black underpants, black bra and black hose pleased all his midnight penitentiary fantasies.

"Haven't you ever seen a woman before, champ? The way you look."

"Not till now," he answered seriously, still unsmiling. And finished his drink without taking his eyes off her. Then he put the glass down and lifted her onto his lap.

She had felt his strength before in a handshake. Now, with both his arms around her, they felt to her like the world's strongest arms. He found her mouth at the same moment that his fingers found the hook of her brassiere. In order to bring her breasts closer to her mouth, she stretched out.

He caressed her left breast firmly yet gently, his palm pressing its small hard nipple. She had never been pregnant and her breasts had remained those of a schoolgirl. Now she felt her nipple stiffening as his tongue began teasing it. She felt him close his lips over her breast and tug slowly upon it.

She raised herself, with eyes closed, high enough to let him get her underpants off. "*Hurry,*" she whispered hoarsely, "*hurry.*"

He would not hurry. He refilled his glass, drank, then stood looking down at her while undressing himself without haste. When she opened her eyes he was standing before her. He was already erect.

She raised his cock to her cheek and began breathing softly upon it, up and down. Although it began trembling, he himself still looked cool. She fitted her lips onto it, closed her eyes and began a slow, soft sucking. For twenty years she had not done this and she had never done it well. Now, for the first time, she enjoyed doing it and was doing it well. Looking down, he saw her eyes, beneath her lashes, were misting. Then she stopped, looking proud of herself. The cock was huge and throbbing.

There was only one satisfactory position in sex for Adeline, and now she maneuvered until she was astride him. She pressed her sex slowly down upon him, her hands upon her knees to lend leverage. His hands pressed her down on her hips.

One position she had always detested, and that was kneeling on all fours while a lover entered her cunt from behind and held her, about her waist, helplessly.

Only one trick had ever gotten away with this. The next one who'd tried it had lost. She'd reached between his legs and given his testicles a terrible twisting. He'd yelped and gone limp. No man had tried it since. Adeline Kelsey was not to be dominated.

Astride Calhoun, she felt a fiery pang when his breathing came harder and his eyes began looking empty. *Who was the athlete now?*

Then those big hands lifted her off him, thrust her onto all fours and entered her, the hands holding her firmly, from behind. He began taking long strokes, bringing her pleasure to the point of pain, then easing off instinctively: this was a joy so sharp she could not endure it and yet she endured it. "*Again!*" she demanded in a hoarse whisper. "*Again! Again!*"

Calhoun prolonged her orgasm with the same cool passion he sometimes worked in the ring, when he had an opponent weakening. He never hurried then and he didn't hurry now. She began beating the pillow with her fists and tossing her head wildly. At last he drew her up to him and released her. She fainted in his arms and rolled onto her back. When she opened her eyes she did not, for a moment, recognize him. Then she put a finger against her lips, recognizing him at last. When he smiled down at her, she smiled back.

"You *are* the champ," she assured him.

She put his head down upon her breast and he fell asleep, her nipple indenting his cheek, like a child.

A tide of love rose within her, like the love of a mother for her child, like the love of a woman for her lover, like the love of a woman for all humankind, in a wave she had never felt in her life before. She had not known herself capable of such warmth toward another human being.

Yet here was an outlaw who had been redeemed and brought back into the fold, and it was herself who had redeemed him and had brought him back. Here was a boy who had been deprived, by the white world, of any opportunity except what he could win by violence, and had then condemned him for that violence. Had it not been for Adeline Kelsey, he would still be in a cell serving life.

It hadn't been the NAACP who'd gotten him free. It had not been Martin Luther King Jr.'s people who'd sprung him. It had been Adeline Kelsey, and no other.

She stroked his arm lightly and said softly, "My baby. My baby."

Calhoun was deep in a troubled dream. He was in a ring with a billygoat wearing blood-red trunks. The goat charged, horns lowered and she heard him cry out without waking, "*Salazar!*"

When he wakened, hours later, the bed lamp was still burning and Adeline was snoring lightly beside him. It was after eleven P.M.

Something he was supposed to have done, someone he was supposed to have talked to—he got up, splashed cold water into his face and took a drink to steady his voice. Then he phoned Jennifer.

Her voice sounded distant and dry, yet he sensed a trembling under it. Her voice was neither cold nor welcoming, like the voice of someone known long ago now forgotten.

"I'm in New York, sweetheart." He tried to feign great warmth, "this is the first chance I've had to phone. We had to wheel right over here to sign for my release."

"I thought that was cleared up this morning in New Jersey."

"Oh yes, *that* was cleared up, but the lawyers had *details* to be attended to. You know how these great legal minds . . ."

There was a silence then, on both ends of the line. He was waiting to be believed. She was waiting to hear whether he had more childish lies to tell.

"Are you coming home, Ruby?" she asked at last.

"If I'm wanted there, yes. If not, no."

He was taking a stronger line now.

"Nobody is going to beg you."

And she hung up. He was left with the receiver in his hand, looking at his snoring mistress. Finally he crawled in beside her and took her.

Then slept upon her breast, dreamlessly.

He wakened to see Adeline in a kimono with a Chinese pattern in black and green, under last night's amber lamp. She came to the bed, sat on its edge and kissed him.

"How you feel, champ?"

"I was never the champ," he reminded her, smiling.

"You're the champ all the same," she assured him, "What do you want to do today?"

"I've never seen a horse race."

"First race is at twelve-thirty. It's eleven now. Get on your horse."

A hot gray sky hung low over Aqueduct. At the rail, she showed him the correlation between the numbers on his program and those on the toteboard.

In the clubhouse it was cool. She took his program and returned it with two fifties enclosed. He put twenty and twenty on something called King Hoss.

The horse broke out in front and held it until the final few yards, then tired and placed second. Six dollars even to place. He returned to their table triumphantly: he'd gotten sixty dollars back for his investment of forty!

They sat out a couple of maiden races, sipping Tom Collinses, until the fourth race. He put ten dollars, across the board, on Sir Norfolk. It won going away and he picked up eighty-one dollars for thirty. The next race he made the same bet on Teddy's Courage. Three horses came in bunched under the wire. Up goes Teddy's number and he came back to her showing a hundred and ten dollars for thirty.

They skipped a race and then, running a finger down the entries for the seventh, he stopped at Funny Peculiar. Adeline consulted the form.

"No way," she assured him, "the horse breaks out in front every race, then tires and winds up sixth, seventh or trailing the field. Last time he ran ninth in a field of ten after leading at the far turn. Early speed but tires is his story."

"This is the day Funny Peculiar forgets to stop," Calhoun decided stubbornly; and returned from the window with twenty to win and twenty to place on Funny Peculiar, off at 9–1.

The horse broke beautifully, three lengths in front of the field as they passed the stands for the first time. At the far turn he was still holding his lead by a length and a half but appeared to be tiring.

At the turn for home, just when it looked like he was about to be overtaken, he began making up ground like a cyclone and swept under the wire five full lengths in front of the field.

Calhoun returned from the window counting a handful of bills and handed Adeline the two fifties she'd put on him earlier. She pushed the bills back toward him, then saw the expression on his face and accepted them.

"There are fights at Madison Square tonight," he told her, "we're going to sit ringside."

• • •

Ringside at Madison Square was like old times. Calhoun shook hands with Joey Gardello, who'd put on thirty pounds and had a light-heavy going in the prelims. Roddy Nims had retained his weight and had built himself a reputation as a trainer. Sammy David Jr. came up smiling with hand extended, and Calhoun turned his back deliberately. He'd once written the man asking his support, and the letter had been returned unopened. Nobody had ever had to warn David about taking risks. He took none.

Gardello's light-heavy, a Jewish youth from the Bronx, kept taking rights and lefts directly into his face for three rounds as though Gardello had failed to inform him that it was not illegal to block a blow with your glove. Then somebody must have filled him in because he came out for the fourth swinging and caught his opponent, a Puerto Rican, with a paralyzing right. The Puerto Rican didn't go down but merely stood, arms dangling helplessly. The Jewish kid stepped back and observed him politely, giving him time to recover. Then, when he had recovered, he stepped in with a left hand to the jaw and the Puerto Rican boy went down on his face. He wasn't going to get up.

Across the street, having dinner at Shor's with half a dozen old-time friends, Adeline began feeling like she was an intruder: an intruder who was going to pick up the tab. Ruby became talkative and gay, among many old friends, accepting their congratulations and goodwill wishes on all sides. Everybody knew who *he* was. Nobody knew who *she* was.

And what *was* he, after all? An ex-prize fighter who'd done prison time, nothing more.

Nothing more than this: a man who, but for herself, would be in prison tonight. A man on whom she had spent a small fortune. The man for whom she had bullied newspaper editors and TV producers and radio commentators. The man for whom she had raised such a political clamor that the Supreme Court of New Jersey had been forced, by public pressure, to review his case. She had gotten him out of prison when the best lawyers had been unable to spring him. His innocence she had presumed. She could just as well, she thought now, have presumed guilt. She had never, until this moment, considered that he was the man most likely to have committed those murders.

Whether Ruby Calhoun had killed three people, or twenty-three, or thirty-three or a hundred and three, made no difference to Adeline Kelsey whatsoever. Had he been miles away from the scene of the murders at that time, made no difference at all.

The man was guilty. Guilty as hell. Guilty through and through. He had swung her, naked, onto all fours, held her immovable by one powerful arm around her waist, then held her head back to watch her emotion while she cried out, in an agony of pleasure, "Again! Again! Again!"

When, back in the hotel room, he stretched out, in his pajamas, ready for sleep, she kept his hand from switching off the lamp. He studied her without a trace of expression.

"Just in case you don't know me," she told him, "I'm a friend of yours. Name of Adeline Kelsey."

Not a flicker of recognition.

"We'll talk in the morning," she assured him, and switched off the lamp. In a matter of moments he was snoring.

She slept only fitfully. Every time she fell asleep, it was into a dream wherein she saw herself crouching, naked, on all fours, in some hall of a thousand mirrors. She would wake up, gasping, beside him. Once she switched on the lamp to see if he were faking that steady, rasping snore. No, it was real. She switched off the lamp.

When he woke, in the nine A.M. light, she was dressed and waiting.

He rose sleepily, mumbled something about something or somebody and went into the bathroom. She heard the shower running.

"I hope you slept well," she said when he came out, with a towel around his middle, looking refreshed.

"I did. I always do. How about you?"

"How *I* slept makes no difference. That isn't the point."

He kept on drying himself. "What *is* the point, baby?"

"The point is this. What do you intend to do?"

He glanced up. "Do about *what,* baby?"

What was so infuriating to her, about this man, was that she had absolutely no way of telling whether he were putting on an act or actually did not perceive anything to have gone wrong.

"About us."

"Ain't nothing to do about *us,* baby. We wanted it. Both of us wanted it. We had it. Both of us. Now it's over." He looked at her steadily: "Done. Finished. Kaput."

"You can't mean that."

He sat on the bed's edge, pulling on his pants. He appeared to be oblivious of her. Calhoun was just as good at shutting other people out as he was at shutting himself in.

"You going somewhere, Ruby?"

He finished buttoning his shirt before he replied.

"Of course I'm going somewhere. Home. To my wife and kid. Where else?"

"I took it for granted you weren't going back to them."

"You took an awful lot for granted then."

"The way you come on, I had a right to take a lot for granted."

He didn't answer that. He merely recalled, in his mind, the passion with which she had confronted him before he had thought of reaching for her. The faint smile of recollection, on his lips, was more infuriating to her than any open protest could have been. She bit her lip to quiet her growing anger.

"No more race track, Adeline," he told her quietly, "no more restaurants. No more cocktail lounges. Back to the old lady. Pick up where I left off ten years ago. That's it."

She shook her head slightly, but he didn't see that. He didn't notice her hand reaching for her handbag, nor did he see her open it. Nor did he see the ivory-handled springblade in it.

"It ain't your wife," she told him, keeping her voice steady. "That's a lie. It's that little country whore."

When he was fully dressed he turned to face her.

"You're an uptown up-tempo woman," he assured her, "I'm a downtown down-beat guy." He extended his hand and she came at him with the springblade.

He stepped inside it as he would step inside any wild-swinging blow and clipped her solidly on the point of her chin. The blade flew out of her hand and she sat down, sprawling ridiculously, eyes goggling in astonishment. He picked up the knife, pocketed it and closed the door behind him quietly.

On Forty-fifth Street a teenage girl caught his eye. She was standing under the traffic light, across the street, waiting to cross. He didn't smile back, but as she came toward him she spoke. He turned his head and asked, "What did you say?"

"I said, 'Jesus loves you,' " she told him.

"He decided to do that too late," Calhoun called after her, and walked on toward his Port Authority bus.

When Calhoun got off the bus in Jersey City he walked directly to Lowry's gym.

Lowry had fought, in the decade before Calhoun, as both a middle and a light-heavy. He'd been the kind of fighter who got his feelings hurt if you didn't bust his nose in the first round. It made him think you weren't taking him seriously.

He'd whipped the heavy punchers and lost to all the boys who could move, stick and jab. Now he'd put on forty pounds, yet moved lightly. He was a direct sort of man, open, friendly and without pretentions.

"Glad to see you on the street, Ruby," he congratulated Calhoun, "you did a hard stretch. You plan to stay out a while?"

"If the new trial goes my way I'm home free, doc," he told Lowry. "You doing yourself any good?"

"This new boy looks like a winner, Ruby," Lowry lowered his voice while indicating the big-shouldered youth skipping rope in a corner. "Whipped everybody in Dublin."

Irish Eddie Sykes was a nineteen-year-old middle weight with slender legs and that breadth of shoulder which indicated he'd soon be fighting light-heavies.

"We're not going to hurry this boy," Lowry assured Calhoun, "he ain't yet twenty. He ain't ready in his head. He don't feel yet he has to *hurt* an opponent. He'll learn."

Between the good gymnasium fighters and fighters who possessed street savagery, the gym fighters always lost.

"What I came up here to tell you, doc," Calhoun explained, "is I'd like to work with you."

"More than welcome as you know. But I can't promise you money right off, Ruby. You help bring along Irish Eddie, we'll talk money when he begins to make it."

Calhoun offered his hand.

"It's a deal," Lowry assured him.

Jennifer did not appear surprised to see him standing in her doorway.

"How you feeling, Ruby?" she asked without embracing him.

Once inside, she came to him. When their long embrace was done, there was nothing more to be said.

Ruby Calhoun had come home.

Every time Calhoun watched Irish Eddie Sykes work out, the boy looked better. He appeared, even in the brief weeks since Calhoun had first seen him, to have grown. He was going to be a full-size light-heavy.

"We're taking our time with Eddie," Doc Lowry assured Calhoun, "putting him on the first time, four rounds, in Paterson. Can you get down to watch him? He says you've taught him a lot."

"I'd like to bring my old lady along. Who you putting Eddie against?"

"Just an opponent. Maybe he'll pick up a trick or two against an older hand. That'll give him confidence. He needs confidence. Winning big, his first time out, that'll give him confidence."

Sitting ringside, between Jennifer and Lowry, with Irish Eddie already in the ring, Ruby saw the opponent coming down the aisle in a green silk robe. He was wearing a dark cap, for some reason, over his eyes, leaving only half his face showing. On either side two corner men, each half a head taller than the opponent, were keeping him straight on toward the ring. Ruby had the impression that, were it not for the two heavies, one black and one white, the opponent would be wavering on his way. Something about him struck Calhoun as vaguely familiar. A corner man gave his man a steadying hand as he climbed through the ropes. Then he took off his cap, and he was wearing hyperoptic lenses. For a moment Ruby got a flash of the man's eyeballs, behind the glasses.

Then he took them off and Ruby heard the snap of the glass case as he pocketed the glasses in his robe.

"I didn't know the man was *blind,* for God's sake," Doc Lowry said aloud to nobody in particular.

"Poor man," Jennifer whispered to Ruby, "he don't have a tooth left in his head. He's gone bald, too."

The man's skull wasn't shaven, that was true: it was bald as a billiard ball. Blind, bald and toothless—but who *was* he? Jennifer sounded as though she knew.

When the man came to the center of the ring Ruby perceived, just by the way he was standing, that he wasn't hearing the referee's instructions.

"I've seen this turkey before," Ruby stroked his chin, trying to recall this battered forty-year-old.

"Salazar," she told him.

"Oh, for God's sake, it really *is.*" Ruby realized that this was the same rough kid who'd cut him up so badly at Madison Square that the fight had had to be stopped. Well, he realized, sitting back, there's a man who's had a harder life than I've had.

It was particularly pitiful because, it was obvious, Salazar was going to take another beating tonight. Salazar's name, on his program, Ruby saw, was simply, "V. Jones." It was plain that Salazar had been barred by the Boxing Commission medics.

Lowry claimed to have no memory of a fighter named Salazar, though he had a good memory. Ruby's conjecture was that he'd known all along who Irish Eddie's opponent would be. It came to Ruby now that Lowry had been looking for an opponent who would test his young fighter for him; that that was what Lowry had meant when he'd spoken of his boy "picking up a few tricks."

Salazar, shoved out of his corner by a handler, raced across the ring and landed a corking left to Eddie's jaw, buried his chin in Eddie's shoulder, cracked a right and a left to Eddie's head, came up with the point of his skull into Eddie's face then held. Eddie was bleeding from a cut above his right eye and there was still two minutes to go in the round. They swung about the ring, holding each other. Eddie couldn't get loose and his right eye began flooding with blood.

Lowry got the bleeding stopped between rounds, but, a moment after the bell rang, Salazar opened it again with a butt. "What has he got in his gloves?" Eddie asked Lowry at the end of the round.

"You got him, Eddie!" someone hollered from ringside. "You're gettin' your blood all over him!"

"He can't even see you, Eddie," the corner man assured Eddie.

"How come then he's knockin' my brains out?" Eddie wanted to know.

"He's *listenin'*, Eddie, he's catchin' vibrations off your feet. Get up on your toes and he won't be able to find you."

Eddie came out for the third on his toes and, for a moment, Salazar was bemused, boggling his head about in search of the blurred shadow he'd been pursuing.

"To your left, José! To your left!" the corner man instructed the old fighter. "In the corner!" Salazar went directly to Eddie then but this time Eddie was ready. He got his glove firmly about Salazar's Adam's apple, which not only kept him from butting but stopped him from breathing as well. Salazar banged both gloves, wide open, against Eddie's ears but Eddie held the Adam's apple as if his life depended upon his grasp of it.

It began to appear as if it did. Between rounds Salazar didn't sit down, but just stood boggling his head, wondering where his opponent has gone.

"I hope he doesn't put his glasses on," Eddie told Lowry.

"If this is how you men want to fight, it's all right with me," the referee told Lowry's corner man.

For the remainder of the fight Eddie's defense was to dig his head under Salazar's armpit and whack away with both hands, blind, in hope of hitting something. Eddie Sykes kept his feet but he took a terrible beating. At the end of the fight the referee waved his hands above both fighters' heads: draw.

Calhoun thought Salazar had won. If what he'd won could be called a fight. He felt badly on the accounts of both fighters: for Salazar, for being still in there taking merciless beatings; for Sykes for having taken a beating which had done him no good whatsoever.

• • •

Had Vincent De Vivani looked up from his deck to see the President of the United States standing, his hand extended in greeting, he would have been hardly more astonished as he was to see Adeline Kelsey, furs and all, smiling sweetly down.

He shook her hand mechanically and motioned her into a chair.

"I'm Adeline Kelsey."

"I know. I know."

"How do you know?" Still smiling sweetly.

"The papers. Your photograph. I saw you several times at the trial." He was regaining control now. "How is your client?"

"I have no client, lieutenant. I'm not an attorney. I'm a bail-bond woman."

"I know. I know."

"So far as I know, Ruby Calhoun is alive and well and living in Jersey City, New Jersey."

De Vivani merely sat there, waiting. It wasn't up to him to ask the questions. She had come to see him. Let her explain herself.

"I came here to let you know you arrested the right man, lieutenant."

"If I was the cause of a man spending one night in jail," he assured her, "for a crime he had not committed, I would feel terrible."

"*I* thought he was innocent. I no longer think so."

De Vivani scented danger. She may have been sent by Nedwick. He waited.

"The man who did the shooting at the Melody Bar and Grill was Ruby Calhoun."

"The court will decide that, madam."

"They will decide it—but will they decide it right?"

"I believe in the jury system, madam. What the jury decides I will abide by."

Adeline had assumed that she could, by surprising him, throw a small scare into this big cop. She perceived now that she may have frightened him more than that. He was backing from her, trying to get away from every question.

"I want to talk to Nick Iello and Dexter Baxter, lieutenant."

"Madam, I cannot help you. For one thing, I have no idea

where either of these men may be. Secondly, if I did, it would not be ethical for me to lead you to them."

"Then the state's attorney will do."

"Will do what?" He was unable to follow her.

"I'll talk to the state's attorney."

She felt his deep sense of relief, at the chance she now offered him, of passing the buck higher up.

"This is De Vivani," he told the prosecutor's office, "have Mr. Scott phone me as soon as he returns."

"He'll be back within the hour," De Vivani told her.

"I'll wait."

He fumbled among his papers, unable to concentrate, while she waited. Every time he looked up, she smiled sweetly.

He didn't smile in return. When Scott phoned back he handed the phone to Adeline and heard her make an appointment for the following morning.

"Thank you, lieutenant," she thanked him when she had risen to leave, "you've been most helpful."

De Vivani sat back and closed his eyes for a full minute after she had left. He felt as if he'd been fanned by the wings of death. Then he grinned to himself. Old Hump Scott was going to have his hands full tomorrow morning.

Hump Scott never gave the lady time enough to make a handful.

He received her courteously, but in the manner of a man whose time is limited. When she said, "I've been badly mistaken about Ruby Calhoun," he showed so little indication of shock that it was almost as though that was what he'd expected her to say.

"He is a dangerous, *dangerous* man," she assured the state's attorney, somewhat taken aback at his indifference. "It is possible that he does not know, even now, that he murdered those people. Ruby Calhoun in subject to ungovernable rages."

"That will be a matter for the jury to decide, madam," he repeated De Vivani's advice.

"I believe that the recantations were gotten by fraud and threats of force. I want to talk to both witnesses."

Scott shook his head sorrowfully. "Madam, for one thing, Dexter Baxter has done a complete disappearing act. My conjecture is that he has left the state and will not reappear until after the trial. I have had no contact with this young man and I doubt the defense will be able to find him. Dexter Baxter has had considerable experience in disappearing himself. I can be of no use to you there at all, madam."

"And Iello?"

"Madam, you are in the wrong office to get information from a recanting witness. Iello is going to testify for Mr. Epstein. The man you want to see is Epstein."

"No, Mr. Scott, the man I want to see is yourself. Because Nick Iello is not going to testify for Mr. Epstein. He is going to testify for the state. He is going to recant his recantation."

"Madam," Scott asked, eyeing her more closely, "what put *that* idea into your head?"

"I know he has already been pressured by your people. I know he is a man who can be made to change his story back to his original one as easily as he was talked out of it by Mr. Kerrigan. All I want you to tell me is where Nick Iello is."

"Madam, I have not the faintest flash notion of where Mr. Iello is. And, if I did, it would not be ethical for me to advise you of his present address."

If this witness recanted his recantation, Scott began thinking to himself, it would be the biggest break of anything that had ever happened to him in his whole career in the courts.

"I'm sorry, madam," he told Adeline, rising to excuse himself, "I can do nothing for you."

Late that night Adeline Kelsey received a phone call from a woman whose voice she did not recognize:

"Go to the Chicken Shack, nineteen-hundred-nineteen Hamilton Concourse, right before you reach the tollway. Repeat: nineteen-hundred-nineteen Hamilton Concourse, right before you reach the highway."

And hung up.

Adeline came into the Chicken Shack wearing shades, in a pair of faded blue jeans and a dark, open-collared shirt. Behind those shades she could have been anywhere between twenty-one and thirty.

"How's the chicken?" she asked the little round man wearing an unclean apron.

"He dropped dead not an hour ago. The end was sudden. How about a duck?"

"Is duck on the menu?"

"Didn't have any when we had that printed. One came in right after the chicken died. Said he wanted to give hisself up."

She knew by his grin that all this was very funny. She smiled.

"Give me the half-chicken."

He held himself back from asking, "Which half?"

Waiting on other customers, after he had served her, he appeared to be forgetting her presence.

"Coffee, please," she reminded him. And, after he'd brought it, she sat stirring the cup thoughtfully until she caught his eye. Then flicked her tongue meaningfully into her spoon. He blinked.

He came to her again after the other customers had left, and his manner had changed.

"Anything else, madam?" he inquired politely.

"Not at the moment." And smiled.

At closing time she was still sitting there, as if waiting for him to make his move. He did.

"Can we have a drink somewhere?" he finally asked.

She looked pleased behind her shades. Her olive complexion, he decided, might be Italian.

"My name is Nick," he informed her.

"Call me Roberta."

They piled into his pickup truck and drove toward Newark with his radio blaring rock and roll. Faintly behind it, from another station, she heard someone singing another song:

You're an uptown up-tempo woman
I'm a downtown downbeat guy. . . .

"I'm trying to stay off the hard stuff," he explained, when they were sitting side by side in a booth in a dimly-lit cocktail lounge off the highway. "It gets me into trouble."

"What kind of trouble?"

"Oh, fights, stuff like that. Last time I got into it with some nigger, I don't even know what about. I wake up in the clink with both eyes black."

"I know how that is," she told him sympathetically, as if she knew exactly how it felt to wake up in the clink with two black eyes, and blew lightly into his ear, "Poor Nicky, poor Nicky."

"Two vodka martinis," he told the waitress.

"Remember that you have to drive, Nicky."

"Drive where?" he wanted to know.

"I live in Ironbound," she told him, mentioning the Portuguese slum of Newark.

"Oh," he seemed to brighten a bit at that, "Portugee?"

She lowered her lids in acknowledgement; and raised her glass to his.

She detected an odor as of frying chicken on him as he pressed her close in the booth. He must have spilled grease on his pants, she thought. Then realized it wasn't an odor of chicken—it was his own odor. His breath was bad. She felt a physical revulsion to him.

"I work in a dry-cleaning joint there," she explained, opening her handbag. "I open the place in the morning." She showed him her key. Then put it back into her bag and left him sipping thoughtfully.

His thoughts were as clear to her as if he'd spoken them aloud:

"I drive this nutty broad to her joint. I wait outside. She goes in because I tell her to go in. I tell her I give her a whistle if I see cops. She comes out with the bankroll. I take her home. She drags me upstairs and gives me a blow job out of this world. It's what she's had on her mind ever since she seen me in the Chicken Shack. I pretend I'm asleep. She turns out the light and falls asleep. I grab the roll and blow. Good-bye Chicken Shack. And thank you, ma'am."

"What," he asked her aloud, "do you have in mind, honey?"

"I want to move into New York City," she confided in him. "I need rent money, clothes, walking-around money. God knows, the way they work me, they owe me *that* much at least."

"How much you think might be in that register?"

"On a Saturday night? Are you *kidding?* They're coining money there, Nicky. *Coining* it. The Brinks truck don't pick it up till eleven A.M. Monday."

"How much you think *is* in there, Roberta?"

"A thousand at least. Maybe more. For the taking."

"Why tell *me* about it?"

"Because you're a man who's been around. I can tell. I need someone I can rely on at the door. Someone to holler cheezit."

He grinned to himself. "I thought all the angels was in heaven," he told her. And thought to himself, "This kind don't usually come out unless there's a full moon."

She kissed him lightly on his mouth to keep him from kissing her on hers. And let her hand fall lightly across his heavy thigh. He rose without being certain of what he intended to do or where he was going.

Neither spoke again until they reached downtown Newark. At her direction, then, he wheeled left onto Kinney Street. She pointed to an all-night neon sign, straight ahead in green and white, inviting everyone in town who owned a pair of unpressed pants:

1-HR. DRY-CLEANING/5-HR. SHIRT LAUNDRY

He parked in the lot behind the store, beside a line of four laundry trucks, and put out his lights.

"Go in and get it, honey," he instructed her. "I'll keep the motor running."

"Just come with me as far as the door," she begged him, "so you can give me warning better," and took his arm. "It won't take but a minute."

She got him to the door before he hesitated. This was too easy, too simple to be true.

"A big fat bundle, honey," she whispered hoarsely into his ear, "they're hauling in so much they don't get time to bank it." She had one hand clasping his arm and her key in her other hand. He had a strange moment when he hoped—he didn't know why—that the key wouldn't fit.

It fitted.

The door swung wide and she stepped in, still holding him firmly. Then swung about, facing him, put her arms about him and drove her tongue between his lips. "Honey," she confessed, "I can hardly wait."

"Not here, babe," he cautioned her, "later. Get the money first."

She didn't let go of him. She drew him beside her to the register. They were both now plainly visible in the green-and-white neon's glow. She gave him a small nudge forward. "*Get* it. Get it *all.*"

He got it. He got it all. He got it in a hurry, dropping a bill, stooping to recover it. He got it so hurriedly he did not even hear the soft turn of the key in the rear door. He was loading his pockets with quarters and halves, confident that she was standing in the shadow right behind him.

Adeline raced around the corner of the plant toward a telephone booth, then switched when she saw a squad car cruising directly in front of it and stopped it by waving her arms wildly.

"Robbing the place!" she shouted, pointing at the dry-cleaning plant. From the squad car, both officers could see the man plainly, in the green-and-white flash of neon, at the cash register.

The officer in the passenger seat didn't wait for orders. He raced around the rear of the plant with his revolver drawn. The driver banged on the front door with the butt of his gun. The man at the cash register looked up. There were bills in his pockets, bills in his hands and his pockets were stuffed with silver. He turned toward the rear, then realized he was trapped. There would be no way out, back or front, either way.

Caught. Caught cold. He tried, feebly, to put some of the bills back, then realized it was no use, no use at all. He went to the front door and unlocked it.

Adeline, watching from a darkened doorway down the street, took off her shades the better to witness the scene. The arresting officer, half a head taller, held the little round man by the nape of his neck, keeping one hand on his revolver, as he urged his suspect into the squad car.

Adeline put on her shades. It wouldn't take long for the Newark police chief to reach De Vivani. De Vivani would do as much, and had done as much, for him.

"Put him in here," De Vivani instructed the same officer who'd pinched Iello earlier. "We'll see what the little wop has to say in the morning."

The little wop had nothing to say by morning. He'd sat on the edge of his built-in cot trying to put two and two together. That little Portugee broad, whoever she'd been, had fled when the cops had trapped him. Couldn't blame her, Iello reflected. What else could she have done?

His recollection of her was vague. Nothing but a pretty face behind a pair of shades and a habit of sticking out her tongue seductively. Let her go. She couldn't help him now.

The tape recorder stood as big as life upon De Vivani's desk.

"Coffee, Nick?" De Vivani asked him.

"If that's all you got to offer," Iello accepted.

"Can you give me a hand here, Greenleaf?" De Vivani asked an officer. "You remember Nick Iello? The Calhoun case? The Melody Bar and Grill. Of course. Nick has something to tell us." He turned toward Nick.

"No hurry, son," De Vivani joshed the pitiable little bum. Over the years he had almost grown fond of him. He'd never seen a man who was such a clown, even in a circus. "Take all the time you want. Think it over. Call your lawyer. Don't tell us anything you don't want to tell us because it may be used against you in court. How did you get into that dry-cleaner's, Nick?"

"Worked the lock with a piece of wire," he assured the lieutenant.

De Vivani poured coffee into a lily cup. "Black with sugar, isn't that it, Nick?"

Iello nodded miserably. De Vivani waited until he'd finished the coffee.

"Sure you don't want time to think it all over, son?"

"Nothing to think over."

Nothing. Of course, nothing. Nothing except an indeterminate sentence, one to fourteen. At least fourteen. With his recantation, how could it be less?

"I'll get you a hundred years," Iello now recalled De Vivani's clear warning.

"What *for?*" Iello had asked him then. "A hundred years? What *for?*"

Now he knew what for.

A good thing about De Vivani was that, when he had you, he didn't rub it in. He didn't say, "Didn't I warn you about drinking, Nick?" He never said, "Look, you bum, I've got you cold." Not De Vivani. "We're not going to pressure you, son," he told Iello now, "this is something you have to make up your own mind about. Fact is we haven't even booked you yet. Had any word lately from Barney Kerrigan?"

Iello looked up. Although his eyes were fogged by misery, he managed to give De Vivani a sick grin. "Let's get it over, Vince," he nodded toward the recorder. "Let her whirl."

STATE OF NEW JERSEY — AFFIDAVIT
COUNTY OF HUDSON — October 1, 1976

I, Nicholas Patrick Iello, in presence of Officers De Vivani and Greenleaf, do hereby attest and swear: The recantation of my original testimony in New Jersey vs. Calhoun, was obtained under duress. Mr. Kerrigan threatened me with violence if I did not sign the statement he handed to me.

Mr. Kerrigan advised me that, unless I signed his document, people in support of Mr. Calhoun would do me great physical harm.

Herewith I swear and attest that my original testimony, offered in New Jersey vs. Calhoun was true. My later recantation was false.

(signed): *Nicholas Patrick Iello*

VIII

Chinatown

MOOKS NEVER LOOKED at the price list. They took the bait by telling the redheaded bartender, "Give the lady a drink."

When Red said, "That will be thirty dollars, sir," they were caught.

If the mook protested, Red called, "Man here, Moon!"

Moon the Bear.

Race: white. Height: six feet five. Weight: 235–240. Hair: blond, worn shoulder-length. Identifying marks: Pancho Villa mustache, also blond. Tattoo on upper right arm above elbow: *Bred to Fight*. Habits: nondrinker, nonsmoker.

Dovie-Jean had been putting in her off week at the Carousel for several weeks and had not yet seen anyone refuse to pay up when confronted by Moon the Bear.

"Mooks put in complaints at the Midtown Station now and then," Red filled her in, "but they don't follow through. They think it over a couple of days then either leave town or decide it's too risky to bear witness in court. So long as Moon don't carry a gun, he's within his rights, speaking legally."

"I've seen you on TV," Dovie-Jean heard one of the B-girls tell a mook, whose head was turned.

"That wasn't me," the mook assured the girl, "that was Art Carney. I ain't Art Carney, I ain't Jackie Gleason. I ain't *nobody.* I never been on TV. If they asked me I'd go on but nobody asked me. I used to work on the Delaware-Lackawan but I don't work no more. All I do is follow horses and screw around. In fact that was what I done mostly on the Delaware-Lackawan—follow horses and screw around."

Then he laughed and, sure enough, he was old Flash-from-the Track. He gave her a hug, then began singing hoarsely:

> *Oh, I get by with a little help from my friends,*
> *Mm, I'm gonna try with a little help from my friends.*
> *Oh, I get high with a little help from my friends,*
> *Yes, I get by with a little help from my friends,*
> *With a little help from my friends.*

"I just got hit three seventy-five for a beer here," he told Dovie-Jean, "so I can't buy you more than one." Then, turning to Red, "Give the lady a drink."

"Remember that 'Dear John' program?" he reminded her. "You know that clown-dressed-like-a-chicken. Kept it up every day until I had to write. He seems to think that a man who comes to a whorehouse wears dark glasses and a false beard, he feels so guilty about it. I been goin' to whorehouses as long as I been goin' to the track, and I never yet felt guilty about either. You put your money down, you make your pick and hope it's a winner, that's all. He seems to think I'm going to give up going to see the girls if he tells my neighbors about it on the radio."

"What you write, Flash?"

"I wrote: 'Dear Mayor, WNYC, New York City. I am in full support of your "Dear John" program. I am a John who patronizes a young woman in midtown Manhattan once or twice a month. I pay her fifty dollars. My name is Arnold Wingate, I live at eighty-two Maple Avenue, Hackensack, New Jersey. I plan to see my friend next week. Shall I call your office first? Photograph enclosed. Cordially yours, Arnold Wingate.' "

"Did he answer you, Flash?"

Flash wrinkled his nose. "Yeah. He thanked me for giving him my support."

Red poured a cheap white wine into a cocktail glass, out of a gallon jar with a screw-type cap.

"That will be thirty dollars, sir," he told Flash politely.

Dovie-Jean felt Flash take a deep breath, then merely sat looking at Red until Red repeated the information.

"That will be thirty dollars, sir."

"No way in the world I'm going to pay you thirty dollars for *that,*" Flash assured him.

Red never argued. He called up front. Here comes the Bear.

The Bear looked Flash over. Flashed looked the Bear over: he didn't appear intimidated.

"You ordered a drink for the young lady?"

"I never offered to pay her rent and buy her a pair of shoes."

"Here's the price list, mister. Tell me what it says."

"I can't read."

"I'm not surprised."

"Even if I could I wouldn't read a price list."

"That shows you're not a gentleman. If you were a *gentleman* you would *always* read the price list."

"I'm not a gentleman."

"Pay for the drink you ordered!" Moonigan bent his big mug right down into Flash's, drew his lips back and hissed so hotly that Flash's thin hair wavered with his breath. Flash himself didn't waver.

"No way."

Moonigan stood up. "Man refuses to pay bill here!" he announced. "Call the squad car! Call the cops! Get the police! Get the law! Take this man away! Lock him up!"

"Flash," Dovie-Jean felt it her duty to support the house, "they'll be here in a few minutes."

"It's all right, honey," the old sport reassured her, "I don't mind getting locked."

"Look, pops," Red leaned across the bar to warn him, "tomorrow's a holiday. That means you won't get into court until Friday."

"I'm not doing anything in particular over the weekend. Being locked is how you get to know new people. Make friends wherever you go. Might meet somebody in the can, see him again at the track, he gives me a hot tip, we go out and celebrate." He turned away from Red and back to Dovie-Jean, "I get by with a little help from my friends." He laughed. Moonigan didn't see anything funny.

"I don't doubt *that,*" he attempted to be cutting. "I'm sure being locked up is an old experience for *you.*"

"What good is a man who *never* gets locked up?" Flash wanted to know. "He just ain't living up to his human potential if he don't."

"You'll be better off paying, Flash," Dovie-Jean cautioned him. "It's their *policy.*"

"*Their* policy ain't *mine,* sweetheart."

The Bear sat down at the comedian's side.

"What they're going to do to you, pops, is *certify* you!"

"*Certify* me? For what? For TV?"

"For Bellevue, old man."

Flash-from-the-Track looked at him in amazement. "*Bellevue,* for God's sake? That's where I'm *from!* I'm on a liberty pass until Monday!"

For the life of him, Dovie-Jean perceived, the Bear couldn't figure this one out. Was he being kidded or was this the real thing in bugs? She saw the doubt in Moonigan's eyes.

"I don't doubt it," the Bear repeated.

"At the other end, Emil," Red told the Bear.

Another mook protesting about the price of a glass of wine. The Bear sauntered down to the Bar's end and shortly reported back.

"*He* paid," he assured Flash.

"Where are them cops?" Flash reminded him.

"I think you're some kind of bug," the Bear came to a decision. "Get out."

Flash rose, yet didn't move toward the door. He went to where Red stood guarding the cash register. The Puerto Rican came and stood in the tavern's door.

"I gave you a ten-spot," Flash reminded Red. "You owe me six and a quarter."

"I don't owe you nothing, mister."

"You been bustin' our balls around here long enough, old man," the Bear gave Flash final warning. So go. *Go-go-go!*"

"You'd best go, Flash," Dovie-Jean stepped in between, and put her hand on his arm.

"Not without my change," he told her, and turned to Moonigan.

"Fuck you, baboon, I'm getting my change."

The Bear looked at Red. There wasn't going to be any change.

Moonigan grabbed the old man by his shoulders, intending to lift him off his feet and hustle him out the door. (It wasn't wise to have a customer hurt.) The old man, feeling himself being lifted bodily, swung with all his force into Moonigan's big nose.

Blood spurted as though it had been broken. Red reached over the bar and clipped the old fool on the side of the head.

Down the old fool went.

A scent rose, into Dovie-Jean's nostrils, of a sick, or dying chicken.

The Puerto Rican bally-man who'd been standing in the door watching switched off the lights when the old man fell. The barflies fled into the dark.

The Carousel had just closed for the evening.

Back in the hotel, Dovie-Jean sat waiting for Red. She was looking at a TV screen without seeing it.

She remembered that she had been pleased to see Flash-from-the-Track again. He had always paid his own way and had never demanded that sort of excessive respect some tricks, being unsure of themselves, demanded from the whores. Flash had been perfectly contented to play the fool.

It was ironic that, tonight, he'd paid so dearly to preserve his dignity.

She became aware of the goings-on on the screen. It was the Uriah Yipkind show. Uriah was explaining to his audience that his guest for the evening was an executive of the business world who had been stone drunk for ten years. Now he had not had a drink for six months. Could he keep it up?

"What are you doing these days, Mr. Markheim," Uriah asked his guest, "other than staying sober?"

"That's a full-time job in itself," Mr. Markheim replied.

Both Uriah and Mr. Markheim laughed over that one.

"Tell us how you got started on your career as an alcoholic, Mr. Markheim," Uriah urged him.

"It began when I was in college," the guest recalled, giving Dovie-Jean an impression that the man had only given up alcohol for pills. He had that glassy look. "I went stone drunk to an examination in the law school, and passed it. Unfortunately, I wasn't in the law school. I missed the examination I was supposed to be taking in agronomy."

Dovie-Jean switched the program off, unable to follow it.

It just goes to show you, she thought, how much it takes to get a spot on TV. Just stay sober for six months and you're a TV celebrity.

She fell asleep in the lounge chair, a reading lamp burning above her, and dreamed.

She dreamed she was in a strange house, up a flight of stairs and into a room where a dozen Puerto Rican women had gathered about a bed.

She could not see their faces, they were all shawled, there was a sense of death in the place. It was lit only by candles, and the women were looking at a sick infant on the bed. By its color, it was either dead or dying.

Above the infant a doctor, dressed in black, stood with a stethoscope in hand. She knew that the doctor was ready to give up hope for the infant's life. The women were about to start grieving.

Suddenly the doctor swung his foot at the infant, kicking it bodily off the bed onto the floor. He had kicked it so violently that it had landed face down—yet not a word of protest or surprise from the women watching.

They understood, and what Dovie-Jean understood also, was that what the doctor had attempted was to shock the infant's system so that death would release its grip and life would return.

It didn't work. Even as she looked, Dovie-Jean saw the small body grow chalk white and *thicken.* It lay there looking as if, were a knife thrust into it, it would not bleed.

She wakened feeling that her own life had gone somewhere far away. Red was sneaking in, shoeless, like a small boy who has committed some mischief. She could *feel* his evasiveness without opening her eyes. She didn't open them until he'd climbed into bed and began pretending to be sleeping. She could feel his fear in the dark.

She waited until he'd had coffee the following morning.

"What happened?"

Red looked at her steadily over the rim of his cup. Then he put the cup down.

"You saw him swing on Moon, didn't you?"

"What *happened?*"

"What the hell do you *think* happened? What do you do with a clown, he drops dead because you slap him the side of the head? You want us closed a month—maybe sixty-ninety days? You think I'm getting paid just to draw beers? What do you think Moon is paid three bills a week for? We're paid to keep the joint *running*. Accidents will happen. Now forget it. It was an accident."

"I knew the old man."

"So you knew him."

"Where'd you leave him?"

Another shrug.

"Where'd you leave him?"

"Where the cops'll find him."

"How much money did he have on him?"

He hadn't expected that one.

Red put his spoon down. "Look, I'm not a jack-roller. It ain't my trade. I never touched the old fool's pockets."

"He was wearing an expensive watch."

"So?"

"If you didn't get it, Moonigan did."

"Moonigan's trade is one thing. Mine is another. He's an honest man. He laid everything out plain as possible for me before I went to work. If I wasn't willing to go along with him, I had my chance to say, No, I won't work with you. I told him I would work with him. I told him so for your sake as well as for mine. Do I have to remind you that we're both wanted in Jersey City?"

"Does Moonigan know about that deal?"

"Certainly not."

Dovie-Jean looked out the window, feeling a slow grief rising. How had she gotten into this in the first place? She had hurt no one; yet now, for the second time, she was involved in a killing.

She didn't understand. How to get away? Where did she have to run to? There was nothing left back home, there was nothing left in Jersey City. Wherever she left a place it was as though she had never lived there. She tried to swallow down her grief, but it would not go down. She put her head into her arms to conceal it.

Red came around the table and put his hand on her shoulder. He didn't perceive what was troubling her so terribly, but he knew she was feeling badly, and that she was a woman who didn't feel badly without good reason. She touched his hand on her shoulder. Not because it was his hand, but because it was somebody's, anybody's. She had never felt so alone in her life.

When she looked up, her eyes were tear-stained.

"He was a *nice* old man," she told Red.

"Sweetheart," he told her, and put out his hand toward her. She rose quickly. "Oh, no, not *that* again," she rejected his sympathy. She went to the bathroom to wash her face. When she came out he had gone.

Dovie-Jean dressed slowly and deliberately. She had not had to make up her mind consciously. Her mind had been made up for her. It had made itself up.

Where she'd go she was uncertain. What she was certain of was that she was leaving Red.

When she was fully dressed she wrote a brief note and put a fifty-dollar bill on top of it:

"This is what I made last night. Now we're square. Good luck. D."

When she reached the door she looked back, hesitated, then returned to the dresser, picked up the fifty and tore up the note.

An iciness began forming about Red's heart as he was rising in the little old-fashioned Hotel Chester elevator. It rose slowly, so slowly, it stopped at every floor whether its bell had been rung or not, its door opened so slowly to nobody waiting there, nobody at all. Then closed so slowly. The iciness began closing in.

That tap he'd laid on the old man had been nothing. He'd hit opponents ten times that hard and they'd done nothing but blink.

It had been enough. "This fool is gone," Moonigan had said when he'd lifted the body.

Old fool running around town with a bad ticker, anything he'd run into would have stopped its beat. He had had to run into the fist of a man hiding out on a murder rap. There's such a thing as bad luck, Red grieved, but this is outrageous.

Moonigan had done the stripping, fast and rough, there in the shadowed place, while Red had kept watch. He'd seen Moonigan's hand move from Flash's pocket to his own, but nothing since had been said about a wallet. Moonigan wasn't being paid just for pitching drunks onto Eighth Avenue.

When the elevator let him out into his own room at last, Red stood looking puzzled. Her clothes were gone.

Red knew then why the ice was closing in about his heart: not out of fear of that old fool's death, but out of fear of losing Dovie-Jean.

Or was that the true fear? Was not his true fear his recollection of her warning: "You letting Ruby take the rap. I won't stand for that."

And yet she *had* stood for it.

She had stood for it because she did not think it had been Red who'd done the shooting. He had never told her he had not. The closest he had come to an explanation with her was, "It must be one of them crazy nigger street kids."

What then was his great need of her? How could he need a *black* woman?

Because she was black, his heart whispered: You need her because she makes you feel *you* are black.

Standing now at the window overlooking the rooftops, chimneys and telephone cables, so black against this gray December sky, and the traffic moving, so far below, as in a slow pantomime, he wondered what it had been that had made such a difference between himself and Hardee.

Of his own mother he had only the dimmest of recollections: only that she had been white. Yet, of Hardee's mother, a black woman, the memory remained vivid. How old had Hardee been the day she had brought him to live with Matt and himself?

And he himself then a lanky fifteen.

Now here he stood, a few brief years after, a washed-up light-heavy, a failed pimp suspected of triple homicide, and Hardee planning to practice law in Jersey City in the spring. What had formed such a difference? Their mothers? The times? Was this

his fear, his great fear, that he was neither white nor black, talking?

Who was he? *What* was he?

She had left only out of being upset about the old fool's death, he decided now. She'd be back tonight or tomorrow.

And when she returned he'd sweet-talk her as he had sweet-talked her before.

If we keep our noses out of Ruby's trial, he'd assure her, Ruby would beat the rap. And everything would be as it used to be, he'd promise her.

Some promise. The girl was so smart, and at the same time so simple, he could never tell what she was going to do or say. But there was no other way to go, so far as Hardee was concerned. His law career would be a shambles before it had even begun unless they all three worked together now.

Dovie-Jean was not, he was sure, the snitching kind. She had no intention of giving evidence which might incriminate either himself or Hardee.

Yet Hardee would have to know, in event she didn't come back. He'd have to find her. If he could not find her he would have to go back to Jersey City and let Hardee know.

He came up the Playmates of Paris stair shortly before midnight and paid fifteen dollars to get into the parlor. Dovie-Jean wasn't working. The other women assured him she hadn't come in. Whether they were fronting for her or not he had no way of telling. He waited until after 1 A.M. before he gave up.

He stood for a moment in the dark of the room, a key still in his hand. There was somebody else in the room.

"Dovie-Jean?" he asked in a low voice.

No reply. He took a step farther, turned about and saw a shadow opposing him.

"Dovie-Jean?"

No reply. He switched on the light and saw his reflection in a mirror. And felt the doggo blues coming on.

"It's going to be a hard night, Edward," he told himself aloud.

He took a shower and tried miming under the water. He sang to himself as the water poured, using Tony Bennett's voice:

From all of society we'll stay aloof
We'll live in propriety up on the roof . . .

He came out of the shower with the towel about him, snapping his fingers in forced cheerfulness, "*The cat couldn't kitten and the slut couldn't pup,*" he sang, "*and the old man couldn't get his rhubarb up.*"

He switched on the TV and caught a fellow jumping up and down behind a storeful of auto parts.

"Wild Willie takes the risk!" the fellow shrieked. "*You* take the profits! Wild Willie is on *your* side!"

"You're on everbody's side, you sonofabitch," Red told him, and switched the commercial off. Then he turned out the light and stretched out naked on the bed.

He became aware of a low murmuring, like that of the crowd seeing the horses approaching the gate, and he looked about for a mutuel window but he could see none, and it was too late, and the murmur rose to a great cheer as the horses pounded to the finish line; but it was too dark to see and the great cheer broke up, then drifted away and everything became still.

He walked through a grandstand looking for a window, but came instead to a high board fence and somebody said, "You can't go through there."

So he went down a darkening way in the dead of night, toward a railroad lantern burning red. Below its glow half a dozen railroaders, wearing blue-striped overalls and brakemen's caps, sat playing cards but he could not make out what game they were at.

"Can you direct me to a mutuel window?" he asked.

The cards made no sound as they touched the chips, red, white and blue in the table's center, and nobody looked up to answer him; and nobody seemed to win the pot.

"Can I make a bet on a horse?" he asked.

He looked up and saw a great toteboard bearing photographs of the next race's entrants, like photographs off the covers of racing programs; but their numbers were unlisted and no odds had been posted.

"Is there a mutuel window near here?" He directed his question now at the only black man among the players, a man no older than himself whom he knew well, yet could not, strangely, quite recall; or what he had to do with him, except that it had been unpleasant.

"On Genevieve," he told the man, offering him a fifty-dollar-bill, "on the nose."

The young black looked at Red steadily for what seemed a long time.

"Who informed on me when I came back from overseas, Red?" he asked quietly. And turned his head away.

A white man, wearing black judge's robes, stood on the big scale at the finishing line.

"Put this on Genevieve," Red told the judge, handing him the fifty, "on the nose."

"Get the stalls cleaned and we'll talk later," the judge replied.

A rider on a gray horse came walking slowly. Red held up the fifty to the rider and said, "On the nose."

The rider turned his face down to Red and it was pale as ashes. His eyes were shadowed by his cap. His lips hung loosely as though he had no teeth. His voice came down to Red in a hoarse warning whisper, "That's a tragic horse," the rider told him, and rode on.

The big board began shimmering as if it were heated and the heat was going out of control. He had a smell of burning and woke to see that the cigarette he'd put out in the tray beside the bed was still smoldering.

In the dim light he saw a figure standing over his bed.

It was himself, yet not himself.

The image faded slowly, as he watched, and disappeared.

It wasn't going to be easy to face Hardee.

When Fortune Foo opened the door, she opened it to Dovie-Jean Dawkins.

"Come in, honey," Fortune invited her, "you look like the wrath of God. What happened?"

Dovie-Jean, looking exhausted, sank back in an armchair and shut her eyes as if gathering strength. Fortune went to her tiny kitchen and lit the gas under the tea kettle.

"Had a fight with my old man," Dovie-Jean told her when she returned to her little sitting room. "He's going to be on the hawks for me all over town."

"Park here until it blows over," Fortune welcomed her without questioning, and switched on the TV, after she had poured the tea, in the hope of diverting her friend from her trouble.

"Catch this creep," she told Dovie-Jean as Uriah Yipkind came into view talking to a man no bigger than himself who appeared to be bored although the program had hardly begun.

"You look to be in good shape, Truman," Uriah congratulated his guest. "You've lost weight. Your eyes are bright. How are you getting on with Gore Vidal?"

"Who is Gar Vital?" Dovie-Jean asked.

"Never heard of her," Fortune answered.

"I know you're not fond of Gore, Truman. You're not fond of many people, are you?"

"I'm fond of many people."

"But who do you *love?* Really *love?*"

"You mean really *really* love?"

"Yes. Really *really.*"

The guest studied his host speculatively.

"I love your wife," he finally replied, "really *really.*"

Uriah looked startled.

"I didn't know you knew my wife, Truman."

"You weren't supposed to know. It's been going on for some years now. But, since you ask who I really *really,* you might as well know."

Uriah's face broke into an uneasy grin.

"You're kidding me, Truman. You're putting me on."

"Aren't you kidding *me?* Aren't you putting *me* on?"

"They're putting each other on," Fortune explained.

"Who are they?"

"TV celebrities."

"Tell us, Truman," Uriah began a new tack, still determined to shake up his guest, "What really happened on that southern campus when you fell off the speaker's platform?"

"I don't recall falling off any speaker's platform, Uriah, north or south."

"Now, Truman, you know what I'm talking about."

"I'm not sure what you're talking about. I do recall a dentist in Gainesville, Florida, giving me a pill so that I dozed, onstage, momentarily. Is that it? I wasn't near enough to the edge of the stage to fall off it."

Uriah snickered knowingly.

"There was more to it than *that,* Truman. Now, *wasn't* there?"

Truman merely shrugged as if to say, "Make what you want of it," so Uriah tried yet another tack.

"What is it you like so much about Studio Fifty-four?"

"What's 'Studio Fifty-four?' " Dovie-Jean asked.

"A classy dance hall."

"Oh."

"I like it because everybody goes there and boys dance with boys and girls dance with girls and everybody enjoys himself—millionaires and taxi drivers, black and white, rich and poor. I always enjoy seeing a lot of different types of people getting along."

"Now come off that," Uriah reproached Truman, "about liking people without money. How many poor people mix with the rich aboard that luxury yacht you sail to the isles of Greece?"

"That luxury yacht isn't mine, Uriah. It belongs to the Whaleys. I just go along for the ride. It's the quickest way of getting to Greece, that's all. I don't organize the guest list. If I did I'd invite your wife."

"She wouldn't accept, Truman."

"On the contrary, she already asked if she could come along."

"But what do you give the Whaleys in return?"

"Conversation. Just conversation. Better conversation, indeed, than this one you and I are having."

"Sure you do. Sure you do. You accepted the Whaley's hospitality and then you wrote about them critically. Was that fair, Truman? Was that *fair?*"

"Who are the Whaleys?" Dovie-Jean asked Fortune.

"Never heard of them."

"Writing isn't a matter of being fair, Uriah," Truman assured him. "If I hadn't've written as I did you'd now be charging me with whitewashing in return for a yacht trip. Anyhow, I didn't make them out to be nearly so vile as you're now implying *I* am: an alcoholic, an addict, an irresponsible ingrate, a narcissist—anything for a cheap thrill."

"What's a narcist, Fortune?"

"Somebody who looks in a mirror all day, can't get enough of himself."

"Why are you so angry, Truman?" Uriah asked.

"I'm not in the least angry. I knew before I came on your show how you operate. And I really don't mind too much. After all, how can *you* hurt *me?*"

"You're telling me I don't respect you, Truman. That isn't true. I love you and respect you."

"I doubt you love anybody, Uriah. I'm sure you respect nobody. However, we can still be friends so long as you don't mind my loving your wife."

Fortune switched the program off.

"What did you switch it off for, honey?"

"There's nothing on the air," Fortune assured her.

"What your trouble is," Fortune told Dovie-Jean the following morning, "is no damned business of mine. But if you want to split the rent on this joint, you'd be welcome."

"I'd love it, Fortune," Dovie-Jean told her, "but all I got in the handbag is a couple of fifties. When that's gone, I don't know. I can't go back to Playmates—he'll be looking for me there. I was working at another joint in my week off, on Eighth. But I sure can't go back there."

"Stick around," Fortune urged her, "you can keep house. Can you cook?"

"Simple things, southern style."

Fortune lived three stories up in one of those airless nineteenth-century tenements shadowed by multitudes who'd been born in these narrow rooms, had climbed these narrow stairs for a lifetime and had died in these small rooms, leaving for remembrance only the odor of cabbage soup up and down the stair.

By morning now, Dovie-Jean walked past packs of instant noodles wrapped in cellophane, and metal tubs holding staring bloody heads of enormous fish; lacquer ware, plastic flowers, and bitter melons would be stacked along the walks.

Before the morning had well begun uptown, it was half over on Mott Street and down Doyers. Purple yams, white radishes, taro roots, fuzzy squash, bokchoy leaves, winter melons, cabbages, garlic, ginger root, scallions and lotus root had been unpacked.

By noon the bustle would die down; an air of somnolence came into her open window above the street. Then, half-sleeping, Dovie-Jean would envision a dim clownish face and hear, far off, a hoarse voice singing:

Oh, I get by with a little help from my friends,
Mm, I'm gonna try with a little help from my friends.
Oh, I get high with a little help from my friends,
Yes, I get by with a little help from my friends,
With a little help from my friends.

IX

Second Trial

THE JURY LOOKED better, to Max Epstein, than the original jury had looked to Ben Raymond. The first had been an all-white jury. The present one impaneled six white men, three white women, an elderly black man, and elderly black woman and a young black man.

Scott built his prosecution upon Violet Vance's identification of the white getaway car, then expanded the case in order to oppose what he termed "the threat of the event-shaping Madison Avenue boys," as he designated New York City's media people who had conducted a campaign of contempt for the New Jersey judiciary, the New Jersey police and, in general, the civilization of New Jersey for many months. He made racial fear a motive of the murders.

Oritano permitted Scott to list all the actors, writers, filmmakers, publishers, studio executives and advertisers who had served on Calhoun's New York City committee. Scott's strongest weapon was the backlash aroused in New Jersey by the New York media.

"As much as I would like to say that the killings did not happen out of revenge," Scott contended, "revenge was the reason they happened all the same."

Max Epstein possessed a disdainful personality and he played it directly into Scott's hands. He kept his back to the jury except for brief occasions when he glanced over his shoulder, as much as to say: "*schmucks*." Scott sat back and watched Epstein destroying his own case.

Neither Scott nor Epstein were aware that Nick Iello had recanted his recantation. Therefore Scott fought to keep him off the stand and Epstein fought to keep him on.

De Vivani had it in hand, and he waited his moment. While he waited he sat and watched the lawyers going at one another like two boxers unaware that each is wearing the other's trunks.

De Vivani cared no more for the prosecution lawyers than he did for the New York Jews of the defense. Personally, he liked Calhoun and respected him; but he had no respect for lawyers at all. He sat at the back of the courtroom listening to Scott pleading, in the jury's absence, to keep the recantation off the stand.

"This man has revealed himself to be a perjuror," Scott was advising the judge. "Whether Iello had been lying in his original identification of Calhoun or whether he had been lying in his recantation, makes no difference. The man is a liar under oath, and if he is permitted to take this stand it will be a mockery of the jury system."

"The credibility of the witness is not the basis, under law, by which identification might be withheld from a jury," Judge Oritano ruled. "The only relevant issue here is whether there have been improper suggestions from the police. This witness's constitutional right to due process has not therefore been violated."

Iello would be permitted to testify.

Epstein, with Iello's recantation in hand, was quietly jubilant. The case, he sensed, was as good as over and he whispered something to Calhoun. "For the first time since this trial began," the press took note, "Calhoun smiled."

Once, while Epstein was giving the judge a long, circuitous argument, Oritano rose and walked off the bench into his chambers.

"Judge!" Epstein called after him. "Judge! I don't like it when you walk off in the middle of a sentence!"

"Too bad," everyone in the courtroom heard Oritano's rumble from somewhere offstage. "Too, too damned bad."

"Was it a two-inch or a five-inch taillight?" Epstein demanded to know of Violet Vance, as if implying that any witness not carrying a tape measure at 2 A.M. must be guilty of complicity.

The witness had been uncertain in her original identification. "It was *like* the same car," she had testified.

"I don't *know,* Mr. Epstein," she now answered, "all I know is that the car I seen leaving and the car I seen returning was the *same* car." And burst into tears. "*I* didn't do anything, Mr. Epstein."

She had done more than she realized. She had greatly strengthened the prosecution's charge that it was the same car. Epstein had frightened her into so stating.

Out of the jury's presence, Scott then requested that the court allow him to introduce an unprecedented motive: racial revenge. When Oritano permitted Scott to use it, Epstein charged Oritano openly with "turning this trial into a racial nightmare."

Scott objected and was sustained. De Vivani covered his mouth with his right hand. Epstein repeated the charge. De Vivani covered his mouth with his left hand. Scott objected again and was again sustained. De Vivani bowed his head forward and appeared to be choking. Epstein persisted.

"Sit down Mr. Epstein," the judge finally instructed him in a bored tone, "sit *down*."

There was no mistaking the threat behind the instruction. Epstein went to his table waggling his head in personal outrage.

"Don't waggle your head, Mr. Epstein," the judge cautioned him.

Epstein sat down and ruffled his papers angrily.

"Don't ruffle your papers, Mr. Epstein."

De Vivani rose and conducted a one-minute check, from a standing position, upon Max Epstein. He did not waggle. Neither did he ruffle.

The trial was not a racial nightmare. There was simply no way of keeping race out of the jury's consciousness. Four whites and one black had been murdered, or had died, since June 17, 1966. One white man had gone to prison for killing a black. A black man was now, for the second time, on trial for his life for the killings of three whites. To conduct such a trial without racial feeling was not humanly possible.

The boredom of the trial was suddenly relieved by the appearance of two clowns.

One was a twenty-eight-year-old New Jerseyan named Joe Hauser. Hauser wore pants of royal blue, a light blue-and-white plaid jacket and a navy-blue lattice tie. He had dressed for the occasion and was obviously enormously pleased with himself. He knew that he had the admiration of everyone in court through his mere appearance. He put one leg up as though inviting viewers to admire the beauty of his knee.

The other looked like something left over from Haight-Ashbury. He wore his hair long, had a single earring and wore a sheepskin and hadn't shaved for days. His name was Sigorski.

"I never put a word into Nick Iello's mouth," Hauser assured the court the moment he got on the witness stand, before being asked anything.

"What is your trade, Mr. Hauser?" Epstein asked him.

"Furniture dealer."

"What is your relationship to Mr. Iello?"

"We planned to make a film. I was his agent. One of his agents. The other was Sigorski."

"Who was Sigorski?"

"Iello's other agent."

"I mean, what was his trade?"

Hauser grinned as at some private joke. "*Sigorski?* That bum never worked a day in his life."

"Since your own trade is that of dealing in furniture, and Mr. Sigorski is unemployed, how did you plan to make a film?"

"I can sell a chair without knowing how to *make* a chair, can't I? Fact is we were going to do a book too. I don't how to write a book either. It don't mean I can't run a tape recorder though."

"You made tapes then?"

"Hours of them."

"With Mr. Iello?"

"Iello is from the basement. Every tape he's telling us a different story."

"With so many versions of the story," Epstein asked him, "what made you think you'd found the true one?"

"With so many versions," Hauser replied complacently, "one of them was bound to be the truth."

Iello's jacket strained across his chest when he mounted the witness chair. He was chewing gum or candy.

"Do you remember being involved in other crimes, Mr. Iello," Scott began on him, "before your involvement in the present one?"

"It's possible," Iello conceded carelessly, "I don't recall at the moment. If I did, I wasn't arrested."

"You've never been arrested, Mr. Iello?"

"Of course I've been arrested. Many times. I'm a thief. I'm a professional thief. I make my living as a thief. When I get caught I go to jail. I serve my time, whatever they hand out. When I get out I go back to thieving. Thieving is my trade. I thought you meant was I arrested in connection with the present case. I've never been arrested in relation to the present case, all I meant."

"Then it is safe to say that there are hundreds of crimes for which you have never been arrested?"

"I object," Epstein interrupted. "Is Mr. Scott merely playing to the audience now? Is he trying to entertain us at the witness's expense? Does Mr. Scott want, seriously, to try this case or not? The question he is putting to the witness is ridiculous, your honor."

"The question is objectionable," the judge agreed. "If Mr. Scott chooses to waste our good time, as well as his own, with such questions, I'll permit him. You do have proof, Mr. Scott, that this witness has committed hundreds of crimes for which he has never been arrested?"

"Your honor, have you listened to the tapes he made with his agents? The material in any one of them is staggering—*staggering . . .*"

De Vivani, at the rear of the courtroom, closed his eyes at the farce being conducted up front. The sight of a state's attorney trying to trap a witness, whom he regarded as having turned hostile, but one who would, shortly, switch to Scott's own side, gave the detective a pang of secret pleasure.

"Will you answer my question?" Scott persisted.

"You'll have to repeat it. I forgot it."

"Are there not hundreds of crimes you have committed for which, sir, you have never been arrested?"

"Objection," Epstein protested. "How is this relevant, your honor? We are now asking Mr. Iello if he wishes to incriminate himself in crimes totally unconnected with the one which this trial is about."

"I'm not going to permit him to go beyond that night," Oritano assured Epstein.

"He said 'hundreds of crimes,' sir," Epstein reminded the court. "Is Mr. Scott talking about hundreds of crimes committed on the night of June sixteenth, nineteen sixty-six; or crimes committed on other nights? I ask the counsel to be specific. This is a court of law, not a cocktail bar for exchange of hearsay."

"Counsel for the witness is agreed," Oritano agreed good-naturedly, "that we should use our sound and good judgment in attempting to save time."

"Do you remember," Scott still addressed Iello, "saying that, on the night in question, you 'were all fucked up,' to use your own phrase?"

"I wasn't messed up on alcohol or on pills, if that's what you mean," Iello replied.

"You were not so messed up that you did not realize it would be an excellent opportunity to rob a cash register?"

"*Mister* Scott," Iello said wearily, shifting his body in the witness chair, "over and *over* I have admitted your charge and I admit it again. *Yes, yes, yes,* I took money from the register of the Melody Bar and Grill. I ran down the street with it. I handed it to Dexter Baxter. I ran back to the tavern. I called the telephone operator. I waited for the cops. I went to the station."

"I see that, after all, you don't have memory problems," Scott complimented the witness.

"My memory is perfectly clear. It was very quiet in the bar. There was broken glass, a beer bottle smashed on the floor. There was a man slumped over the bar like sleeping. There was another man flopping around with blood down his face. There was a woman lying on the floor. The man with the blood on his face began mumbling."

"You told Assemblyman Rawlings you had seen a colored male," Scott asked, "wearing shades and a sports jacket, five foot eight inches in height, did you not?"

"I did not swear everything exactly true to Rawlings. I had a reason for saying whatever it was I said to him at that time. Joe Hauser was right outside, we had rehearsed what I was going to say to Rawlings. I was looking to get even with Hudson County at that time. I had these two guys on my back who wanted a book. Some of the things I said to Rawlings were complete lies. They were said to make an exciting book."

"Who were these two guys?"

"Hauser and Sigorski. I was working for them at the time and they suggested a book. They said the actual story they couldn't do anything with. They sent a letter to some guy Truman Capote. He was a writer, they were looking for a writer to write it."

Oritano swung about toward the witness, supporting his cheek upon his palm. This might be the first time, his attitude suggested, that he had had before him a witness who not merely identified himself as a liar and a thief, but proclaimed it. Iello revealed not the faintest trace of embarrassment.

"Mr. Hauser made you say those things?" Scott asked.

"I can't say anyone *made* me," Iello answered, "I could say we discussed them. Hauser said, 'If you get in there and tell them what actually happened, forget it. Do the right thing and we got a good story we can sell to anybody.' All the tapes were rehearsed with Hauser and Sigorski. It was why on the tape I said I never seen Calhoun. That made a better story, Hauser said, more mysterious-like."

"But that part was true—that you never saw Calhoun," Epstein asked.

"*What* was true? That I never seen Calhoun? Calhoun was in the white car when he passed me. Just like I told it to Lieutenant De Vivani. And when they brought the car back Calhoun was still in it."

"I don't understand what you're trying to say," Epstein protested. "Your failure to identify Calhoun, as you swore in your recantation . . ."

"Mr. Epstein, I just got through explaining: that was *bunk*. Pure *bunk*. The recantation was Joe Hauser's idea, for the book. 'Tell Kerrigan you were lying when you originally identified Calhoun,' Hauser told me, 'think of the publicity in *that!* And it'll make you look good, too.' Then I thought to myself: Look what it will make them stupid cops look like. Them that promised me so much then left me hanging . . ."

"You don't seriously expect us to believe what you're telling us now, Mr. Iello?"

"Objection," Scott switched fast to the witness's side.

"I don't give a good goddamn whether you believe me or not, Mr. Epstein," Iello assured the defense. "You asked me so I told you, that's all."

"Your recantation," Scott put in almost breathlessly, "is then a complete falsehood?"

"Look," Iello replied with the note of utter weariness returning to his voice, "look, we had a contract, they were supposedly my agents and they were in contact with different people in New York. They went over but I didn't. I didn't want to go way over there.

"What Hauser had in mind was to start a big argument going on the tapes calling De Vivani every name in the book—it ain't hard to get De Vivani hot you know—and then putting weight on him with that recantation play. Hauser said, 'Good, now if we can get Newark involved in this, we get all the free publicity and who the hell cares who goes free or who doesn't go free, we got a good book to sell. We got the story, them guys in New York got nothing, they got to come to us.'

"That was how it started out. Then Sigorski comes to me and says, 'What do we need Hauser for? We drop him and me and you split fifty-fifty.' I said, 'Okay by me.' Then Hauser comes to me and says, 'What do we need that stupid Polack for? We drop him and you and me split fifty-fifty.' I says, 'Okay by me.'

"Then they get together and decide the one they really don't need is me. So they go over to New York with the tapes and come back with so much money they'd bought new money clips. The day Hauser declared hisself bankrupt in New Jersey, he was shopping for a new Lincoln in New York and Sigorski was pricing a twelve-room house in Montauk. No, I don't know where they got it but I'm sure they never used a gun."

"Have you no shame, Mr. Iello?" Epstein asked the witness.

Iello chewed leisurely, studying the lawyer. After a while he shifted the wad in his cheek and asked quietly, "Do you really want me to answer that?"

Epstein evaded the challenge. "Sir," he asked, "are you trying to tell us that your recantation, which you swore on oath to be true, was actually false?"

"Actually and absolutely, Mr. Epstein. There was not one line of truth in that recantation. The first story I told Lieutenant De Vivani was true."

Epstein, pale as ashes, started circling the courtroom and waggling his head. Everyone watched him wondering where he thought he was going. He himself didn't know. Judge Oritano watched him with a flicker of sympathy. De Vivani watched with no sympathy at all. Finally Epstein turned back to the witness.

"Mr. Iello, did you apply for a reward of twelve thousand dollars for your identification of Ruby Calhoun?"

"I forgot about that years ago."

"Why were you applying for it then in nineteen seventy-four?"

"To rattle Hudson County's cage. I felt Hudson County had gave me the shaft. I was having a lot of problems. I was sick at the time. I came out of a hospital. These two guys kept telling me we can get quite a few dollars. You yourself were even calling me."

"Did you not swear, before Investigator Kerrigan, in an affidavit on October first, nineteen seventy-four?"

"I was lying."

"You swore to this story in order to further your financial possibilities—is that what you're telling us now?"

"Now you've got it."

"No, mister, I have *not* got it," Epstein's voice reflected his rising anger. "You will now explain the statement you just made, to the effect that your recantation, the one sworn and notarized before Mr. Kerrigan, is untrue. If I'm not asking too much."

"Not at all. Don't mind at all. I've had people after me, ever since that first trial, to get me to recant. One person after another, a newspaperman, a TV producer, a state investigator. Once three came in on me at once, when I was locked in the Bergen County jail. Kerrigan was one of them. I was ill and despondent. The newspaper dude offered me a job on his paper if I would recant. It would mean a lot to him, personally, he said, if I would. When I got out I'd go to see him and he'd take good care of me. 'Between you and me, Berwyn,' I told him, 'the man who committed those murders was Ruby Calhoun.' You know what *he* said? He said, 'Jesus Christ, Nick, don't ever let anyone hear you say *that.*'

"The TV producer promised me a thousand bucks for a documentary about the murders. Then Kerrigan put it to me, 'You need money, Nick?' Who doesn't need money? 'What do you mean by "money"?' 'I can't put it on you in here,' he tells me, 'but I can open an account for you to draw on as soon as you get out.' "

"Your honor," Scott came to life at last, "these men—this reporter, this producer, this investigator—are the worst kind of lying opportunists. They think that by labeling themselves 'liberals' they gain immunity from the law. This recantation of Iello's was worked up at WNIT and calculated to get as high a rating as *Kojak*. Trial-by-television, your honor: Calhoun would be exonerated without benefit of jury. Rather, the viewing public would be his jury. Thumbs up, thumbs down.

"What are our courts of law *for,* your honor? Leave us bring men to trial by media. Leave the public decide innocence or guilt. If a man is found guilty he can then be executed under TV lights, in prime time! Think of the sponsors ready to pay big money for *that!* If he is innocent he can sign a film contract and perform in nightclubs.

"Your honor, I can understand why Mr. Iello would be tempted by the opportunity offered him by the New York media to be a TV hero, a man of stricken conscience finally redeemed by testifying for the man against whom he had once testified falsely. Barbra Streisand would be fine as the feminine lead. Carol Burnett would be even better.

"Your honor, this producer, this reporter, this investigator seek nothing but their own aggrandizement and their own enrichment. They manufacture news and sell to the highest bidder. They pervert justice. Before this trial is over each and every one of them is going to be subpoenaed."

The crowded courtroom, until now in complete support of Calhoun, was shaken. In the uneasy silence that followed Scott's address, one could feel the sand shifting under the feet of the defense.

More than sand was shifting beneath Epstein's feet. With Iello's repudiation of his recantation, his whole case began collapsing.

He had been cordial to Dovie-Jean Dawkins but had not considered her testimony vital to Calhoun's defense. Now, that suddenly, she was all he had.

And he had no idea how to find her. And find her fast.

Hardee Haloways, watching him from a corner of the corridor, read Epstein's anxiety when he was talking to Jennifer. He saw Jennifer shaking her head, No.

Hardee approached her after Epstein had left her. Yes, he had been asking for Dovie-Jean but she had not been able to help him. "All I could tell him was I suppose she was in New York," Jennifer informed Hardee. "She came out one weekend but she didn't say where she was staying. Or what she was doing."

"I know what she was doing," Hardee decided. "Did she come alone?"

"No, she was with a little friend. A Chinese woman. I forget her name."

"Thank you," Hardee told her, and walked away.

Hardee Haloways drove his half-brother out to his new suburban home. Hardee had married and was as proud of his bride as he was of his new Peugeot. He'd sold the Paradise and was doing well in his law practice.

After his wife had served drinks, and Hardee had tapped the ash out of his cigar, he studied Red a long minute.

"How's the girl making out?" he asked at last.

"It's what I come to see you about, Hardee," Red told Hardee miserably. "I don't know where she is. She took a powder last week. Well, a week and a half. Two weeks say."

No use, Red thought, going into that scene with Moonigan in the areaway.

"What does the trial look like to you, Edward?" Hardee sounded Red out.

"It looked pretty good, by the papers, yesterday," was as far as Red would commit himself.

"What do you think happens if Calhoun beats the state?"
"He goes free is all I know."
Hardee offered him the box of panatelas. Red declined. Hardee lit one himself, blew out smoke and came to a decision.
"What a lousy pimp *you* are, Edward."
"Pimping isn't my trade, Hardee," Red assured his half-brother. "I'm a bartender."
"It looks to me, Edward," Hardee answered with a smile, "like Calhoun is going to beat the state. Which means that there's going to be a warrant out, triple homicide, for a crazy nigger who used to be a sparring partner of Calhoun's."
"It might be your ass too, Hardee."
"Never, Edward. I am no way involved. I have a solid alibi for that night. You have not. Do you think you still beat the lie test, Red?"
Red shrugged. Hardee gave him the answer.
"No way. Neither did Calhoun. If that girl gets on the stand, Red, Calhoun will beat the state. Or don't you think she'll testify for Calhoun?"
"I see," Red acknowledged, "I see what you mean. She'd take the stand for Calhoun all right. She said she would, way back."
"Would she take the stand for you?"
Again the shrug.
"Would she take the stand for you?"
"If she took the stand for Ruby, how could she take the stand for me?"
"Now, you're beginning to see your situation, my dear brother."

Fortune Foo came down the stairwell of Playmates of Paris at four A.M. with a small umbrella folded beneath her arm. Facing the morning fog, she hesitated as to whether she should open the umbrella for the short walk to the bus. "Good morning, baby," a black man's voice greeted her, but she could not make out his face. She kept the umbrella closed but held its point in the direction of the voice. One funny move and he'd get it.
"Let me talk to you, baby."
She made no reply and he fell in at her side. The lights of Fifth

Avenue, bemooned by mist, glowed hopefully ahead. A car wheeled to the curb, a big figure emerged and the black man's voice said, "Easy, Moon. Take it easy. Nobody gets hurt."

Fortune jabbed at the big figure, saw it leap back and cry out in pain. Then the umbrella was wrenched from her and she was in the rear seat of the big car with the big man holding her fast and the one with the black voice at the wheel.

"Nobody going to get hurt, baby," the driver reassured her, and in the shadowy light she saw a trickle of blood down the big one's face where she'd caught him with the umbrella.

At Washington Square they wheeled to the curb and the driver turned about to face her. The big hand across her mouth moved to the nape of her neck. It felt as if it could snap the neck like a rabbit's.

"You got the wrong party, fellows," Fortune assured them without permitting a hint of fear into her voice.

"All we want is my old lady's address," the black man told her, "Dovie-Jean. She's living with you. Nobody gets hurt."

"If nobody gets hurt," Fortune asked, "what is this big ape holding me by the neck for?"

The hand on the back of her neck eased slightly.

"Address, baby?"

No reply.

Mott Street was starting to lighten. It is a narrow, dingy street whose unswept litter is less noticeable under the bright glow of its commercial evening than now, when all the lights were out and all the tourists gone. Great trucks bearing Italian names were making early-morning deliveries of seafood. The neon of the Jade Room, Chinatown's only topless bar, had been darkened. The driver pulled to the curb on Mulberry and Mott.

In the growing light she saw that the trickle of blood on the big one's cheek had dried. He tossed her handbag to the driver. A slip from her dry-cleaner's was all he needed: 22 Doyers Street.

Not a cop in sight.

The dark and narrow doorway to 22 Doyers looked ominous to Fortune. She got out of the car only when the big one got his arm about her waist and had put her handbag back in her hand.

Red went up the stairwell before Fortune. Behind her came the big blond. At the first landing Red looked back and told the big man, "You wait there, Moon. I'll handle her."

Fortune paused then, but the big man shoved her ahead. He was not the waiting kind.

There were two doors to every flight. On the third flight the driver—she could now see he was a redheaded black man—read her name on a small metal panel. For some reason he did not knock at the door, but scratched at it, like a cat, with his fingernails.

Dovie-Jean, in a blue bathrobe, opened the door, then tried to shut it, but Red had his foot in.

"They *made* me, honey!" Fortune called to Dovie-Jean. "They *made* me!" Then Red was inside and Fortune was after him, with the big blond pushing in heavily and closing the door quietly behind him.

Dovie-Jean sat on the bed's edge trying to make sense of this early-morning visit. The only one who fitted the scene was Fortune. What, in God's name, had Red brought along the Bear for? Her fear of this man was so great she could not, even now, look at him as he went prowling about the room, lifting small objects here and there and setting them down.

Fortune sat in a corner of the divan, her umbrella still in her hand. It was not the redheaded driver on whom she kept her eye, but the big blond.

"Say what you're doing here, Red," she heard Dovie-Jean tell the redhead, "then get the hell out. This is my home. I don't want you in it. I don't have to tell you why."

Red sat in an armchair looking like a schoolboy being reproached by a teacher.

"You're my old lady, Dovie-Jean, I want you back."

The big blond turned slowly, eyeing first Red then Dovie-Jean. He did not have to ask, "Your *old lady*?" His expression was incredulous. At last he turned to the liquor cabinet, took a long drink straight from the bottle and put the bottle back. When he turned he made a sudden lunge at Fortune's umbrella, then drew back grinning. She had had it half-raised.

"It don't matter what you want, Tiger," Dovie-Jean assured Red, "if you want to play white, that's all right. If you want to play black, all right too. But you can't play it both ways. Not with me, you can't. I'm a *nigger* woman, mister. I always been. I always will be. You want to pass, pass. But pass me by."

The big blond took another drink. Fortune kept the umbrella in hand. He turned toward Red.

"I gave you the benefit of the doubt, mister. Now you got me locked into a deal with a nigger and a chink. How am I supposed to handle a deal like that?"

"You got no deal with me, Tarzan," Fortune assured him, "you muscled me here, you muscled me upstairs, and now you're hanging on as though you'd been invited. Where's the deal in that?"

"I'll leave when I think it's time to leave," Moon replied, seating himself with the bottle.

"Here it is Easter again," he announced solemnly, "and all of you, whoever you are, sit around here looking like the wrath of God. I took a scratch in the face and a kick in the balls from this little chink, and I still look better than all of you."

All three looked at him without the faintest understanding.

"I said Easter is here again," Moonigan persisted, "so here come the Easter creeps."

"Easter creeps?" Fortune asked.

"It's what I said. The creeps who write the governor, this time every year, how it's time to abandon capital punishment. Don't you creeps even read the papers? You did, you'd know what I was talking about. Easter creeps I call them because every Easter they come creeping out of the wallpaper. They write the governor. What would have become of Our Lord had capital punishment not been the style then? How could the Son of God become the Son of Man? Do you realize what a blessing capital punishment has been to man?"

"This bird is bonkers, Fortune," Dovie-Jean told her friend, "I've heard him come on before. The sonofabitch has eaten so much cunt he can't get it up naturally anymore. He needs medical attention."

Words that should not have been spoken, Dovie-Jean knew, as soon as she had spoken them.

The big man put the bottle down slowly and rose, slowly,

toward her. Fortune, on her feet, felt the umbrella broken in her hands while he shoved her to one side. Red rose, apprehensively. "Nobody gets hurt, Moon, nobody gets . . ." One big hand sent him stumbling backward. Dovie-Jean rose before him and held her hands to her breast as though protectively. She caught a curious odor, heavy and sweet as if from some far-gone time.

Even when she felt his great hand holding the nape of her neck she kept her hands to her breast. Red put his arm tentatively against Moon's. Fortune rose, her broken umbrella in her hands, and for the first time she felt afraid.

"She didn't mean anything, mister," she began, and it was as though she felt that big hand upon her own nape. She caught the flash of the blow without seeing it. Dovie-Jean saw a white hen flutter up, up and up but she never saw it come down. When Moon stepped back she fell forward and for a moment an appalling stillness rose in the little room. The girl lay entangled in her blue bathrobe with her head held loosely to one side.

Moon looked down. He had not meant to hit that hard.

Then he saw, and turned slowly toward the door. He did not close it. Fortune went to the window and began screaming, "They're killing a woman here!" into the empty night.

Red, ashen-white, stood looking down. Dimly behind him he heard heavy steps moving down the stair. But he could not follow. He knew what he saw.

Then Fortune's scream aroused him and he turned, went slowly to the door and went down, in the early morning light, like a man walking in darkness.

The police found him huddled against the building's wall and lifted him to his feet, mistaking him for a drunk.

In that black-and-white throng outside the courtroom, only guards and matrons looked like people who still believed in the triple murder charge against Ruby Calhoun. Even the journalists, so long aloof from commitment, had swung to support of the defense.

A hope (as yet too dear to speak aloud) was in the very air. Everyone was hoping for acquittal.

"It'll be a Christmas verdict," strangers kept assuring Floyd Calhoun, meaning that the state of New Jersey was going to give him his son back for Christmas. Floyd looked grateful, yet not believing.

The jury had been out since noon. It was now six P.M. By the time the jury got back from dinner it would be eight o'clock. By ten the judge would send them back to their hotel. The possibility of acquittal appeared to be growing by the hour.

Floyd Calhoun was not a man who danced easily or lightly. In his upbringing, dancing had been sinful. Yet, in the restaurant, before the jury had come in, Floyd rose quietly from the table and began dancing, to a jukebox's tune, solemnly, with himself:

Night and day

the juke box sang,

You are the one . . .

It was slow, heavy-footed old man's dance,

Only you beneath the moon
And under the sun . . .

Floyd was five inches taller than his son and forty pounds heavier. In all his seventy years he had had nothing to dance about. Now he had.

And he danced his solemn joy out about the room, his eyes closed and hands extended, palms turned upward as if accepting some divine gift.

Nobody laughed at the old man. Everyone caught his immense dignity. It was a dance that might have been named: Dance of an old man's joy upon the release from prison of his son.

He returned to his table and sat down as though unaware that he had done anything unusual, or even that he had been watched, in hushed astonishment, by everyone in the room.

"I had a strange dream once," he told Barney Kerrigan, "during Ruby's first trial. I dreamed I was an American soldier. I was in uniform and I had a gun. We were firing at some enemy. The enemy kept firing at us.

"We were fighting across a plain. I put my gun down and started walking toward the enemy lines. Who the enemy was I have no idea.

" 'Don't harm a hair of his head,' I heard an enemy officer command, and the firing stopped. I reached the enemy lines.

" 'What are you doing here?' the same officer's voice asked me, 'Why did you leave your own lines?'

" 'I don't belong there anymore,' was all I was able to tell him.

" 'Lie in the ditch,' the voice commanded me. I lay down in a shallow trench. The firing began again over my head. Again the firing stopped.

" 'Go back to your own lines,' the enemy officer's voice ordered me. Behind me his voice repeated, 'Don't harm a hair of his head.'

" 'They aren't going to electrocute Ruby,' I told my wife when I woke up, 'he's going to come home in time. I don't know when. In time.' "

Wooden barriers, the kind used to block off streets, had been set up in the lobby. Twenty-two Hudson County sheriff's officers circled the inside of the courtroom.

When the jury filed in they seemed to be walking on eggs, eyes downcast.

Calhoun rose to face them slowly.

A short, stout matron of sixty, the jury forewoman, rose and read the jury's verdict in a voice only just audible:

"Ruby Calhoun: for the murder of Donald Leonard, we find you guilty as charged.

"Ruby Calhoun: for the murder of Nicholas Vincio, we find you guilty as charged.

"Ruby Calhoun: for the murder of Helen Shane, we find you guilty as charged."

For one long moment there was nothing, nothing at all.

Just a group of people, in seats, looking at a smaller group in the jury box.

Then a small crippled wind, like a wind off some old half-sunken grave, began limping soundlessly about the courtroom. A young white girl began sobbing hysterically and a matron cautioned her to control herself. A black woman, beside the girl, put an arm about her. The girl regained control yet continued weeping softly.

Max Epstein rose to ask the judge to take his client's excellent prison record into consideration when resentencing him. He then asked whether sentencing could be postponed long enough to let Calhoun spend Christmas with his family; but the judge shook his head, No.

Somebody leaned across the rail dividing the courtroom and handed Calhoun a Christmas stocking, red and white, filled with nobody knew what.

Then he stood, straight and expressionless, while cops took the ridiculous Christmas stocking from him and began stripping him of his personal possessions publicly. Everybody stared helplessly and reluctantly at this demonstration of the state reducing a man to a number.

Floyd Calhoun handed him a couple of bills as the police turned the number around and marched it out.

Judge Oritano congratulated the jury upon the "trauma," as he termed it, that they had endured. He congratulated them also upon voting their consciences. He was proud of them, individually and as a group.

"We've come a long way in ten years in race relations in this town," Humphrey Scott assured the press. "We didn't try for an all-white jury. We had three blacks who didn't vote their color. People are proud here of the fact that black and white have now come to trust one another in Jersey City. The celebrities never bothered to acquire the facts. And it's going to be a cold day in hell," he added with his voice rising, "before Madison Avenue hucksters try to take down an honest cop again."

"Another kangaroo court," was how Floyd Calhoun saw it, and added bitterly. "You can't fight them on their grounds." He was, obviously, not among those blacks, observed by the state's attorney, who had come, through Calhoun's trial, to love and trust all whites.

"Iello," Scott continued, "was just part of the case. The defense could have expressed reasonable doubt without attacking the police. They could have said certain officers had been mistaken instead of charging them with conspiracy to frame a suspect. The American jury system, to my judgment, is the greatest instrument of justice in creation. The contest between the Madison Avenue hustlers and the American jury system was no contest."

"After twenty-seven months of being castigated and maligned by the New York media," Vincent de Vivani agreed, "it is indeed a grand relief to be absolved by our jury system."

"Of course I feel bad, *very* bad," Max Epstein acknowledged. "It doesn't look like anything in America has changed. It is still too easy to make people feel that blacks will kill whites for race. Apparently the jury didn't hear it the way we heard it. It was numbed by Iello's lies. It accepted a perjuror's word even though the man himself admitted to have lied, under oath, at every opportunity given him."

"It's like walking around in a circular tunnel, around and around," was Calhoun's reaction. You think you've come to the end and you find yourself right back where you started."

"He wanted a new trial and a new trial was what he got," was how the governor let it be known that he would no longer consider Calhoun for clemency.

Security at the New Jersey state prison is both too loose and too tight. When Kerrigan entered the main gate, a guard asked him casually, "You got a gun or knife?" He could have been holding two grenades, five shivs and a police special, but he said No and passed on.

There were half a dozen women and children in the visitors' room waiting to see husbands, brothers or sons. One guard was supervising; he had one ear bent above a small transistor. Kerrigan got tired of waiting, went to the door and found it locked.

Locked! The women smiled knowingly; they'd known it had been locked. Kerrigan thought: What do you know, I'm doing time on an unspecified charge.

He went to the soft-drink machine and put in a quarter. No drink. The quarter was returned. He repeated it in another slot. The quarter came back. On his third try there was no drink and the quarter was not returned. He turned to the guard, a burly young buck with a beard.

"I lost two bits in the machine," Kerrigan told him.

The guard continued to lean across the thin, faint music but made no reply. No sign he had understood. Kerrigan repeated the information.

No reply and no expression. The man wasn't, apparently, deaf. Kerrigan came up closer and repeated himself, "I lost two bits in the machine."

Kerrigan saw the women smiling and understood at last. He was telling Kerrigan that the machine was no business of his, the guard's. He was telling him that no man, woman or child was any business of his. His business, the man was telling Kerrigan, was with himself, and with himself alone. And that was his *only* business. He was never going to get involved, he was determined, with anything, or anybody, for any reason, outside of himself. Living was a matter of keeping yourself shut up tight within yourself.

Kerrigan had observed many people playing it safe. But *this* safe? Of walking around dead years before the funeral?

Kerrigan turned away from the machine that had stolen his quarter with the realization that these dummy-uppers, wearing the uniforms of security guards, were as fully prisoners of the establishment as were the prisoners.

He was carrying a book and also a magazine report on the second trial he wanted to give Calhoun. When the visitors' door was unlocked he told the clerk at the visitors' window, "I'd like to leave these for Calhoun."

"You can't."

"Can't?"

"Can't."

"No?"

"No."

"Might I ask why not?"

"Because what you have to do with books is mail them."

"I see. What about this?"

Kerrigan showed him the magazine. Consultation was now required. A decision was at last handed down.

"Yes. You can take it. You can show it to Calhoun. Calhoun can read it in front of you. But he can't keep it to read by himself."

"I'll mail it with the book."

Kerrigan was then escorted to a dining room where guards were being served lunch in cafeteria style. A restaurant-sized coffee urn stood beside their table, with cream, sugar and paper cups at hand.

"Do you mind," Kerrigan asked courteously, "if I help myself to the coffee?"

"No," a guard told him firmly, "you can't."

"Can't?"

"Can't."

"Might I ask why not?"

"Because the coffee is just for security guards," one explained.

"If I pay for it, can I have a cup?"

"No."

"No?"

"No."

"Water," one of them told Kerrigan.

"Water what?"

"You can have water. That's all."

Kerrigan helped himself to a cup of water, shaking his head sadly. He couldn't quite believe that any one group of men could get this tight up.

Kerrigan had read that Calhoun was now living, without contact with either prisoners or guards, in a small one-man cell, and living by night. He had become estranged from his wife and daughter. They no longer visited him. Nor did any of the media celebrities who had once borne witness for him. He subsisted on canned foods, brought to him once a month by some devoted fan, so he no longer had to leave his cell.

He was waiting, looking owlish, when Kerrigan returned from the water cooler. Kerrigan filled him in on the dummy-uppers but Calhoun didn't think it funny. He didn't laugh.

"I live with that, Kerrigan." He explained, "They're crazy as Dick's hatband. This is an insane asylum where the patients have taken over the administration. Prisoners, after all, are *forced* to live here. The guards prefer spending their lives between walls. Who is crazier? If every prisoner were set free tomorrow, there would be guards who would want to remain. They would be afraid of the risks they would have to take in the outside world. It's why we don't call the P.B.A. the Police Benefit Association. We call it the League of Frightened Men."

Losing his second trial had left Calhoun undismayed, Kerrigan perceived. The appeal he now planned to file would be upon the contention that Iello had disqualified himself, as a witness, before the trial.

His problem was money. The trial transcripts, which the defense would have to have to write the appeal, cost ten thousand dollars. Calhoun didn't own a nickel. Every dollar contributed to his defense had been appropriated by Adeline Kelsey.

"She must have cleared a hundred thousand," Calhoun conjectured, yet without apparent bitterness. He'd declared himself indigent in hope of having the county put up the ten thousand for the transcripts.

"For sure, Iello didn't do you much good," Kerrigan acknowledged, "and Epstein looked like he was patterning himself after a TV soap opera. But the who lost you case was yourself."

"How?"

"Because, after nearly ten years of proclaiming your innocence, you fail to take the stand and tell the jury, 'I never shot those people in the Melody Bar and Grill.' Had you done so, it may well have made all the difference. Whose idea was it not to testify? Yours? Or Epstein's?"

"Epstein *begged* me to take the stand. I refused."

"I don't understand you, Ruby."

"They had witnesses backed up, for one thing and another, for two decades back. They would have hit me with *everything*."

"So let them hit you with everything. Then you turn to the jury, admitting all charges, and tell them, I am not the man who should be standing trial. The fact is, Calhoun, I can't understand how you could *not* take the stand. When you think of the people who have borne witness for you, who have invested belief in you, you had no choice except to bear witness for yourself."

Calhoun merely sat studying Kerrigan.

"Look at the position you put *me* in," Kerrigan added. "Scott wanted me on the defensive, and that was where I was. 'Where are receipts for the money you handled for Calhoun? Was this recorded on your income tax, Mr. Kerrigan?' He put me into the light of a man seeking money and personal glory and nothing more. If you had taken the stand, you could have given me support, but you didn't. You could have explained that Kerrigan handled your money for you because you had nobody else you could trust. But you didn't. You sat there while Scott kicked my ass, threatened me with subpoenas. I just don't understand you, Ruby."

Calhoun studied Kerrigan a long moment.

"If I had to do it all over again," he finally decided, "I'd do it the same way."

Kerrigan looked like he could not believe what he had just heard.

"You would do it the same way," he repeated, trying to grasp it, "and you're now eligible for parole in nineteen hundred and ninety-eight. And you would do it the same way?"

Calhoun looked away as though Kerrigan were no longer there.

"Lord," Kerrigan heard him say as he rose, as though he were praying. "Lord, I don't ask you to move mountains. Just give me the strength to climb this one."

Kerrigan left without shaking hands.

The madman stood naked before his window bars, wondering at the midnight moon.

He did not see the midnight moon, no more than the moon saw him. He saw an image of a black girl's face, eyes wide but pupils rolling.

His hair had turned snow white.

Now a man in his forties, yet his face had become that of one in his twenties. No lines of anxiety across his forehead, nor lines of worry about the mouth.

His mouth, indeed, was held in a childlike half-smile, lips partly parted. The eyes no longer held the shadow of depression.

There was nothing left to depress.

He returned to his bed, switched on his light and sat looking, for a long while, at the calendar on his wall. The days had been marked off, day by day, above the colored photograph of a brown cow in a green field.

Finally, having ascertained the date beyond all doubt, he turned off the light, and slept.

Slept, yet had no dreams.

In the morning he washed and dressed himself carefully, then sat in his armchair in his stocking-feet, waiting for his attendant.

When the attendant arrived he greeted Red with a hearty, "Good morning, Edward!"

If spoken to harshly, tears might come into Red's eyes. If spoken to softly, he smiled faintly.

The attendant waited for him to put on his tennis shoes, which took a couple of minutes more than it would have taken another man, because the knots had to be tied so carefully. Then Red stood up and they walked slowly toward the Coffee Cup, a small building in which vending machines stood against the walls, where paperback books, newspapers and magazines were sold, and where there were tables and chairs for patients.

The attendant brought Red a copy of the *New York Times*. Red scrutinized the date to be sure it was not yesterday's edition. With the paper folded beneath his arm, he stood before the coffee machine with the attendant beside him.

There was black coffee with sugar, black without, coffee with cream but no sugar and coffee with cream and sugar. The attendant always gave Red time to choose. He was paid by Hardee to give small services, beyond those of his regular duties, to Red. He waited now for Red to point to his choice. Then he put in the coin, Red picked up his cup, his paper still under his arm, and moved to an empty table. If no table were empty he would drink standing against the wall. If he was joined by another patient, he would rise slowly, say "excuse me" and finish his coffee standing.

Once, seeing a group of people approaching, he drew to one side and waited for them to pass.

"What's the matter, Edward?"

"They might hurt you."

"Nobody is going to hurt you."

"If they want to, they can."

The attendant would leave him at the Coffee Cup for half an hour, while he tended to other patients. Red preferred the table under the radio and the attendant knew the station Red preferred. It was a local station that played old-time popular tunes all day. No rock and no classic. Sometimes Red would hum to the music above him:

Nights are long since you went away
My buddy
My buddy.

Or:

Make my bed and light the light
I'll arrive late tonight . . .

One morning a little aging man, in his late sixties, approached Red's table. He was dressed neatly in a white shirt, dark bow tie, dark trousers carefully creased, but without socks or shoes. Red started to rise when the old man sat down, but the old man stayed him, with a sly expression.

"I don't have to be here," the old man informed him, "I committed myself."

Red nodded.

"Because of the niggers. I committed myself to get away from the niggers."

"How about you?" the old man asked.

"I wanted to get away from niggers too."

"You always did."

"*I* always did?"

"Don't you remember when you used to take the mike and pretend to be Eddie Arnold, Red?"

A faint memory fled through Red's mind.

"Oh, yes." He stood up and began moving his mouth to the tune being played from above:

Don't the moon look lonesome
Shinin' through the trees . . .

"Sing it like you used to Red," the old man encouraged him.

But the song faded, the memory gave out, the mime's mouth ceased to move and he sat down, a faint blush spreading into his cheeks as he stared into his paper cup.

The little old man smiled as though he had won some secret prize and left in his bare feet, shuffling cheerfully among the mad and the half-mad and out the door.

Red waited for his attendant without opening his paper. He did not open it until he was back in his small room and the attendant had closed the door behind him. Then he checked the paper's date, once again, with the calendar on the wall.

He spread the paper's section out on his bed and sat in his armchair before them. He began stripping the business section first, into long, neat strips, When it was done he gathered the strips and put them into the waste basket. He took a drink of water then, and began on the sports section, and again put it carefully into the waste basket. And took another glass of water.

It was slow work, because each page had to be stripped neatly and scissors were not allowed. When he had finished the metropolitan section there remained only the news. This was the biggest section and it was almost noon before he had it done.

Once the attendant stood outside the door and listened. When he had heard the sound of tearing paper he had opened the door and asked courteously, "Excuse me, Edward, but is there some purpose in tearing the paper into strips like that?"

Red looked up and gave him a grave smile.

"Of course. They fit better into the waste basket this way," and returned to his meticulous task.

"That's the sanest thing been said around here in years," the attendant's supervisor commented when Red's curious explanation had been reported to her.

Everything is different yet everything is the same.

The tavern that once was the Melody Bar and Grill is now the Aquarius Lounge.

The changes have been great. There had been no change at all.

The pool table remains in the middle of the room; but the players now are black. Budweiser ads still border the walls but the handsome young marrieds in them are, again, black.

The jukebox has forgotten the songs of the sixties. Now it plays "The Games That Daddies Play" and "Don't Break the Heart That Loves You."

"Isn't this the place that got into the papers some years back?" Kerrigan asked, sitting at the bar waiting for a beer.

The bartender was a black woman who had read Frantz Fanon.

"Maybe it is. Then again maybe it isn't," she replied, concealing her hostility beneath the guise of courtesy. "We don't know anything about this place when it was a white bar. I'm sure I couldn't tell you."

"I heard there was a triple homicide in here."

"Mister," the woman came close to her white customer, "I don't know what you're after but you won't find it here."

"I just thought . . ."

"When you finish your drink, mister, feel free to leave."

A young black man, cue in hand, was holding the door open for Kerrigan.

Kerrigan grinned at him, smiled at the bartender and took his time finishing his drink. He gave the youth holding the door a broad wink as he passed him into the street.

"Thanks, buddy."

All, all is changed. All, all is the same.

The sound of a revolver's blast was faded across the years. The people who heard it are dead, jailed or gone mad. The old faces fade; new faces take their place.

All, all is changed.

And everything remains the same.